CW01497690

DEVILSTON

J.J.Greenwood

For My Dearest Parents and Family

1

A TALE OF THREE ISLANDS

The hot summer of 1940 would have been perfect, but for the shadow of war. Now a ripe autumn warmth oppressed the audience in the little theatre.

Applause dribbled into expectant silence. A thin black-haired youth in a tweed suit placed a music sheet on the stand in front of him then cleared his throat.

"Good evening, ladies and gentlemen. My name is Daniel Rosenbaum and I am going to play Bach's Prelude to his Suite Number One in G major. This piece is usually performed on the cello but since I no longer possess one I shall be playing it on the violin."

Now he surveyed the gathered. Herr Bruschell, his music tutor, smiled up at him from beneath a cloud of hair. Also on the front row sat the plump Commandant in army uniform and, next to him, a slim woman in a cream dress. She had pale skin and long red hair, like Rita Hayworth. She could have been an angel, but for her scarlet lips and the darkness of her eyes.

Some of the audience were fanning themselves with their programmes. Dan could sense the voltage of expectation in the room. He felt like the magician in the Berlin nightclub where his father used to play, entertaining Wehrmacht officers. In his right hand was the saw; in his left, his voluptuous assistant. Would he remember where to place his fingertips on her slender neck? Or would the magic fail him and the horse hair merely scrape against the sheep gut, reproducing the terrible animal cacophony of their final moments...?

He lifted the violin to his chin and began to play. The music came to him, but not easily. His body was tense, his arms stiff, his fingers slow. It didn't feel right.

This piece is usually performed on the cello.

The staves reminded him of the high barbed-wire fence around the camp. His concentration snagged on the notes as he thought of his father in another camp, far away. Even as he weaved the web of music, he was anticipating the mistake that would cause the fragile tapestry to unravel.

The door of the theatre opened, disturbing the warm soup of air and causing his music sheet to fall to the floor.

He stopped playing.

There was a murmur of displeasure in the audience. Someone coughed. He contemplated walking off the stage, but then he saw familiar faces at the back. His friends had arrived - late, as ever - and his heart leapt. Among them he thought he'd glimpsed his father.

The violin seemed to nestle under his chin of her own accord, her strings attracting his bow as if now induced with supernatural magnetism. He closed his eyes, tuning into her voice, allowing her to lead him on...

Sometimes she moaned, low and slow, as if suffering under the friction of the cruel bow. Then, as his fingertips pressed on the base of her neck, her song would soar to a new pitch of agony. At the climax the bow see-sawed with frantic urgency, as if he was struggling to cut himself free from her curse. His face shone with sweat as his head bobbed and nodded, his hair splayed like crow feathers.

He found himself playing his father's gypsy music. Now the gathered clapped and stamped in time, all animated by the heartbeat of rhythm, all bound together by the melody's invisible thread. But while joy propelled his audience, the young violinist was driven by darker forces.

When the end came, he felt a great weight lifted from him. He opened his eyes and remembered where he was. The audience had risen to its feet, vigorously applauding. He saw his friends at the back of the hall, grinning and whistling and clapping madly. His father wasn't with them. He'd only imagined it.

But the red-haired woman was still there, her dark eyes penetrating his soul.

Lady Charlotte Smythe-Morrigan sipped her dry martini while the Commandant nursed a mug of cocoa on his lap. They sat at each end of the sofa, in his drawing room. The scent of her perfume hung in the air, like a spirit.

The Commandant watched his guest light a cigarette, inhale deeply then blow the smoke forcefully upwards. He noticed a small smudge of lipstick on the cigarette's filter. He usually prohibited smoking in his house, but there was something about this woman that stifled his will.

"So you enjoyed the concert, Your Ladyship?"

"Very much, Major. But I must confess an ulterior motive to my visit…"

"I presumed as much. An internment camp is hardly top of the list of the Isle of Man's attractions."

He laughed nervously, coughing a little as her smoke found the back of his throat.

"Our school wants to do her bit for the war

effort," she continued. "We have a scholarship place available for a disadvantaged boy."

He noticed she was seeking somewhere to deposit her ash. Improvising quickly, he requisitioned a small heart-shaped bowl from the drinks cabinet.

"Thank you."

She played along with the pretence that this was a proper ash tray and not a receptacle intended for stuffed olives. It was part of the silver cocktail set that had been a wedding present from his mother-in-law.

"Tell me," she asked," how old is the violinist?"

He resumed his place on the sofa.

"Rosenbaum? Seventeen, I think. And sharp as a knife, as they tend to be. Picked up English in no time. His father was a professional musician, before the Nazis caught up with him."

"And the rest of his family?"

"Still in Germany. The lad was the only one young enough to qualify for the Kindertransport programme. He was on the last train out before the balloon went up. Seems rather cruel really, packing him off to a strange country like that. But I suppose they have their own ways..."

"A good mother would do anything to protect her young," she countered. "And terrible things have been happening in Germany of late."

"I suppose so…"

"You don't sound very convinced."

"Germany is modernizing, and you can't make an omelette without breaking a few eggs…It's the bloody Ruskies we should be fighting. Communism will consume us all if we don't halt its advance." He felt his face flushing. "But of course that's only my personal opinion…"

"And you have every right to it. Freedom of expression. That's what we're fighting for, after all…" She took another drag on her cigarette, her cheeks hollowing slightly, emphasising the fine structure of her face. "And I must say, I was extremely impressed by Rosenbaum's musical expression this evening."

"Yes. He's certainly a talented chap."

"A talent that's rather wasted here, I'm sure you'll agree. Which is why I'd like to offer him the scholarship. Considering his age he would only be with us for a year, but we could do a lot with him in that time…"

The Commandant made a slight grimace.

"A most generous offer Your Ladyship, but I'm afraid that wouldn't be possible. You see, he's due to be transported imminently. The PM wants all German nationals out of the country."

"But he's a Jew. He hardly presents a threat."

"He's also a citizen of a state we're at war with. We can't afford to take the risk."

"So where is he being transported to? My God, it makes them sound like cattle…"

"Canada, I believe. The *Star of the Ganges*, if my memory serves me correctly. Sailing from Liverpool."

"When?"

"I'm afraid that's classified information. 'Careless talk' and all that…I've probably said too much as it is."

"But can't you just have him removed from the roster?"

"Far beyond my jurisdiction. Of course he could make an official request for naturalisation but I doubt we'd get a response before his ship sails. These things tend to take an awfully long time."

"Isn't there some way we could speed up the process? Oil the cogs, so to speak?"

"Well, I do have an old school friend at the Home Office…"

He wasn't quite sure why he'd said that. This woman seemed to have cast a spell over him, loosening the reins between his mind and his mouth. He felt compelled to please her.

"That's interesting. So why don't you telephone this friend of yours?"

"On a Friday evening?"

"Well, no rest for the wicked, as they say…" She took another draw of her cigarette, all the time watching him intently. "Are you married,

Major?"

He nodded, his fingertips instinctively finding his wedding ring, cold and hard.

"She's in London. City girl. Says she'd sooner suffer the Luftwaffe than be stuck on some Godforsaken little island."

Another uneasy chuckle.

"Children?"

"Three boys, all at boarding school."

"You must get terribly lonely here."

"Well, I keep myself busy enough…"

Now he found himself fixed in her dark stare, like a rabbit in the glare of black-out headlights.

"Could I make you a proposition, Major?"

"A proposition?"

"Why don't you telephone your friend and make the necessary arrangements? Then you can introduce me to Rosenbaum. And after that…well, perhaps you and I could get to know each other a little better…"

The Commandant's mouth dried. He took another gulp of cocoa. It was nearly cold.

"Forgive me but I was under the impression you were married too…"

She indicated mild surprise.

"I was merely suggesting a political discussion, Major."

Again his face reddened.

"I do apologise, Your Ladyship. I must have got the wrong end of the stick…"

"Mind you," she continued, "considering our differences, there's always the possibility that our debate might get a little...heated."

"Right..."

"Though I'm sure we'd find some common ground. In the end."

She stubbed out her cigarette in the heart-shaped bowl then elegantly re-adjusted her legs. Then he felt the weight of her gaze resting on him again. He had to say something. Anything.

"You must be hungry...I mean, with all that travelling..."

"Ravenous. I had to skip dinner to make it here in time for the concert."

"Well then, how about a spot of supper? My cook is an Italian internee. She works wonders with the local fish."

"Sounds divine. So...shall we get down to business?"

"Sorry?"

"You were going to telephone your friend."

"Oh yes. Of course..."

Krystallnacht. The Rosenbaums stand at the window of their apartment, watching in disbelief.

The street that had once been so familiar and safe is now a vision of Hell. Men of the Sturmabteilung in brown uniforms and black

boots are smashing up shops and dragging people outside to beat them, spurred on by crowds of onlookers. Tongues of flame writhe from the windows of the synagogue at the end of the street.

Father pulls the curtains. But they can still hear the screams and the cheers, the crackling of fire and the shattering of glass. And then comes the sound they dread the most: the rapid beat of heavy boots on the stairs.

The Rosenbaums stare at each other in petrified silence. For the first time in his life, Dan sees real fear on his father's face.

The lights were snapped on, releasing Dan from the nightmare like a click of fingers. Others in the dormitory stirred and mumbled in their beds.

Two soldiers had entered. They wore khaki uniforms and round helmets. Each had a rifle slung over his shoulder, bayonets fixed.

"Which one of yous is Daniel Rosenbaum?"

"Why do you want to know?" slurred a sleepy voice.

"Just tell us where he is!"

Dan sat up, rubbing the sleep from his face.

"I'm here."

"Right. Put something on and make it sharp. You're coming with us."

Dan pulled his old coat over his pajamas and slipped his bare feet into his cold shoes.

As the soldiers escorted him downstairs other internees emerged from their rooms, watching them leave.

"Where are you taking him?" one of them called out.

"I thought you were supposed to be fighting the Nazis," sneered another, "not imitating them."

"Get back to bed!" barked the soldier behind Dan. Then his bayonet caught on a door frame, to the amusement of the onlookers. Even his oppo in front of Dan laughed.

"I hope you're more careful with your own weapon, Taff."

"Shut your cakehole, you bloody scouser. Unless you want a bayonet up your fundament..."

The night was cool and moonlit, and sprinkled with stars. Dan remembered his mother's words in the letter she'd slipped into his suitcase:

"Whenever you are missing us, look at the stars and the moon. When you look up at them, my dearest one, remember that it is the same sky that I can see. Then we will feel like we are together. I will send my love by the moon and the stars."

Above the crunch of the soldier's boots on the road to the golf course he could hear a faint rumble. Glancing over his shoulder he saw distant flashes on the sea's horizon.

"Is that a thunder storm?"

"Nope," said Scouser. "That's Jerry visiting Liverpool."

"Jerry?"

"You know," said Taff. "Your lot."

The club house was now the commanding officer's residence. The fairways and bunkers were a convenient space for the garrison to practise repelling invaders, and the Commandant to work on his swing.

After ringing the bell, the guard at the front door exchanged light banter with Dan's escort. Dan compared these fresh-faced recruits in their baggy uniforms with the battle-hardened German troops who'd boarded the Kindertransport train. It wasn't a favourable comparison.

The door opened and the Commandant looked Dan over.

"You could have let him dress properly."

"Sorry sir," said Taff. "We thought it was urgent."

"Not that urgent. Anyway, come in young man..."

The Commandant's tone was unusually warm. He led Dan into the drawing room. Its fine furnishings and tasteful décor were of another world after the starkness of the internee quarters. The woman he'd seen on the front row at the concert was sitting on a sofa.

"Rosenbaum, this is Lady Smythe-Morrigan."

"Please, call me Charlotte..."

Smiling, she rose to her feet and shook his hand, then indicated for him to sit next to her.

The Commandant felt a pang of jealousy. Rosenbaum sat closer to her than he had; nor had she invited him to use her first name. He stood in front of the fireplace and consoled himself with the promise in her earlier words, and her eyes.

"Daniel, you play beautifully," she said.

"Thank you."

"So what made you choose Bach?"

"The Prelude is one of my father's favourite pieces."

"It is lovely, isn't it? But you must experience mixed feelings when you play the German composers..."

"I'm proud to come from the same nation as such great artists. I'm only sorry that I didn't really do justice to Johann Sebastian."

"That wasn't your fault. You lost your music. But, my word, you found something wonderful to replace it."

"It was one of my father's tunes. He's a Romany. It's in his blood...and mine, I suppose. He toured all over Europe, and performed with Yehudi Menuhin and Pablo Casals. Have you heard of them?"

She smiled.

"I've met them. My husband and I are great music lovers. It's one of the fortunate privileges of our position that we're able to meet such talented people in the flesh...But your father was a Romany, you say? I thought he was Jewish..."

She glanced at the Commandant.

"My mother is Jewish," said Dan. "My father converted so he could marry her. He even took her surname. He could have given it up to avoid being arrested but that would have made their marriage...aufhebung. Sorry, I'm not sure of the English word..."

"Annulled."

"My mother begged him to do it for his own safety. They would have been married still, just not officially. But my father refused. He can be very stubborn."

"Your father sounds like an extraordinary man."

"He's still alive, you know. All of my family is still alive."

She was impressed by the certainty in his eyes.

"You've heard from them?"

"No. But I know it, in my heart."

There was a pause in the conversation. The Commandant took the opportunity to chip in.

"Excellent. And you'll be pleased to hear we've got some very good news for you."

Dan's heart lurched.

"About my family?"

"I'm afraid not." Charlotte placed her hand on his. "But I'm sure you'll be with them soon, when this awful war is over."

There was no other good news he could possibly hear now. Anything else would be mere information.

"Daniel," she continued, "have you heard of a place called Cornwall?"

Despite his disappointment he was unable to resist the opportunity to exercise his knowledge.

"Yes. It's where King Arthur was supposed to have come from. And Tristan and Isolde. My father played under Herbert von Karajan in the Berlin State Opera's production."

"Really? Well, if you like legends then I'm sure you'll love Cornwall. And we have the most beautiful beaches, and a lovely rock pool. Do you enjoy swimming?"

"Of course. But we're not allowed to bathe in the sea here in case we try to swim to England."

The Commandant guffawed.

"Oh come now, young man. You make this place sound like a prisoner of war camp."

"Isn't that what it is…?"

Another uncomfortable pause.

"Daniel," Charlotte said, presently. "How would you like to come to Cornwall?"

"I can't. I have to go to Canada."

"Not if you become a British subject…"

"But I don't want to be a British subject. I'm a German citizen."

Now she looked puzzled.

"After all that they're doing to your people?"

"Germany is my home." The emotion rose within him. "What's happening there could happen anywhere. Here, even. It's just a disease and it can be cured. One day Germany will be free again, and I will go back to my family. In Berlin, where I was born."

"I'm sure you'll go back Daniel, as soon as Hitler is gone. And if you stay in England you won't be very far from your family. But Canada is such a long way away…"

He had already resigned himself to going. Part of him was even looking forward to the adventure: a new life in a land of lakes and forests and wolves, and freedom. But he also knew that any hope of seeing his family again would be as distant as the Rocky Mountains seemed to him now.

"Daniel, my husband is headmaster of a boarding school in Cornwall. In the light of your special circumstances we're offering you a full scholarship, so you won't have to pay any fees. We'll help you develop that talent of yours, and you can sit the entrance examination for a college of music. Perhaps even the Royal

Academy..."

"I must say, this is a brilliant opportunity," the Commandant chipped in. "If I were you Rosenbaum, I'd grab it with both hands!"

"But what about my family? If I become a British subject, will they be able to live here too?"

The Commandant glanced at Charlotte.

"Well, I'm sure it would make things easier," he said, uncertainly. "That's if they manage to get out of Germany, of course..."

"Daniel, I'm afraid you'll need to decide immediately," said Charlotte. "Term begins on Monday. We'll have to catch the morning boat if we're to make it in time."

"I've already decided. I'll come with you."

The Commandant clapped his hands together.

"Very decisive, young man. Well done."

And very brave, he thought. *I know where I'd rather be, and that's on the other side of the Atlantic, well out of range of the bloody Luftwaffe.*

"I have no choice. I'll be closer to my family in Cornwall than Canada."

"Indeed," said Charlotte. "Now, the Major has kindly prepared a letter in case we're questioned by the authorities on our way down..."

Dan read the letter carefully. He could sense the impatience of his audience but his father was always thorough about anything he signed, a trait he had inherited. He was aware of the traps that might lie within the forest of words, and he understood the power wielded by the bureaucratic machine. Before the soldiers had taken him away, his father had been forced to sign papers granting them permission to arrest him. Even in the most brutal regime, there always seemed to be due legal process.

But the letter looked harmless enough: a simple statement transferring responsibility for Dan's welfare. He signed it, beneath the Commandant's pedantic script and Charlotte's flamboyant scrawl.

"Well, that's that then," said the Commandant. "My friend at the Home Office will send you all the paperwork, Your Ladyship. And I'll arrange for my driver to take you both to Douglas first thing in the morning, in time for your boat."

"That's very kind of you, Major." Charlotte placed the letter in her handbag and snapped the clasp closed. "But now that Daniel is officially my responsibility I'd prefer him to stay with me in Douglas tonight. I'd hate to miss the boat."

"But…what about supper?"

She raised a finger to her temple, wincing slightly.

"Forgive me but I think one of my migraines is coming on. If you don't mind I'd really like to get back to my hotel for an early night. Daniel and I have a very long journey ahead of us."

"But…"

"But I'd love to visit again. Perhaps you'll show me the sights another time soon…?"

"Yes," said the Commandant, dazed. "Of course."

A farewell committee gathered on the doorstep in dressing gowns, pale faces glowing in the moonlight. As he embraced each of them Dan felt a familiar sadness welling up which his throat could barely suppress. A battered violin case was pressed into his arms.

"No," he protested. "This belongs to the Music Society."

"And as President of said society I hereby decree that she's now yours." Herr Bruschell's old eyes gleamed as he winked. "Just promise to remember us whenever you play her."

As the Commandant's car drove away Dan watched his waving friends diminish.

"You would have been leaving them anyway," said Charlotte, seeing him wiping away tears as he turned from the rear window.

He shook his head.

"They're all going to Canada."

A sentry saluted as the car left the camp. Its blacked-out headlights had little effect on the ocean of night beyond and now the interior of the car was flooded with darkness. Dan felt the first pricklings of panic. He fought to smother it with happy memories of holidays by the sea. But the fear kept returning, in waves greater each time as if having fed from the troughs, until he was sitting bolt upright, breaths shallow, fists tight, jaw clenched.

"What's the matter, Daniel?"

"It's so dark…" His voice was weak. "So close… I can't breathe properly…"

Charlotte wound down the window a little and he felt a cold rush of wind on his face. Presently he sat back in his seat, relieved but now very tired.

"I know what it's like," she said. "I'm rather claustrophobic myself."

Trapped in a small place, with no prospect of escape.

"We had a secret hiding place in our apartment," said Dan."For when the soldiers came. But there wasn't enough room. There wasn't enough air…"

He closed his eyes, struggling to suppress the memory. Again he felt her hand on his.

"There's no need to worry, Daniel. You're quite safe now."

Father replaces the pantry door with a panel

he has covered with wallpaper to match the rest of the kitchen. The family conducts a rehearsal, squeezing into the tiny space: his parents, his three older sisters, and himself. There is much restrained hysteria, and when the exercise is over they burst out of the tiny cell with noisy relief. Amid the clamour, Dan reads the secret look his parents exchange.

Too small.

Then, Krystallnacht. As fists hammer on the door of the apartment Father shepherds his family into the pantry. Now there is no hilarity, only horror. They enter in silence, eyes wide with fear, limbs trembling. Only when Father fixes the panel in place from the wrong side do they speak, begging him to join them.

"Quiet!" he whispers as he slides a folded table against the panel. He places a vase of flowers on it and some books, as if the table has always been there.

The Brown Shirts smash open the door. To the family in their hiding place, the voices sound so close.

"What took you so long?" their leader demands. "Hiding your money from us, were you?"

"I'm sorry," Father says. "I was in the bathroom..."

"Where are the others?"

"Abroad."

"So why are you still here?"

"My work is here. I'm a musician."

"Really? More like you're sitting on all that cash you can't take out of Germany..."

The officer barks an order and the family hears the apartment being turned over, on the other side of the thinnest of walls.

The safe is soon found, concealed behind a picture of the Rosenbaums smiling on a beach.

"Buried treasure," says the officer, with glee. "Now open it."

When the safe has been emptied of their meagre savings a document is produced, and a pen.

"What's this?" Father asks.

Hearing a hard slap, the family winces as one.

"Just sign it or we'll beat the shit out of you..."

When peace returns they remain in the pantry for some time, fearing the men might be waiting for them, like cats outside a mouse hole.

It's Dan who eventually opens the panel, unable to stand the heat and the darkness and the stale air any longer. He has to push hard to shift the table on the other side. The vase falls off and smashes on the floor.

He fills his lungs with new air then looks

around.

Their apartment has been ransacked. Father has been taken away.

Dan woke with a start. For a moment he wondered if he might be in heaven, before his memory re-occupied the space vacated by the nightmare.

The hotel room was as big as the dormitory he'd shared with twelve others.

Was this what Hitler meant by Lebensraum?

A full English breakfast was delivered by a pretty maid with a bright smile. Sitting up in bed with the tray on his lap - a luxury in itself - he ate everything, including the bacon. It had a salty richness which made his tongue sizzle.

Though his family had never been devoutly religious, they had always kept kosher. But the foster parents he'd stayed with in London observed the traditions with clockwork devotion. They hadn't treated him badly, but they didn't seem to care much for him. He'd felt like just another ritual obligation.

So, while he was sure his foster parents would have condemned him to Hell, he knew his real family would have forgiven him. And would God - if He even existed - be so horrified to see one of His subjects eating pork, compared with all that was happening in Germany...?

After breakfast a uniformed porter carried his suitcase and violin down to the foyer, where

Charlotte was waiting. When the porter had loaded their luggage into the cab, she tipped him and he touched his forehead in deference.

She seemed so at ease in the world, as if all of life was scripted and rehearsed, like a film. She wore red, with a fox fur draped round her shoulders. The animal's head, limbs and tail were still attached, its mouth frozen in a snarl.

Victoria was an old but elegant steamer which might have arrived at the quay from another age. Beneath a low grey sky she slipped her bonds again and turned seaward. Leaning on the rail of her promenade deck, Dan watched the island recede into the mist, like a mythical place.

The freshening wind drove him inside, among the dark wooden panels and leather upholstery of First Class. With a pianist playing Schubert on a baby grand, it seemed like an extension of the hotel they'd just left.

Charlotte was sitting in an armchair, smoking a cigarette as she read a newspaper. She registered Dan's arrival with a brief smile. He glimpsed the headline on the front page:

BRITAIN ON YELLOW ALERT: INVASION IMMINENT

As *Victoria* left the shelter of the bay, she began to nod and sway on the swell. A waiter delivered Charlotte's martini without a drop being spilled, but the frequent crashes from the galley suggested the cooks were enjoying less success.

The drunken roll of the lounge and its smoky stuffiness conspired to concoct a growing nausea within Dan, to which he eventually yielded. Passengers lined the promenade rails so he made for the stern, just in time for his breakfast to re-appear in a spectacular encore.

Afterwards - purged - he stared mesmerised into the boiling white mass of the ship's wake, feeling the throb of the boat's iron heart, tasting her acrid smoke on his tongue.

Above him a red flag flapped in the breeze, its colour faded, its trailing edge ragged. In the flag's top left corner he recognised the union jack, representing the country that had taken him in and then almost regurgitated him. But the image on the flag's red field remained a mystery, even though he'd seen it many times on the island. He'd never enquired about the origin of the three legs joined at a single hip. It reminded him too much of a symbol he feared and hated.

"Wherever you throw me I will stand."

He turned to see an old and wiry deckhand

standing nearby, his face creased and tanned, his legs set apart to provide stability as the ship moved beneath him. A roll-up cigarette hung from the corner of his mouth.

"Sorry?"

"It's the Manx triskelion."

Dan watched as the sailor pulled down the flag and replaced it with one he'd been holding under his arm.

"About time the old girl had a new ribbon…"

Now he yanked at the halyard and Dan watched the bright new flag ascend, flying with what appeared to be greater vigour than its predecessor.

"It looks a bit like a swastika."

"Nothing so sinister, lad. Just means we'll be alright, no matter what…"

As the sailor folded up the old flag, the ship leaned over at its steepest angle yet. Fearing a capsize Dan gripped the rail, while the sailor casually shifted his stance to take account of the list, took a last drag on his cigarette then flicked the stub over the side. As the ship righted herself he grinned, revealing a black gap in yellowy teeth.

"Don't worry, lad. This lady's seen a lot worse than this. She was at Dunkirk, ferrying our boys back to Blighty."

Dan recalled the newsreel footage of retreat celebrated as victory.

"Were you there?"

"Certainly was. Suppose I'm hitched to the old girl now. Through Hell and high water, 'til death do us part..." The sailor patted the hand rail. "Her first taste of war that, but not mine." He pulled up his sleeve to show off a tattoo: a silhouette of a battleship across a lean bicep, with **Jutland 1916** written beneath. "Never saw the enemy that time. Too busy loading shells in the bowels of the *Iron Duke*. But we heard the guns right enough, and the ships exploding when their magazines were hit. Like the gates of Hell slamming shut..."

As he spoke the sailor gazed at the horizon, as if seeing it all re-enacted there.

"Dunkirk was different though. Out on this very deck in the fresh air, with Stukas screaming down like bloody vultures. How we weren't hit while we hauled those boys aboard, God knows. And you couldn't see the deck for khaki. Hundreds of 'em, all fast asleep like babies. Not surprising really, considering what they'd been through. I swear, if we'd gone down there and then, none of 'em would have as stirred. Then we went back for seconds. And thirds..."

"It must have been frightening."

In his mind Dan was comparing the horror of anticipating a direct hit to that of waiting for your enemy to find your hiding place.

"Fear comes later, when you've time to wonder what might have happened. But I was glad to play my part..." The sailor turned away from his memories. "So, where are you heading?"

"Liverpool."

"We're all going there, lad. But a rich one like you won't be hanging around for long, I bet. Not with the Luftwaffe doing its worst."

"I'm going to Cornwall. And I'm not rich."

"Course not, son." The sailor glanced at the door to First Class then winked. "Cornwall, eh? But that's not where you're from, is it? I'm usually good with accents but can't quite place yours..."

"I'm from Berlin."

The sailor's smile vanished. Now Dan's fear had nothing to do with the pitching of the boat. This man looked strong enough to throw him over the side with ease. But the grin soon returned to the sailor's face, its natural habitat.

"Funny old world, that's for sure." He pushed the rolled-up flag into Dan's hands, and winked again. "Here you go, lad. A bit of Manx for you."

Liverpool appeared ahead like a heavenly city, bright in the new sunshine which had broken through the cloud. But as they came closer Dan noticed changes since his last visit, on his way to the camp. Now a multitude of barrage balloons hung in the air, like a school of strange fat fish above a reef. Palls of thick black smoke billowed from wrecked warehouses, and from a hulk half-sunk alongside. And there were many more ships in dock than before, and anchored out in the river: big rusty merchantmen and sleek grey warships were gathering into the beginnings of a convoy; a ragged herd of sheep and their escort dogs preparing to brave the wilderness and the wolf packs.

As *Victoria* came alongside, Charlotte joined Dan on the promenade deck. He was staring up at the statues of two graceful birds on top of the tall building by the quayside. He couldn't help imagining a flock of German eagles swooping down on them and tearing them apart.

"There's your boat..."

Charlotte pointed at a large passenger ship tied up nearby. Dan read the fading name on her stern: *Star of the Ganges*.

"My ship?"

"The one that was going to take you to Canada."

He saw anti-aircraft guns on her deck, pointed at the sky, and helmeted sailors. Soon - like the *Mayflower* - she would be heading into the New World, while he remained behind in a ravaged land, with the forces of darkness amassing beyond.

But he recalled what his mother had written:

"Do whatever you can to get us to England, my darling one."

How could he do that, on the other side of the world? And then there was the letter he'd signed. He'd given his word, and his word was all he had.

They took a taxi from the docks to the station. Despite all that his family had suffered, he still felt shame for what the German bombers had done. He saw a shop demolished in an otherwise untouched street, as if the hand of a vengeful god had punished only that one particular address. In an exposed bedroom, clothes hung forlornly in an open wardrobe.

Perhaps they were Jews who hadn't kept kosher.

Further on, a double-decker bus had fallen into a huge crater in a road, its rear end still visible as if being consumed by the Underworld. He saw firemen trying to douse an angry fire with a pathetic spout of hand-pumped water. Casualties were being carried away on stretchers.

"Copped it bad last night," said the cabby over his shoulder as he drove. "Wave after wave of 'em. Never thought the Jerry bastards would stop, 'scuse my French."

"We can take it," said Charlotte, staring

impassively out of the window. There was a hint of annoyance in her voice at having to conduct a conversation.

"Just as well yous are passing through. Wouldn't be surprised if we get another visit tonight..."

Lime Street Station was crowded and noisy. Parents were seeing off their children, dispatching them to the safety of the countryside. Dan noticed the evacuees had numbers on tags round their necks, just like he'd been given in Berlin.

The crowd on the platform parted for Charlotte like a sea of grey at the bows of a beautiful galleon. A porter followed her, his trolley piled high with luggage.

First Class was a haven of peace. They were shown to their sleeping quarters, each a private little room with a single bed, a small corner-sink and a window.

"I'll see you at dinner," said Charlotte before disappearing into her compartment.

"Could I get sir anything?" asked a smart waiter in red waist coat and white gloves.

"What is there?"

"Tea, coffee or cocoa, sir. And a full selection of alcoholic beverages, of course."

Now Dan was intrigued.

"What kind of alcoholic beverages...?"

He was thwarted by Charlotte's muffled voice from the next compartment:

"No alcohol!"

So, as the train prepared to leave, Dan sipped real coffee from a bone china cup and watched the goodbyes on the platform outside: the tight smiles and anxious eyes that said so much more than words.

His window seemed like a cinema screen. Once he'd been one of the actors in the film. Now he was just a spectator, viewing the sadness of others.

Almost exactly a year before, on a platform in Charlottenberg Station, Dan hugs his mother and sisters. He's wearing the tweed suit his father bought himself during a concert tour of Britain. The suit has been altered but he still feels uncomfortable wearing it. It seems like unspoken acceptance that Father isn't coming back.

"You look like a proper English gentleman," his mother says proudly, fussing with his tie. "It will help you to fit in quickly."

"I don't want to go." He fights back the tears. "I don't want to leave you."

"Don't worry, my darling one." His mother smiles but she can do nothing to hide the pain in her eyes. "It won't be for long. You're the advanced party, remember? Just as soon as we

get our papers we'll be with you. Be brave for us, my dearest. And for your father."

Dan is the last to board. The conductor slams the door shut with great force as if to express his displeasure at having to wait. As the train jolts into motion, Dan claws at the strip of metal at the top of the window. His mother and sisters begin to walk along the platform to keep up with him, their faces contorted with distress.

Then the train gathers speed and they slip out of view.

One of the volunteer escorts comes over to help: an old man with kindness in his eyes. He slides the window down so that Dan can lean out and catch a final glimpse of his family, before they are lost in a cloud of smoke.

The bruised grey cityscape gave way to rich green countryside. Now the war seemed only a dark nightmare: the concern of cities and people, not trees and animals. The sun was beginning to set, gilding the scenery rolling past.

Before dinner, Dan ventured along the narrow corridor to the next carriage. The long space was crammed with child evacuees, stretched out on the seats or on the floor, their heads resting on their little suitcases. Some even lay in the luggage nets above like landed fish, rocking gently. It was strangely quiet, the children exhausted by the upheaval in their lives. He knew that when they awoke and remembered where they were they'd suffer the same pain he still felt every morning.

As he turned to leave, Dan noticed a girl sitting by the door, an infant asleep on her lap. She looked about the same age as him and he felt a pang of guilt. He should be here in this carriage, not in a private compartment with waiter service. But the girl smiled at him, not caring where he'd come from or where he was going. He returned the smile, and remembered another girl on another train, one year ago…

He joined Charlotte for dinner in the softly-lit dining carriage. The scrape of silverware on fine china and the low hum of polite conversation were accompanied by a selection of Beethoven's piano pieces. The occasional jump of the needle on the record was the only disturbance to the genteel atmosphere.

Rationing had yet to reach Pullman restaurant carriages. They ate steak, tender and succulent. For dessert Dan enjoyed a delicate crème caramel which he sliced with the edge of his spoon, thinking of Hitler consuming Europe in a similar fashion.

Charlotte made some effort to engage Dan in polite conversation, enquiring about life in

Berlin - without inviting too much detail - and discussing favourite composers. But now it seemed she was only fulfilling the demands of good manners. She didn't appear to be as interested in him as when they'd first met.

The train stops at the Dutch border. Soldiers in grey uniforms and black jackboots clamber aboard, rifles slung over their shoulders. They clump along the aisle, grinning and laughing, drunk with boredom and power. Dan glimpses the insignia on their collars: the skull and crossed bones of the Waffen SS.

The whole carriage seems to have sunk under their weight. They are looking for adults trying to escape, and smuggled valuables. Any abuse of the Kindertransport programme will result in the whole train returning to Germany.

The children sit quieter than they ever have, hardly breathing. Even the infants are still, sensing the danger.

A soldier takes Dan's cello out of her case and holds her up to his chin like a violin, to the amusement of his comrade. Beneath the frost of his fear Dan feels the heat of a dangerous anger. His father gave him the cello, the day before he was taken away.

"She's yours now, Daniel. Look after her."

Now the soldier studies the instrument, thick fingers with dirty nails violating her strings.

"How much is this worth?"

"Not much."

"He's lying," says the other soldier. "I can see it on his face. I bet it's one of those Strudelvalkyries..."

"She isn't a Stradivarius," Dan says. "She isn't worth much at all, in fact. Just a family heirloom..."

"Female, eh? And you have a good play with her, do you?"

The soldier nudges the other and they both laugh.

"Not in that way."

Now they regard Dan with mock astonishment.

"Is the Jew daring to answer back?"

The tip of the cello's spike touches Dan's throat.

"How would you like a ticket back to the Fatherland to teach you some manners?"

"I'm sorry. I didn't mean to be rude."

The soldier lowers the instrument.

"Tell you what...We'll give you a chance. If you can play this thing well enough we'll let you cross the border. But one bum note and it's back to Berlin for more practice..."

So Dan takes the cello, picks up the bow

and positions himself for the most important performance of his life. His whole body is trembling but as soon as the bow kisses a string and the instrument begins to hum, he feels a calm settle over him.

He finds himself playing an old folk song his father taught him, passed down the generations like a living inheritance. It is a warm and slow lament: a nomadic voice from the past comforting another huddle of terrified migrants on the brink of deliverance.

As he plays he glances up at the soldiers. At first they are entertained by the way he sits with the instrument between his legs, and how his right hand works away suggestively at the cello's neck while his left attends to the bow. But they are soon stilled by the musical spell, staring in silence at the beautiful body of wood which is producing such a deep and sweet resonance. He even thinks he sees a softening in their features, as if they are remembering something...

Then one of the soldiers snaps out of his trance and snatches the cello from Dan, gripping her neck and strangling the sound.

"That's Jewish music!"

"With respect, sir," Dan says, "it's a Romany tune."

"Gypsies?" The other soldier's top lip curls. "Even worse. At least Jews have houses we can confiscate."

The cello is thrown to the floor. A heavy boot crashes into the heart of the instrument, splintering the thin wood. The cello's strings protest in a final discordant groan. Dan feels a sharp stab of pain in his chest, as if the jackboot has entered his own ribcage.

"Just checking for hidden treasure," grins the perpetrator. He carries the splintered carcass to the door and throws it into the night. "That'll teach you for playing the Devil's music."

"We should really send you back," says the other. "Just be thankful we can't be bothered with the paperwork."

They are walking away - laughing - when a voice stops them.

"You're the devils."

It belongs to the girl who smiled at Dan when he first took his seat. Now the two soldiers stand over her.

"What did you say?" says one.

"That was an evil thing to do. You murdered his music."

Her eyes are wide and she is shaking with fear and anger, but pride raises her chin.

"I don't mind!" Dan insists, trying to diffuse the tension. "It's only an instrument, after all. I can get another one…"

But his words are futile. The girl is grabbed

by the hair and dragged out of the carriage.

Some of the younger children sob softly, hearing her screams.

The shriek of the brakes woke Dan. He was lying in complete darkness and stillness, like death. He threw off his bedclothes, fell out of bed and fumbled round the tiny compartment. Finding the heavy black-out curtains at last, he pulled down the window and gulped in the fresh night air.

The train had stopped on a stretch of curved track. Ahead he could see the dark shape of the engine, breathing out steam like an iron dragon at rest. Beyond, the horizon was glowing with an eerie orange light, pulsating with brighter flashes. He heard distant explosions and a deep throbbing hum. Columns of light swept the sky, criss-crossing each other like the start of a Twentieth Century Fox picture. It looked like the beginning of the end of the world.

"Frightening, isn't it?" said a voice nearby. Charlotte had her window down, too. She was smoking a cigarette, her face softly illuminated by the light of the fires. "And yet quite spectacular..."

"What's happening?"

"They're bombing Bristol. We're waiting until it's over."

He tried to imagine what it would be like to be caught in such an inferno.

"All those poor people…"

"Indeed." The glowing remains of Charlotte's cigarette died in a tiny explosion as it hit the ground. "I just hope there's a station left or we're going to struggle to make our connection…Now get back to bed. We've an early start in the morning."

Her window slid up, leaving him to watch the spectacle alone. Today he'd seen the effect of the bombers. Now he was witnessing the Luftwaffe at work.

His enemy was getting closer.

Dawn revealed a huge pall of black smoke hanging over Bristol, like the finger of some dark and accusing god. Temple Meads Station was undamaged but departures had been delayed. So, before changing trains, they were able to enjoy a leisurely breakfast.

"They're checking the track for bomb damage, madam," explained the waiter as he poured the tea. "I shouldn't imagine it will take too long."

"I hope not," said Charlotte. "We still have a long journey ahead of us."

She wore a dark blue outfit which looked almost black. She said very little now, gazing out of the window with what appeared to Dan like sadness in her eyes.

After breakfast they crossed the station to board the Penzance Express. As they took their places in the day compartment a whistle blew and the train began to move. Dan wondered if the driver had been waiting for them to finish their breakfast and change trains. It would have been entirely in keeping with Her Ladyship's way of doing things.

But they'd only travelled a few yards when the train lurched to an undignified halt.

Charlotte sighed.

"What now...?"

Dan glimpsed a brown-skinned youth and a short stocky man of lighter complexion hurrying across the platform. A door slammed, the whistle blew again and the train resumed its slow acceleration.

The compartment door slid open and the late-comers entered. The youth was perfectly turned out. His shoes shone, his grey trousers were sharply creased, his black blazer was perfectly tailored and the tight knot of a red and black tie protruded from a starched white collar. He had an athletic build, and large dark eyes with prominent eyebrows which gave him a predatorial look. Out of breath, he smoothed back a lock of black hair dislodged in the rush.

"Phew. That was close."

"I did warn sahib not to leave the train," said the man accompanying him. He too was smartly dressed, in a dark suit with a green and black tie. He had a broad face with high cheekbones and almond-shaped eyes.

"Had to stretch the legs, old boy," the youth replied. "Getting a little cabin crazy, cooped up like a chicken off to market. But now we've some company to share our discomfort..." He beamed down at Charlotte and Dan, his teeth bright in his broad mouth. "How do you do? My name is Jai Rana and this is Jomsom."

The new arrivals shook hands with Charlotte and Dan.

"I'm Daniel Rosenbaum and this is Charlotte - "

"Lady Smythe-Morrigan," she cut in.

"Smythe-Morrigan, did you say?" Jai and his companion sat down on the long seat opposite. "Any connection to this place...?"

Jai tapped the red badge on his blazer.

"My husband is Headmaster."

"Gosh!" Jai's eyes widened. "Better watch my peas and queues, then. And this is your son, I presume...?"

Charlotte seemed slightly amused by the suggestion.

"No."

"My apologies. I assumed you were travelling together..."

"We are," said Dan. "Charlotte - I mean - Lady Smythe-Morrigan has very kindly offered me a scholarship place."

"So we're all heading for the same destination. Well, that's rather splendid, isn't it?"

"Your father was unable to make the trip?" Charlotte asked.

"Unfortunately not. Heavy gambling session last night, you see. The old man rather over-indulged on the Scotch... So I've borrowed his batman instead, and a better companion you will not meet. Ex-Gurkha Rifles. Pater couldn't possibly function without him."

"So how will he cope when he finds his servant gone?"

"Oh, Pa always sleeps through after a bout. I'm sure Jomsom will be back home in time to pour his first drink of the day."

"Where do you live?" asked Dan.

"Well, my father has a house in Kensington for society parties, and another in Suffolk where he pretends to be lord of the manor. But my real home is Rajputana, in the North West of India."

"I think Mister Rana is being rather modest," said Charlotte. "His father is the Maharaja of Jaisalpur. I believe he rules a kingdom the size of Wales, if I'm not mistaken...?"

"Thereabouts," said Jai, "though much of it is desert, of course....So tell me Dan, from where do you hail? You don't sound English..."

"Germany."

Jai's eyes widened again.

"Really?"

"He was one of the Kindertransport," Charlotte explained.

"Oh yes. I read about that in the paper. And here's me thinking we were lucky getting out of London without incident."

"But you have some experience of escape yourself, haven't you Mister Rana?"

"Oh dear. I fear my reputation precedes me..."

"Remind me again. How many schools have expelled you?"

Jai held up two fingers victoriously.

"Eton and Westminster."

"Your father must be running out of patience."

"Patience isn't a favourite of his, true enough," Jai grinned. "He much prefers poker."

"So what is it about school that you take such exception to?"

"Rules, Your Ladyship. I'm allergic to them, you see. They bring me out in awfully rash behaviour. I don't mean the ones that ensure we live together without killing each other, of course. I mean petty rules which make no sense."

"Well Mister Rana you'll be pleased to learn that all our rules make perfectly good sense." Charlotte smiled coldly. "And I should warn you that we have a great deal of experience in dealing with difficult pupils. I believe this is the main reason your father chose our school…"

"And its distance from London, so I won't be lured by the flesh-pots of the metropolis." Jai winked at Dan. "And he won't have to visit me so often."

Jai was like a bright shaft of Indian sun slicing through the gloom Dan had been feeling since leaving the Isle of Man. As the train sped westwards the two compared notes on their respective countries, while Jomsom gazed out of the window at the rolling greenery and Charlotte read a novel.

Germany and Rajputana seemed like different planets: one orderly and functional, with clean cities and punctual trains, where crime - for most - was rare; the other, a place of chaos and colour, her land parched and harsh, her people wild and sensuous. But while Jai was proud to talk about the country he loved, for Dan it was painful.

"What's happened to Germany?" asked Jai. "Has she gone mad?"

"I suppose that's one way of putting it," Dan replied.

"Well, I hope she recovers soon so you can return."

"Yes. So do I."

The train accumulated school pupils at each station along the way. Mountains of trunks and tuck boxes grew in the luggage spaces. The younger boys were in shorts, the older ones grey trousers, but all wore the dark blazer with its scarlet badge which looked like a wound.

It was quite evident who the new ones were: generally the quiet ones, accompanied by parents or guardians, their uniforms pristine but their faces creased with uncertainty. In contrast, the old hands piled noisily onboard, punching each other affectionately and tossing casual goodbyes in the direction of those who'd seen them off.

Now the train rattled along the coast. Dan glimpsed great rocky headlands and lines of white waves storming ashore. Rain clouds hung over the dark sea like a funeral veil and he watched water droplets racing horizontally across the sooty window.

Why such a hurry to get to the edge?

The train slowed into a small country station, crawling to a halt with a creaking sigh. The signs had been removed to make it harder for an invasion force but it was clear from the ensuing pandemonium that this was journey's end.

The carriages disgorged their contents onto the platform and the passengers were herded to a line of buses parked outside the station. Porters piled the luggage on to the roof racks, including Dan's suitcase and violin. He joined Jai and Jomsom in the queue for a bus then felt a hand on his arm.

"You'll come with me."

Charlotte gestured towards a huge black motor car parked nearby.

"But my luggage is already onboard…"

Her dark eyes regarded him sternly.

"That wasn't a request."

"I'd take the Roller if I were you," said Jai. "Make the most of a bit of luxury, while you can…"

A tall grim-faced man in grey uniform was holding open the door of the Rolls Royce.

"Thank you Garsten," said Charlotte as she got into the car.

The chauffeur smiled slightly and touched the peak of his cap. He didn't bother to acknowledge his other passenger.

Dan found himself ensconced within polished wood, smooth leather and gleaming chrome. He remembered his school in Berlin where he was made to sit in the corner of the class, the focus of the teacher's anti-Semitic jokes. But now he was being driven to his new school in the finest motor car in the world, with its angelic bonnet crest with wings of silver; even finer than the Fuhrer's Mercedes Benz he'd watched cruising past the adoring crowds on Wilhelmstrasse. The pendulum seemed to have swung the other way.

The Rolls Royce soon lost the trundling convoy of buses. The winding road was flanked by high hedges but through gates Dan glimpsed wheat fields and - beyond them - the grey and ancient cliffs.

The car carefully negotiated the sharp elbows of a steep road which descended to the sea, where a white-washed village surveyed a broad bay embraced by two headlands. At the end of the longest of these - on the right of the bay - he saw a white lighthouse, and three jagged outcrops of rock.

In the middle of the bay lay an island. It was surrounded by sand bejewelled by pools gleaming in the sun, the sea having temporarily retreated to permit the passage of mortals. On the seaward end of this island was a hill and at its top stood a castle of such antiquity it might have grown out of the rock, like a dark crystal.

Skirting the harbour, the car passed weathered fishing boats, and a pub called the King's Head, its fading sign depicting a bearded man wearing a crown and holding a sword. Then the wheels of the Rolls Royce rumbled on the cobbles of a stone causeway, splashing through puddles of sea water, its expensive suspension unperturbed. The island grew in front of the tiny figurine on the bonnet until they were passing between the thick stone walls of another, smaller harbour.

Now the road zig-zagged sharply, up through an orchard of apple trees bearing ripe fruit until it reached a plateau. Here, as if in reverence, the car drove slowly around the edge of a flat expanse of manicured grass.

"Top Pitch," said Charlotte. "Where the First Eleven play their cricket matches."

"What's that?"

Dan pointed towards a small mound on the far edge of the pitch, with a circle of standing stones at its top like a gathering of people turned to rock.

"That's the Crown of Stones," she replied. "Built by Ancient Britons. It's supposed to be older than Stonehenge."

Driving through a gateway with a raised portcullis like the upper teeth of an open mouth, they entered a broad space within the castle walls where regimental lines of vegetables grew. Dan spotted a small church, with all the usual trappings of a Christian place of worship but for a stone dome in place of a tower.

"Looks like a synagogue," he thought aloud.

"The Chapel was a Roman temple once upon a time," Charlotte explained. "But I'm sure the Reverend will tell you about that…"

The Rolls Royce had come to a smooth halt at the foot of steps leading up to the entrance of the inner keep. In the open doorway an elderly man in a grey pin-striped suit was leaning on a walking stick. As the car stopped he descended the steps and opened Charlotte's door. Now Dan saw he wasn't that elderly at all; it was his white hair and stick that had made it seem so. His eyes were a cold blue.

"What took you so long?" he asked with a lop-sided smirk, taking Charlotte's hand to help her from the car.

"We were delayed," she replied. "They bombed Bristol last night."

"Really?" He kissed her lightly on the cheek, his arms only half-embracing her, like the two headlands around the island. "How inconsiderate."

Dan had let himself out of the other door. The driver wore a slight sneer on his face, as if in disgust at Dan's temerity.

"I'll need to change," said Charlotte.

"No time for that, I'm afraid. They'll be arriving any minute."

"Ralph, these are my travelling clothes..."

But her protest was half-hearted, as if she'd already resigned herself to compliance. She seemed to have shrunk before Dan's eyes from the formidable woman with whom he'd travelled.

"My dear, you look quite presentable... Garsten, take Her Ladyship's luggage to the house, will you?"

As the Rolls Royce swept away in a graceful arc the man turned to Dan, regarding him with curiosity.

"So this is our new scholar..."

"Rosenbaum," said Charlotte, "this is my husband, Captain Smythe-Morrigan. Our Headmaster."

"Welcome." The Captain displayed an impressive set of teeth, and his handshake was tight. "But let's get inside. There's a chill in the air. Before we know it, winter will be having her wicked way with us..."

Dan followed the Captain and his wife up the steps. Crossing a stone-floored hallway they re-emerged in an area enclosed by high walls. Two towers loomed above them, the one they'd just passed through forming the third corner of the space. A multitude of dark windows - half-choked by ivy - overlooked the flagged courtyard.

"This is the Triangle," said the Captain. "I like to think of it as the heart of our school."

In spite of his limp he moved quickly, like an impatient tour guide, leading the way across the Triangle and into the shadows of the arched cloisters. Climbing another flight of stone steps, they entered a long room with a high vaulted ceiling and a huge wrought iron chandelier. Tapestries on the walls celebrated great battles, hunting scenes and riotous feasting. Thick rugs covered the wooden floor and a large fire crackled in a huge stone fireplace.

In the centre of the room a long table was adorned with plates of sandwiches, cold meats, tarts and cakes, attended by uniformed servants. The music of a clarinet and a harpsichord trickled down from a filigree screen high up at one end of the room.

"The original minstrels' gallery," the Captain explained. "Travelling troubadours carried all sorts of nasty diseases so they had to be kept separate."

"That's Quirk and Buttermere up there," said Charlotte. "They came on an earlier train so they could play this afternoon."

"Now that's dedication for you." The Captain turned to Dan. "You're a musician yourself, I believe?"

Dan nodded.

"Rosenbaum is highly accomplished," said Charlotte. "He'll make a fine addition to the ensemble."

"Splendid. Our little orchestra would certainly benefit from an injection of talent." The Captain grimaced slightly as the harpsichord stumbled over a wrong note. "They're keen but a little creaky..."

But the beauty of the music - the Adagio from Mozart's Concerto in A major - shone through the cracks, filling Dan's heart with a sad warmth. Looking into the fire he saw again the synagogue in flames, its books and scrolls burning in the street.

"When will the rest of my family be able to come to England?"

"I'm sorry?"

"I was told it could be arranged."

"Were you...?"

"Actually, that was the Commandant's suggestion," Charlotte replied to her husband's quizzical glance. "I made no promises."

"And rightly so," said the Captain. "But first things first Rosenbaum, you must remember to address me as 'sir'. I'm sure our rules are similar to those of your last school..."

"I hope not all of them. Sir."

"Well, perhaps not all of them." He smiled briefly. "As for your family coming here, you must understand there's a war on."

Dan thought this a curious thing to say, considering all he'd been through.

"It would be extremely difficult for anyone to leave Germany now," the Captain continued. "But that's not to say there's no hope. Personally I think there will be peace negotiations soon, in which case I'm sure some kind of a deal will be struck..."

"Would that mean the Nazis would keep everything they've taken, sir?"

"Sometimes in life compromises have to be made, young man. But bear in mind a peace treaty would make your family's safe passage here a very real possibility. Ah, here they are..."

Dan looked towards the door, almost expecting to see his family enter. Because of the steepness of the road and the sharpness of its bends, the buses were unable to drive up to the castle so their passengers had walked. Now they began to fill the room, flushed and breathless from the climb, looking round in wonder at the historic interior and the lavish feast before them.

When all were in, the door was shut with an ancient clunk. The Captain stood on the raised hearth of the fireplace. The music stopped and the murmur of the gathered hushed so that for a moment only the business of the fire could be heard. Then, with the easy charm of one well-accustomed to such occasions, the Captain spoke:

"Good afternoon, ladies and gentleman. Considering what is being done to our cities at present, I'm glad to see you've all made it here safely. Welcome to our school, and congratulations to all you parents and guardians for making an excellent choice..."

A smattering of laughter passed round the hall and the Captain employed his smile, relishing his hold upon his audience.

"This is indeed a great school, manifested by our many old boys serving their country even as I speak, among them some very brave pilots currently giving Goering a bloody nose."

"Bravo!" someone shouted and applause broke out spontaneously.

"Of course we're also doing our bit for the war effort," the Captain continued. "All our spare land has been given over to growing crops and raising livestock, and we conduct regular fishing expeditions. In fact, I'm proud to say that most of the fine fare you will be enjoying shortly has been produced on this island..."

Another enthusiastic round of applause.

"I'll address my final words to all of you new boys. Remember that you are all extremely privileged to be here. Our school is a very special place, with a long and proud history which binds all of us together, like one family..."

For a moment all was quiet. The Captain seemed to be looking directly at Dan. Then he clapped his hands together, breaking the spell.

"Now I'm sure you'll all be ready for some refreshment after your journey, so do please dig in...for victory!"

The tables were immediately besieged. While the gathered ate, the Captain and his wife circulated, but Charlotte lacked her husband's effervescence. To Dan she looked drawn and tired, a weariness that seemed deeper than the demands of a long journey.

"Well…" Dan turned his attention to the pile of crabmeat sandwiches on his plate,"if this is going to be the standard of food then I think I might enjoy it here…"

"Make the most of it, my friend."

Jai was contemplating a strawberry jam tart crowned with fresh cream.

"What do you mean?"

"I've attended too many of these functions to be lulled into a false sense of culinary security. But what I take particular exception to is having to stand whilst one eats. Quite barbaric."

He placed the whole tart into his mouth and winked. Jomsom smiled, clearly in agreement.

"Why isn't your friend having anything?" Dan asked quietly.

Jai swallowed.

"Believe me I've tried to persuade him but Jomsom considers it disrespectful for a servant to dine before his master. Hence the reason I'm eating so fast…"

Presently a spoon tapping on a glass brought a hush over the assembled.

"Ladies and gentlemen," said the Captain, "I hate to break up the party but I'm informed that the tide is on the turn…"

A long line of guests, disappointed at having

to abandon an excellent spread, made its way back down to the harbour. Dan watched the awkward goodbyes. Most shook hands stiffly, some hugged. A few of the younger boys were crying.

"Goodbye Jomsom," said Jai, shaking his escort's hand.

"Goodbye sahib." Jomson bowed his head, wearing a smile that seemed to be of an altogether finer quality than the Captain's. "And goodbye sahib."

He shook Dan's hand, likewise bowing and smiling. Dan noticed his jacket pockets were stuffed with sandwiches.

As Jomsom walked away, past the buses, Jai called after him in Hindi then laughed at his reply.

"What did you say?" asked Dan.

"I asked him why he wasn't taking the bus. He said a Gurkha prefers to walk."

"But it's a long way to the station."

"A mere stroll in the park for our Jomsom. You know, he walked halfway across the Himalayas to join the British Army."

When the parents and guardians had boarded the doors were closed and the line of buses pulled out of the harbour and trundled along the stone road, the sea lapping at each side.

Soon Devilston would be an island again.

J.J. Greenwood

2

FIRST DAY AT DEVILSTON

The Head of School stood on the harbour wall, arms folded and feet set apart like a general surveying his troops. He wore a red and black striped blazer with matching cravat, a purple waistcoat, grey trousers with creases sharp enough to slit a throat and shoes gleamed with the sweat of a lower-school lackey. His ginger hair was greased back, his hairline an arrow's tip. Cruel grey eyes, hungry for prey, scrutinised the crowd of new arrivals gathered on the quayside below.

Behind him stood a line of twelve seniors. Their waistcoats were an assortment of colours, like a row of signal flags proclaiming war. Now their leader cleared his throat and the crowd beneath him fell silent.

"So...now that your dear parents and guardians have departed, I shall be your new daddy. And these..." he jabbed a thumb over his shoulder, "are your surrogate mummies."

The line of seniors grinned at the joke: the same one they'd heard when they'd been anxious newcomers themselves.

"They are my Praeposters and what **I** say they'll ensure **you** do. Is that understood?"

The gathering muttered a meek response, like the bleating of a flock of penned sheep.

"There are three houses in our school: Prophets, Philosophers and Privateers. You will now muster in front of your respective Head of House and await further instructions."

Three Praeposters with clipboards began to shout out names and numbers as pupils frantically jostled to find their correct line. Dan and Jai were pleased to learn they were sharing a dormitory-study in the same house. But the Head of Prophets was the most intimidating of the three: a lumbering specimen called Tattersall with a thick mass of black hair, small eyes and the gait of a bull.

"Wipe those smiles off your faces," he snorted at Dan and Jai, "or I'll wipe your faces off your heads. You're not on a honeymoon."

When the divisions were complete the Head of School spoke again:

"That took far too long so I shall time the next task..." He extracted a gold watch from his waistcoat pocket and consulted it. "You have exactly twenty-five minutes to get all this detritus up to school." He waved a hand towards the sprawl of trunks and tuck boxes on the quayside, lying like treasure chests washed up from some stricken wreck. "Any junk remaining when the time is up will be dumped overboard. So what are you waiting for? The twenty minutes have already started!"

The pupils dashed for their luggage.

"Aren't you going to carry your trunks up first?" asked Dan, seeing Jai picking up his tuck box amid the frenzy.

"This takes priority, old chap. There are certain things that are simply irreplaceable."

As they negotiated the steep road up through the orchard, Dan struggled with his suitcase and violin. The handle of the violin case had broken so he had to wrap an arm round it awkwardly. When he stopped to adjust the load, Jai took the violin case and placed it on his tuck box.

"Thanks."

Jai winked in reply.

Depositing their luggage in the entrance to Prophets they hurried back down to the quayside, against a flow of pupils struggling like ants with their loads. After carrying one of Jai's trunks up to school, the pair returned in time to see two Praeposters standing on the harbour wall, swinging Jai's second trunk between them. Tattersall stood by, in command:

"One…two…**three**!"

The trunk rose as gracefully as it could into the air then dropped out of sight. As Dan and Jai ascended the steps they passed the three Praeposters on their way down, laughing.

The trunk had split open on the rocks below. Clothes were swirling around on the incoming tide like spilled guts.

"Pretty sure that wasn't twenty minutes," Jai sniffed casually, apparently unperturbed by the loss.

Dan didn't reply. He was remembering the soldiers throwing his broken cello into the night.

Their dormistudy was located high up in Prophets' tower. It took some effort for the two of them to carry Jai's surviving trunk up the narrow spiral stairway. At the end of a dark corridor a door marked with the number thirteen was slightly ajar.

The room beyond was small and crammed with furniture: a narrow wardrobe in each corner and - squeezed between them - two bunk beds and four sets of desks and chairs. High up in the wall opposite the door - in a deep alcove - glowed a small window filtering a meagre supply of daylight into the space. The smell of mould stained the air.

"This isn't a room," said Jai with disgust, "it's a

bloody cell."

Dan spotted two trunks beneath one of the bunk beds. Each had a name stencilled on its front.

"*T.W. Barrow* and *S.P. Yorke*," he read. "Hard to believe there's space for two more in here..."

"What's that?" Jai's attention had switched to a flat wooden box with slits in the front, fixed above the door. "Some kind of listening device...?"

Dan squinted up at it.

"Looks more like a loudspeaker than a microphone."

In order to gain access to the window, Jai had to climb onto a desk and pull himself up into the tapering alcove above it. The castle's wall was so thick that this space was big enough to accommodate him quite comfortably. He opened the window and looked out.

"Ye Gods!

"What is it?"

"See for yourself..."

Jai climbed down to make way for his friend. The sight made Dan's head reel. It was a drop of over fifty feet to the base of the tower, then at least another hundred to the bottom of a sheer cliff where black rocks were tearing the grey sea into white shreds. He could just make out a narrow path around the foot of the tower, offering little hope of interrupting a long plummet down to the salivating rocks far below.

Now looking out to sea Dan breathed in the fresh air, savouring the wind on his face and the tang of salt on his tongue.

"*The Count of Monte Cristo*," he thought aloud, closing the window and climbing down.

"Who?"

"It's a book by Alexander Dumas, about a man who's betrayed and imprisoned on an island."

"Ah yes. Dumas. *The Three Musketeers*." Jai raised a clenched fist. "All for one and one for all!"

At that moment, as if summoned by the call, a plump youth shuffled into the room. He had large sad eyes which seemed resigned to all the miseries of the world, prominent ears, and a mop of unruly hair so blond it looked almost white. He wore scuffed shoes, a crumpled blazer and a miscreant collar and tie.

"Hallo there. I'm Tom Barrow. You must be my new room mates…" Dan and Jai shook hands with him and introduced themselves. "I'm an old hand here. Bit of a shock to the system at first but you'll soon get used to the place."

Dan noticed Tom had a different accent to the other pupils. Warmer somehow, with flatter vowels.

"Jai had one of his trunks thrown into the sea," he said.

"Oh dear," Tom replied. "They did that to me on my first day, too. Took me ages to get all my gear back. Do you want a hand finding yours?"

"No thanks," said Jai. "I wouldn't want to give them the satisfaction of seeing me splashing around in the water."

"But what about your stuff? You'll be in for a real beasting if you haven't got the right uniform."

"All my school kit is in this one." Jai tapped his remaining trunk with his foot. "The other had a few extra luxuries in it. I suppose I'm just like everybody else now…"

"Not quite," said another voice, intruding.

The Head of School had appeared in the doorway, a group of Praeposters looming behind him. He extended his hand, smiling.

"Smythe-Morrigan. S-M to my friends though you'll call me Sir. Just doing a quick round, meeting all those new to school. Or newts, as we call them. You must be the chap from India. Your old man's a margarina or something, isn't he…?"

"A maharaja," Jai replied.

"Is that like a king?"

"I suppose so."

"So that makes you a prince?"

"Of sorts."

"Well here you're just an ordinary pleb I'm afraid. Well a bit darker than the usual, perhaps. The Prince of Darkness even...." The Praeposters laughed. Smythe-Morrigan patted Jai on the shoulder. "Only having you on. No hard feelings, eh?"

Jai smiled faintly.

"Not really. But tell me, why are we Seniors in our final year treated the same as the Juniors? It wasn't like that at my previous schools..."

"Because privilege doesn't grow on trees here, old fruit. It must be earned. Shame about the trunk business, though. Mind you, if you'd only brought the one then you wouldn't have had a problem. One trunk per elephant...You look like a sportsman. Rugger?"

"A little."

"Excellent. Only, we don't use human heads here..." The Praeposters guffawed. "Oh, take no notice of me. I'm just pulling your leg. You're a good sort, I can see that. We're going to get along splendidly." Now Smythe-Morrigan regarded Dan. "And you'll be...?"

"Daniel Rosenbaum."

"That's the one!" He winked at his grinning Praeposters. "They tell me your dad works for Hitler..."

"My father is in a German labour camp."

"That's what I meant!" Again the Praeposters exploded with mirth. "Just jesting, Rosamunde. Glad to have you aboard." Smythe-Morrigan extended his hand. Dan shook it uncertainly. "I hear you like a fiddle..."

"I play the violin," said Dan, "if that's what you mean."

"So, a musician and a sportsman for Prophets. But poor old Wheely here isn't much good at anything, except stuffing his guts. He can put it away for England, as you can see." Smythe-Morrigan jabbed Tom in his stomach. "Wheely's from Up North...Yorkshire, isn't it?"

"Lancashire sir."

"Same difference. His old man used to work down t'pit but apparently he's flying Spits now, out of Saint Eval. Isn't that right Wheely?"

"No sir."

"But I thought you said pater was a pilot...?"

Smythe-Morrigan glanced knowingly at his audience.

"He is, sir," Tom replied, "only he used to work in a cotton mill, not a coal mine."

"I see. So he's good at spinning yarns then...?"

The Praeposters found this hilarious.

"It's not a yarn, sir. It's true."

"Really Wheely? So what rank is your pa then?"

"Flight Sergeant."

"Sergeant eh? But according to my father only officers fly planes. And he should know, having flown Sopwith Camels in the last one..."

"They come from all sorts of backgrounds nowadays, sir."

"Do they?" The Head Boy eyed Tom doubtfully. "Only the thing is, you don't look very much like the son of a fighter pilot to me. Though I have to say, with ears like yours you wouldn't need an aeroplane." More laughter. "What do you think, Your Highness? Is old Wheely here telling porkies?"

He gave Tom another poke in the stomach.

"I've no reason to doubt him," said Jai.

"Well, as they say, there's one born every minute. Actually Ramadan, it's every second in your country isn't it...?"

"My name is Rana."

Smythe-Morrigan's grin disappeared.

"Your name is exactly what I say it is. But mine is always Sir..." The smile returned. "Anyway, I can see you three are going to get along famously. Remember Wheely, as dormistudy skipper it's your job to see these two swabs learn the ropes as quickly as possible..."

"Yes sir."

"Splendid. Well, must dash. Plenty more newts in the pond, as they say..."

He turned to leave.

"Sir, one question before you go...?"

Smythe-Morrigan turned back to Tom.

"Better be a good one, Wheely. I'm a busy man."

"I was just wondering when Yorke's due to arrive, sir..."

"Who?"

"Yorke sir. The other new one. His trunk's here but there's no sign of him."

"Ah yes." The Head of School clicked his fingers. "Forgot about him...Well, apparently his luggage was sent ahead then the poor chap bought it in an air raid."

"Is he...?"

"Very much so, I'm afraid. But at least you'll have a bit more space in here. And you might as well have his uniform Rosalyn, since you've clearly none of your own."

"But he can't wear the clothes of a dead person," said Jai. "It wouldn't be right."

"Why not? I believe his family was killed in the raid so there's no-one to send it back to... Besides, Rosencrantz here is Jewish so he won't want to see anything going to waste. And he's a Jerry to boot, so he won't mind taking other people's property..."

"You know, you really shouldn't say such things."

Smythe-Morrigan took a step closer to Jai. He was taller than Jai and his manner was suddenly threatening.

"I'll say whatever I want to, Mowgli. I'm Head of School, remember...?"

Jai said nothing but stood his ground, returning the stare. Jai glimpsed a flare of fear in the grey eyes. Then Smythe-Morrigan's face broke into a grin again as he playfully touched Jai's shoulder with a fist.

"I'm only larking. Look Rosetta, you don't have to wear Yorke's clobber if you don't want to, but turn up for Roll Call tomorrow morning without a uniform and you'll be first on my Cutter list come Sunday. Cheerio chaps! And Wheely…"

With that Smythe-Morrigan marched away, his entourage of Praeposters following.

"I really don't like that one," said Jai.

"Best to keep in his good books though," said Tom. "He is the Head of School, after all."

"Nothing to do with his father being Headmaster, of course," Jai sneered. "And there's him lecturing us about working for your privileges…"

"Arbeit macht frei," said Dan, pulling Yorke's trunk out from under the bed.

"What?"

"Work sets you free. One of the many slogans of the National Socialist Party…"

Dan opened the trunk and lifted out a blazer.

"You're not going to wear that, are you?" asked Jai.

"I don't believe in superstition." Dan was already putting the jacket on. "There. What do you think?"

With his hands by his sides only the tips of his fingers could be seen sticking out of the sleeves, and the shoulders drooped. Jai remained doubtful.

"It's a bit big..."

"As my mother always says, I can grow into it."

"And you haven't disappeared in a puff of smoke so I don't think it's cursed," said Tom. "Anyway, I doubt if poor Yorke would mind."

"Well," said Jai, "I only hope you're both right."

At six o'clock the following morning the box on the wall above the door resonated with a bugle call: a strained sound, like a dying cockerel.

"So that's what it's for," Jai mumbled.

The three dragged themselves out of their bunks to join the rest of the school for Roll Call on the Triangle. The three houses had assembled in front of their respective entrances in each corner of the yard, shivering in gym kit in the brutal chill of dawn.

Standing on the doorstep Tattersall was like a bear prematurely disturbed from hibernation. When he reached the last name on his house list there was no response. He looked up, grunting the name again.

"Yorke!"

"Sir," said Tom meekly, remembering his responsibilities,"Yorke's not here."

"So where the Hell is he then?"

"Sir, he's…"

"He's what? Still stinking in bed, waiting for Mumsy to bring him breakfast…?"

"No sir. He's…"

"Well come on then, you fat oaf. Spit it out!"

The other two houses had completed their roll calls and now the whole school had tuned in with interest.

Another voice spoke up.

"Yorke's dead."

Tattersall's glare shifted to Jai.

"And who asked you?"

"I was just trying to help."

The Head of Prophet's eyes narrowed.

"What's your name again…?"

"Jai Rana."

"Sir!"

Tattersall's roar echoed around the Triangle.

"Oh, that's quite alright," said Jai loudly, knowing he commanded the attention of the entire pupil body. "No need to call me that…"

The school seemed to gasp as one. Tattersall stared at Jai with disbelief, his mouth opening and closing several times. He'd only been Head of House for a matter of hours yet already he was feeling the deep and secret fear of a leader in danger of losing control of the mob. He wanted this foreign upstart to be pulled from the crowd and beaten but decided to postpone his revenge.

"Congratulations Rana." Tattersall smiled. "You're my first customer for the Cutters..."

During the morning exercise regime the duty Praeposters patrolled the groaning lines, barking obscenities and dispensing summary justice to those showing insufficient effort. Inevitably Tom was one of those targeted for punishment. He trotted miserably around the courtyard, ordered to repeat between wheezing pants:

"I'm a...fat...lazy....useless...pleb..."

The routine always culminated in a sprint down to the harbour and back, the slowest having to repeat it. But today the Praeposters were denied their full gratification. Dan and Jai fed Tom a constant supply of encouragement, and when their new friend seemed close to collapse, they took an arm each to support him.

"Thank you..." Tom gasped, as the three of them recovered on the steps of Prophets. "First time...I've not had to...do it again..."

A shadow fell across his face.

"I see you've got yourself a couple of guardian angels now Wheely," growled the Head of House.

"All for one..." said Jai.

Tattersall stared down at him, unamused.

"The joker in the pack, eh? Well, here's a warning: you'd better wind your neck in Gunga Din or this place is going to be Hell for you."

"Wind my neck in...?"

The expression had drawn Jai's attention to Tattersall's own neck, or - rather - the lack of it. His head seemed to have been attached directly to his body.

"With respect, sir..." Tom wheezed, "...but Rana has a little trouble with the language... He's not trying to be funny or anything..."

"Isn't he? Could have fooled me."

"That wouldn't be too hard," muttered Jai.

"What was that?"

"I said, you shouldn't be too hard on yourself. You seem so angry all the time." He paused before adding: "Sir."

Tattersall's eyes grew even smaller.

"Mark my words, darky. Pretty soon you're going to be wishing you were back home in whatever armpit of the Empire you came from. And as for you..." Now he was addressing Tom again. "You'd better get your fat backside upstairs pronto and start running my bath..."

"A little trouble with the language?" said Jai when Tattersall had lumbered away. "I speak the King's English better than any of these Preposteruses."

"I know," said Tom, "but you've really got to watch your tongue in this place."

"My tongue is like a serpent not easily charmed..."

"Well, if you can't control it," said Dan, "then at least keep the lid on its box."

"Basket," Jai corrected him.

"No need to be rude," said Tom.

Now Jai laughed loudly, his anger discharged, but Dan didn't get the joke. Sometimes English seemed like an impenetrable code.

The warmth of a new friendship was temporarily doused by icy water. As Leavers the three shared the corridor with the four House Praeposters, including Tattersall. Each prefect enjoyed a room to himself, and a priority claim upon the four iron tubs in the bathroom. But the capacity of the boiler was only enough for four baths, and there wasn't time for the ancient geyser to re-heat before breakfast commenced.

"Tom, why do you have to run their baths?"

Dan was swiftly towelling himself dry, trying to rub some life back to his limbs after the shock of the cold.

"Well, they do have plenty of Juniors to do jobs." As he dried himself, Tom couldn't help comparing his own flabby body with Dan's wiriness and Jai's lean build. "But I suppose it's convenient for them to have somebody on the same floor..."

"But you're a Leaver," said Jai. "You shouldn't be fagging for anyone."

Tom shrugged then plodded back to the dormistudy to dress, his towel wrapped round his ample waist.

The Dining Hall had a high vaulted ceiling with thick rib-like beams, like the abdominal cavity of some great monster. On the stone walls hung a selection of antique swords, muskets and rifles arranged in the shape of giant flowers, each weapon a petal. Between these clusters were lines of shields bearing various heraldic emblems, dragons the most common motif.

The breakfast duty party emerged from the kitchens carrying large deep pans. When the lids were opened, great clouds of steam billowed upwards like the vapours from a witch's cauldron. A thick glutinous substance was spooned into bowls and passed along the tables.

Dan and Jai stared doubtfully at what had arrived in front of them as Tom dug in.

"Porridge," he said through a full mouth. "Get stuck in lads, before it goes cold…"

The porridge was quite adhesive, clinging to the roofs of mouths and burning the backs of throats as it was swallowed down. Jai pulled a face as he ate.

"Tastes like boiled books…"

"That might make it easier to learn things." Tom was scraping the last remnants of the sticky substance from his plate. "I mean, if you could eat books instead of having to read them..."

Jai contemplated the cooling sludge in his bowl.

"I'd hardly call this easy."

"In Berlin they burn books," said Dan.

"Why?" asked Tom. "Not enough fuel?"

"No," said Jai. "Too many fools..."

The main course was a small island of an insipid yellow hue in a red sea of tinned tomato, in which wallowed a raft of deep-fried bread and a thin sausage like a beached submarine. The Dining Hall rang out with the sound of steel on plate as knives cut through the brittle bread, sending fragments flying like shrapnel.

Jai studied the yellow blob on the end of his fork.

"Powdered egg," said Tom.

Jai grimaced.

"More powder than egg, I fear..."

Dan was tackling the sausage, tasting fat and gristle and little else. Now he recalled the meals on the Isle of Man with longing: plain country food, fresh and plentiful. And then there were the delicacies he'd enjoyed during his journey here.

"So where do the Praeposters eat?" he asked, noticing only a handful of duty prefects were present."

Tom swallowed a mouthful.

"Oh, they use the Staff Dining Room upstairs, where you had your reception yesterday. They even have their own kitchens up there..."

"You mean, they don't eat the same food as us?" asked Jai.

"Of course not. And they have their own cooks and waiting staff as well."

The duty breakfast party cleared the tables then brought round large aluminium tea pots, half-filling tin cups with a dark brown concoction of weak tea and powdered milk.

"I have to say..." Jai was struggling to remove a stubborn morsel from between his teeth with his thumb nail, "...of all the school meals I've had to endure, that one easily qualifies as the most repulsive."

"Well, there is a war on," said Tom.

"There is indeed." Jai nodded in the direction of the kitchens. "Chemical warfare waged on our stomachs by the deranged army on the other side of that door. They should be shot for crimes against gastronomy."

"I suppose they're just doing their best. They're only pupils, after all..."

Dan and Jai exchanged an astonished look. Tom laughed.

"Didn't you know? There's a rota. We take turns to do the cooking. Except the Praeposters, of course..."

The Reverend Edward Monmouth was a tall middle-aged man with a large once-lean frame now surrendering to the fat of time. His dark suit appeared about to burst at its seams and his white dog collar chafed at his neck. From his broad shoulders hung a black gown, like the withered wings of some giant but ageing bat which had long abandoned the dream of flight. His unkempt grey hair and short beard were flecked with dying embers of red, his face a constellation of small angry blotches within a nebula of general redness. And yet - illuminated by a shaft of sunlight shining through the stained glass and invigorated by the sacred text before him - his green eyes still shone with some vestige of youth.

The bronze lectern at which the Reverend stood took the form of a golden dragon with wings spread, bearing a large Bible on its back. The dragon's head was turned to one side, mouth open and tongue extended, as if in protest at its sacred burden.

Now a deep and rich Welsh voice echoed round the Chapel:

"The lesson is taken from the Book of Revelations, Chapter Twelve..."

The Reverend cleared his throat - a formidable sound in itself, like a boulder being rolled from a cave entrance - then commenced reading. He pronounced each word with exactness and relish; and every time he raised his eyes from the text, his stare would be directed at a random member of the congregation, striking fear into the boy's heart lest he be struck down there and then by a bolt of lightening.

"*And there appeared a great wonder in heaven,*" the Reverend boomed, "*a woman clothed with the sun, and the moon under her feet, and upon her head a crown of twelve stars. And she, being with child, cried, travailing in birth, and pained to be delivered. And there appeared another wonder in heaven: behold a great dragon, and the dragon stood before the woman...for to devour her child as soon as it was born.*"

"*And she brought forth a man child, who was to rule all nations with a rod of iron. And there was a war in heaven: Michael and his angels fought against the dragon, and the great dragon was cast out into the earth....*"

Frequently striking the lectern with his palm so that it wobbled as he reached the crescendo, the Reverend thundered:

"*Woe to the inhabiters of the earth and of the sea, for the Devil is come down unto you, having great wrath, because he knoweth that he hath but a short time...*"

He paused to survey a congregation riveted by his words but - for the most part - utterly ignorant of their meaning.

"Here endeth the lesson. We will now sing the school hymn: number two hundred and ninety three in your books…"

Though some of the words were different, Jai recognised the hymn. It was as if Devilston was claiming it for herself, slowly altering its form like creeping ivy:

Who would true valour see,
Let him go under;
One here will constant be
Come storm, come thunder;
There's no discouragement
Shall make him once relent
His first avowed intent
To serve old Devilston!

Dan knew that the main function of this hymn was not to invite reflection on its meaning, but to bind the gathered together in the coils of a rousing melody. It was a mechanism of social control with which he was familiar.

Whoso beset him round
With dismal stories,
Do but themselves confound;
His strength the more is.
No dragon can him fright;
He'll with a giant fight,

But he will have the right
To serve old Devilston!

To Tom, the hymn was a familiar part of the furniture of the school and - hence - meaningless. But he sang with great vigour all the same, roaring the final line of each verse like a battle cry:

No maudlin nor frail friend
Can daunt his spirit;
He knows he at the end
Shall death inherit.
Then, fancies fly away;
He'll not fear what men say;
He'll labour night and day
To serve old Devilston!

As the final note swirled around the Chapel's ancient dome the Captain made his way to the front, his steel-rimmed heels clicking unevenly on the stone flags as he limped. For a moment he cast a critical eye over his audience, then he spoke.

His voice lacked the deep mellifluousness of the Reverend's, but it possessed a piercing quality just as penetrating:

"The Reverend's reading spoke of a new-born child being brought into the world. For me that child represents this new term - Michaelmas -

and the start of another academic year, with all the promise that entails. We also heard mention of a dragon, reminding us of the challenges in this year ahead; and - of course - our nation is confronting a great challenge herself at this time: a struggle bigger than any of us but involving all of us, and one which I'm certain will end in victory...

"And what were those final words of the lesson? *Because he knoweth that he hath but a short time...* You may think your lives stretch before you to infinity, but mark my words: all of your days are numbered..."

The Captain had lifted his walking stick and was slowly moving it in an arc in front of him, like the barrel of a gun selecting its target. For a moment its end seemed to be pointing at Dan.

"So don't be wasting a single second of your time here..."

Now the Captain lowered his stick, its end striking the ground with an echoing report.

"I hereby declare Michaelmas Term officially begun. Work hard, play hard and pray hard, with all your mind, body and soul; a message enshrined in our school motto: Usquequaque Tria Via. Always Three Ways..."

The striped-blazered prefects at the back of the class ignored the black-blazered non-entities in front of them. They laughed and joked amongst themselves, relating their summer antics. The war was only mentioned as a back-drop to lurid tales of drunkenness and easy girls. And in the midst of this rowdy gaggle of back-slapping self-congratulation presided the Head of School: the young prince indulged by his fawning courtiers.

The Praeposters seemed in no hurry to acknowledge the arrival of their new form tutor. They rose slowly to their feet, their conversations dribbling to an end in their own time. They were clearly signalling to the entrant that - although he was a Member of Staff and hence higher in superiority - their respect would still have to be earned.

The master was youthful if not young, of average height and build, with eyes and hair somewhere between dark and fair, and features on the ordinary side of handsome.

"Good morning gentlemen," he said and the class mumbled a reply. "Sit down please."

Chairs scraped on the wooden floor. The room was quiet now but there was a palpable tension in the air. The teacher knew that how he handled the next few minutes could well define his relationship with his new class for the whole year. But deep within himself he feared he lacked the essential requirement of the effective pedagogue: that basic desire to impose one's will upon a group of individuals. As he spoke he hardly recognised his own voice. It was as if he was listening to an actor delivering someone else's lines.

"My name is Mister Alderley and I'm your form tutor. As you all probably know, I'm new to the Staff so hopefully you won't be too harsh on me if I happen to get things wrong..."

Most of the room stared back at him in silence. Only a black-blazered trio on the front row responded, providing a degree of encouragement with their smiles.

"So I'm looking forward to meeting you all and helping you to get the most out of your final year at Devilston. Yes...?"

Someone had put a hand up at the back.

"Could I ask you a personal question...?"

"That depends on how personal." Alderley smiled uncertainly. "What's your name, by the way?"

"Smythe-Morrigan. Head of School."

"Ah yes. Of course. And your question is...?"

"Why are you here?"

The Praeposters sniggered.

"Now that's rather a philosophical one, isn't it...?'Why are any of us here?' you may ask, and I think the Reverend might be better qualified to answer that one..." Alderley laughed nervously. "But if you mean, 'why have I come here to teach?' the answer is, I was a pupil here myself, a long time ago. I left in Nineteen Eighteen, in fact..."

"Actually," Smythe-Morrigan closed in for the kill, "I meant, why haven't you joined up...?"

An awkward silence. A window was partly open and in the outside world - above the whisper of the sea - the call of a gull could be heard, like a rude laugh.

"Well," said Alderley, "for a start I'm a little too old..."

"Oh, I wouldn't say that. Your predecessor Mister Buchan was older than you and he's in the Navy now. On convoy patrol I believe, hunting U-Boats in the North Atlantic..."

Alderley braced himself.

"Alright, I'll be honest with you." He took a deep breath and the whole class leaned forward. "I'm a pacifist. I don't believe war is the solution to humanity's problems."

"A conchie...?"

"That's right. A conscientious objector."

Someone at the back of the class began slowly clucking, just loud enough to be heard at the front, yet quiet enough for Alderley to pretend not to notice.

When he'd finished taking the register he dismissed the class. The room swiftly emptied, like reluctant witnesses vacating the scene of a crime as quickly as possible.

Alone again at last, he walked to a window to

look out over the blue expanse of Devilston Bay, beyond the diamond lattice of lead. His hands shook as he fumbled for a cigarette. His instinct was to get out right now, to pack his suitcase and flee across the Causeway. The tide was out again and the mainland looked temptingly close.

Go while you can. Before you're sucked down any further...

He searched his pockets for matches. Then a hand appeared in front of him and expertly manipulated a brass army lighter: flipping open the lid, flicking the flint then presenting the flame to the tip of his cigarette.

"Thank you."

The slim young woman next to him lit a cigarette for herself.

"You're welcome."

She wasn't beautiful in the conventional sense - her black curly hair was boyishly short, her nose prominent, her eyebrows thick - but he was immediately intrigued. Her skin was olive-brown and her eyes so dark they seemed black, like pools of oil. She wore a light summer dress and cardigan.

"This is a beautiful place," she said, looking out of the window as she smoked.

He was relieved to have been offered a way in to a conversation.

"The island or the school?"

"You don't like it here?"

"Now I never said that…"

She smiled. One of her teeth was slightly crooked, only adding to her attractiveness. She held out her hand and he shook it.

"My name is Elena Montserrat. I teach languages. My form room is next door."

"Michael Alderley. Science. How do you do?"

"I do very well, thank you."

He placed her accent somewhere on the Iberian peninsular. There was also a slight hoarseness to her voice.

"Are you from Spain?" he asked.

"Not quite."

"Portugal?"

"Not at all."

"Oh dear. I'm not doing very well, am I…?"

"I'm from Catalonia."

"Really? I followed the Civil War in the papers. Such a tragedy…"

"Yes. It was."

He felt suddenly foolish. His words had sounded trite. *I followed the Civil War.* He could have been talking about the football.

"And where are you from?" she asked.

"Truro. And here."

"Here…?"

"I'm an Old Devilstonian."

"Ah. Now it begins to make sense…So, what brought you back?"

"I don't know, really. I just saw the advertisement and it felt like the right thing to do. Perhaps I'm a masochist. Or perhaps it's just fate..."

"Fate?" She was looking deep into his eyes now. "I didn't think you Anglo-Saxons believed in such things."

"Actually, I was born in Cornwall so I'm probably more of a Celt..."

"Ah Elena, there you are...." Distracted, Alderley hadn't heard the Captain enter the room. "I was going to introduce you to our new science teacher but I see you've pre-empted me..."

"Mister Alderley and I were just discussing fate," said Elena.

"Is that so? Not a fan, myself. I like to think we're in charge of our own destinies. God may have built the ship but He has given us full command of the tiller..."

"Well, I certainly can't rely on God to do my work for me." Elena stubbed out her cigarette in the ash tray on the teacher's desk. "If you'll excuse me gentlemen, I have lessons to prepare..."

"So, what do you think?" the Captain asked after she'd gone.

"She's delightful."

"Actually, I meant your opinion of the school. Whether you think it's changed for the better, since you were last here..."

Alderley flustered, embarrassed by his spontaneous confession.

"Oh yes, definitely. It feels like a new place, Headmaster."

"Really? I was hoping we'd preserved some of its ancient essence. That indefinable something which makes Devilston so special..."

"Oh, naturally. That hasn't changed at all."

"Plus ca change, plus c'est la meme chose, eh...?"

"Quite."

Alderley had little knowledge of French. The Captain looked at him for a moment, as if gauging him.

"Well, I'd better let you get on. But one last word, old boy. Just between you and me..."

Alderley felt a hand on his shoulder, the grip tightening as the Captain displayed his teeth.

"The Spaniard's spoken for. If you get my drift..."

The Reverend Edward Monmouth strolled slowly between the lines of desks, his long cape swinging, a yard ruler in his hand like a magic wand. In registration the Leavers had been restless and impudent but now, in the huge presence of the Reverend, they were quiet and submissive. Yet a tiny hint of irreverence remained, for the class sensed their history teacher was in a good mood. Term had begun, and consequently some purpose and structure had returned to his life.

"So someone tell me," he rumbled, relishing the return of his audience, "what is history...?"

"What's already happened, sir," said a black-blazer sitting at the front of the class. He was thin and gawky, with large teeth and thick spectacles.

"Indeed, Mister Quirk. But that's not the whole story. You see, everything we are today - our language, our culture, this very school - was forged in the crucible of the past. We are standing on the shoulders of giants...Who said that, by the way?"

"You did, sir," said Smythe-Morrigan, from the back. "Just then."

The class laughed, in a restrained manner.

"Very funny S-M, but watch yourself. Quirk?"

"Sir Isaac Newton, sir."

"Newton indeed. And what do we see from this lofty height...?"

"Sir, the sea?" the Head Boy ventured.

"The future, lad!" the Reverend bellowed. "History is not only our understanding of who we are, but what we will be!"

"So what's the history of this place, sir?" asked Dan, inspired. The class groaned.

"Quiet!" The Reverend turned to regard Dan.

"Name?"

"Rosenbaum, sir."

"So can anyone answer Mister Rosenbaum's question? Not you, Quirk." The room remained silent. The Reverend sighed. "Quirk...?"

Quirk pushed his glasses up the bridge of his nose and pulled his chair in.

"Well sir, the Devil was abroad one stormy night, doing evil deeds, when he came to the sea. He saw the waves crashing on the shore, ships being broken up, people drowning and such like, and it made him angry to see something more powerful than he was. So he picked up the nearest rock - actually, it was the size of a hill - and threw it at the ocean. It landed in the bay and created this island: The Devil's Stone. Or Devilston."

"Well done, Quirk. Concise summary of an ancient legend."

"Of course," Quirk continued, "the island was really created millions of years ago by an eruption of magma to form the granite plug on which the school stands..."

"Very good, but I think we'll leave all that to the Science Department. Wouldn't want to steal their thunder..." A sudden loud crack made the whole class jump. "Wake up, lad!"

The Reverend's yardstick had made violent contact with the top of Tom's desk, blasting him out of his doze.

"Sorry, sir."

"You will be. A candidate for your Cutters, Mister Smythe-Morrigan."

"Thank you, sir."

"There's only one category of person allowed to rest in peace in my lessons. Isn't that right Mister Quirk?"

"Sir, the dead."

"The dead, indeed. Which rather conveniently brings us to the first occupants of this place...The Ancient Britons are said to have used this island as a burial site, though this has never been corroborated since no such chamber has been found to provide us with primary proof. All we have are unreliable writings produced centuries later. What we call secondary evidence..."

Dan spontaneously voiced a thought:

"Avalon..."

The master eyed this new specimen.

"I've read about it, sir," Dan went on. "Avalon means 'The Isle of Apples', doesn't it? And there are many apple trees on this island..."

The Reverend resumed his slow prowl around his domain.

"Arthurian legend does indeed tell of an island where the dead are taken, but I'm afraid we'd need more evidence than the existence of large quantities of fruit.We are now entering the realm of myth, which we shall call tertiary evidence: the most unreliable of all..."

"Sir," said Quirk, aware of a new rival and keen to score more points, "isn't there supposed to be a secret tunnel, connecting the island to the mainland?"

Another collective groan from the class. Most had heard this story many times.

"Pipe down!" the Reverend roared, then rumbled on: "In answer to your question Mister Quirk, Ancient Britons are indeed said to have carved a passage from this hypothetical burial chamber to the shore, perhaps so that the living would be able to stay in touch with the souls of their ancestors, and vice versa... However, it is also believed by some that a monster lurks in a certain Scottish lake, fairies reside in the gardens of fortunate people and an old man dispenses gifts at lightening speed on Christmas Eve..."

"Sir, are you suggesting Father Christmas doesn't exist?" asked Smythe-Morrigan with mock affront.

The Reverend acknowledged the joke with a smirk.

"Proper history is rational, rigorous and resolutely unromantic." The alliteration rolled off his tongue. "We know for a fact that the Ancient Britons were extremely limited in their use of technology, so you can banish from your tiny minds all notions of a secret passage."

"But they built Stonehenge, sir. And the Crown of Stones..."

The Reverend stopped and turned to consider Dan again. He was irritated by this new pupil's petulance but - at the same time - gratified by his engagement. This was what education was about, after all: questions begetting questions.

"Don't you think that if it existed then we would have found it by now?"

"But just because it hasn't been found," Dan countered, "doesn't mean it doesn't exist. No-one has primary evidence for the existence of God, but that isn't proof there isn't one."

The Reverend stared at Dan like a toad about to consume a fly.

"And which god would that be, Mister Rosenbaum...?"

It was meatloaf for lunch, a dark concoction with the consistency of dry soil which fell to pieces on the plate. The potatoes and cabbage had been mercilessly boiled until they were pale ghosts of their former selves. Jai grimaced as he forced the food down.

"I thought it couldn't get any worse than breakfast. One shudders to think what's in store for supper..."

"Tell you what, Dan," said Tom through a mouthful, "when you were going on about God in that history lesson I thought Old Monster Mouth was going to eat you alive…"

"Do you believe it exists?"

"God? I suppose so…"

"Not God. The tunnel."

"Well, according to Monster Mouth there isn't one."

Jai raised his fork.

"But why not? My city Jaisalpur is riddled with underground passages, like a Swiss cheese."

"So if you know about them they're not secret any more, are they?" Tom snorted triumphantly, spraying some meatloaf. "Monster Mouth was right. If a tunnel existed, it would have been discovered by now."

"Ah," countered Jai, "but its existence might only be known by a select few."

"And look at this…"

Dan pointed to the red ellipse on his blazer pocket. Now Jai and Tom studied their own badges in detail for the first time. As an old hand, Tom felt a little ashamed he'd never done so before.

Most of the badge consisted of a mermaid with long hair barely covering her bare breasts. She was wearing a crown and holding a trident. The top of her head protruded from the surface of the sea so that it resembled an island, her crown a castle on top. The three points of her weapon also broke the surface, like three rocks.

"Nope," said Tom. "Can't see any tunnel there. Anyway she's half-fish so she doesn't need one. Quite tasty too…"

"Look closer," said Dan. "Beneath the mermaid…"

Now Tom saw beneath the curled fish tail a kind of chamber in which a small red dragon cowered.

"Doesn't that look like a tunnel? Underneath Devilston, represented by the mermaid…?"

"Could be, I suppose," said Jai. "Or it could be Hell…"

"And how did that hymn go this morning?" Dan quoted the first two lines: ***Who would true valour see, let him go under…*** Under where?"

Tom was puzzled.

"Underwear?"

"Underground!"

"Or underwater," said Jai. "Sorry, Dan. Just playing Devil's advocate."

"I think he has enough of those already…"

Dan gathered up the remnants of meatloaf with his knife and fork, then gave up on the small pile.

"Well, I still reckon the tunnel's just a legend," Tom re-assured himself. "Like the Devil throwing his rocks into the sea. And the Mad Monks…"

"Mad Monks?" said Dan and Jai, together.

"That's right. This place was a monastery once, until some king closed it down."

"Why?" asked Jai as the plates were passed to the end of the table.

Tom shrugged.

"Henry the Eighth wanted to divorce his wife," said Dan, "but the Pope wouldn't let him. So he made himself head of the English church and dissolved all the monasteries."

"So how come you know so much about British history?" Tom asked.

"You mean, for a foreigner?" Dan smiled. "We had a library in the camp and plenty of spare time. Ironic I suppose, to be learning about a country that wanted to kick me out…"

"So what happened to the monks?" asked Jai.

"Well," said Tom, "they weren't for giving up their home so the king sent his soldiers in. The Mad Monks are the ghosts of those who were killed. They're said to haunt Devilston to this day, seeking revenge…"

"Have you ever seen one?"

"No, and I don't want to. Anyway, let's not talk about it anymore."

"You brought it up first," grinned Dan.

Jai was eyeing the suet pudding that had just arrived.

"Might not be the only thing being brought up…"

From the open window of the Music Room tiny creatures could be seen laying claim to a small corner of Neptune's kingdom. Since Top Pitch was preserved for cricket and there was insufficient space elsewhere on the island, every games afternoon (exact time and location dictated by the tide) a temporary rugby pitch was created on the exposed sand. Seaweed was cleared, lines drawn and goal posts raised, great care being taken to avoid areas of deadly quicksand.

The click of heels on stone disturbed the three musicians' observation of proceedings.

"Ca-ve!" whispered Quirk. "Lady Carrot!"

They hurried from the window to their seats as Charlotte swept in. She wore a variety of green hues, perfectly complimenting her flowing red hair and pale skin. The three were enchanted by her beauty, seasoned with a dash of exotic perfume, but their rapture was instantly dispelled by the staccato tap of a baton on a music stand.

"Absolute attention," she instructed them sharply. "We've a lot to practise this afternoon..."

Under Charlotte's firm steerage the trio - Dan on cello, Quirk on harpsichord and a mousy junior called Buttermere on clarinet - navigated their way through a hazardous selection of chamber pieces. Though the best of what was available in school, Quirk and Buttermere were several leagues below Dan in ability. Charlotte's face frequently creased when a piece floundered, Dan having to repeatedly rescue his partners by varying his tempo accordingly, like a life boat dragging a pair of stricken vessels off the rocks. But just to be in command of a cello again more than compensated for the inconvenience.

By the end of the session, with notes dancing before exhausted eyes like tadpoles, Charlotte had discarded the more complicated pieces from the list.

"You'll just have to repeat your repertoire when you get to the end..."

The music - so faint it seemed almost like a product of his own mind - reached Tom's large ears as he laboured in the vegetable plots, rendering his chores slightly less unbearable.

In the afternoons pupils like Tom who lacked any sporting or artistic aptitude were put to work, learning a range of practical skills in farming, fishing and general fettling. This also had the beneficial side-effect of saving the school a considerable amount of expense; the more cynical might have concluded that this was actually the primary aim of the arrangement.

The workers toiled under the cantankerous guidance of Trevail, the Head Groundsman: a small humourless man with big hands, rickety legs and a wispy chin-beard, giving him the look of a garden gnome who'd lost his rod. He squeezed every drop of sweat he could from his work parties.

"...and don't you dare be lettin' those hogs scoff any of 'em!" he shouted as the apple-pickers wobbled precariously on their stepladders. Often they'd have to swiftly descend to rescue any fallen fruit before the school pigs got there. An ancient breed with thick coats, sharp tusks and a mad look in their little eyes, they had more in common with their wild boar ancestry than any pink and benign domesticated type. Roaming freely in the orchard they had developed a territorial attachment to the place, and the sweet red globes that dropped from the sky at this time of year.

Tom discovered just how jealously they guarded these treasures when he attempted to retrieve one from under the snout of a large male. The grunting beast shot towards him, butting him in the leg with a force that sent him toppling over. The creature gobbled up the apple and ran off, snorting with what sounded uncannily like piggy laughter. As he got to his feet - shocked and shaken - Tom felt another blow, on the back of his head.

"Idiot!" barked Trevail. "You better get quicker than that lad, else I'll stake you the ground and let the hogs eat you..."

The choicest of the day's fruit and vegetables was delivered to the small kitchen adjoining the Staff Dining Hall, the rest to the main school kitchens. While he worked Tom could hear noisy skirmishing, battle cries and the piercing shriek of a whistle from the direction of the sands. As bad as his lot felt, one simple thought gave him some consolation:

At least I'm not playing rugby...

It didn't take long for the Reverend to realise he had a singular talent on his hands. In baggy shorts and cricket sweater he was coaching the training session, his voice fog-horning across the sands, his whistle shrilling above the call of the seagulls.

The skipper of the First Fifteen was also very much aware of a new planet in his solar system. There seemed to be no position that Rana couldn't play. He had the speed and agility of a winger, the strength and aggression of a forward, and - most disconcerting of all - a natural instinct for leadership wherever he was placed. So Smythe-Morrigan stuck him well out of the way.

But even at full back Jai excelled. The ball seemed to home in on him, as if longing - like a little lamb - to nestle in his arms alone. And he was willing to tackle the mightiest of opponents. As Tattersall charged past him Jai dived at his thighs and hung on - in the manner of a panther at the haunches of a buffalo - until his Head of House came crashing down.

"Black bastard," Tattersall grunted as he picked himself up, dusting the sand from his thick hairy legs.

"He's certainly a fearless tackler," coach commented to skipper, "but I think Rana's skills are rather wasted back there. Don't you agree, S-M...?"

"On the contrary, sir," said Smyth-Morrigan with some irritation. "I'd say he's an invaluable last line of defence."

"Well I'd like to see him back in the fray. Let's try him at scrum half..."

"Bones and beans!"

Tom rubbed his blistered hands together with glee, a quarry of hunger yawning in his belly from an afternoon of hard graft. He was referring to a grey and murky slop of haricot beans and rabbit bones, the latter with tiny shreds of flesh on them like shipwreck survivors clinging to flotsam. The surface of the soup glistened with a thin oil-slick of fat. The meal was accompanied by brown gritty bread with margarine, and carrot jam with too much artificial colour, looking more like freshly-clotted blood than the strawberry preserve it was supposed to resemble.

"So the Staff and Praeposters get the pick of the crop while we have to make do with the cast offs," said Jai with anger when Tom had described his work.

"I suppose it's a reward for their responsibilities..."

"What responsibilities do Praeposters have Tom? Apart from shouting a lot...?"

"Keep your voice down Jai..."

Tom glanced around fearfully. Jai ignored him.

"And the Staff get paid for teaching us so why do they need any more reward? And it's our parents who pay them!"

"Not mine," said Tom. "The RAF pays for me."

"Nor mine," said Dan. "I'm on a scholarship."

"Well, my father pays," Jai responded, "and if he had any idea of the conditions here..."

But even as he spoke he knew in his heart that his father wouldn't be bothered. This simple truth was the real fuel of Jai's anger, not the injustice. He remembered his father thumping drunkenly on the dinner table, at the head of a host of fawning guests:

"The British Public School is the greatest educational institution in the world! What was good enough for Winston Churchill is good enough for my son!"

"Anyway, it's always been this way," said Tom as he gnawed on a bone. "What can we do to change it...?"

After tea, Dan learned why the trio had been rehearsing so intensely that afternoon. The three musicians collected their instruments then Charlotte escorted them to the Staff Dining Hall. In a long cream evening dress, she resembled a Celtic goddess.

The banquet table was covered with fine white linen and set with crystal glasses and silver cutlery. A warm glow was provided by hosts of candles on the table and from the flames in the huge fireplace. Here a whole pig had been rudely skewered on a spit, slowly revolving by means of a mechanical device operated by cogs, pulleys and weights. Globules of fat would regularly drip from the roasting carcass onto the fire, causing flames to flare up, hissing and spitting like fiery serpents. Invisible tendrils of deliciousness found their way up the noses of the three as they passed by, as potent as Charlotte's perfume.

She led them to a far corner of the Hall, lifting the corner of a tapestry to reveal a secret entrance. They ascended a narrow winding staircase, to a small room with a filigree screen in one wall. Here in the minstrel's gallery the three set about tuning their instruments and preparing their music sheets on the stands.

"Now remember what I told you," said Charlotte. "Let Rosenbaum take the lead, and concentrate. And if you play well enough you might just be in for a little reward..."

"I wonder what she'll do to us if we don't play well enough," said Buttermere with apprehension after she'd gone, her perfume lingering like a spicy afterthought.

"Well, Buttery," said Quirk, peeved by her favouring of the new pupil and in need of a discharge of spite, "you see that spit down there...?"

As they arrived, the guests were presented with glasses of champagne on silver trays by the uniformed waiting staff. The ladies wore evening dresses (though none quite as elegant as Charlotte's), the gentlemen black tie and - but for one - black dinner suits. The exception was the Captain, sporting a cream jacket which complemented his wife's dress. He stood behind his chair in the central position at the table, facing the fire, with Charlotte to his left: the white king flanked by his queen.

At the far end of the table towered the Reverend while facing him at the opposite end stood Doctor Pottinger, the thin and grey Head of Science. Alderley was at a corner of the table, next to Pottinger. The discomfort of his starched wing collar, the heat of the fire on his back and the prospect of suffering his superior's moaning Caledonian monotone was offset by the deep pleasure of seeing Elena opposite him.

She was wearing a black dress beguiling in its simplicity, and - unlike the other women at the feast - no make-up. The candle flames reflected in her dark eyes as she smiled at him.

The tapping of a fork on crystal glass brought the music and conversation to a pause, and woke Alderley from his daze.

"Esteemed colleagues," said the Captain, "welcome back to a new Michaelmas term... And speaking of Michaels, I'd also like to extend a special greeting to the new member of our Science Department. As an Old Devilstonian himself, Michael Alderley is already steeped in the customs and curiosities of our school, and I'm sure he won't take long to settle into Her ways again..."

Alderley nodded and smiled, uneasy in the limelight.

"So, without further ado I shall propose the

toast. Ladies and gentlemen, the King…"

"The King," mumbled the Staff, raising their glasses.

"…and Devilston."

"To Devilston!"

A much more enthusiastic response.

"And in keeping with tradition," the Captain continued, "I shall now invite the Reverend to say the Latin grace…"

Having drained his glass following the toast, the Reverend was having it re-charged with champagne by a particularly charming young waitress. Now startled by the sudden mention of his name, his hand moved and a stream of effervescence flowed onto the table, splashing his trousers. He'd completely forgotten about this duty, the requisite words lying in a neglected heap in the cluttered attic of his memory.

"Er…thank you, Headmaster…"

He looked around. All had now bowed their heads, except for the Captain who was regarding him with a wry smile, and - inevitably - Rex Elgin. The beady eyes of the ancient and marble-pale Head of Classics scrutinized him over half-moon spectacles.

The Reverend closed his eyes. This was less in spiritual communion with God, more to aid recall of his own bastardized version of the prayer: the only means by which he could remember the turgid liturgy. And to cut off Tyrannosaurus Rex's cold stare.

He had always hated Latin, avoiding the intimidating ranks of its text during his ecclesiastical education like a druid evading the advancing legions of Rome. Now he was thankful for the generous measures of fine cognac he'd awarded himself following an afternoon of heroic refereeing. The effect of this dosage allowed him to slur his words without effort, thereby diminishing the ability of his audience to properly distinguish the nonsense that now spewed forth.

"Benny, Dick, Dom and Amos," he mumbled, hiccupping softly, "ate hake and tuna, Donna quail and two large tatties, summer: some touring, I nominate Pat Rhys (Aunt Filly), a spirituous aunty, pearl crystal diamond nostril..." He rounded off the performance with a confident rendition of that part he could fully recall, burping simultaneously: "Amen!"

"Amen," the gathered solemnly repeated, then sat. Few had even noticed the Reverend's eccentric version of the benediction and now - with an enticing starter of pork liver pate and warm bread rolls before them - even fewer cared. However, even as he avoided his eye, the Reverend could feel the hostile glare of the Head of Classics boring into him.

"So which King do you think our Headmaster

meant?" Pottinger muttered in his Scottish drawl, tearing his bread apart. "The present incumbent, or the one who ran off with that American woman?"

"Well, King George I should think."

Alderley was uncomfortable in the knowledge of who was within earshot. The Captain appeared able to maintain one conversation whilst monitoring others, his awareness like a hawk hovering above the proceedings, scanning for prey. But Alderley was also annoyed by the distraction that was Pottinger. He was itching to talk to Elena, if only he could think of a suitable opening gambit...

"Don't be too sure," the Head of Science droned on. "There's a lot of sympathy for the Duke of Windsor in these parts Michael, mark my words. Didn't you notice the lack of enthusiasm when glasses were raised to our monarch just now? That pig on the spit is getting a better toasting…"

"Quite right, Angus," said the Captain loudly, and a hush descended on the table. "We all know the Duke would have made a better king than this one. Poor old George can hardly string a sentence together."

A cold squall of cruel laughter passed across the table.

"I don't think he likes speaking in public."

"What was that, Angus?" The Captain cupped

his ear theatrically. "You'll have to speak up."

"I think the King is a little shy, Headmaster…"

Fidgeting with his bread, Pottinger was blushing now.

"Well, timidity has no place among the qualities of a king," the Captain continued. "Wouldn't you agree, Edward…?"

"Most definitely," the Reverend boomed from the other end of the table, keen to make amends for the abomination of his grace. "Monarchs have it far too easy these days. The last time a king led an army into battle was George the Second, two hundred years ago."

"Ah yes," said the Captain. "Wasn't he German…?"

The Reverend nodded, suddenly uncomfortable again.

"Why do we need kings anyway?" said a new, female voice.

Eyes darted from Elena to the Reverend, at the other end of the table. He replied slowly and patiently, as if addressing a wayward child.

"Because, my dear, it is the natural state of things. A people must have a leader."

"But one who is unelected?"

"A monarch is part of the people, like the heart is part of the body. The other organs don't vote for the heart."

"A cancer is also part of a body. But if the rest is to survive healthily, it must be cut out."

Now the table was stunned. The Reverend hadn't expected such a ferocious response. He looked to his Headmaster for support.

"Harsh words Miss Montserrat," said the Captain. "We've always tolerated a broad spectrum of opinion here, but this is language of an extreme nature…"

All eyes turned back to Elena. To Alderley it seemed she was contemplating the consequences of pressing forward with the assault. Then she smiled.

"Forgive me, Headmaster. I didn't mean to cause offence. Perhaps the appendix would be a better analogy…"

The Captain nodded, acknowledging her apology like a gracious king. The hum of conversations resumed.

"You see Michael, we're like one big happy family here," said Pottinger nervously, and with more than a hint of irony. "We have our disagreements, but we all love each other really…"

"Families can be the worst," said Elena. "Our civil war has split many in two. Hate is the other side of love."

"England had a civil war as well." Alderley was pleased to be able to establish a beach-head in the discussion. "This very castle was a Royalist stronghold."

"Ah yes Mister Alderley, but yours was a long

time ago. I think you British have forgotten how brutal people can be to those who are closest…"

"Please, call me Michael."

She leaned towards him and he reciprocated, like two conspirators.

"So you want to get closer, do you?"

"Well, I think it's worth the risk."

"I must warn you, I'm not the easiest of people to get along with."

"I wasn't intending to get along with you." He was aware of the champagne beginning to take effect. "I was intending to get to know you…"

"Really? And why would you want to do that?"

"Because I think you're beautiful."

"That's not a very original line…"

"I'm a science teacher, not a poet."

"Then as a scientist you'll know that the concept of beauty is a subjective notion, and no indicator of any inherent goodness. In fact, external beauty can often lead to the spoiling of the interior substance."

"So, you're spoiled goods then…?"

She ignored the question.

"Tell me, Michael. What is your definition of 'beautiful'?"

He shrugged.

"Full of beauty, I suppose."

"So for something to be beautiful it must possess beauty not only on the surface but within...?"

"Well, I couldn't possibly comment on the quality of your inner organs."

"No, you couldn't. Nor my private thoughts. In fact, it isn't possible to conclude that a person is beautiful - that is, full of beauty - until you have knowledge of the nature of that person's soul. And, even then, how much of that beauty is determined by the prejudices of the observer...?"

Now she raised her glass, holding its stem between her finger tips and scrutinising its contents like a connoisseur.

"This champagne, for example. See the light that seems to come from within, as if all that sunshine the grapes have absorbed has suddenly been released again...? Pure illusion, of course. This apparent latent beauty is really only illumination by those candles. Its true quality can only be tested by tasting it, and even that is tainted by my own bias..." She took a long sip. "Very good, though personally I prefer red."

"But haven't you demonstrated to me your inner beauty, in what you've just said?"

"Not really." She smiled again, this time with a hint of sadness. "All I've demonstrated is a refined appreciation of aesthetics, which is the product of a privileged education. There are Nazis with a similar love of philosophy and art who are laying waste to civilisation as we speak.

In my book, true beauty lies in our actions. The rest is merely the reflection of candle light in a glass of champagne..."

She took another sip and he found himself lost for words. He was saved by the arrival of the main course. The pig had been carved and now great steaming slices of it were being served up to the Staff, accompanied by glazed roast potatoes, a selection of fresh vegetables and rich thick gravy.

The meat was utterly delicious. He savoured the tenderness of the flesh, the divine complexity of its flavour (with the faint suggestion of apple) and the pure decadence of the juices that oozed across his tongue.

But even as he ate he was disgusted by his complicity. The nation was under siege and most people could only dream of such a feast. It was also very warm and close in the room; a damp patch of sweat had formed on his back, and his collar was cutting into his neck. It felt like a kind of purgatory for his gluttony.

He found some relief from his discomfort in the music. The mournful call of the clarinet, the ponderous hum of the cello and the strange almost supernatural clatter of the harpsichord - though not entirely harmonious - seemed to cast a spell over him. The notes gently descended onto the diners like invisible petals of sound. But even as he listened he couldn't prevent his eyes from being drawn to the woman opposite him.

Now Elena was discussing politics with a female member of Staff next to her whose presence Alderley had hardly noticed, but whom he now deeply despised for robbing him of her attention. Occasionally his gaze would meet Elena's and his heart would leap, though he wasn't sure she was looking at him out of attraction, curiosity, or simply because he was looking at her.

Her eyes were wide and her hands animated as she explained her point to her neighbour. As he watched her he ached with a hunger not even the choicest cuts of meat could satisfy, and the champagne did little to loosen the tightness of desire in his chest.

She was right: he had no knowledge of the consistency of her soul and thus the true depth of her beauty, but he very much wanted to find out.

"For God's sake man, keep away from there!" hissed Quirk. "If Sticky sees you…"

Dan ignored the warning. He was standing at the filigree screen, taking the opportunity between pieces to survey the banquet below.

"You should see what they're eating down there. You wouldn't think there was a war on."

"Well, it's none of our business," said Buttermere. "We should be thankful we're getting out of Prep. And you heard what Lady Carrot said. If we play well enough we might get some grub..."

"How easily the human soul is purchased," said Dan, wistfully. "We should be playing for the pure joy of it."

"Well, joy might fill your heart," said Quirk, "but it doesn't fill my stomach. Now come on. She'll be wondering why we've stopped for so long..."

In fact, Charlotte was generally pleased with the trio's performance over the course of the evening. When the dinner was over, she instructed a plate of pork sandwiches to be sent up to the gallery.

"Have you ever tasted meat so sweet?" said Buttermere as he chewed, closing his eyes to invest his full attention in the experience.

"Delicious," said Dan.

"If you don't mind me asking, Rosenbaum..." Quirk was in the process of swallowing a particularly large mouthful, "but doesn't your religion prohibit you from eating pork...?"

"Yes it does."

"So what'll happen to you?" Buttermere was intrigued. "Will you roast in Hell...?"

"I don't know, and I don't really care. What kind of a God is He anyway, spying on us all the time, making sure we're always doing the right thing...?"

Dan was standing by the screen again, looking down at the waiting staff clearing up the aftermath of the dinner. He was experiencing some degree of guilt, though it had little to do with eating pork, more to do with not saving some for his room mates.

"It isn't fair," said Buttermere, the taste of proper meat suddenly awakening some revolutionary zeal. "That lot scoffing fine food like royalty while we have to survive on bones and boiled cabbage like peasants."

"I suppose that's the way of the world," said Quirk, licking his fingers. "But look at it this way: if we work hard enough we could be down there ourselves one day, enjoying the fruits of our labour..."

"You mean, the fruits of someone else's labour," said Dan.

"Where does it all come from anyway?" Buttermere wondered, his indignation emboldening him. "The champagne, for instance? And those fat cigars they were smoking at the end...?"

"Not to mention all that brandy and chocolate," Dan added. "I thought there was supposed to be a shortage of luxury items..."

"Catalonian," said Elena as Alderley watched her pouring out the red wine into two tumblers. "Stronger than French because our sun is fiercer. I think it's better, but then I'm biased."

To his deep satisfaction she'd invited him for an after-dinner nightcap in her cottage, at the end of the terrace that lined Devilston's little harbour. They were sitting on an old leather sofa in front of an open fire. He'd removed his jacket, collar and bow tie and - for the first time that evening - he felt relaxed. She handed him a tumbler and he thrilled at the fleeting touch of her hand.

"You don't use wine glasses?"

"Where I come from wine is an everyday staple, not just for special occasions." She clicked her glass against his. "Salud."

"Cheers."

They stared into the fire for a while, Alderley wondering where the evening was heading.

The flames of triumph or the ashes of disaster...?

"Do you play chess Michael?"

"Yes but not very well." He was disappointed yet relieved by this sudden distraction. "I'm a little out of practice..."

"Then let's practise!"

She fetched a chess set. He admired the movement of her firm body in her loose dress, and her bare feet now that she'd removed her shoes. A thick curl of hair hung over her eye.

"Black or white?" she asked.

"Black. It's my lucky colour."

He didn't really have a lucky colour, or lucky anything for that matter. But he was keen to impress, to compete with her mystery.

"But if I'm white then I get to make the first move," she said. "Are you comfortable with that?"

"Yes," he replied, uncomfortably. "I think so…"

From the start it was obvious she was in a different league. She played aggressively, surging forwards and immediately forcing him on the defensive, putting him under pressure at every opportunity. He couldn't remember the last time he'd worked so hard at playing a game.

At last, with his queen and most of his major assets fallen and her pieces closing in on his king for the kill, he held up his hands.

"I surrender! You win!"

"Really? You shouldn't give up so easily. It's not over yet."

"Give up so easily? I'm exhausted! Where did you learn to play like that?"

"From my father. He was an excellent teacher."

"He's…no longer alive?"

"He's dead, yes. And my mother. My whole family in fact…"

He was toying with the few pieces he'd won

from her, feeling awkward now.

"Aren't you going to ask me how they died?"

"I wouldn't want to pry into your business…"

"But it's everyone's business, Michael. If the Nazis invade they'll do the same here."

"Did they kill your family?"

"Falangists, our local variety of fascist. But they were trained by the Germans."

"I'm sorry to hear that."

"You English…always apologising, even for things you aren't responsible for. Mind you, your government could have done a lot more to support our cause…"

She got up and picked up a poker. For a moment he thought she was about to strike him with it. Instead she thrust it into the fire, the flames rearing up as if siphoning off her anger. When she sat down again she was calmer.

"Now I'm sorry for getting angry."

"That's alright. It's quite understandable. Please, don't feel you have to talk about it."

"I want to talk about it, if you want to listen. But I must warn you, it's no fairy tale…"

"I'd like to hear it, all the same."

"Very well."

She offered him a cigarette, took out one for herself then lit them. She took a deep drag, exhaling the smoke from her nose. Then she lay back, resting her head on the back of the sofa and closing her eyes.

"My father was a diplomat: First Secretary in the Spanish Embassy in Paris, then London. Of course he took his family with him, which is how I learned French and English. He would probably have become an ambassador but he grew tired of all the diplomatic hypocrisy. So he retired and we moved back to Catalonia, to our family's ancestral home. It was an almond farm and our life was very good, though I didn't think so at the time. I was still a teenager and after all the excitement of city life I hated living in the country. At first anyway, until I learned to love the wilderness...

"I was a little wild, you might say. There were a lot of quarrels with my parents. They wanted to marry me off to someone well-heeled and respectable, someone who would keep me in check. They were always lining up prospective suitors, bless them, but I was having none of it. I had no intention of getting married, at least not yet. Life lay in front of me, fat and ripe. I wanted something more than my parents could offer me."

"Adventure?"

"Yes!" She opened her eyes. "I wanted to be an actor. I wanted to escape into other people's lives. But my father wasn't impressed. For him, acting was akin to prostitution. For me, I was fighting for my independence...

"Then came the Civil War. My father wanted

to keep out of it but this was a conflict no-one could avoid. So he made preparations for us to leave. England was his first choice because he knew France would quickly fall. Once it gains enough momentum, fascism is an unstoppable force. A mad bull...

"My father had made many friends in London and the immigration formalities were swiftly arranged. And so, on Christmas Eve, our family sat down to eat, knowing it would be our last Christmas on the farm...but not knowing it would be our last meal together. I remember it all, vividly. It was raining outside. Everyone was happy enough, in the circumstances, except me. I'd had another argument with my father, you see. And then they came..."

Now she was sitting up, gazing into the fire, her dark eyes gleaming.

"Workers from the fields given uniforms and guns, and an excuse to hate. Some of them had even worked on our farm. They'd been brainwashed into believing we were Communists. Ridiculous, really. Father was a diplomat, a landowner, a member of the ruling elite. But some bright spark had noticed that a left-wing newspaper was delivered to us. Father read newspapers right across the political spectrum, you see. He always said it gave him a better perspective on the world, like a ship taking several fixes to determine its true position. But that was all the fascist bastards needed to reach their verdict. You might say it was a red rag to the bull…"

She gave a fleeting crooked smile.

"I'll spare you the details of what they did to my family. I was the only one who survived because I was upstairs at the time. After arguing with my father I'd stormed up to my bedroom to sulk. I even remember wishing he was dead. Of course, I didn't mean it. I loved my father, but at that moment I hated him also. Love and hate, you see…? Sometimes I wonder if I conjured up the Falangists myself…"

There was a flatness to her voice. She seemed to have detached herself from the horror.

"That's impossible."

She shrugged.

"Maybe…But they were real enough. I saw them through my bedroom window: a truck full of drenched and drunken soldiers. I knew immediately what they were going to do. And do you know what I did, Michael?"

He shook his head.

"Nothing. I hid under my bed, curled up like a little child with my eyes closed and my hands over my ears. But I couldn't shut out the sounds: the shouts, the screams, the gun shots. Then, when they'd finished, they set fire to the house. But still I didn't move. I wanted to stay under my bed and burn for my treachery."

"Treachery?"

"I'd done nothing to help my family."

"But what could you have done?"

"Nothing, of course. But rationality doesn't rule in the mind of a teenaged girl whose family has just been slaughtered. Then the smoke began to invade my room, which brought me to my senses. I had to step over the bodies to get out. I knew I'd lost all that I loved, but I also knew I had to escape."

For a while she said nothing. He noticed her tumbler trembling as she drank more wine.

"I'd like to think I was driven by the hope of one day seeing justice done, but really it was the pure will to survive that saved me. I travelled north, through the Pyrenees, crossing the border and making my way to Paris. The Spanish government hadn't yet fallen to Franco's rebels so the embassy was still a friendly place, and some of the staff still remembered me. I'd like to have stayed in France but I knew the Nazis were coming. Everyone did. So my passage to England was arranged. I wanted to get as far from war as possible and Cornwall looked a suitable distance away from anywhere. I never wanted to be helpless again, as I was under my own bed, hearing them butchering my family."

She finished her wine then gazed into the tumbler.

"You probably wonder why I don't weep," she said at last. "That's because the girl who used to love and laugh - and feel - was left behind to burn in that house, along with my family. The woman who escaped is just an empty vessel…"

He struggled for the right words, then gave up.

"I really don't know what to say."

"You don't need to say anything, Michael." She smiled sadly. "So, to conclude what we were discussing at dinner, any beauty I may possess is merely superficial. Inside there is nothing."

She stood and went into the kitchen.

"What are you doing?" he asked presently.

Her reply was the sound of a cork being pulled, then she returned and filled their empty glasses. Small talk seemed pointless now, like fine drizzle falling on a fresh bomb crater. It was Elena who broke the silence.

"So you think you've lost, do you?"

She was studying the chess board.

"Well, I don't see any way out."

"There's always a way out, Michael." Carefully she turned the board. "I'll be black…"

So they played on. For a while he retained the upper hand, but he couldn't quite deliver the finish. His head was growing fuzzy. It could be the wine, he thought, but it could also be love. He smiled to himself. The terrible images her story had conjured in his mind were now dispelled, replaced by a warm glow of contentment within him.

"Are you alright?"

"Yes," he replied, his own voice sounding different to him, distant. "In fact I can't remember when I've felt this good…"

"Even though you're being beaten?"

She was using her remaining pieces to their full potential while he was quickly squandering his advantage. He was just too interested in her, marvelling at the miraculous architecture of her hands as she moved the pieces, and the intensity of her concentration. Soon she'd managed to get a pawn to his side, exchanging it for the black queen.

"That's why I love chess," she said, kissing the heroic little piece. "Even the lowliest can play a part in the grand scheme of things. And the queen can move so much further than the king…"

Her new queen went on to lead a swift and victorious counter-attack, fatally pinning him down in check mate.

"I told you I wasn't any good," he laughed as he sat back.

"You took your eye off the game."

"I was distracted by you."

She smiled.

"Do you like to dance, Michael?"

"Yes but I'm not very good. Two left feet, I'm

afraid..."

She rose and moved over to an old gramophone player. He watched her select a record then carefully rest the needle on the track. A slow guitar played an intro, then male voices sang a sad melody in warm harmony:

I don't want to set the world on fire
I just want to start a flame in your heart...

"The Ink Spots," he said as he took her hand.

She looked into his eyes as they slowly danced, his hands on her waist, her hands resting on his shoulders.

"You're not bad," she said.

"I can just about manage slow ones..."

He felt wonderful. His head was light. He didn't want the dance to end.

"So what about you, Michael?"

"What about me?"

"Well, you know all of my history now but you've told me nothing about yourself..."

"Oh, I couldn't possibly do that. It's all very hush-hush, you see."

"Hush-hush?"

"Yes. Hush-hush..."

He found the phrase suddenly very amusing. He began to laugh, a giggle at first which grew into something quite uncontrollable so that eventually - as much as he hated to - he had to break away from her. Soon he was gripped in a manic seizure, the contractions so painful he thought his stomach might rupture and spill the beans. *Spill the beans!* The image generated more laughter, and more excruciating spasms. Eventually he collapsed onto the sofa. Elena looked down on him, smiling patiently.

When at last the waves subsided he felt a huge relief.

"I'm so sorry about that," he gasped, wiping away tears. "I don't know what came over me..."

"It's just all that tension being released," she said.

"Yes, I suppose it is...This damned place...I feel so tired now...So bloody tired..."

Now she was kneeling by the side of the sofa, her face close to his.

"This is very embarrassing," he slurred. "I never normally get this drunk...You're right...That wine of yours is very strong..."

"Of course it is, my darling," she said, gently stroking his forehead. "It's from Catalonia..."

His eyelids were heavy. He was fighting against the drowsiness.

"The Headmaster told me...you were spoken for..."

"Spoken for?"

"I mean...seeing someone...."

"I'm never spoken for, Michael. I speak for myself. And at this moment I'm seeing only you…"

"Oh Elena," he sighed. "You're so bloody beautiful…"

"And you are so bloody secret."

She leaned forward until their lips made contact. She opened her mouth to him as they kissed. Then she broke off, to study him again.

"So tell me, my darling. Who is Michael Alderley…?"

3

THE MAD MONKS

"So," said Jai, lying in the darkness of the dormistudy, "while the cats gorge themselves, the mice nibble on the fallen crumbs..."

But then he remembered his father's lavish feasts, and the left overs tossed like manna from the palace walls to the famished far below.

Dan was grappling with his own guilt, having omitted from his account of the banquet any mention of the pork sandwich. He opened his mouth, intending to fill the pause with a confession, but it was Tom who spoke.

"So, what do you two think of this place then...?"

"A most singular pile of old stones and bones," Jai replied. "All bound together with yarns. Rather reminds me of home, in fact..."

"I imagine you have many ghost stories in India," said Dan, relieved the conversation had changed direction. "With so many souls living there."

"And dying...Yes, the night is a veritable cocktail of demons, djinns and churels...."

"Gins?"

Tom was reminded of the drink that made his mother miserable.

"Evil spirits," Jai explained, only reinforcing Tom's misunderstanding.

"And churels?" asked Dan.

"Female phantoms with back-to-front feet, who feed on the blood of young men..."

"Sounds like my kind of girl."

Tom was keen to lighten the tone. Now he and Jai laughed raucously. They were silenced by Dan.

"What was that?"

Tom's levity was instantly doused.

"What?"

"I heard something outside. Like a splash..."

Nimbly traversing from top bunk to window ledge via a desk, Jai opened the window and peered out into the night. Thin cloud leaked light from the waning moon, like milk through muslin. He could just make out a dark shape moving slowly on the calm water.

"It's a small boat...and there's a bigger one beyond it, out to sea. Trawler, perhaps. Damn..."

"What now?"

"The small one's gone out of sight, behind some rocks. I think it's coming ashore..."

Jai descended from the window ledge, clicked on the lights and began to dress over his pajamas.

Dan cringed in the cruel glare.

"Where are you going?"

"Where do you think?"

Tom was shielding his eyes from the light.

"But we're not allowed out at night."

Jai glanced at his wrist watch.

"Well, officially it's still evening. So who's coming...?"

"I can't," said Dan. "If I get caught they'll send me to Canada."

"Quite understand. Tom?"

"I don't know...My dad would be angry if he found out."

"But would he, really?" Jai was tying his shoe laces now. "Or would he not be proud of an adventurous son? I mean, he's a fighter pilot after all..."

The Head Boy's taunts still haunted Tom.

"Alright," he heard himself say. "I'll come with you."

"Good man!" Jai slapped him on the back. "Get dressed. Dan? Hold the fort..."

Tom hoped Prophet's door would be locked, but his prayers went unheeded. So he trailed his new friend into danger, keeping within the shadows of the castle walls.

Passing beneath the raised portcullis of the gatehouse they turned right, taking the path that followed the castle's outer perimeter.

"Hang on," Tom wheezed and Jai stopped. "Need a rest…"

But as soon as his backside made contact with what appeared to be a rocky outcrop it came to life, shooting into the dark orchard with a squeal. Tom lay sprawled on the floor, startled.

"It's alright," Jai chuckled as he helped his friend to his feet. "It was just a pig."

"Those aren't any old pigs," Tom mumbled, collecting his scattered wits. "They're the hogs from Hell…"

They continued along the path until they reached the corner of the tower that was Prophets. The orchard on their left had now given way to a cliff, and an open view.

Crouching behind the cover of a buttress, the two surveyed the small beach below them. A rowing boat had been pulled up the shore. Dark hooded figures were unloading a long box.

"It's them!" Tom whispered fearfully. "The Mad Monks!"

The boat was pushed into the water and the figure within began to row away. The other four hoisted the box onto their shoulders then proceeded along a path, up the far side of the cove.

"That path leads up here," said Tom. "We'd better go."

"Not yet."

Jai took hold of Tom's arm and guided him into the darkness of the orchard.

"But what if they see us?"

"They won't if we keep quiet."

"Why can't we just go back, Jai? We've seen enough, haven't we?"

"Shush. They're coming..."

Because the path had narrowed the load could only be carried by two monks now, one at each end. The tallest of the four led the way. Then, within spitting distance of Jai and Tom, the leader stopped.

A hooded head turned slowly towards their hiding place, as if sensing the pair's presence. The leader's face - if it had one - was concealed within the hood, but the nature of the box the figures carried was now evident.

Tom shut his eyes. Only when the procession had moved on and the sound of their footsteps had diminished into nothing did he open them again...to find himself alone.

Now the trunks and branches of the orchard resembled the dark faces and twisted limbs of a cursed multitude, its voice the sad whisper of the wind in the leaves.

Then an owl screeched, jolting Tom into motion.

There was no sign of his friend at the gatehouse. Standing in Devilston's mouth - with the great iron fangs of her portcullis poised above him - Tom found himself frozen in fearful indecision.

A hand clamped his mouth.

"Only me." Jai released his grip and Tom relaxed. "Sorry. Couldn't risk you calling out."

"Where the Hell have you been?"

"I went ahead. Didn't want to lose them."

"But it's alright to lose me, is it?"

"Keep it down. They're not far away..."

Tom followed Jai into the graveyard. Peering over a tomb they saw the Chapel door was open, a faint glow spilling out. Tom imagined the monks had now slipped out of their robes, their supernatural radiance permitted to shine forth unhindered.

The light went out and figures emerged from the Chapel. Jai and Tom ducked behind the tomb. They heard the door close, a key being turned then the sound of footsteps receding.

"Jai, what are they up to?" Tom whispered.

"No idea but we'll have to leave that for another time. They've locked the door."

Keeping within the sanctuary of the shadows, the pair returned to the Triangle. Jai turned the handle of the door to Prophets and pushed. It didn't yield and he cursed.

"We'll just have to knock," said Tom, feeling a

growing instability in the pit of his belly.

"And what do we say?"

"We tell the truth. We saw some strange goings on and came down to investigate."

"And if it's one of them who answers the door...? No. We'll just have to find another way in..."

"There isn't another way in."

But Jai had already moved on. They retraced their steps through the gatehouse and along the path until they were standing beneath the tower again. The only open window was high above them.

"Prophets is practically impregnable," Jai observed.

"Hardly surprising." Tom was trying to ignore the cliff edge close behind him. "This is a castle, after all..."

Jai began throwing small stones at the open window. It took several attempts before he found his target.

"I hope it's the right one..." said Tom.

For a moment even Jai had his doubts. Then a familiar head appeared.

"Where have you two been?" Dan called down, as loud as he dared. "I thought something had happened!"

"It has!" Jai's hands were cupped around his mouth to amplify his forced whisper. "Someone's locked the front door! Go down and see if the key's been left in the lock!"

Dan returned with bad news. Jai cursed under his breath.

"Well, that's that then," said Tom. "We'll just have to wait until someone unlocks the door."

"They'll only unlock it for Roll Call." Now Jai was studying the wall of the tower, his head tilted back. "Shame those gargoyles are too far apart…"

Tom could just make out a vertical series of carved heads protruding from the wall at equal intervals, originally designed for the dispersal of waste water - and other things - from each floor into the sea. The drain holes had long since been blocked up, but their conduits had survived. Centuries of weathering had taken a toll but the dragon features were still recognisable on the lowest ones.

"Too far apart for what, Jai?"

Now Jai pulled at a rusty iron drain pipe, testing how firmly it was fixed to the wall. Tom followed the line of the Victorian structure up to the roof. It passed quite close to their window and he laughed nervously.

"You're not thinking of…?"

"Why not? Many a night I've scaled the palace walls after a spot of nocturnal naughtiness. Believe me, I am well trained in the dark arts of clandestine operations. Largely thanks to Jomsom, it must be said…"

"Johnson?"

"Oh, you didn't meet him did you...? He was at Gallipoli. The Turks were on top of a cliff blasting away at the British below, then the Gurkhas came along - our Jomsom one of their number - and promptly shinned all the way up a crevice to take the position. To this day it's known as Gurkha Bluff."

"Nice story Jai, but what about me? I can't climb to save my life."

"Worry not, my friend. Just wish me luck and I'll see you at the summit..."

Jai pulled himself up to stand on one of the brackets which fixed the pipe to the wall, one foot wedged into the gap. He rested for a moment before repeating the process, gradually moving closer to his goal.

From his vantage point, Dan could see the concentration etched into his friend's face as he climbed.

Now level with the window, Jai reached out with his right hand, his fingers finding a firm purchase on the window frame. Then he stretched across the space until he was perched on the gargoyle beneath the window, praying the dragon head would hold.

In a final surge of effort - face contorted in a rictus of pain - he heaved himself up and wriggled through the open window.

"That was remarkable." Dan patted Jai on the

back as his friend descended from the window ledge. "Well done."

But there was no time for celebration. Jai began to pull the bedclothes off the bunks.

The horizon glowed with the first hint of dawn, though not nearly enough to ease the cold in Tom's bones.

Something heavy and white landed on his head, waking him from his upright stupor. He began to fight off what he believed to be a huge seagull, before realising he was wrestling with a long line of sheets, tied together.

"It's a safety rope!" Jai called down. "Tie it round your waist then climb up the drain pipe like I did! I'll maintain the tension so if you do slip you won't fall very far!"

"Jai, I can't!" Tom was looking up. His friend looked impossibly distant. "I hate heights!"

"Then don't look down!"

"Come on Tom!" Jai's head had now been replaced by Dan's at the open window. "You can do it!"

"Easy for you to say," Tom mumbled as he tied the sheet-rope around his waist. Then he reached up and gripped the pipe with both hands, just above a bulge where two sections met. He tried to heave himself up to get his foot into the first bracket, but his arms lacked the strength and he slipped back to the ground.

"I can't do it," he told himself, then called up: "It's no good! I'll just have to wait 'til they unlock the door!"

"Don't give up!" Dan called down. "Remember Dunkirk!"

Tom was angry now. What had climbing a drain pipe got to do with thousands of soldiers being evacuated from a beach? And why did his mother and father have to row all the time so that he had to be sent to this place, out of the way? But most of all he was angry at himself, for being fat and weak and too ready to give up.

Fury surged through his body like steam. He took hold of the drain pipe as if he wanted to rip it out of the wall, and - with a stifled growl - hauled himself up. Thrusting his foot into the gap between wall and pipe, he found himself standing on the first bracket.

"Well done!" said Dan. "Just keep doing that and Jai will pull each time!"

Jai had passed the sheet-rope a turn around the thick heating pipe in their room; the iron artery was never warm enough but at least now it was serving a useful purpose. The end of the sheet-rope was wrapped round his waist and as Tom embarked on each section of the climb Jai took up the slack, hoping the twist around the pipe would be a sufficient brake in the event of a fall.

In this way Tom slowly ascended - Dan relaying his progress to Jai - until he was level with the window. He was breathing heavily now as he stood on the narrow bracket between pipe and wall, his face glowing red.

"I don't like this," he whispered shakily. "I don't like this at all."

"You've nearly made it," said Dan. "Just don't look down..."

Until that moment, Tom hadn't even considered doing so. But now something made him want to feel the full force of his fear. He needed to look death in the face.

Far below him he saw the thin line of the path, and - beyond that - the slavering rocks, for the tide was creeping in. His mind reeled. A part of him wanted to let go and fall into the sea. To counter this urge, he closed his eyes and hugged the drain pipe tightly.

"Oh God..."

"Nearly there," said Dan, softly. "Give me your hand..."

"I can't," Tom moaned. "I'll fall."

"Trust me, Tom. You're not going to fall. I promise."

Tom opened his eyes and looked at his friend across the apparent gulf that separated them. He saw a calmness in the dark eyes, settling him enough to allow him to reach out with his right hand. Guided by Dan, his fingers hooked themselves onto the window frame.

"Now put your right foot on that dragon's head..."

Tom glanced down to where Dan was pointing, forcing himself not to look beyond it.

"And remember," Dan added, "there's a rope tied round you."

"You mean, there's a sheet tied round me..."

Against his instincts Tom lifted his right foot from the safety of the bracket and moved it towards the dragon head. He felt the sheet tightening around him as Jai pulled, and the pain in his fingers from clinging to the window frame, and the strain in his right leg as it delivered its foot onto the target. Then, allowing the gargoyle to take his whole weight, Tom lifted his left foot from the bracket.

But something wasn't right. In his haste to span the space, Tom had placed his foot not on the dragon's head but on its snarling snout.

"Not there!" Dan called out, but too late.

The ancient spout cracked and fell, bouncing off the path below then spinning over the cliff edge to be consumed by the sea: an appetizer before the main course.

The sheet-rope jerked tight, cutting into Jai's waist with the full force of Tom's weight. He felt himself being pulled forwards, the turn around the pipe proving inadequate as a brake. He was in a desperate tug of war: his ally friction, gravityhis enemy.

Had anyone in the dormitory below been awake, he would have seen a plump blond youth swinging to and fro past the window, like a pendulum.

But Tom hadn't cried out. Eyes squeezed shut, he had resigned himself to his fate. He was waiting for one of the knots to give, most probably the one he himself had tied around his waist. And as he swung - the sheet-rope digging into his armpits - his mind's eye pictured this knot being slowly pulled apart by his own treacherous weight...

Yet no fall came. Instead, as the arc of his swing lessened, Tom felt himself being lifted. Opening his eyes, he saw the window ledge above getting closer - in jerking increments - until his chest was pressed against it.

Jai was sitting on the floor now, his legs straight, his feet firmly planted on the pipe, his upper body straining like a fisherman fighting to land the biggest catch of his life.

"Pull him in," he gasped, a vein protruding in his forehead, "before I'm bloody well cut in half..."

Dan hooked a hand under each of Tom's armpits and dragged him through the open window.

For some time Tom lay face down on the ledge, as if kissing the ancient stone in gratitude, his feet sticking out of the window. When he'd recovered his breath, he allowed his friends to help him down.

"Thanks," he said, at last. "I couldn't have done that without you." After a pause he added, addressing Jai: "Come to think of it, I wouldn't have had to do it without you..."

Jai grinned.

"What happened?" asked Dan. "What did you see?"

"The Mad Monks," said Tom.

"Ghosts?"

"We couldn't see their faces. We got a good look at what they were carrying though..."

"So what was it?"

Still shaken by his near-death experience Tom was unable to utter the word so Jai delivered the line.

"They were carrying a coffin."

4

GUNPOWDER AND TREASON

The Science Room was crammed with intimidating scientific apparatus and assorted bottles of chemicals, like an unholy marriage between a torture chamber and a medieval apothecary. The smell of sulphur hung in the air, not unlike the Dining Hall's permanent stench of boiled cabbage.

The shelves above the blackboard held the most-prized exhibits. Glass jars of various sizes housed a macabre museum of biological specimens, grotesquely magnified by their preservative solution: insects, fish, reptiles, mammalian organs and - taking pride of place in the largest receptacle, like a clock on a crowded mantlepiece - a human foetus.

In a corner by the blackboard a skeleton lurked, eternally leering. It wore a red and black school cap and scarf.

"Where the Hell is he?" Tattersall grumbled. "I can't believe he's late for his first lesson with us."

"Could be stage fright," said another Praeposter.

"That's it!" Smythe-Morrigan was suddenly inspired. "Cowardly Alderley!"

The spontaneous birth of a new nickname was celebrated by bellows of laughter and the thumping of tabletops.

"I know. Let's make a little surprise present for him…"

The Head of School produced a small package from his pocket and tore it open to reveal a sheath of thin latex rubber. Its appearance was met by a lusty roar of approval.

"The last one of summer…"

He filled the prophylactic with water from a tap. It swelled into a wobbling globe, shifting shape in his hands like a living creature. When it was on the verge of bursting he sealed the bulging balloon with a knot then presented it to Quirk.

"I'll let you do the honours, Quirky. Stick it on top of the door, there's a good chap…" Seeing Quirk's face draining of blood, Smythe-Morrigan added: "Don't worry. We won't split on you. Will we boys…?"

All but three of the class rumbled in agreement. Dan, Jai and Tom were weary from lack of sleep, and singularly unimpressed. After the magnificence of last night's caper this prank seemed mean and unoriginal.

Of course Quirk had no choice. Refusal was unconscionable. He would be challenging the Head of School, with all the ramifications that involved. Why make life harder than it already was?

Urged on by calls of 'Go on, Qwerty!' and 'Attaboy, Q!', Quirk opened the door slightly then - standing on a stool - set the booby trap in place. It sagged over the top of the door like an ample bottom.

Just as he stepped off the stool the door swung fully open. Quirk received a punishing blow to the head from the ancient oak, while the balloon of water toppled off its perch to land on the entrant's head, bursting spectacularly.

A triumphant cheer went up. Two hits for the price of one.

Alderley was stunned. He'd walked onto the stage with no understanding of the scene or knowledge of his lines. As cold water flowed down his spine, he could only stare at the thin bespectacled youth who'd emerged from behind the door. The rest of the class was now silent, tense with anticipation.

"I'm so sorry, sir..." Quirk mumbled meekly, his eyes charged with tears.

Alderley dried his face with a cloth from the teacher's bench. The sniggers in the audience and the bitter tang of chalk on his tongue informed him he'd used the board-wiper.

There seemed to be a considerable delay in his reactions to events. It was as if he'd left his brain in bed, steeped in the dregs of last night's wine. It had been a dreamy evening in Elena's company, but now he'd woken to a nightmare.

Always the payback.

His body ached for coffee - or at least tea - but he'd slept in and there hadn't been time.

"Here you are, sir..."

Alderley snatched the paper towel offered by Tom and dried his face. Then he did what he invariably found to be the best course of action in such situations: he bought himself time by postponing a decision.

"Sit down," he instructed Quirk sternly. "I'll deal with you later..."

Quirk returned to his place, miserably contemplating the irreversible chain of events that had now been triggered: a taste of the cane, then likely expulsion followed by a swift descent into a life of dissolution. And then the final ignominious end, rotting in some back-street gutter...

Alderley noticed that his delaying of judgement appeared to have exerted a calming effect upon the class. Apparently the Leavers were still uncertain of the true mettle of their form teacher: useless ditherer, or calculating disciplinarian biding his time? He wasn't sure himself. Yesterday's registration hadn't been a promising start in establishing his authority, but neither had it been a total disaster. As for the water bomb, wasn't this just a case of good-natured high jinx? A final fling of summer frivolity...?

Whatever the truth, he knew it was now imperative to commence the lesson as swiftly as his sluggishness permitted. He was thwarted by a raised hand.

"Yes?"

"Sir, it was Smythe-Morrigan's idea," said Jai calmly. "He made Quirky plant the bomb."

"Damn you, Rana!" the Head of School growled from the back. "You filthy snitch!"

"Silence!"

Alderley was feigning anger. A fault line had appeared which might be exploited to his advantage.

"I want to hear nothing more on the subject. Is that understood?"

The class muttered in the affirmative.

"However, I would like to hear more on the subject of bombs, since this happens to be the theme of today's lesson. Specifically, explosives..."

It was as if a magic word had been spoken. Heads perked up, ears pricked, backs straightened. Meanwhile Alderley was donning his white lab coat (inside-out) and shepherding his wandering wits.

"So tell me, someone. What makes a bomb explode...?"

He opened a large book on the bench in front of him and leafed through it in search of the right recipe.

"It's a chemical reaction, sir."

"That's right, Quirk..."

Now he was scanning the shelves for the right ingredients, cursing himself for not getting in early to prepare properly. He knew that the attention of the class could only be held captive for a finite period of time. Already he could sense the beast straining at the flimsy cage of promise he'd thrown together.

"Not all explosions require a chemical reaction, sir," said Dan. "In theory, an atom bomb could use the energy stored inside a single nucleus to begin a chain reaction..."

"Well, that's very interesting," Alderley replied, disinterested, "but - as you've just said yourself - it's only a theory..."

"But it could happen, sir. Have you read *The World Set Free...?*"

"Can't say I have."

"It's by H.G. Wells. It's about atom bombs changing the whole balance of power in the world."

"Didn't he also write about men visiting the moon...?"

A murmur of amusement.

"But they've already split an atom, sir. It's only a matter of time before they make a bomb..."

Alderley's head felt like it had split yet he didn't feel the least bit energised.

"So how do you know all this, Rosenbaum?" asked Smythe-Morrigan.

"Because many of my father's friends were scientists."

"And were they German, by any chance?"

"Of course."

"So your father was talking with German scientists about making bombs?"

"My father is a musician."

"And Hitler was an artist..."

"Sir," said Tattersall, getting bored, "are we going to do a practical?"

"Yes. We're going to make gunpowder."

Alderley's announcement galvanised the room's attention again.

"Now gunpowder was invented in Arabia thousands of years ago..."

Quirk found himself caught in the pincers of another painful dilemma. After what had happened earlier he had no wish to contradict his teacher, and yet there was a glaring error to be addressed. In the end his arm made the decision for him.

"Yes?"

"Sorry sir, but wasn't it the Chinese who invented gunpowder...?"

"Quite possibly. My history is quite hazy..."

"So is his science," the Head of School commented under his breath, for the benefit of his Praeposters. "Does he actually have a clue what he's doing...?"

Now Alderley had managed to assemble the raw materials on the bench: three large jars containing black, white and yellow powder, and a set of weighing scales. After yet another consultation of the book, he weighed out a quantity of the black substance.

"So what's this? Any ideas...?"

"Is it coal dust?" Smythe-Morrigan chipped in. "I believe they make bread out of it where Wheely comes from."

His cronies cackled.

"That's enough," Alderley snapped. "Actually it's charcoal: the fuel of the reaction."

Now he measured out a pile of powder from the second jar. It was a considerable amount but he had faith in the book. It said the experiment was designed for the classroom, after all...

"It's very white, isn't it?" said Smythe-Morrigan."Unlike Rana."

More chuckling. Alderley sighed.

"How many times do I have to warn you...?"

The Head of School shrugged. Alderley referred to his book, as if the answer might be there.

"This is potassium nitrate, also known as salt petre. It provides the oxygen for the reaction."

Finally he weighed some of the yellow substance.

"And this is sulphur. It's a..." Again Alderley consulted the text, like a magician unsure of his spells, "...catalyst."

"Yellow is the colour of cowardice, isn't it? For those who won't fight..."

Now a hush fell on the class. A line had been crossed. Alderley glared at Smythe-Morrigan.

"I thought you were supposed to be Head of School, not the class clown..."

"And you're supposed to be a science teacher," Smythe-Morrigan retorted coldly, "but you don't seem to know very much about science."

He held Alderley's stare.

"You know, just because you're the Headmaster's son doesn't mean you can say whatever you want."

"Doesn't it?"

Smythe-Morrigan smirked. Some laughed, nervously. Then the Head of School closed in for the kill.

"So, tell us then. What is a catalyst...?"

Alderley could feel the tide turning against him.

"Look, I don't need to prove anything to anybody."

"But I wasn't asking you to prove anything. It was just a simple question."

Dan hated it when a class was unruly. It reminded him of his school in Berlin; only there it was the teachers who invoked the malice, invariably directed at him. Now the tension in the air felt like a storm about to break. He very much wanted the lesson to finish.

"A catalyst is something that speeds up a reaction," he said.

"Correct." Alderley smiled gratefully at Dan. "Now, let's get on..."

Using a spatula he mixed the ingredients together on a heat-proof slate. The resulting grey hill seemed rather a lot, but he trusted the book.

"I don't suppose anyone has a light on them...?"

He was fumbling in his pockets. Jai threw a match box to him.

"Thank you. I shan't ask why you have these."

Then, stepping back a few feet from the bench, Alderley struck a match.

"Here we go..."

The fragile peace of a Devilston morning was instantly torn asunder. Many feared the commencement of the German invasion. The Headmaster's house was far from the epicentre of the explosion yet the Captain's tea trembled in his bone china cup.

Instinctively the students had ducked down behind their benches, prior to ignition. Thus they escaped the full force of the blast but still felt the air being sucked from their lungs.

But Alderley hadn't the luxury of cover. He was lifted off his feet and flung backwards against the blackboard like a rag doll. A fiery cloud of combusted gas passed over cowering heads like the wrath of God, punching through the leaded windows. In its wake, thick black smoke poured out of the Science Room and billowed skywards.

Warily the class raised their heads from behind their tables to survey the scene, a haze of acrid smoke hanging in the air.

All the jars in the laboratory had shattered and liberated liquids were cascading from the shelves. Alderley sat slumped on the floor beneath this waterfall, surrounded by a gruesome picnic spread of pickled specimens as if caught in a biblical plague. A snake hung round his neck like a scarf, he wore a jellyfish on his head at a rakish angle and in his lap lay a human foetus.

"Your explanation better be bloody good..."

The Captain glared across the neat empire of his desk.

The sickly-sweet odour of formaldehyde

lingered in the air around Alderley. His face was smoke-blackened and his ears still rang from the blast.

"I misread the instructions, Headmaster. The quantities in the book were in percentages, not ounces..."

"I'll come to that presently. But how dare you suggest the Head of School enjoys some kind of special immunity?"

Alderley was caught off guard.

"I will not tolerate any suggestion of nepotism in this school, Alderley. Sebastian is Head of School because he is quite simply the best man for the job. Do I make myself clear?"

"Yes, Headmaster."

"Granted, his wit can be a little barbed at times but that's a reflection of a keen mind. Or would you rather we suppress independent thought, like Herr Hitler is doing...?"

"No, Headmaster."

"So...what exactly were you hoping to achieve in that abortion of a lesson?"

"I was trying to capture the attention of the class."

"By blowing them up? You were damned lucky there were no injuries or fatalities, your own included. And it would have been my job to explain to parents why their precious darlings had been wiped out by a clumsy and incompetent science teacher."

"I'm sorry, Headmaster. It won't happen again."

"Well, there's certainly one way of ensuring that..."

"By sacking me?"

Alderley found himself unperturbed by the possibility.

"And why shouldn't I? You've only been here a matter of hours and already you've arrived late to a lesson, laid waste to a science laboratory and endangered the lives of an entire class. And - to top it all - you had the temerity to defy a direct order..."

"A direct order, Headmaster?"

"You blatantly ignored my instructions concerning Miss Montserrat. And don't try to deny it. I was watching you at the dinner last night. You were practically drooling over the woman..."

"We were having a conversation. Isn't that permitted?"

"And afterwards...?"

My God. He must have spies everywhere.

"We played chess and drank wine. Then I fell asleep."

Now the Captain sat back in his chair.

"You know, from what I've seen of you so far, I actually believe you."

He smiled. Alderley reciprocated nervously, relaxing a little himself. Then the Captain's smile vanished.

"I know why you're here."

"You do?"

"This is a forgery, isn't it?"

Alderley had noticed his degree certificate on the desk.

"Though I must say, it's a very good one. Almost had me fooled. And no doubt the story you span at your interview was equally fake: all that nonsense about resigning as a government scientist because of your pacifist tendencies. Well, evidently you're no scientist, and I'd wager you've never even set foot in Cambridge..."

The Captain crumpled up the certificate then tossed it into the waste paper basket.

"So tell me...what were you really doing, before you took this job?"

"I was a newspaper reporter."

"Ha!" The Captain clapped his hands together in triumph, his face beaming. "I knew it! You look like a hack. It's those shifty eyes..."

"Thank you."

"Which rag...?"

"*The Guardian.*"

"Manchester?"

"Cornish."

The Captain chuckled.

"A mighty organ, indeed. So presumably you're after the undercover story on Devilston? What really goes on behind the doors of an exclusive boarding school on a mysterious island..."

"I said I **was** a reporter."

"So why did you give it up?"

"I suppose I'd had enough of prying into people's lives."

"Is that so? Or was there another reason...?"

"What do you mean?"

"Well, journalism isn't protected employment, is it? And you saw the conscription age slowly creeping higher: an approaching tsunami of khaki about to sweep you away to a war you want no part in. But teachers are a precious species, vital to the effort on the Home Front, nurturing the next generation of cannon fodda..."

The Captain leaned forward.

"Though just between you and me, I think it's more to do with controlling our wayward youth. Potentially a very explosive material..."

He sat back.

"So here was the perfect bolt hole for you. Somewhere you could keep your head down while this mad war runs its course. Only problem was, it was a science job: a subject you clearly know very little about. I must say though, you were quite impressive in your interview. A result of some pretty frantic cramming, I should think. Of course I saw through your little act right from the start..."

"So why did you give me the job?"

"Well, firstly you're an Old Devilstonian. You were here before my time admittedly, but we like to look after our own..."

"And secondly?"

"I rather like the cut of your gib, Alderley. You're a survivor, like me. But you're not really a conscientious objector, are you...?"

"I'm a pacifist."

"I see. Still clinging to that flimsy olive twig, are we? So tell me, what kind of a pacifist gives lessons on gunpowder...?"

"There are many non-military uses for explosives, Headmaster. Mining, for instance..."

"So you're against taking up arms under any circumstance, are you...?"

As he spoke the Captain stood and made his way round the desk, to loom threateningly over Alderley.

"That's right..."

The Captain lifted his walking stick then brought it down at speed. Alderley raised his left arm to parry the blow then - bristling with a sudden anger - swung a punch with his right. But the Captain moved swiftly, catching Alderley's fist in his hand like a cricket ball. Alderley was aware of a great strength behind it.

"A pacifist, eh?"

The Captain stared down at him, eyes wide with triumph.

"That was unfair. It was instinctive. I had no choice."

Releasing Alderley's fist the Captain returned to his seat. He ran a hand through his hair, re-positioning a displaced lock and regaining his composure.

"You're absolutely right, of course. Sometimes one must act not with the heart or the head, but from the gut. Pure survival instinct....So what does your instinct tell you about this war? And don't think about it, just tell me now."

He clicked his fingers impatiently.

"I'm not sure what you mean..."

"It's a simple enough question, Alderley. Do you think this little island will defeat the might of the Third Reich?"

"Do you mean Devilston or Britain?"

"You know exactly what I mean..."

"I think we'll win."

"We? But you're not even in the fight."

"Alright. I think Britain will win. Eventually..."

"I don't believe you. And I don't believe you're a pacifist either. Do you know why? Because just then I saw the fire in your eyes...I think you would be willing to serve your country, if you thought your country had a chance. But you know very well, deep in your gut, that Britain has had it, and you don't wish to sacrifice your life for what you perceive to be a lost cause."

"That's not true."

"See? You're doing it again. Instinctively defending yourself. And yet you're all too aware of the facts. Dunkirk was celebrated as a great victory. What was it Winny said....?" The Captain gave a good imitation of Churchill's deep growl: "**From the jaws of defeat**... Poppycock. The truth is, the British Army suffered a total collapse in France. The RAF have managed to fight off the Luftwaffe for a while, but how long are we going to put up with our cities being smashed to pieces and our ships being decimated? And meanwhile the Nazi War Machine is building its boats, fuelling its tanks and sharpening its bayonets, ready for the final onslaught. It's the age-old story, you see. The strong prevailing over the weak...

"Of course you've thought about the future - who hasn't? - and an intelligent man like yourself is bound to conclude that the odds simply aren't worth the stake. Then there's your gut feeling, and that's in agreement too, isn't it...?"

Alderley didn't answer. He was shocked by the Captain's words. He'd heard doubts expressed before, but never with such candour and conviction.

"Which leaves one's emotions. One's love of country. But what does that even mean, exactly?

Love of Britain? England? Cornwall...? How is it possible to love something so large, consisting of so many people you don't even know? I think love on that scale demands too much of the average human being. Ask any soldier what he's fighting for and he'll tell you three things..." The Captain counted them off on his fingers. "Himself, his comrades and his loved ones. I think you'd find King and Country languishing a lot further down the batting order..."

"The Germans love their leader," said Alderley. "Hitler's their number one batsman."

"That's not love," the Captain replied coldly, "that's fear. But here in Devilston our motive is much deeper than fickle emotions. For millennia we've been fighting for our survival: a struggle that has bound us together as One..."

He placed his hands together, his fingers tightly interlocked.

"Devilston has been forged under a perpetual state of siege. There have always been forces on the mainland striving to destroy us: Romans, Saxons, Normans, Tudors, Parliamentarians, Progressives...all plotting our downfall and yet we've always survived. And we'll survive the Germans too, because we're strong. Not physically - we're a tiny community, after all - but here..." He tapped his head with a finger. "And here..." He touched his chest with a fist. "So put it this way, Alderley: your objections to the war - whether conscientious, pragmatic or purely visceral - will be respected in these parts, as long as I can count on your loyalty to Devilston..."

"So...you're not going to sack me?"

"No, though of course I shall have to dock your wages to cover the repairs. To be honest, I'd struggle to find a replacement at such an early stage in the academic year, and with a war on as well. And as they say, better the Devil you know..." He smiled. "The priority for me is that you fit in here with our way of doing things. You're an abysmal science teacher, true enough, but there are ways round that..."

"Are there?"

"Friends in high places. Or rather, an Old Devilstonian at the Examination Board...Let's just say - strictly between the two of us - that the contents of the exam papers don't come as a complete surprise..." He winked. "So, will you join us?"

"But I've already joined you. Haven't I...?"

The Captain didn't reply. Instead he selected a cigarette then pushed the silver box across his desk towards Alderley, watching him with amusement.

5

THE CUTTERS AND THE CRYPT

Sunday brought a brief break in the dreary trudge of scholastic servitude. The whole school filed across the grounds to the ancient Chapel, like a worm consumed by a great stone beetle.

Dan enjoyed the respite of the Christian service: the archaic English of the lessons, the templar timelessness of the Chapel itself, and - despite its stubborn amateurism - the hymnal music: plodding melodic anthems clawed out by Quirk on the organ.

Tom was contemplating the turnip field of cropped heads in front of him, and the prospect of Sunday lunch. He knew the reality would be a dry nut roast with powdered mash and vegetables boiled into ghosts, but it was something to look forward to before the horror of the Cutters.

Jai was trying to make sense of the large circular window above the altar, its primary colours glowing richly. At its centre stood a figure in a white gown holding what looked like a cross above another figure cowering prostrate on the ground. From this central image a number of panes radiated like petals, each containing a hooded monk kneeling in prayer.

But there was something wrong about the pattern.

When the service was over the three remained seated - the organ's rumble reverberating in their chests - while the pews emptied of pupils. Praeposters stood by, monitoring the drainage. Outside, the Reverend was busy dispatching his flock to the world.

"What music is this?" Tom asked Dan. "It's quite scary."

"Bach's Toccata and Fugue in D Minor. Or at least I think it is. Quirk adds so many notes of his own..."

"Dan, tell me what's wrong with that window above the altar," said Jai. "It's making my brain hurt."

Dan contemplated the circle for a while, then smiled.

"It's asymmetrical."

"What?"

"There are only eleven panes. That's why it doesn't look right."

Tattersall appeared at the end of their row.

"What are you three hanging around for?

Christmas?"

"We're listening to the organ," said Jai.

"Are you now?" the Praeposter sneered. "Well, you listen to this: disperse pronto or you won't have those organs on the side of your head to listen with."

"I'm sorry." Jai wore an expression of mock confusion. "I don't understand…"

"What I mean is Sambo, I'll bloody well box your ears if you don't shift your backsides."

Dan was genuinely perplexed.

"Put our ears in a box…?"

The Praeposter's face twitched. Before he could respond the Duty Master arrived. It was Alderley in his Sunday best.

"So what are these three reprobates up to, Tatters?"

"Apparently they're listening to the organ," said Tattersall with contempt.

"Really? Taking an interest in a bit of culture, eh?"

"But they're supposed to be going back to Prophets, sir."

"Oh, let them have a few minutes. It's not going to hurt anyone, is it…?"

As Alderley walked away, Tattersall glared down at Dan with malevolence.

"Quite the brave one, aren't you? I'd have thought being a Jerry Jew would have been two good reasons to keep your head down."

"Sorry sir," said Tom, keen to douse a dangerous situation. "He didn't mean to be rude."

"He's the rude one."

"For God's sake, Dan…"

Tattersall took out a piece of paper and a pencil from his top pocket and scribbled on it.

"His God's not going to save him this time. Rosebum, you're on the Cutters for gross insubordination."

"Well, that's all three of us now," said Tom when Tattersall had gone. "You should have kept quiet, Dan."

"I know but their arrogance makes me angry. They remind me of…"

"Of what?"

"Never mind."

His defiance felt pathetic compared with the girl at the Dutch border.

Suddenly Jai darted from his seat, in the direction of the empty choir stalls. Tom sighed.

"Where's he off to now…?"

They found him in front of a small arched door. The music reached a crescendo then ceased. Its echo haunted the Chapel for some time, as if in search of escape.

Jai turned the iron ring on the door and pushed.

"Damn. It's locked."

"Can I help you?"

The Reverend was standing behind them, looking huge but ridiculous in red cassock and white surplus. Like a big sherry trifle, Tom thought. He could even smell the alcohol.

"Sir, we were just wondering what's behind this door," said Jai.

"Why?"

"Oh, just curious."

"But don't you know what Curiosity did to the Cat...?"

The Reverend should have been angrier but the sermon had gone well and he was in good spirits. The communion wine had been a fruity little Spanish number. Why use cooking wine when there was so much of the quality stuff available?

"That," he said, "is the door to the Crypt."

"What's inside?"

"Dead Morrigans, lad. It's the family vault."

"Could we have a look...?"

"Certainly not. How would you like some filthy oiks poking around while you're trying to get some well-earned R.I.P....? Now get back to Prophets before I lock you in there and throw away the key."

The three filed along the path between the vegetable plots, in no particular hurry to return to their house.

"So those Mad Monks we saw the other night…" said Tom. "Do you think they were carrying one of the Morrigans to the Crypt?"

"I'm not sure that would make chronological sense," said Dan.

"What do you mean?"

At that moment a Leaver overtook them, walking quickly with his head down, a collection of music manuscripts clutched to his chest.

"Quirky!" Dan called out.

Quirk stopped and turned, clearly irritated by the interruption to a busy Sunday schedule.

"When did the Morrigans first come here?"

Quirk consulted the relevant section in his mind.

"In the reign of Queen Elizabeth. She gifted the island to Lady Caitlin Morrigan for services to the Crown. A portrait of the First Duchess of Devilston hangs in the Library, should any of you philistines ever venture in that direction…"

"She must have done something special to earn such a reward," said Dan.

"Well, apart from being a particular favourite of the Queen, she was one of the most successful privateers of the Spanish Main…and, by all accounts, one of the cruellest. So you see gentlemen, Devilston has piracy in Her blood. Now if you'll excuse me, I have work to do…"

"So," said Dan, watching Quirk hurry on,

"whatever your ghosts were carrying in that coffin, it wasn't a Morrigan."

"They weren't ghosts," said Jai.

"But if it was a real coffin," said Tom, "why were they transporting it in the dead of night?"

"Well, you Christians have some strange customs, and that's coming from a Hindu. You know, it's so much easier to burn the dead rather than all this body-in-a-box malarkey..."

"There's only one way to find out what's in that coffin," said Dan.

"By getting into the Crypt."

"Count me out," said Tom. "Places like that are given unpleasant names to keep the curious away..."

"That reminds me," said Dan as they came to the entrance of Prophets. "What exactly did Curiosity do to the Cat...?"

After lunch a dozen and a half miscreants of varying size and age mustered on the quayside in gym kit. The sun shone in a blue sky in which cumulus cloud floated like heavenly galleons at anchor; but there was an autumnal bite in the wind and the thinnest were shivering.

A black Rolls Royce glided along the opposite side of the harbour and came to a halt. Garsten's funereal figure got out and opened the door for the Captain and his wife. Then the three descended the stone steps to a pristine motor boat, Garsten carrying a large picnic basket and a folded blanket.

Llamrei was fashioned from rich red mahogany, with a varnished sheen in which the lapping water admired its reflection. Her lines were classically beautiful: her stern rounded and shapely, her sides slightly concave, tapering to sharp bows. Her chrome fittings gleamed and the sun glinted off her polished windscreen, testament to Garsten's loving attention. The car and the boat were both his responsibility but he'd yet to decide which of these glamorous mistresses reigned supreme in his affections.

The Captain - wearing a blazer, cravat and a naval officer's cap - took the wheel. Charlotte sat next to him, in a floral dress and tweed jacket. A silk scarf protected her hair from the wind and her eyes were shielded from the glare by sunglasses. Jai was reminded of the glamorous couples he'd seen promenading in Monte Carlo while he accompanied his father on his disastrous gambling campaigns.

The engine coughed into life, then idled with a deep and muscular throb. Garsten untied the ropes then waved the couple off. With a roar the boat proudly lifted her nose and powered out of the harbour, a boiling mass of white water surging from her stern, the ensign fluttering above it like a red ribbon in a thoroughbred's tail.

A thin cloud of blue smoke drifted across to the other side of the harbour, where the admiring gaze of the gathered was now disturbed by the shriek of a whistle. The Head of School had arrived, accompanied by his guard of Praeposters.

"Without rules civilization would quickly dissolve into chaos," Smythe-Morrigan bellowed with unnecessary volume, strolling along the line of offenders. He had his hands behind his back, reminding Jai of how his father would inspect his troops. "You have all chosen in some way to ignore Devilston's rules, so now you will suffer the consequences. Then hopefully we won't need to meet here again on a Sunday afternoon..."

The Praeposters smirked, knowing that every week there would always be a sufficient quota. Since the criteria for earning this punishment were not fixed, the prefects were always able to arrange the requisite numbers.

"For those newcomers amongst you, allow me to introduce our Cutters..."

Smythe-Morrigan gestured with a sweep of his arm towards three large rowing boats tied up at the quayside.

"*Faith, Hope* and *Charity*. Once upon a time these three lovely ladies hunted whales, but today it's you lot who will be doing the wailing…"

The Praeposters laughed dutifully. The joke wasn't new.

The Head of School enjoyed the privilege of being the first to choose his crew. He stopped in front of Jai. Now his voice was low.

"You think I've forgotten about you splitting on me, haven't you? What, with the explosion and all that…" He smiled. "Just biding my time, though. Revenge is a dish best served cold…"

The two stared each other out. Smythe-Morrigan was the first to blink.

"You're in my crew," said the Head of School.

Jai climbed down the rusty iron ladder and carefully took his place on *Faith*'s starboard side, near the stern. Dan thought he glimpsed some unease in his friend's manner, an uncharacteristic nervousness in this new environment.

Jai was followed by five more rowers, representing the strongest of the gathered. Then the Head of School and the Head of Prophets joined them: Smythe-Morrigan in the bows facing his crew, Tattersall manning the tiller at the stern.

Jai saw that Dan had been assigned to *Hope*, Tom to *Charity*. He also noticed much discussion and the exchange of money between the remaining haggle of Praeposters on the quayside.

The crews were instructed to hold their oars vertically while the boats cast off. As they drifted, awaiting starter's orders, Smythe-Morrigan stood up in the bows of his boat to address the little flotilla through a conical loud-hailer:

"Do you hear there? The crew of the first boat to circumnavigate the island will have completed their punishment. The two runners-up will then race each other again, and the losing boat of that contest will do another lap. So you'd better put your backs into it or you'll find yourselves doing this three times!"

Sitting down, Smythe-Morrigan quietly instructed his crew to lower their oars and begin rowing.

"I say!" a new boy shouted. "They're cheating!"

"Of course they're bloody cheating," grumbled Tom. "This is Devilston."

With a head start and the strongest crew, Smythe-Morrigan relished the sight of blue water opening up between *Faith* and the other boats.

"Pull!" the Head of School roared at his crew from the bows. "Come on, you weaklings!"

Swiftly mastering technique, Jai fell in with the rhythm of the strokes. Then a thought occurred to him: if his boat lost then one of his friends would be spared another circuit of the island. And there was that mad look in Smythe-Morrigan's eye, a desperate lust for victory at all costs...

So, as *Faith* left the harbour, Jai suddenly accelerated his rowing rate. Its propulsive symmetry upset, the boat began to veer towards the harbour wall.

"Rana!" Smythe-Morrigan screamed. "What the Hell are you doing, you bloody wog?"

"Sorry sir," said Jai, ceasing his efforts, the damage done. "Rather carried away there. Never done this before, you see..."

"They're over-taking us!" Tattersall shouted from the helm.

Smythe-Morrigan pushed the bow away from the wall. By the time the boat was pointing in the right direction again, *Faith* was third, and last.

"Row, you bastards!"

Now the Head of School had unbuckled and withdrawn the belt from his trousers. Walking up and down the length of the craft, he thrashed this way and that with the leather strap, with a vigour that even Tattersall found disturbing.

"Steady on, S-M..."

"Just steer straight," Smythe-Morrigan snapped, "or you'll be rowing yourself!"

Throwing up cold spray, *Faith* nodded through the waves as she rounded that part of the island exposed to the open sea, passing the beach where Jai and Tom had seen the Mad Monks landing. Under the ambivalent gaze of the castle's windows, *Faith* overtook *Charity* and quickly closed in on *Hope*. But as *Faith* drew level with the lead boat, the end of Jai's oar kept striking the oar of the rower behind. Again *Faith* turned off course, allowing *Hope* to surge away.

Seized with a blind fury, Smythe-Morrigan laid into the offender with his belt.

"You black...useless....imbecile!"

Jai held up his arm to shield himself, drawing most of the sting out of each lash.

Noticing the rest of his crew laughing - even Tattersall at the helm - brought the Head of School to his senses. *Charity* cruised past, her crew jeering and wolf-whistling at the sight.

"Don't just sit there!" Smythe-Morrigan was struggling to pull his trousers up. "Get after them!"

But the race was lost.

As *Faith* came alongside in the harbour - in third place - her skipper launched a tirade of abuse at his crew, reserving the brunt of his anger for Jai. Spittle flew from the Head of School's mouth as he raged.

"I am so sorry," said Jai, head bowed and palms together, "but - as I previously indicated - this is my first time in a small boat. We have little call for such vessels in the desert..."

"Right," said Smythe-Morrigan hoarsely,

regaining some composure, "we're going to make some changes…" He called over to *Charity*: "Rana's going in your boat and I'll have one of yours." He pointed at the strongest-looking of *Charity*'s crew, sitting next to Tom in the stern. "Him."

"Oh come on, S-M," protested *Charity's* skipper. "You can't change your crew. It's against the rules."

The Head of School glared across the water at the Praeposter.

"And who makes the rules…?"

So, as the winning crew - Dan among them - collapsed exhausted onto the quayside, Jai changed boats. He shared a quiet word with his new skipper.

"Sir, we won't win through strength alone. But if we use our heads…"

When he'd explained his idea Jai took his place next to Tom. His friend was wheezing heavily, red-faced and sweat-soaked.

"I'm…absolutely…knackered…"

"Hang in there, old chap," said Jai quietly. "If all goes to plan this will be your last time…"

Again Smythe-Morrigan allowed his boat to steal ahead before officially starting the race, and again *Faith* began with a decent lead. Without Rana his crew was now rowing in good time, and he congratulated himself on an excellent tactical move. This time victory would be his, and he'd also recover the substantial amount of money he'd lost in betting on himself in the last race.

His satisfaction was short-lived. As *Charity* cleared the harbour, Smythe-Morrigan watched it swing away from them.

"Where the Hell are they going?"

"The other way," Tattersall replied from the stern.

"It was a rhetorical question, you moron. But they're not allowed to do that."

"Why not? It's the same distance."

"Because I said so. Well, we'll beat them anyway... Come on, you miserable lackeys! Pull!"

Rounding the top of the island the two boats closed on each other, on collision course. Each hugged the shore to minimize the distance to cover, their oars inches away from rocks.

"Keep this course!" Jai instructed *Charity*'s helmsman, the other five rowing in time with Jai's now strong and regular beats. "Aim straight for them!"

"But we'll ram them!" cried the skipper from the front.

"No we won't! They'll break first! And when they do, make sure you steer inside them!"

As *Faith* drew closer Smythe-Morrigan's voice boomed through the loud-hailer.

"Give way, you bloody cheats!"

"Ignore him!" Jai shouted. "Just hold this course and keep rowing!"

"As Head of School I command you to yield!"

"Hold your course!"

Now with only a boat's length between them *Faith* reacted first, her bow swinging seaward.

Indecision had frozen *Charity*'s helmsman so Jai reached over to push the tiller and steer her between *Faith* and the rocks. As the two boats passed, their oars clattered together. Then *Charity* powered on, while *Faith*'s crew fumbled to recover from the near-miss.

Smythe-Morrigan berated his crew.

"Sort yourselves out! If they win I'll have you all flogged!"

Faith quickly made up the debit. By the time the two boats were converging on the harbour entrance, they had an equal distance to cover to the finish.

"Faster, boys!" Jai urged. "We're nearly there!"

"I can't..." gasped Tom, his stroke falling behind the others. "My arms..."

"Move up then!"

Tom slid up the bench to allow Jai to take hold of his oar as *Faith* and *Charity* entered the mouth of the harbour, side-by-side. Again their oars clashed as each crew fought to get the upper hand. The spectators on the harbourside - Praeposters and *Hope*'s crew alike - cheered on a fine spectacle of maritime battle.

With the intention of taking over the helm from Tattersall, Smythe-Morrigan had moved to *Faith*'s stern...tantalizingly close to Jai's position in *Charity*.

Jai spotted the opportunity immediately. Using his oar with some force, he prodded *Faith* just below her gunwale. The boat pitched over, catching the standing Smythe-Morrigan off his guard. His arms windmilled in a desperate attempt to regain his balance, but in vain. With a cry he toppled over the side and splashed into the water and a deep cheer of surprised delight went up from the spectators.

"Help me!" Smythe-Morrigan glugged, struggling to keep his head above the surface, his clothes like dead hands dragging him down. "I'm drowning!"

Charity extricated herself from *Faith* and continued into the harbour, while *Faith*'s crew watched their skipper floundering; fascinated by the sight of one so powerful reduced to such a pitiful state.

Then a stream-lined sliver of fine craftsmanship appeared on the scene, her engine rumbling. Having carefully steered *Llamrei* alongside the flailing Head of School, the Captain leaned over to open the long seat behind the driver's position. Taking out an emergency oar he offered its end to the stricken Smythe-Morrigan.

"What the Hell are you playing at...?"

"Sorry...Father..."

Smythe-Morrigans's teeth were chattering as he slithered into the boat.

"You poor thing," said his mother, handing her son the picnic blanket. "We'll drive you up to school."

"No we won't," said the Captain. "He's going to finish what he started. Aren't you, Sebastian?"

"Yes...of course..."

"But he'll catch his death," Charlotte protested.

"Better to gain a cold than squander respect, my dear."

The boat came alongside the harbour steps. As Smythe-Morrigan stepped ashore the Captain snatched the blanket from him.

"Never show weakness, Sebastian."

"Yes Father."

With sadness Charlotte watched her shivering son secure *Llamrei* to the quayside then make his way round to the other side of the harbour, to re-join the noisy throng.

"You never cut him any slack, do you?"

The Captain switched off the engine.

"Molly-coddling the lad won't do him any favours." He helped his wife from the boat and they ascended the steps to the quayside. "But let's not spoil a delightful afternoon with another argument, shall we?"

"A delightful afternoon...?"

"I'll say. Luncheon of champagne and cold meats on a secluded beach, followed by the most delicious of desserts....what more could one wish for on a Sunday afternoon...?"

"A choice," Charlotte replied coldly. "Oh, but I forgot. A wife is the legal possession of her husband, to do with as he wishes. Presumably your other women enjoy more freedom...?"

She felt his grip tightening on her elbow as he guided her towards the Rolls Royce.

A sizeable group of pupils had now congregated on the harbourside to investigate rumours of a drowning. Now the swollen crowd celebrated as *Charity* came alongside, *Faith* following forlornly in her wake. Since he was always entitled to the strongest crew, the Head of School's boat usually won. Today was the first time it had ever come last.

"Great plan, Rana!" gushed *Charity*'s helmsman as he pumped Jai's hand.

"I have to say," said her skipper, slapping Jai on the back, "that was definitely worth losing the bet for. But that's just between ourselves, of course..."

The Praeposter had bet on *Faith* to win. But today pride had prevented him from simply capitulating and cashing in, and a deeper desire to get one up on his leader. Seeing the Head of School thrashing helplessly in the water had been the baptism of an already special day.

Now a dripping Smythe-Morrigan stood on the quayside, glowering down at the two boats. A hush descended upon the horse shoe of spectators gathered around him. The two crews prepared to receive the Head Boy's wrath.

But then a strange thing happened. Like a shaft of sunlight breaking through a storm cloud, his face split into a broad smile.

"Well," he laughed, a little too theatrically. "I must say, that was a great lark, wasn't it? Well done, everyone! Splendid sport!"

He clapped enthusiastically and a smattering of uneasy applause accompanied him. The crowd was anticipating the punch line.

"Nevertheless," he continued, "since you're here to learn the importance of obeying Devilston's rules, I'm afraid *Charity* must be disqualified for going the wrong way round the island. Therefore I declare *Faith* the winner of Round Two!"

A cheer of relief from the crew of *Faith* was drowned by the groans of disappointment and disbelief from the rest.

"Silence!" Smythe-Morrigan held up his hand until order returned. "However, in recognition of their initiative and enterprise, I shall grant a reprieve to the disqualified crew. For this week only, another circuit of the island will not be necessary."

Only the Praeposters clapped now. Most felt robbed of a moral victory; the sight of their leader skippering his boat on an ignominious circumnavigation of the island would have been one to cherish.

"Clever bugger," Tom muttered to Jai. "He managed to save face there."

"Not entirely," Jai replied, catching the Head of School's eye. Smythe-Morrigan was still shivering from his unscheduled swim. "Revenge is a dish best served cold..."

The Reverend swayed slightly as he stood at the open window. A set of antique brass binoculars hung from his neck and in his trembling hand he held a crystal glass of fine cognac. Watching the Cutters was the high tide of his Sunday afternoon, before his inevitable marooning on a mudflat of loneliness, with only his books and gramophone for company. And his brandy.

No bloody good at all...No bloody God at all...

The location of his rooms at the top of Prophets' tower meant he commanded a grandstand view of the entire race circuit. He only needed to move from one room to the next in order to follow the progress of the boats around the island. On this particular Sunday he'd relished the surprising spectacle of two boats on head-on collision course. And then - to crown it all - there was the Head of School's impromptu immersion.

In truth he'd experienced a mixed reaction to the mishap: the deep amusement which reverberated in his chest as he watched Smyth-Morrigan cartwheel overboard was followed by a jolt in his heart, as if he was suffering Sebastian's shock by delayed proxy.

The crowd on the harbourside began to disperse. The Reverend was about to re-fill his glass when he glimpsed a flash of white in the walled garden of the Headmaster's house. Raising his binoculars again, his shaky view came to rest on a pale pair of buttocks. The figure was bending over but he knew immediately to whom the bare bottom belonged.

Seeing the Rolls Royce pull up outside the house, the Reverend anticipated a little more entertainment to enliven his solitude.

Lady Jennifer Smythe-Morrigan - the Dowager Duchess of Devilston - was devoted to her garden. In the summer she'd often work in the nude, indifferent to the possibility of being observed, though not entirely oblivious to it.

Naked horticulture was a habit she found difficult to curtail as the season waned. The walled garden was a sun trap, accumulating a pool of still and pleasant heat even on windy days. So whenever she had the house to herself she made the most of her freedom, exposing as much as she could to the attentions of the ailing sun.

Though her dishevelled hair was as grey as sea mist and the skin of her face had dried and coarsened like driftwood, her body remained firm from regular exercise: nocturnal horse-rides on the beach, early morning swims in the rock pool and - of course - gardening; all conducted without clothing, if she could get away with it.

Now she paused in her work, hearing the crunch of wheels on gravel.

"Good afternoon, Rebecca." Charlotte removed her sunglasses as she and her husband entered the hall. "Where's the Duchess?"

"In the garden, ma'am..."

The Captain read the maid's blushes.

"She's out there again without a stitch on, isn't she?" He turned to his wife. "Get her inside. This isn't a nudist colony."

Charlotte smirked.

"Bit hypocritical of you, Ralph..."

"We'll take tea, Rebecca."

"Yes, sir."

The Captain waited for the maid to leave before continuing.

"How many times have I told you not to discuss personal matters in front of the staff?"

Charlotte laughed scornfully as they walked through into the drawing room.

"Remarkable. From rogue to prude in the blink of an eye..."

"We weren't in plain view of a boys' boarding school this afternoon." The Captain's attention was shifting to the Sunday newspaper, and his favourite armchair. "It's about keeping the public separate from the private...and shut that bloody door, will you?"

"Of course, darling..." Strolling into the garden she closed the french windows behind her and removed her head scarf, shaking the sand from her hair. "After all, we've so much to hide, haven't we...?"

From a wrought-iron seat on the patio she picked up the silk dressing gown her father had brought home from the Orient. Her mother was kneeling by a flower bed.

"You'd better put this on, Mother. Ralph's rather irate."

The Duchess planted her trowel and slowly stood up, supporting her back with her hands.

"Your father didn't mind."

"No...I wonder what he'd think of how things have turned out..."

The Duchess placed a palm on either side of her daughter's face and studied her intently.

"Divorce him," she said quietly. "You're still young. You shouldn't be so miserable."

"I can't."

"But he treats you abominably..."

"I know. It doesn't make any sense, does it?" Charlotte caressed the dressing gown, as if seeking consolation in the smoothness of the silk. "And anyway, what about Sebastian?"

"He'd be better off away from that man's influence. Such a lovely boy once, but so much cruelty in his eyes now..."

"If I left Ralph he'd have Devilston all to himself."

"No he wouldn't. You're the rightful heir. It's in the will."

"But he's my husband. He'll get everything, Mother. He always gets everything..."

They'd had the same conversation many times before, and always it ran aground on the same rock.

"Besides," Charlotte added, "he'd make sure everyone knew the truth, including Sebastian. I couldn't live with that."

"The truth will always find a way out, my dear."

"I know, but I want to protect him from it for

as long as I can. He isn't strong enough yet."

"Do you think he'll ever be?"

As usual Charlotte avoided the question, instead holding the dressing gown up, the Chinese dragon resplendent.

"Come, Mother. Put this on. The boys might see you."

"Well, let them, I say. It'll give them something to write home about…"

Now the Duchess turned towards the school and waved vigorously.

The Reverend lowered his binoculars, startled by the sudden unadulterated view of Devilston's matriarch gesticulating in his direction. Had she seen him at the window? Raising his spy glasses again with some trepidation he watched Charlotte helping her mother into a dressing gown.

How ironic, he reflected. For all her eccentric ways, the Duchess still managed to display the most dignity…

He put his binoculars down then drained his glass, the brandy helping to anaesthetise the dull pain he'd felt in his chest upon seeing Charlotte.

Re-filling his glass from the decanter, he wound up the gramophone and - with a shaky hand - placed the needle on the spinning disc.

Then, easing himself into his armchair and squashing tobacco into his pipe, he strained to listen beyond the hiss and crackles to the opening he so loved: the Prelude to Wagner's *Tristan und Isolde*; its melody struggling to soar, but each time thwarted by the jarring discord.

From a small window two floors below the Reverend's chambers a cricket bat emerged, a shaving mirror attached to its handle with a rubber band. Dulled by drink the Housemaster of Prophets had left his black-out curtains open, providing Jai with a convenient means of determining exactly when Monster Mouth turned in.

Packing the bat had been an act of great optimism on the part of Jomsom, believing Jai would still be at Devilston for the Summer Term, and the playing of cricket still permitted in England. Now Jai was thankful for the old soldier's foresight.

"You never know when a cricket bat might come in handy, sahib…"

"Bloody Hell, Jai." Tom yawned as he lay in his bed in the darkness, his body stiff and his hands raw from the oar. "I wish I knew where you got your energy from."

"Beedis, old chap."

Jai was coiled up in the window space. He

blew a final puff of smoke out of the open window then flicked the butt of the Indian cigarette into the night.

"Ideal for staying alert. But that was my last, sadly...Ha! Bingo!"

"What is it?" Dan mumbled drowsily.

"Monster's light's out." Jai retracted the cricket bat and closed the window. "I'll give him a bit of time before I go up, just to be on the safe side..."

"Not like you," said Tom.

"Taking risks is like telling lies, old boy. The bigger they are, the more thought they require."

"Did Johnson tell you that?"

"Jomsom lie? Never. No, that's one of my father's old chestnuts. Only, he's not very good at eating them. You wouldn't believe how much money he's frittered away on the cards over the years..."

"What does your mother think about that?"

"Which one?"

"Which one?" Tom was astonished. "How many have you got?"

"My father has many wives. Consequently I have many mothers."

"But only one brought you into the world."

"Yes but I was never told who she was. And there are many women in the zenana..."

"What's one of those when it's at home?"

"The zenana **was** my home, Tom. It's where

my father's wives live. A palace within a palace, really."

Curiosity now lured Dan from the hinterland of sleep.

"So how many wives does your father have?"

"Twelve, last count. And then there are the concubines, and the nautch girls..."

"Now you've lost me," said Tom.

"Concubines are mistresses," Jai explained. "They're a bit lower down the pecking order to wives."

"And the match girls light his cigars, I suppose...?"

Jai laughed.

"Nautch girls are entertainers. Dancers, singers, musicians and such like."

"All those women for one man..." Tom mused dreamily.

"It sounds like the harem in *One Thousand and One Nights*," said Dan. "And no men are allowed in this place, except for your father...?"

"Well, there are the eunuchs, of course," said Jai. "They run the place, and a zenana with over a hundred women under one roof takes a lot of running..."

"Lucky you-nooks," said Tom.

Simultaneously Dan and Jai burst into laughter.

"Alright, what's the joke?"

"I'll leave Dan to explain," chuckled Jai. "Time

to go."

He descended from the window ledge and carefully opened the door. After checking the corridor was safe he slipped out, closing the door quietly behind him.

"I wish I had his courage," said Dan.

"He's a brave one, no doubt about that," said Tom. "Then again, he's got nothing to lose…"

"What do you mean?"

"Well, I'm only here because the RAF pays my fees and you're only here because you're on a scholarship, so we wouldn't get a second chance if we blew it. But if Jai's expelled, his dad would only have to find another school…"

"I'm not sure there are many schools left he hasn't already been to," said Dan, slurring now as sleep re-claimed him.

"Dan?"

"Tom, I'm very tired…"

"Just one more question."

"Yes?"

"What's a you-nook when he's at home…?"

Jai crept silently up the spiral stone staircase, past Alderley's door and onwards to the top floor of the tower. He was now in forbidden territory and the thought thrilled him.

Pale milky moonlight from a tiny window provided just enough illumination. He turned the handle and gently pushed against the Reverend's door. To his delight, it yielded.

So the Monster sleeps with his door unlocked. But why shouldn't he? Who would be so bold as to dare enter his realm...?

The door creaked like a living thing, protesting at being forced to labour at such an ungodly hour. Jai paused, ears straining the night for any sound from within. Then he entered the Reverend's chambers.

Glimpsing a dark and headless figure lurking in the corner of his eye he turned to confront it, fists raised. But the figure remained hanging, motionless.

Again Jai silently rejoiced; the operation might be easier than he'd expected. He rummaged in the duffle coat's deep pockets, his fingers delving amongst coins, a pipe, a matchbox and numerous sundry items. But no keys.

Moving deeper into enemy territory Jai negotiated the dim corridor, each foot testing the floor for creaks before committing his weight to it.

He entered a room. Within, like crouching creatures, he saw the dark forms of furniture. On a window ledge - silhouetted against the night sky - a bird of prey stood with wings half-outstretched, as if about to take flight. Jai caught his breath, anticipating its alarm shriek, before realising he'd be waiting for ever.

Shelves of books covered the walls, with more tomes piled precariously around the floor like booby traps. How could he hope to search this room without knocking over a column of volumes and alerting the enemy?

He was distracted from his thoughts by a sound: a deep and rhythmic rumble which drew him further along the corridor, like a knight of old approaching the lair of a slumbering beast.

It was his intention to close the bedroom door, thereby diminishing the chances of waking the Reverend while he searched his rooms. But as he stood in the doorway, Jai found himself consumed by an overwhelming curiosity. He wanted to see his Housemaster sleeping. He wanted to witness this formidable man in his most vulnerable state…

Moonlight beaming through the bedroom's leaded window illuminated another stuffed bird, this one perched on the bedside table: a white owl which glowed angelically, wings folded, head turned towards the bed as if watching over its sleeping master.

The Reverend was lying on his back, a huge and mountainous form. His mouth hung open like a dark cave, emitting a cycle of rattling snorts and deep sighs. But the sound was almost too snore-like and Jai wondered if the Reverend was only pretending. He feared the eyelids might flick open at any moment...

The Reverend's pajama shirt was undone, revealing a chain around his neck with a ring attached which lay on the vast and forested chest. On this ring Jai saw three large keys.

He stood motionless for some time, steeling himself.

The bigger they are, the more thought they require...

Now Jai leaned over the sleeping body, his fingertips homing in on the keys. It would require perfect timing, for the prize was rising and falling with each of the Reverend's snores. He counted three breaths, hooked his little finger through the ring to lift the keys, then froze.

His Housemaster was stirring.

Standing as still as the owl at his elbow, Jai waited.

The Reverend turned onto his side, mumbling in his sleep.

"Charlotte..."

This movement caused some disturbance within the great body and the bed reverberated loudly. Jai held his breath for some time; partly for fear of rousing his Housemaster as he rose close to the surface of consciousness, mostly to avoid inhaling the noxious fumes of the flatulent eruption.

Resuming his task, Jai lifted the chain until

most of it was clear of the Reverend but for the section that lay beneath his head. Looking round the room for inspiration, Jai's eye was caught by the barn owl's glassy stare. He reached over with his free hand and selected a suitable feather on the bedside owl: a downy one from its breast, small enough for its absence not to be noticed. Plucking it, he half-expected a squawk.

Apologies, old bird. Needs must…

Now armed with this little wisp of fluffiness, Jai gently tickled the Reverend's bulbous nose. It twitched but nothing more so he attempted a bolder approach, carefully inserting the tip of the feather into one of the Reverend's nasal caverns.

The result was spectacular. His nostrils flared, his eyebrows arched and his top lip rose to reveal stained teeth. Then, with great sound and fury accompanied by a cloud of warm spray as from a whale's blow-hole, the Reverend sneezed.

For an instant his head parted from the pillow, allowing Jai to fully extricate the chain.

"I thought you were visiting Monster Mouth." Tom was squinting in the sudden harsh light. "Not Cowardly…"

"So this is what you've woken us up for?" Dan

was equally unimpressed."A white feather?"

Jai brought his other hand from behind his back and jangled the keys on their chain. Tom's eyes grew wide.

"You did it..."

Dan took the chain from Jai for closer scrutiny.

"Three keys. But what do they open...?"

"I reckon one for Prophets, one for Chapel and one for the Crypt." Jai reclaimed the chain and hung it round his neck. "Right, I'm off."

"Where are you going now?" asked Dan.

"To test my hypothesis..."

"On your own?"

"Not quite. I'll be taking a couple of friends with me..."

"Well, you can count me out," said Tom.

"I don't mean you."

Tom felt a lurch of disappointment, despite himself.

Jai had turned his tuck box over. He slid its bottom panel out to reveal a secret compartment. The other two - now out of their beds - peered in, fascinated. Tom was particularly taken by a magazine's front cover: the legendary temptress Gypsy Rose Lee reclining in red bodice and black stockings. He only just avoided getting his fingers trapped when Jai slid the panel home.

"No time for that."

Jai had extracted two objects from the hiding place. One was a flat metal box the size of a hip flask with a round lid in it. He flicked the lid open to reveal a lens which lit up when he pressed a switch.

"German field torch from the last war."

Jai illuminated his friends' faces in turn.

"Jomsom took it from a dead soldier after the Battle of Ypres. It's my second most-prized possession…"

"So what's your first?" asked Tom. "Apart from the obvious…"

Jai passed him the torch then held up a long sheathed knife. Like a stage magician he slowly withdrew the steel blade from its leather scabbard until almost all of its length was revealed, gleaming in the torch's beam. It had a graceful curve not unlike Gypsy Rose's leg, Tom noted.

"Jomsom's kukri," Jai explained. "They say a Gurkha charge with knives unsheathed is the most frightening sight an enemy could ever witness…"

The three admired the broad and lustrous blade, wondering whose insides it might have violated. Then, with a snap which returned them to the moment, Jai slid the blade back into its home.

"Well chaps, wish me luck…"

Pushing the sheathed knife under his belt and

retrieving the torch from Tom, Jai was about to open the door when Dan spoke.

"Wait. I'm coming with you. I want to see what's in that Crypt."

He began to dress over his pajamas.

"Thought you might." Jai grinned. "Cheerio Tom. Hold the fort, won't you?"

"Not a chance."

Now Tom was hurriedly dressing. He was disturbed by the thought of what might lie beneath the Chapel but he was more worried by the prospect of being left alone, even with Gypsy Rose Lee to keep him company.

Unlike on their first foray, Prophets' door was locked. Jai tried two keys, without success.

"Well, if it's not this one then it's an early bath..."

Dan was puzzled.

"An early bath?"

"He means the game will be over," Tom explained, secretly wishing for it.

The third key turned in the lock and Jai opened the door.

"Phew. That saves us having to use the window again..."

His friends weren't entirely sure he was joking. Jai locked the door behind them then led the way to Chapel. They took the long route round again, using the shadows of the castle wall as cover.

"I don't mind admitting it," Tom whispered breathlessly, "but I'm scared."

"Only the foolish and the dead feel no fear," Jai replied. "But don't you feel really alive at the same time?"

"Yes," said Dan. "I do."

"Well, make the most of it," said Tom, "because we're going to be really dead if we're caught…"

Now they'd reached the Chapel door. The second key Jai tried turned in the lock and the three entered. He quietly closed the door behind them then locked it.

"Aren't you going to switch your torch on, Jai?" Dan asked.

"Not yet. Don't want to advertise our presence…"

Dan and Tom followed Jai down the side aisle, behind the choir stalls. Above them the arched windows glowed dimly like spectral forms. Tom found himself wishing it was an ordinary boring Sunday morning with the Chapel full of people, and light.

"Well," said Jai, fumbling for the right key as they stood in front of the door to the Crypt. "This is it…."

He inserted the key and the lock clicked as it

turned.

"Acha!" said Jai.

"Wunderbar!" said Dan.

"Isn't this trespassing?" asked Tom.

"In our own home...?"

Jai slowly opened the door. In the faint light of night they saw stone steps descending into a pool of black. They crossed the threshold then he shut the door behind them.

Tom had thought it dark enough when they'd first entered the Chapel, before their eyes had become accustomed, but now the three stood in a blackness that was of a different quality altogether. It was absolute.

"Switch the torch on, Jai..."

There was a tremble in Dan's voice now.

"Will do, at the bottom of these steps..."

They began to slowly descend, hands extended either side to feel the walls. Then Jai switched on the torch and the three blinked in the brightness. They were standing in a long chamber with a low vaulted ceiling. The air had an ancient and organic smell to it, of damp and decay. The torch beam swept across the walls, illuminating an array of inscribed stones. The dates varied but all the surnames were the same.

"An assortment of Morrigans," said Jai. "And the future resting place of our noble Head Boy..."

"And not a day too soon, if you ask me," said Tom. "Dan, are you alright...?"

Tom had noticed their friend was breathing heavily. When Jai shone the torch on him they saw his face was deathly pale and shining with sweat.

"It was the dark." Dan sat down on what looked like a long wooden seat. "Like Krystallnacht..."

"Like what?"

"When they came into our homes. We hid in that place in the kitchen...Die Spiesekammer...I don't know the English word...Where you keep the food...?"

"Larder."

"There was no room for my father. He promised he would hide somewhere else but when they came he gave himself up. He sacrificed himself so that his family would survive..."

"I'm so sorry," said Jai. "I didn't realise..."

"It's alright." Dan smiled up at his friends. "But I'll just sit here for a few moments, if that's alright...?"

Jai scanned what Dan was sitting on with the torch beam.

"Actually, it might be better if you didn't..."

"Oh dear." Dan stood up quickly. "It must be at least one hundred years of bad luck to sit on a coffin."

"Make that two hundred," Tom corrected him. "There's one underneath it, too..."

"Well, if it's any comfort," said Jai, "it can't be too much bad luck if you live for two hundred years."

The coffins were made of rough pine with rope handles. When Jai flashed his torch around the floor of the Crypt they saw many more.

"Jai, you don't think there are actually... " Tom paused, horrified by the thought, unable to even say the word. "I mean, inside them...?"

"Hold this."

Jai handed Tom the torch. Then, positioning himself at one end of the coffin Dan had sat on, he gripped the rope handle with both hands and lifted.

"Well, there's something in it alright."

Jai lowered the end then retrieved the torch.

"The question is, what?" asked Dan.

"You mean, who?" said Tom. "I think it's time to call it a night, lads."

"But don't you want to know what's inside?"

The torch shone in Tom's face.

"No Jai, I don't." He shielded his eyes. "And stop doing that. It hurts."

"Oh, come on." Jai pressed on with the interrogation. "At least a part of you wants to know..."

"You're right. The stupidest part. Tell him, Dan. We're not opening that coffin."

Dan shrugged.

"Why not? It can't be much worse than sitting on it."

Jai smiled at Tom. In the torchlight his face looked demonic.

"It would appear you're outvoted, my friend."

He handed Tom the torch again then drew out the kukri from its scabbard, its crooked blade flashing in the light. He carefully inserted its sharp tip into the slight crack where the lid didn't quite meet the side of the coffin.

"Jai, this isn't right," said Tom. "This isn't right at all."

"Just be quiet and keep the torch still. Every time you talk it moves."

Now Jai carefully worked the knife along the crack to widen it - each nail groaning in protest at being prematurely raised from its grave - until the lid was loose. Before sheathing the kukri, he pressed the end of his thumb against its tip. A small bead of red appeared which he licked away.

"An unsheathed blade must always taste blood," Jai explained to his astonished friends. "Now Dan, if you would kindly give me a hand...?"

Dan and Jai positioned themselves at each end of the long box. On a nod from Jai they lifted the lid.

Tom kept his eyes shut, holding his breath

and anticipating his friends' cries as they beheld the slumbering vampire, or rotting corpse. But there followed neither scream nor smell, only a low chuckle from Jai.

"Well, how about that...?"

Tom opened his eyes and deflated with relief.

"Thank God..."

There was no body. Instead, the coffin was tightly packed with merchandise. Dan pulled out a bottle and studied its label in the torchlight.

"Champagne."

Jai picked out a cylindrical container, twisted open its lid and extracted a sample. He sniffed the fat brown sausage under his nose then sighed.

"Finest cigars, rolled on the thigh of a beautiful Cuban girl..."

Not wanting to be left out, Tom selected a flat rectangular package.

"Chocolate..."

"Swiss," said Jai, reading the label. "Those ghosts of yours certainly enjoy the finer things in life, don't they?"

"Now I never said they were definitely ghosts," Tom protested. "I just like to keep an open mind..."

"What better cover for clandestine operations than an ancient legend? And look at those..." Jai pointed the torch beam at a cluster of garments hanging in a corner. "They really ought to hide their dirty habits better…"

"So where's all this stuff coming from, anyway?" asked Tom.

"Probably some neutral country. Ireland perhaps, or Spain. Smuggled here in that fishing boat I saw."

"Smugglers. Who'd have thought it, in this day and age…?"

"So this is where the Staff get all their luxury goods," said Dan.

"Not only the Staff, I wager." Now Jai shone the torch around the Crypt. "If all these coffins are full then there's too much booty here even for those greedy bastards. They'll be moving some of it on to the black market, I'm sure. And I think I know how they get it to the mainland, out of sight of prying eyes…"

"So, another successful mission accomplished."

Safely back in their room in Prophets, Jai was perched in the window space again. He was puffing on one of the Cuban cigars he'd pocketed, blowing the smoke out of the window as he pontificated. The bottle of champagne was safely stowed in the secret compartment of his tuck box. As fruitful as their recce had been, he wanted to save it for a truly special occasion.

"Quite successful," said Tom, through a

mouthful. "But we didn't find your tunnel."

He was on his bed, celebrating with chocolate. He savoured each delicious chunk as it melted in his mouth, forming a stream of heavenly sweetness which flowed over his tongue and down his throat, bestowing warmth and comfort within him. He'd given Dan and Jai a part of the slab and had intended to save the rest. But now the chocolate was exerting its seductive influence upon him, and the precious ingot was rapidly shrinking.

"Ah," Jai countered, "but just because the entrance wasn't in the Crypt doesn't mean the tunnel doesn't exist."

"So we've eliminated one possibility," said Dan. "But what about these...?"

Dan was sitting at his desk, toying with the keys. He'd arranged them so that their shafts were splayed out like the three legs on the Manx flag the old sailor had given him. The tattered red ensign was pinned on the wall above his desk, adding a little colour to the grey room.

"What about them?"

Tom swallowed.

"We can't keep them, Jai. They'll search high and low for them. When the kitchens were raided last term they turned the school upside down and shook it."

"Did they find the culprits?" asked Dan.

"Eventually, and only after they'd put us all

on bread and water. Except the Praeposters and the First Eleven cricket team, of course. It was over a week before someone split."

"Well," said Jai, "we won't be splitting, will we...?"

"No, but I don't fancy living on a starvation diet until Christmas."

"But we won't have to, Tom. With these keys we have access to all those goodies, whenever we want."

"You'd better take them back Jai," said Dan. "They're bound to suspect us. We're only two floors below Monster's rooms, after all. And you've already showed them you're willing to challenge the system..."

"But we won't be able to get into the Chapel again. Or find the tunnel entrance."

"So you're still convinced the entrance is in the Chapel?"

"I'll tell you where it is," said Tom, tiring of tunnel talk. "Up my bum, that's where."

Jai ignored Tom.

"I'm sure it's somewhere close to where the treasure's kept."

"Just like I said," Tom grinned, his mouth stained with chocolate.

"There are many graves in the Chapel floor," Jai continued. "Any one of them could be the entrance..."

"Look, I hate to be the Doubting Thomas but

there's no bloody tunnel. It's just a legend."

"So how are they getting all that contraband to the mainland, Tom?"

"The same way it got here. In a boat. I bet if we wait and watch long enough we'll see a coffin being carried away..."

"Well you can wait and watch all you want," said Jai, annoyed, "but I prefer action."

"Alright." Tom was equally irritated, not least at himself for gorging so greedily. "If it's action you want then let's go to the police and report what we've found."

Jai was appalled by the suggestion.

"What? And tell them I sneaked into our Housemaster's rooms and pinched his keys? And how do we prove what's in those coffins is smuggled goods? They could just say it was bought before the war or something....No, we need to find out where that stuff is going. And we need those keys..."

"Well, if you keep them I want nothing to do with it!"

"Keep it down Tom," said Dan.

"Look, it's one thing borrowing something without someone else's permission." Tom's voice was quieter now though the heat remained. "But keeping it is a completely different kettle of fish."

Dan was puzzled by the image.

"So you're only borrowing all that chocolate

you've just scoffed?" Jai asked mischievously. "You're going to return it all, are you?"

Tom pulled his bedclothes over his head, mumbling to himself. Already he was feeling sick from the chocolate overdose.

"Are you really going to keep the keys?" Dan asked as he got ready for bed.

But Jai didn't reply. Seeing the way Dan had left the keys on his desk had given him an idea. Throwing the stump of his cigar out of the window he descended from his ledge and - while Dan and Tom drifted into chocolate dreams - he set to work with paper and pencil.

The Reverend was still deeply asleep.

"So now we know what your game is, boyo," Jai whispered, carefully passing the chain over as much of the Reverend's head as he could, as if endowing him with some sacred investiture.

He knew he should have left it at that, but the way a section of the chain lay on the pillow instead of behind the Reverend's neck indicated a job half done. So Jai plucked another feather from the owl's breast and repeated the tickling procedure.

It seemed the slumbering Reverend had become somehow wizened to the ploy. Each time Jai applied the tuft to a nostril the twitching nose was turned away from the foreign invader. After several attempts Jai gave up on the feather. Instead, he gently lifted the Reverend's huge head...

It was as if a large voltage of electricity had suddenly surged through the Monster. The Reverend sat bolt upright, his eyes open, his hair sticking up in a multitude of directions as if charged. For a moment Jai froze in the Reverend's unblinking stare: the great mouth gaping open, the face pale like a death-mask. Then he turned and fled.

"What?" Tom sat up in his bed as the door burst open, striking his head painfully on the bottom of the bunk above him. "Ouch!"

"He looked right at me," Jai gasped, having closed the door and now leaning his back against it.

"Was he awake?" Dan asked sleepily from his bunk.

"I don't know...I really don't know..."

6

SKELETONS AND KEYS

A desert storm was choking Jaisulpur, red dust swirling in the air like a mist of blood. From a window high up in the palace wall Jai watched a stray cat playing with a rat in the street; then - bored of the game - the cat pounced, administering a lethal bite.

In the days following Jai's incursion into enemy territory the Reverend exhibited no particular hostility towards him, other than the general distaste he showed for all but a select few of his favoured scholars. But Jai feared Monster Mouth was merely biding his time, toying with him before striking.

Then, during supper on a Sunday evening, Tattersall plodded over.

"Rana, the Rev wants to see you. Now."

"Well, this is it chaps." Jai gulped down his tea. "Wish me luck."

He'd decided his best defence would be a

flat denial, hoping the Reverend would have to conclude that the dark figure by his bed had been a dream, or a ghost.

The door to the Reverend's rooms was ajar. Jai knocked.

"Come!" a voice boomed from within.

Following the smell of tobacco smoke he found the Housemaster seated at his desk in his study, his back to the doorway. The desk stood beneath a leaded window, looking out over a grey sea.

The revolving chair turned creakily, like the gun turret of a battleship, until the Reverend's eyes were trained upon his visitor. The mouthpiece of his pipe pointed in Jai's direction, a wisp of smoke rising from it.

"Well don't just stand there, lad. Come in."

Jai entered the study, anticipating the broadside.

"This has come in the post for you..."

The Reverend gestured towards an open shoe box on the desk. Inside it - on a bed of white tissue paper like a heavenly cloud - lay a small statue. Jai smiled with recognition, and relief.

"We have to check all incoming parcels, you understand."

"Of course, sir. You wouldn't want any illegal goods being smuggled in, after all..."

Jai couldn't resist the quip. The Reverend eyed him over his reading spectacles.

"Quite," he said at last, apparently satisfied that the remark was innocent. "Nor do we permit improper material."

"Improper material, sir...?"

The Reverend lifted the statue from its box, a look of distaste on his face.

"This effigy is entirely inappropriate for a place of learning, Rana. She's practically nude."

This Jai couldn't deny. But for a gruesome necklace of human skulls, the six-armed woman was stark naked. Riding a tiger and brandishing a selection of items in her six hands, she looked like a travelling trader from Hell. Her black skin gleamed with gloss varnish like a sheen of sweat and she displayed a large red tongue to the world.

"So what's the meaning of having such a salacious object sent here?"

"She's my murti, sir."

"Your what?"

"My personal god, sir. Every Hindu has one."

"I should remind you this is a Christian school, Rana. We have no place for false idols."

"With respect sir, but she's very real. Many call her the goddess of destruction but I like to see her as Mother Nature herself, in all her worldly glory."

"So what's the severed head all about?"

"That represents her fierceness in battle, sir. The other hand holding the cup is collecting the blood to drink, you see...?"

"How vile."

"It's symbolic, sir. Your enemy's energy makes you stronger."

"My God but you're a rum lot, aren't you? So what made you choose this one, anyway? I'm sure there are plenty of nicer deities."

"There's something vital about her, sir. And she's also very beautiful."

"Really? Can't see the attraction myself. I mean, six arms? And that ghastly tongue sticking out..."

"For me her beauty lies in her honesty, sir."

The Reverend returned the statue to her bed.

"Well, this is all very interesting but the question is, am I going to allow you to keep this abomination? I don't want some heathen cult taking root here, Rana..."

"I'll see that she's kept safely under lock and key, sir."

"In that case I'm going to permit my respect for historical artifacts to over-rule my spiritual concerns." He handed the box to Jai. "Bit of a weight, isn't it?"

"Indian plaster, sir," said Jai as he took possession of the idol. "Much less refined than Parisian..."

"She looks quite a handful," said Tom.

In their room the three were contemplating the new arrival.

"So what are you going to do with her?" asked Dan.

Jai's expression was enigmatic.

"You mean, what is she going to do for us…?"

"Don't tell me," said Tom. "You rub her belly and she grants us each a wish."

"And yours would be an evening with Gypsy Rose Lee, presumably…?"

"Actually, I was thinking more of Helluva."

"Who?"

"You know. Elena Montserrat."

"Ah yes. She's quite something, isn't she…?"

"I know what my wish would be," said Dan.

The other two didn't need to ask. Now their secret desires seemed rather trite.

"Anyway, please explain how this little statue is of help to us, Jai. I don't believe in magic."

"It's all in here…"

Jai handed Dan the letter that had accompanied the statue. The writing was small and neat, like troops on parade. It came as no surprise to learn that its author was a soldier.

"Read it out," Tom urged Dan.

He sighed then began again, aloud:

"Dear Sahib,
Please find enclosed the statue, as requested. May she provide you with help when you need it.

I hope you are settling in well to your new school. We have been watching the Spitfires fighting the enemy bombers in the skies above us. Such brave boys. I hope and pray we will survive, but I think we are going to need the Yanks with us if Europe is to be free again.

Bombing raids are an almost nightly occurrence here. We have been making frequent visits down to the cellar, and your father always takes the opportunity to open a bottle or two from his collection of fine wines."

"That's pretty typical for him," said Jai. "The old soak..."

"Your father's social diary is as hectic as ever. Only last night he threw a party for a host of dignitaries, including our parliamentary representative for Kensington South and the famous poet Tagore.

Many of his friends have de-camped to America but your father refuses to 'chicken out', as he puts it. He wants to do his bit for the Empire. He is planning to travel to India soon in order to whip his men into shape for battle. I think he will miss London, despite all the bombs. You know how much he loves the night life here...

Well, that is enough for now. Take care of yourself and do write if you need anything else.

Down with Adolf and up with the King!

I remain your honourable servant,
Jomsom."

Tom looked puzzled.

"He doesn't say much about the statue."

Jai smiled.

"Perhaps you need to look closer…"

Dan held the letter up to the light.

"But don't waste your time looking for invisible ink. The message is hidden in the letter itself. Or - rather - letters…"

"Oh come on, Jai," Tom protested. "Why don't you just tell us?"

"Because that would be too easy," said Dan. "And we all know how Jai loves his little games…"

Jai maintained his smile, like the cat who'd acquired the cream.

"So there must be some kind of secret code…"

Dan pulled his chair up to his desk in order to scrutinise the letter laid before him. His eyes darted across the page, seeking secret passages, hidden signposts and subtle patterns within the text. His nimble mind worked at the words like the fingers of a praying monk fumbling with a rosary. And as he toiled he mumbled to himself as if in a trance, rocking gently in his seat.

"What did he mean by your father whipping his men into shape?" Tom asked.

"My father has his own army," Jai explained.

"He's offered its services to the Mother Country."

"His own army?" Tom was astonished. "How many soldiers?"

"Oh, about a thousand infantry," Jai replied casually. "They're modelled on a British Guards regiment, only they wear turbans. Bearskins aren't very practical in the heat...Then there's the Household Cavalry. A few hundred of those, I think..."

"A few hundred horses?"

"Camels, mostly. Very good in the desert."

"Camels...?"

"Oh, and not forgetting the elephants, of course."

"Elephants!"

"I suppose they're the equivalent of tanks, though I suspect pachyderms wouldn't be much good against Panzers...But why don't you visit and see for yourself?"

"You mean, come to India...?"

"I do indeed."

"I'd love to!"

"Capital! And Dan too, of course..."

"Did you hear that, Dan? Jai's invited us to India..."

Dan grunted a response, still hunched over the letter. His concentration was converged upon the forest of words like sunlight focused through a magnifying glass.

"Capitals..." he muttered, suddenly inspired.

"Tom, write these letters down as I read them out, will you?"

"Right."

Taking a piece of paper and a pencil from Dan, Tom began noting down the dictation.

"D...S...P...M...I..."

"Hang on, Dan. Slow down."

"W......S......S......I......oh, never mind."

Impatient, Dan snatched back the pencil and scribbled the rest down himself. Then he inspected the letters lined up before him:

DSPMIWSSIIYEBWYOKSTMAHEHIILYWTD AKIJ

"Well, if this is an anagram it's going to take a long time to find the message. And how long must it have taken Jomsom to compose a coherent letter around so many capitals...?"

Then Dan struck his forehead with the base of his palm.

"Of course! It's only the proper nouns! We have to ignore the personal pronouns... and the beginning of sentences..."

Dan worked through the letter again, this time only picking out the first letters of the proper nouns:

SSYEKSTEAILAKJ

Now he set to work trying to solve the anagram, scribbling down combinations of letters in his search for meaningful words, his mind like a mill grinding grain.

Presently he sat back in his chair.

"The best I can get is 'SS takes Yekl, Jai'..."

"Who's Yeckle when he's at home?" Tom asked sullenly, his mood darker now.

"He was a character in a novel I read: a Russian Jew who went to America to escape persecution..."

"Sounds familiar," said Jai.

"But of course this isn't the right solution. What has this phrase got to do with getting into Chapel? It only demonstrates where my thoughts lie at present. Freud would have had a field day..."

"Floyd?" asked Tom.

Dan was astonished.

"You've never heard of Sigmund Freud?"

Since failing at dictation, anger had been simmering within Tom. Now it was vented.

"No!" His face glowed red. "As a matter of fact, I haven't! In fact, I don't know very much at all! I'm just bloody backward, aren't I?"

"Tom, of course you're not..." Jai began, but he was interrupted.

"Backwards!" Dan cried. "That's it!"

"That's what?" sniffed Tom, diverted from his misery.

"I'm making it too difficult for myself, looking for anagrams. It's much more obvious than that..."

Now Dan scribbled down the sequence of letters in reverse order:

SKALIEATSKEYSJ

"And if you get rid of the first S and the last J - because all of his letters would start with 'Sahib' and end with 'Jomsom' - you get the message..."

"What message?" asked Tom.

"Kali eats keys!" Dan announced triumphantly. Then his forehead furrowed again. "But who - or what - is Kali...?"

Smiling, Jai caressed the statue with his fingertips as enlightenment dawned on Dan's face.

"Of course..."

"Of course what?"

Tom was tiring of the game.

"**That's** Kali..."

"The very same," said Jai. "Goddess of Destruction; and - in the guise of Shiva - Creation. Nice work, Dan."

"You two are so good at stuff," Tom mumbled. "But look at me. Good for nothing..."

"Don't be ridiculous! There's plenty of things you're good at..."

"Such as?" Before Jai could answer Tom had

embarked upon a rant: "Admit it, I can't keep up with you both. You saw it just then. All those letters got jumbled up in my head and I couldn't write them down quick enough. And then there was that night we climbed the wall and you had to pull me in. And the morning runs when you drag me up that hill. And the Cutters when Jai took my oar....You're carrying me, lads. I know it...I'm just a dead weight..."

Sitting on the edge of his bed Tom rested his head on his hands, contemplating the bare floorboards.

"Tom!" cried Jai.

Tom looked up to see the statue arcing through the air towards him. He moved to catch it but he wasn't quick enough. The effigy slipped between his hands and hit the floor with a sound like the cracking of a bone, smashing into pieces. A small cloud of plaster-powder billowed upwards, like magician's smoke.

Tom looked down at the fragments in dismay.

"See? I can't even catch. And now the statue's broken. How much bad luck is that going to bring us...?"

"It's alright," said Jai. "I didn't want you to catch it."

Dan had crouched down to inspect the debris. Kali's head remained intact, still sticking her tongue out as if in defiance of death itself. Among the other pieces he spotted three black objects. Bits of plaster were still stuck to them in places, but there was no mistaking what they were.

"Now I get it," he said, picked them up and cleaning them off. "Kali eats keys…"

"See, Tom?" Jai took one of the keys and held it up triumphantly. "In Destruction there is also Creation…"

Tom took a key from Dan and studied it.

"But…aren't these Monster Mouth's…?"

"Exact reproductions," Jai explained. "I traced around each original key then sent the drawings to Jomsom who had these copies made."

"But how did you get them past Monster?" asked Dan. "He checks all the letters before posting them."

"I'll show you…"

Jai placed his key on a piece of paper and traced round it. Then - around this outline - he sketched one of the legs of the Manx triskelion: the oval ring of the key was in the leg's knee, its shaft inside the lower leg with the business end jutting out into the foot.

"See? And I did the same for the other two keys: one in each leg. When I coloured it in you could hardly see the outline. And in the accompanying letter I referred to Jomsom's interest in flags of the world, to put old Monster off the scent…"

"That was handy," said Tom, "him liking flags,

and all."

"Actually, I'm not sure he does. Nepal is full of flags and he's probably sick of the sight of them. It was just a cover story. A false flag, as it were..."

"And presumably Jomsom was alerted to your plan by means of a coded message within your letter," said Dan.

"Correct. We've used our code system many times."

"And no-one has ever broken it?"

"Not until now. And you had the advantage of knowing you were looking for one. Well done, though. You cracked it quicker than I expected. And well done, Tom..."

"Me? What did I do?"

"You revealed Kali's secret."

"Only by accident."

Jai smiled.

"Where I come from, nothing happens accidentally."

They each held a key and now Jai had an idea.

"We'll be a secret brotherhood, bound together by these keys. So let's make a pledge..."

Directed by Jai, they aligned the oval rings of the keys.

"All for one and one for all!"

There was a doubtful pause.

"It's a bit over-used," said Dan.

"Well you think of a better one then..."

Dan looked around the room for inspiration. His eye was caught by the Manx flag, and the words of the old sailor came back to him.

"Wherever you throw us, we shall stand…"

Later that night, while the rest of the school slept, the three consummated their new union with another visit to the Chapel.

"Start in that corner and work your way across the floor," Jai instructed his friends. "Remember, we're looking for a stone that's been recently lifted…"

He handed the torch to Dan then departed its pool of light.

"Where are you going?" Tom asked with unease.

His reply was the gentle opening and closing of the Chapel door, then all was quiet.

"Well," said Dan, "we'd better make a start…"

Crouching, the two began to examine the floor, paying particular attention to the gravestones but finding no sign of any disturbance.

Presently Dan stood up, his back beginning to ache. His eye was caught by a white square of marble in the wall which seemed to glow in the torchlight. Joining him, Tom read the inscription:

In Memoriam
Lord Julian Alfred Morrigan, VC
1862 – 1927

Seventeenth Duke of Devilston
Headmaster of Devilston School
Served with Great Honour at Omdurman,
Mafeking and on the North West Frontier

Beloved Husband of Jennifer
Devoted Father of George and Charlotte

Taken Too Soon, and So Deeply Missed.

"Jam," said Tom.

"Jam?"

"It was his nickname. His initials, see? He was Headmaster before Sticky. A good one too, or so they say..."

"What does 'VC' mean?"

"Victoria Cross. The highest award for bravery you can get."

"Taken too soon," Dan read. "I wonder what happened to him..."

"Apparently he went for a walk one day and never came back. They say it was the quicksand that got him because they never found his body, but some think it was suicide."

"Why would he have killed himself? He doesn't sound the type."

"They reckon it was losing his son in the war that did it..."

Now Dan noticed another inscription near to the memorial, carved into one of the wall's stones at shoulder height and much less obvious:

FINALITER LUX

JUDAS ULTIMUS

1540

The words meant little to Tom, but the small skull and crossed bones above the inscription was familiar.

"Pirate...?"

"Death, more likely."

Dan remembered a similar symbol on the collars of the German soldiers at the Dutch border.

Now Tom focused on the numbers, the least hostile of the assembled figures.

"1540. That's exactly..."

"Four hundred years ago," said a third voice. Startled the two turned to see Jai's grin.

"Do you have to do that?" Tom's heart was pounding. "And where have you been...?"

"On an errand...So what does it mean, Dan?"

"Not sure. I don't know much Latin. I've

missed a lot of school..."

Jai studied the inscription.

"Is it 'The Ultimate Judas'...? Sounds like someone might have done the dirty on someone else..."

"More likely 'The Last Jew'," said Dan. "That would explain why there's only one year. No-one would have been concerned with when a Jew was born, only the year of their death. It would have been a date to celebrate, like the end of a plague."

"But why would a Jew be buried in a Christian church?"

"Perhaps this one converted. I believe torture was the usual method..."

The three silently contemplated the horror implicit in Dan's suggestion, then Jai spoke.

"I wonder what the top bit means..."

Dan ran his fingers over the inscription, as if their tips might be able to read them.

"'At the end there is light'. I think..."

Jai's mind had been wandering. Though interesting, the stone was a diversion in their quest, but now Dan's translation had seized his attention.

"This isn't a tomb," he thought aloud. "The skull and the last Jew thing is just a means of keeping people away..."

"So what is it then?"

"Think about it, chaps. What has light at the

end of it…?"

Tom shrugged.

"A lighthouse?"

"A tunnel!"

Tom remained unconvinced.

"But what about the date? According to the legend the tunnel was built by the Ancient Britons. Now even I know that was a long time before 1540…"

"1540 might be the year in which this particular entrance was made." Dan was warming to Jai's hypothesis. "It's also an explanation for why there's only one date."

Jai ran a finger round the periphery of the stone.

"And look at its edges…"

Unlike its surrounding companions there was a definite groove around the stone, as if it had been removed from the wall then replaced.

"But why would the entrance to a tunnel be in a wall and not the floor?" asked Tom.

"Because an entrance in the floor is too obvious," Jai replied. "But put it in a wall and most people would overlook it."

"Underlook it," Dan corrected him.

"Alright," said Tom, "so if it **is** the tunnel entrance, how are we going to shift this stone? We'll need a crowbar for starters…"

Dan's mind conjured an image of a drinking establishment for carrion, then Nazis flocking out of beer cellars in search of undesirables.

"To quote Jomsom," said Jai, "prior planning prevents poor performance…"

In the dim light and all the distraction, Dan and Tom had failed to notice the object Jai was holding. Now he held it up. It was the size and shape of a small pick-axe.

"Had a choice of three but *Faith*'s seemed the most appropriate…"

He located one of the anchor's arrow-shaped tips in the gap beneath the engraved stone then pulled on its shaft like a lever.

The stone didn't move.

"Need a hand here, boys…"

"But what if this isn't the tunnel? What if this really is a tomb…?"

"Tom, it isn't a tomb," said Jai emphatically. "Tell him, Dan."

Dan despised having to make a decision based on insufficient information.

"I don't know…"

Jai sighed.

"Come on Dan, get stuck in. We haven't got all night."

Cursing under his breath in German, Dan took hold of the anchor's shaft. Together they pulled but still to no effect.

"Tom, we need you."

"But this isn't right, Jai. I can feel it in my bones."

"Remember the coffin? I was right about that, wasn't I?"

"Oh…bloody Hell!"

Now Tom gripped the anchor too.

"By the six hands of Kali." Jai grinned. "Right, after three…Three!"

Very slightly, the stone shifted.

"That's it, chaps. She's coming…"

Working at it with the tool - and careful not to damage its edges - they eased the stone out, until there was enough protruding to get a proper hold on it with their hands.

"Right." Jai put down the anchor. "This is it…"

"But won't the wall collapse if we take it out?" asked Tom.

"Well, it's been removed before and the Chapel survived."

Jai took the middle while the other two manned an end each. Together they slid the stone from its home and carefully lowered it to the floor. Then the three stood in silence, contemplating the dark square before them. They could feel a faint draught on their faces from some opening in the exterior wall, like a cold breath.

"So, what are we waiting for…?"

Picking up the torch Jai peered into the hole. Then he stepped back, almost falling over his friends. His mouth was open, his eyes wide.

"Well? What did you see?"

Tom hoped it was just another of Jai's little jokes.

Taking the torch now Dan looked into the hole. Then - as Jai had done - he recoiled, wearing the same expression. He passed the torch to Tom.

"If you think I'm looking in there after seeing your faces..."

And yet Tom felt the black hole pulling at him irresistibly.

The light of the torch illuminated a tiny rectangular space. Tom saw a table, a stool, and - lying on a low bed - a skeleton. Its black eye sockets stared at him, as if distracted by the intrusion.

Tom stumbled backwards. He felt a grip on his arm. For a moment he feared it was the skeleton's claw.

"It's alright," said Dan.

"Is it?" Tom's voice trembled. "So much for your tunnel, Jai..."

"Well, I can't be right all of the time, can I?" Jai shot back. "Not even a god is right all of the time..."

"Let's just put the stone back and get out of here."

"Not yet..."

Taking the torch from Tom, Dan looked into the tomb again.

The skull seemed to be compelling him to

confront its countenance so Dan forced himself to concentrate on the bony hands instead. They were clutching something close to the rib cage.

Passing the torch to Jai, he stepped on the stone they'd removed and began to pull himself head-first into the hole.

"Dan, what are you doing...?"

Tom was appalled by the sight of his friend being consumed by the hole. Dan's feet disappeared into the darkness then his head appeared in the gap.

"My curiosity has overcome my fear." His voice was dampened by the tiny space. "Anyway, if this is a Jewish grave then I should be alright. Torch please..."

"You'd better be quick," said Jai. "The battery's dying."

The light had a jaundiced hue. Dan took the torch then braced himself. He could feel the panic growing within, as it had done in the hiding place in their Berlin apartment, with death so close he could almost hear its breaths...

Then he sealed his emotions. He would undertake this task clinically and forensically. This corpse had something important to tell him, from across an ocean of time.

"Dan," he heard Tom mutter outside, "remember what Curiosity did to the Cat?"

"And as you British also say, there isn't room to swing one in here..."

Dan was sitting on the small table that was directly beneath the hole in the wall, his feet on a stool. Next to him was the bed, as wide as the space itself, as if built to fit it. He smelt a damp mustiness, tainted with the faint yet sharp edge of death.

Again he looked upon the corpse, though carefully avoiding the glare of the eye sockets. The tremulous torchlight seemed to animate the bones from which hung remnants of cloth like tattered sails from the rotten hulk of a shipwreck. Now he saw what the corpse had been holding close to its chest for all those years.

Taking a deep breath he crawled along the bed to extract the small book from the skeleton's grasp, managing to avoid its touch.

"Well?" asked Jai. "What have you found?"

Dan turned the book the right way up.

"It's a Bible."

"So he **was** converted."

"But it doesn't make sense…"

Dan had opened the book. The torch light began to flicker in its final death throes.

"You're damned right this doesn't make sense," Tom mumbled, behind Jai. "Meddling in someone's grave without their permission…"

"This Bible was only printed in 1813," said Dan. "That's nearly three hundred years after this person died. Why would someone open a grave then put a Bible in it...?"

"Perhaps they thought eternity was a long time without something to read," Jai pondered.

"So just put it back and get out of there," said Tom, "before he notices..."

Dan closed the Bible and returned it within the clutch of the claws, now the right way up. In replacing it he had to lift the fingers and he felt their cold touch . A shiver passed down his spine, as if the latent power of death had been conducted from the corpse's bones into his own.

When Dan turned back to the hole he saw his friends' faces looking in on him.

Then the torch died, plunging him into darkness.

A loud crack woke Tom. The Reverend was looming over him, brandishing a yard stick.

"Am I boring you, Barrow?"

"No, sir. Just tired, sir."

"Been burning the midnight oil, have we?"

"Yes, sir."

"Very commendable, but I won't tolerate pupils sleeping in my lessons."

"I wasn't asleep, sir. I was just..."

"Resting your eyelids?"

There was laughter at the back of the class.

"I was still listening to what you were saying, sir."

"Splendid. So you'll be able to give me a definition of the Reformation…"

"Sir?"

"I've just been talking about it, boyo!" The Reverend pointed his stick at the blackboard on which the word was scrolled in large letters. "Or do you fancy another appointment with the Cutters come Sunday…?"

Behind the teacher Tom could see Jai desperately miming the action of breaking a stick.

"Sir, does it mean…bent…?"

Tom's answer was met by hoots of derision.

"How appropriate!" Smythe-Morrigan called out. "Those three are always hanging around together!"

"Silence!" the Reverend thundered and all was quiet again. Dan put his hand up. "Rosenbaum…?"

"I think Barrow is referring to King Henry the Eighth's refusal to bend to the will of Rome, sir."

"Yes, sir," Tom nodded, relieved. "That's exactly what I meant, sir."

"Sir, the Pope was trying to bully Henry, wasn't he?" Jai chipped in. "But Henry stood up to him…"

The Reverend turned slowly to engage Jai, like a battleship.

"Rana, if you've something to say you should put your hand up."

"Sorry, sir."

"I should remind you that family background has no influence upon our rules here."

"Really, sir…?"

Jai shot a look across the classroom at Smythe-Morrigan. The Head of School glared back.

"I detect a stubborn streak in you, lad." There was now a serious bow in the Reverend's yard stick as he applied pressure to each end. "I suggest you need to do some bending of your own if you are to fit in with our way of doing things…"

With a loud snap the stick broke. The Reverend didn't blink.

Dan saw defiance in Jai's expression. A diversion was urgently required and he raised his hand again.

"Yes?" the Reverend growled.

"Sir, who was the Last Jew…?"

The Head of School pounced on the gift.

"That's you, isn't it?"

His comment triggered another chorus of cackles.

"Quiet you imbeciles!"

In the silence the Reverend tossed the pieces of his stick into the bin then turned to regard Dan.

"There's an inscribed stone in the Chapel wall, sir," Dan continued. "It says 'The Last Jew' in

Latin, and the year 1540 - "

Now a high-pitched giggle pierced the air.

"Something amusing you, Mister Quirk?"

"Sorry sir but Rosenbaum has clearly made a simple translation error. I've seen the inscription myself. 'The Last Jew' would be 'Judaeus Ultimus'. But what it actually says is 'Judas Ultimus' meaning 'Jude the Last'..."

"Indeed. There were no Jews on this island during the Reformation, Mister Rosenbaum. In fact, as far as I'm aware, no Jews have ever resided here. Until now, of course..."

The Reverend's mouth flickered with a slight smile. He walked over to the blackboard and scribbled another word on it, the chalk squealing under duress.

"Jude was what is known as an anchorite, meaning...? Rana?"

"Is it something to do with anchors, sir?"

Jai glanced over at Dan and Tom. Beyond them he saw Smythe-Morrigan making a W sign with his fingers followed by an unambiguous gesture, to the delight of his Praeposters.

"Wrong!" chimed the Reverend. "Quirk?"

"Someone who lives in self-imposed solitude for religious purposes, sir."

"Spot on. Behind that tombstone is a tiny cell in which a Benedictine monk called Jude resided for many years. His food and water were passed through to him as if he were a prisoner, which I suppose he was, of sorts. A prisoner of his own conscience..."

"What about going to the toilet, sir?" asked Tattersall.

"Trust you delinquents to think of that. He used a bucket, lad!"

The class reacted predictably to this revelation.

"Must have been very boring," said Smythe-Morrigan, "stuck in a cell for all that time."

"Boredom was a luxury Jude could ill afford." The Reverend was now slowly pacing between the desks again. "You see, just as a pupil writes lines as punishment so Jude had set himself a task to accomplish in order to redeem his sins."

"What sins, sir?"

"Oh, the usual I expect, S-M. But Jude was an unusual man. While most would seek forgiveness in Sunday confession then continue their wicked ways for the rest of the week, Jude sought complete spiritual redemption. A deep clean, as it were. This he could only achieve by removing himself from the world and embarking upon a monumental feat..."

"Sir, Tatters has monumental feet."

"Thank you S-M but I'll do the jokes. Quirk?"

"What did Jude have to do, sir?"

"He didn't **have** to do anything, but he **chose** to translate the entire Bible. Both Old and New Testament. Absolution through translation, you might say..."

"From Latin to English, sir?"

"You'd think so, wouldn't you? After all, that's the direction in which the river was flowing. But Devilston was a Benedictine monastery remember, and thus still loyal to the Pope in Rome. No, Mister Quirk. Jude was swimming against the current. He was translating the King's Great Bible from English back into the original Latin..."

"He must have done a lot of sinning to deserve a punishment like that, sir."

"Yes," said the Reverend. "I imagine so."

"But didn't they have printing by then, sir?"

"They did indeed, and it came from Mister Rosenbaum's neck of the woods. But what kind of a penitence would that be? Knocking off a copy on a press doesn't require much effort. Of course he could have copied a Latin Bible by hand - an accomplishment in itself - but, as I've already said, Jude was an extraordinary man. He wanted to show God he was truly repentant, and strike a blow against the Protestant reformers to boot...

"You see, the Great Bible he was translating was aptly named: a huge printed edition in English commissioned by the King's chief minister, Thomas Cromwell. Here was the English crown imposing its authority on its people, and thereby undermining a thousand years of Rome's dominance. Think of it like a bomb dropped on every parish in the kingdom, destroying all texts that had gone before it…

"So, in translating the Great Bible back into Latin, Jude sought to turn back the clock. A purely symbolic act of course, but nevertheless a deeply subversive and courageous one. Discovery would have led to his prosecution as a heretic, and the inevitable fate…" The Reverend slowly drew his finger across his throat. "Rosenbaum?"

"What happened to Jude's Bible, sir?"

"Good question…"

Now the Reverend opened the door and gestured for the class to follow him.

"A slight intellectual digression, Headmaster," he replied to the Captain's quizzical expression as they passed him prowling the cloisters.

With his gown now billowing in the breeze like great black wings, the Reverend led the Leavers across the castle grounds to the main gates. They entered a dark entrance in the left-hand tower and ascended a spiral flight of stone steps. Halting in front of an arched door he delved in his trouser pockets then patted his jacket, cursing under his heaving breath.

"Damn. Left my key…"

"Use mine, sir."

Quirk had produced a ring from which hung a

large key and a smaller one.

"Good man." The Reverend unlocked the door and opened it. "Now wait here you lot."

"Nice one, Rosebum," sneered Smythe-Morrigan when the heavy door had closed. "Now we're going to be bored to oblivion with Bible stories because of you..."

There was a general grumble of agreement.

"What is this place?" asked Jai.

"Don't you know?" the Head of School mocked. "It's Monster Mouth's private harem. He's just gone in ahead to warn the women..."

"You mean, warm the women!" Tattersall guffawed. He was immediately disarmed by a withering look from his superior, then Smythe-Morrigan turned back to Jai.

"So Rana, is it true your father has his own harem...?"

"It's called a zenana."

"And is that where your mother lives?"

"It's where all the women of the palace live."

"And do you know which one is your mother?"

"I have many mothers. I love them all equally."

"I'm sure you do." The Head of School grinned. "So I suppose that makes you the son of a hundred whores...?"

His words were met by a shocked silence. Even the Head of School's closest allies knew that Smythe-Morrigan had crossed a line. All eyes were now on Jai.

Jai remained expressionless but Dan sensed a darkness in his friend he'd never seen before: the shadow of a great anger. Then the moment passed and Jai smiled.

"You know, where I come from there is a proverb that says, unless cared for the spoken word lives a short and useless life. So I choose not to water your words with the attention they crave and hence they will wither and die, like sour grapes..."

Before Smythe-Morrigan could respond a great voice bellowed from beyond the door.

"Right you miserable mob, you can come in now!"

The Leavers entered a large circular room which spanned the entire width of the tower. Shelves radiated from the centre of the space like the spokes of a wheel, crammed with books. Dan filled his nose with their smell in the manner of an addict returning to the intoxicating fumes of an opium den.

The Reverend stood before a table on which lay a big black book. Behind him, above a large fireplace, hung a life-sized painting of an Elizabethan woman. Dan was immediately intrigued by her, and what she was wearing. Or - rather - wasn't wearing.

She was dressed not in the usual elaborate gown of a lady of wealth, but thigh boots, tights and puffed pantaloons, her upper body encased in a shining armoured breastplate. A helmet was tucked under her right arm - its hand resting on the hilt of the cutlass hanging from her belt - while her left hand was spread across a globe, as if laying claim to the whole world. She stood before the very same fireplace that the Reverend was now guarding. In the picture a spectacular fire burned eternally, but in reality the iron grate stood empty and cold.

For Dan the most striking feature of the painting was the woman's face: long and angular with a strong nose. Her luscious mouth was slightly twisted in a sneer; very possibly the side effect of a scar down her cheek. Her red hair cascaded over her shoulders in thick curls - the same hue as the fire - while in her green eyes there was the look of deepest experience. She bore a close physical resemblance to Lady Charlotte Smythe-Morrigan.

Near the fireplace stood a large wooden cabinet with glass doors. It contained an enormous mechanism consisting of a multitude of cogs, wheels and pulleys. From the bottom of this instrument hung a long weighted pendulum, slowly swinging. Each swing was accompanied by a noise not unlike a deep voice, tirelessly repeating the same word:

...clock...clock...clock...

The Leavers clustered round the table,

generally disinterested though some were feigning their boredom, in keeping with expectations.

"So, gentlemen. This is it…"

The Reverend's large hands gently caressed the dark leather binding of the book, as one might a slumbering creature easily disturbed.

"The very Bible that Jude the Last devoted the best part of his life to creating. And if I was to open it Barrow, what would I see…?"

"The first page, sir?"

"Of which book, you moron?"

"The Bible, sir. You just said…"

The Reverend raised his eyes heavenwards.

"Oh Merciful God, deliver me from this wretched pit of ignorance…" Then he barked at Tom: "The Bible consists of many books, lad! I'm asking you which is the first?"

Dan whispered under his breath and Tom repeated what he thought he'd heard.

"German…Hiss…?"

"Speak up, man!"

"Sorry, sir. I don't know, sir."

"Dear God!" the Reverend exclaimed. "How you've managed to blunder through all your years on this Earth without that enormous fact striking you between the eyes is utterly beyond comprehension… Quirk?"

"Genesis, sir."

"Genesis!" The Reverend brought his hand

down on the table with a force that shook the disengaged from their vertical doze. "In the beginning God created the Heaven and the Earth..."

Now, with great care, the Reverend opened the book at the first page.

"According to Genesis it took the Almighty six days to create the Universe, whereas poor old Jude toiled for many years on his creation. And what a wondrous thing it is to behold! Look at the care and attention he has invested in the illumination. Without doubt, a true labour of love..."

Not even the most philistine of those gathered could deny that the opened book was, indeed, a beautiful sight. While it couldn't be said that the Latin text had been assembled with architectural precision, the eye was distracted from the unevenness of the letters by the shining glory occupying the top left hand quarter of the first page. The first letter of the Bible had been incorporated into the trunk of a tree, sprouting leafy branches from which red apples hung. Above this canopy an angry old man glared down from the sky, while next to the tree stood a naked couple, holding hands. The woman was reaching up with her other hand, her fingers about to pluck a low-hanging fruit.

And within the foliage, if one looked close

enough, there could be seen the shape of a red snake, coiled round the trunk. Then Dan corrected himself.

No. It has limbs, and wings. Not a snake but a dragon...

The attention of the class had increased considerably. Comments were muttered about the ampleness of the woman's breasts and the obviousness of the man's gender.

"So who are the two skinny dippers, sir?" asked Tattersall.

The Reverend regarded the Praeposter with an expression of pitiful exasperation.

"I truly despair... Adam and Eve, you great buffoon! They partake of the Forbidden Fruit and hence lose their innocence."

"Sir, can you turn the page please?" A leer lurked in Smythe-Morrigan's smile. "I'd like to see them losing their innocence..."

"I'm sure you would, S-M."

"Did he succeed, sir?" asked Quirk.

"Of course he did!" the Reverend boomed. "How else do you think Cain and Abel came into existence? My God, you lot are obsessed with sex..."

There was an awkward pause.

"Actually sir," Quirk ventured, "I meant, did Jude finish his translation of the Bible...?"

"Oh...I see...." The Reverend's face flushed. "Well, very nearly. He made it to the penultimate book: that of his namesake, the General Epistle of Jude. Only one book is missing..."

"The Book of Revelation, sir?"

"The very same."

"Is that why he's called Jude the Last, sir?" Dan asked. "Because he left out the last book...?"

"Nice idea Mister Rosenbaum, but the truth is rather darker...When King Henry the Eighth sent his soldiers to destroy the monastery of Devilston, the monks put up quite a fight. But they were no match for the King's men, of course. All were slain, except Jude. Then the invaders set fire to the Chapel, with Jude still in his cell. He managed to survive the inferno but the smoke fatally damaged his lungs. He lived for only a few more days, unable to escape his cell. That's how he became Jude the Last, you see? Because he was the last monk of Devilston to die...

"When a few brave mainlanders finally dared to venture over here, they found Jude lying dead in his cell with his precious Bible clutched to his breast. And that's exactly how they left him. A stone was placed in the hole that had been his only connection to the outside world - bearing that simple inscription of remembrance - and thus his cell became his tomb. The place he'd inhabited for so much of his life became his grave for all of eternity..."

The Reverend gazed out of the window, momentarily lost in his thoughts.

"Sir...?"

"Rosenbaum."

"If he was dead when the locals found him, how do you know he survived the fire?"

"Glad to see someone's still awake. The answer is, because we have primary evidence..."

"What evidence, sir?"

But the Reverend's only reply was to tap his nose and smile wryly.

"Who found this Bible, sir?" asked Quirk, keen also to demonstrate his attentiveness.

"Well, we can thank the Thirteenth Duke of Devilston for that." The Reverend nodded towards a nearby painting: a portrait of a thin pasty-faced man, in a pink silk gown and a purple turban. "Lord Percival Morrigan. Third-rate poet, second-rate opium-eater...and first-rate squanderer of Devilston's riches."

"Steady on, sir," said Smythe-Morrigan. "That's one of my ancestors you're talking about..."

Dan noticed more than a passing resemblance. The Head of School and Lord Percy possessed the same lazily arrogant eyes.

"Actually," the Reverend continued, "we've great reason to be thankful to the old wastrel. After all, had this irresponsible scoundrel not frittered away all of his inherited wealth then his ancestral pile would never have become a school in order to save it from the Receivers, and consequently none of us would be here...

"Having exhausted his inheritance, Percy had begun to raid Devilston's graves for more funds with which to sustain his vile appetites. Perhaps he was attracted by the skull and crossed bones on Jude's tombstone and thought there might be treasure in there, left over from Devilston's pirate heritage. X marks the spot and all that..." The Reverend jabbed a thumb over his shoulder at the portrait of the lady behind him. "But all he found was this Bible. Fortunately for us, he didn't see much value in an old book and didn't bother selling it."

"Or perhaps he thought it too beautiful and important, sir," said Dan.

"Possibly. They do say, for all his faults, he was something of a romantic in the Byronic mould..."

"So Percy opened Jude's tomb and swapped this Bible with another...?"

The Reverend eyed Dan with curiosity before replying.

"I couldn't possibly say, having never seen inside Jude's tomb for myself..."

"Just speculating, sir," Dan added hastily. "I imagine Percy wouldn't have wanted to leave Jude empty-handed, as it were..."

"No. Probably not..."

The Reverend's stare lingered on Dan, his brow furrowed, his eyes slightly narrowed. Jai came to his rescue.

"Sir, what happened to Lord Percy?"

"Died young. Ruptured liver, I believe. The obvious explanation would be his dissolute existence, but some say it was the curse of Jude the Last. Righteous punishment for violating his resting place…"

Dan, Jai and Tom exchanged glances. at that moment the clock mechanism nearby clicked and whirred into life, marking the hour like a toll of doom.

"Sir, can we look at some more pages in your next lesson with us?" asked Smythe-Morrigan above the striking of the bell.

The Reverend smirked.

"So you can view some more naughty pictures, S-M…? I'm afraid not. This is a precious artifact. We need to keep exposure of its pages to a minimum." He closed the Bible with a deep thud. "Here endeth the lesson."

As the final chime died the Leavers vacated the Library, Dan stealing a last glance behind him. The Reverend was still standing at the table, waiting for his audience to leave the theatre before safely stowing away his precious prop.

"That was close, Dan," said Tom as the three made their way to their next lesson. "I thought Monster Mouth was on to you there when you were going on about swapping the Bible..."

"Yes. Sorry about that. Wasn't thinking..."

"Not like you," said Jai.

But there was something more serious on their minds and now Tom voiced their fears:

"So...do you think we're cursed then, for opening Jude's tomb...?"

"Probably just me," said Dan. "I was the only one who entered, after all..."

"I don't think there can be more than one curse on a place," said Jai. "Take King Tut's tomb, for instance. Lots of people have been in there since it was found. They can't all be cursed."

"And the substitute Bible was placed upside down in Jude's hands," Dan added, seeking further re-assurance. "That can't have done any good..."

"That's a point," said Tom. "Why did Lord Percy do that?"

"Maybe he was in a hurry," Jai pondered. "A tomb isn't the kind of place you want to hang around in, after all..."

"I can vouch for that," said Dan. "But there might be another reason..."

"Which is?"

"Not witches, Jai." Dan was beginning to get the hang of the British love of puns. "Devil-worship..."

"Are you suggesting Percy was a Satanist?"

"Well, he was the Thirteenth Duke, after all. And an upside down Bible could be a sign of the Devil's work. Like inverted crosses and backwards prayers..."

"What a pleasant thought," said Tom, grimly.

"I'd love to have a proper look at that Bible..."

"You mean go back into that tomb, Dan? You must be mad..."

"Not Percy's Bible. I mean Jude's. I think there's more to it than the Word of God..."

"How can you have more than the Word of God?"

"You could have the final thoughts of a humble monk, Tom...How else does Monster Mouth know that Jude wasn't killed in the fire? Just think about it. If you were trapped in a cell and slowly dying, wouldn't you want to write a final message? To leave something personal for posterity? Monster was waiting for us to go so we wouldn't see where he hides it. So we wouldn't be able to read Jude's secrets..."

"Or he just wants to keep it safe," said Jai. "It is four hundred years old after all, and hand-written by the last monk to live on Devilston. It must be worth a king's ransom."

Tom grinned.

"I think he doesn't want us to see it because it's full of naughty pictures. Like that one on the first page of Jenny Sis."

"Well," said Dan, "if we want to get our hands on that Bible then Quirky is our key..."

7

COMETH THE HOUR...

As usual on a Saturday afternoon Quirk was executing his duties as Head Librarian, manning the same desk on which Jude's Bible had been displayed to the Leavers. Now another large book lay open upon it, this one infinitely more mundane than the Reverend's historic volume: a tally of books borrowed and returned, recorded in Quirk's spidery scrawl.

Nevertheless - he pondered - who was to say that his lowly ledger might not one day become a precious artifact in itself: a unique record of the reading habits of a remote boarding school in the mid-Twentieth Century...?

The door opened then softly closed. Another pilgrim had entered to pay homage in this church of knowledge.

"Rosenbaum," said Quirk when Dan was within earshot. "May I help you?"

"No thanks, Quirky. Just browsing."

Dan was waiting for the others to leave before he could move in for the kill.

"Well, you haven't much time," said Quirk. "I'm closing early today."

"Really? Why?"

"The First Fifteen are playing Rockenough at home. Didn't you know?"

"No," Dan lied.

"They're our arch rivals, and the whole school has to be out there supporting our team. You see," Quirk added with a hint of disdain, "rugger takes priority over all other pursuits here, including learning..."

Sport versus Literature. For Dan there was no contest. He remembered the book burning in the streets of Berlin, the flames gorging on the pages. By the end - after his father had been forced to sell their collection on the black market in order to pay the bills - the only books Dan had left were his school texts, full of the glories of the Third Reich and the menace of the Jewish race.

Now he found himself amongst a silent multitude, waiting with infinite patience on their perches to spread their wings and sing.

But he had a mission to fulfill. Aware of Quirk's beady eye Dan began to scan the shelves, though he suspected his quarry lurked in a more secure place.

Something snagged his attention: a uniform

row of slim black books with the same title embossed in red along the spine: The Devilston Chronicle. As Dan ran his finger down the line he could see a gradual deterioration in their material quality, like the cross-section of a forest floor. He paused at the 1927-28 edition, remembering the date on the memorial plaque in the Chapel. He slid out the thin volume and opened it.

On the first page was a black and white photograph of a man in uniform on a beautiful white horse. Beneath it the text read:

Lord Julian Alfred Morrigan, VC
1862 - 1927

I am certain our late Headmaster would have loathed to have had space devoted to him in a publication celebrating the achievements of his pupils, but I feel it my duty as his successor to include a tribute to this extraordinary man: a man whom I was fortunate enough to call not only my father-in-law but a very dear friend.

An Old Devilstonian himself, Lord Morrigan excelled both on the sports field and in his academic studies, yet always made time for the service of others: the very personification of our school motto.

After Cambridge, His Lordship attended Sandhurst then joined the cavalry. Horses have been a passion throughout his life; I shall never forget the magnificent sight of Lord Morrigan on his favourite grey, Merlin, galloping across the beach of Devilston Bay.

His Lordship served on the North West Frontier of India, in the Second Boer War and the Sudan Campaign. Attached to the 21stLancers he took part in the final mass charge by a British cavalry regiment, at the Battle of Omdurman in 1898. Observing that a war correspondent (a certain Mister Winston Churchill, now Chancellor of the Exchequer) had been struck off his mount and surrounded by the enemy, Lord Morrigan fought off the dervishes, took the stricken man onto his own horse and delivered him to safety. For this supreme act of valour His Lordship received the highest accolade this nation can bestow upon one of her soldiers.

Lord Morrigan's age and his commitment to Devilston prevented him from serving in the Great War, which in my opinion was a blessing. I can vouch from my own service in the Royal Flying Corps that this was a very different kind of warfare to anything mankind had faced before. Nevertheless, His Lordship was not spared the suffering of that terrible conflict: his only son was killed during the Somme Offensive of 1916.

Lord Morrigan was deeply affected by his experiences on the battlefield, and of course the loss of his beloved George. He saw education not merely as an instrument for the moulding of minds but as a means of nurturing the flame of love in the hearts of the young, so that the horror of war might finally be consigned to the crypt of history.

So it is with the heaviest of hearts that I commemorate the life of a truly great man, tragically taken from us when he had so much more to give. He is survived by his devoted wife and daughter, and a formidable legacy that I shall do my very utmost to preserve.

Captain Ralph Smythe-Morrigan,
Headmaster of Devilston School,
July 1928.

Dan replaced the book on the shelf then withdrew the 1917-18 edition, now curious as to what kind of a pupil his hapless Form Tutor had been.

It didn't take long to find Alderley. He had been Head of School and Captain of Rugby, Cricket and Soccer. A series of photographs depicted him in action: hugging a rugby ball to his chest while fending off marauders; booting a football with great ferocity; brandishing a cricket bat like a two-handed sword, and engaging in a quasi-ritualistic display which Dan understood to be the bowling of a cricket ball. Other pupils featured too, but Alderley was undoubtedly the star of the show.

He had altered in the years since the photographs had been taken, but the eyes were the same; and yet there was something wrong about these images, and it wasn't merely the absence of any justification for the nickname Smythe-Morrigan had coined. An unidentified anomaly had lodged itself in Dan's sub-conscious, like a tiny fragment of school dinner trapped between his teeth.

His thoughts were interrupted by the clock mechanism springing to life, striking a quarter to the hour. The loud speaker above the Library's door crackled.

"Do you hear there?" Electrification rendered the Praeposter's voice flat and nasal. **"The whole school will muster immediately on the rocks. Late-comers will be punished severely. That is all."**

Quirk rang a little bell on his desk.

"Time gentlemen, please!"

Clutching the Chronicle, Dan waited at the end of the small queue at the Librarian's desk. Quirk was employing his mechanical stamper on each book then recording the name of the borrower in his ledger. As he wrote, the tip of his tongue peeped out from the corner of his mouth.

When it came to Dan's turn, Quirk's stamper paused in mid-air.

"Can't you read, Rosenbaum? This is a reference book."

"But I only want it for a short time. Cowardly's in it, you see. I was going to show the others…"

"Sorry. Rules are rules."

Quirk smiled smugly. He closed his ledger and put it in a drawer in the desk, along with his precious stamper and bell.

There was a time when Dan would have simply accepted this inconvenience and replaced the book. But now something fundamental seemed to have changed within him, quite possibly a consequence of Jai's influence. He remained standing in front of the desk.

They were alone now. Quirk looked up at him, questioningly.

"What's your price?" asked Dan.

"Sorry?"

"How much to let me borrow this?"

Quirk laughed, incredulous.

"Rosenbaum, are you trying to bribe me?"

"Yes."

The Head Librarian studied Dan for a moment, trying to gauge his seriousness.

"I'll give you my pudding at dinner tomorrow," said Dan. "I believe it's your favourite. Apple pie and custard…"

Quirk didn't immediately reply. His eyes were blinking rapidly behind his spectacles and Dan felt a sudden sickness of uncertainty. He knew Quirk was the type who'd take great pleasure in reporting the attempted bribery of a school official.

"A week's worth," said Quirk.

"What?"

"All your puddings for a week. Except Spotted Dick." He shuddered. "I hate raisins..."

"Alright," said Dan, relieved.

They shook on the deal.

"But don't you dare mention this to anyone. It would cost me my job."

Now Dan smiled.

"And then you'd have to do games on a Saturday afternoon like everyone else..."

A look of dismay passed across the Librarian's face as he contemplated the horror.

"Anyway, we'd better be going." Quirk rose and pushed his chair under the table. "The match will be starting soon..."

But Dan stood his ground.

"There's something else," he said. "Where does Monster Mouth keep Jude's Bible?"

Again Quirk laughed in disbelief.

"How do you expect me to know that?"

"Because you're Head Librarian."

"Just because I'm Head Librarian doesn't mean I know everything, Rosenbaum."

"I don't believe you," Dan pressed. "I bet the other key on your ring has something to do with it…"

"Rubbish!" Quirk protested. "I've no idea where he keeps his bloody Bible. And even if I did, I wouldn't tell you."

"Wouldn't you?" Dan was astonishing himself with his own bravado. "Not at any price?"

"No."

Quirk crossed his arms.

"Not even if I threatened to report you for accepting a bribe…?"

Now the Librarian's eyes widened.

"That's blackmail!"

"Probably. And?"

"So what evidence have you got? A reference book in your possession? I'd just say you stole it. It would be my word against yours. And who are they more likely to believe? The Head Librarian or a bloody - "

Quirk hesitated.

"Jew?" Dan smiled. "Don't worry, I won't tell anyone about our deal. But I have another offer for you…"

"What's that?"

"Knowledge."

"Knowledge?" Quirk scoffed, gesturing at the shelves. "I've already got plenty of that, thank you."

"I mean, secrets…"

"What…secrets?"

Quirk was feigning disinterest but it was a poor act. He was nibbling at the bait.

"There's something in Jude's Bible that Monster Mouth doesn't want us to see," said Dan.

"You're right. Lots of rude pictures."

"Not just the illuminations. I think Jude wrote something else in that Bible other than religious scripture. Something about himself…"

Quirk stared off into space, his imagination suddenly unleashed. Then he reined himself back to reality.

"Not now, Rosenbaum. We have to go to the match."

"Now is perfect. We won't be disturbed."

"But what if they notice we're missing?"

"We were reading and we lost track of the time."

"And then it'll be the Cutters for the both of us. I'd say such a big risk requires some further incentive…"

"How much incentive do you need? I'm talking about the final thoughts of the last monk of Devilston. Knowledge is power, remember?"

"Power perhaps, but not puddings…"

"What?"

"All of your desserts until Half Term."

"But that's a month's worth!"

"As I said, it's a big risk…"

"Alright." Again they shook on the deal. "You know Quirky, I never imagined you were so easily corrupted."

"And I never imagined you had such criminal tendencies, Rosenbaum. I think it's this school. It brings out the worst in people."

"And the best. So...where's the Bible?"

"I told you. I don't know."

"What? Do you mean I've promised you a month of puddings for nothing?"

Quirk smiled.

"You promised me a month of puddings to let you look for it, that's all."

"In that case you're helping me. Lock the door..."

On the sands a group of First Form boys were struggling to raise the goal posts while a Praeposter bellowed instructions at them.

"Two big H's," Tom muttered to himself as he watched the cross beams being added. "Heil bloody Hitler..."

The area was cleared of debris and seaweed, a rope laid out to mark the pitch's perimeter and lines drawn in the sand. Visiting teams complained routinely that the home side possessed an unfair advantage, being accustomed to playing on a beach. But Devilston needed every bit of help She could get.

The Staff sat on chairs lined up near the touchline while the rest of the school took up position behind them on the rocks which formed a natural terrace. Sitting was prohibited since all pupils were expected to cheer with maximum force, though very few posteriors would have braved the sharp rock bristling with barnacles and mussels even if permitted.

Praeposters prowled amongst the pupil body, ensuring appropriate behaviour and a satisfactory level of vocal support for the First Fifteen. A pair took some interest in Tom.

"Wheely," said the first, "I hear your father's doing a fly-past today..."

"That's right, sir."

Tom's father had promised in his last letter that he'd conduct a flying visit at fourteen hundred hours, weather and Luftwaffe permitting.

"Oh come on," said the second Praeposter. "You don't expect us to believe your old man's a fighter pilot, do you? I mean, if he's as fat as you, how would he ever take off...?"

Recalling Jai's indifference in the face of the Head of School's outrageous provocation, Tom said nothing.

"So where's your Jewish friend? Come to think of it, I don't see Quirky around either..."

"I think they went to the bog, sir."

Tom knew exactly where they were.

"Together…?" The Praeposter smirked at his colleague. "Well, you tell them to report to me as soon as they get back."

"Yes, sir."

"And it's 'the toilets', by the way. You're not up North now…"

"No, sir. Sorry, sir."

As the prefects moved on, Tom cursed his lack of imagination. Dan or Jai would have come up with a much cleverer excuse.

The clock on the Library tower struck two o'clock. Tom squinted into a deep blue sky, straining to hear above the gannet chatter of the pupils surrounding him. With every minute that passed his heart grew a little heavier. It had been a huge risk telling others about the fly-past; but if he'd left it until after the event, who would have believed him?

Now a cheer went up, spreading through the crowd like the wind through wheat. Tom scanned the sky expectantly, but there was no plane. The crowd was greeting the entry of the gladiators into the arena, studs clattering on the steps cut into the rock. Rockenough were in blue, Devilston red and black stripes.

Tom's enthusiasm surged. He held up his scarf and shouted along with the rest of the school.

He'd spotted Jai.

Dan and Quirk were interrupted in their quest by the shriek of a distant whistle, the thump of a boot hitting a ball and a lusty cheer.

"They've kicked off!"

From an open window Quirk watched the players scurrying around like beetles in pursuit of a dung ball, the great black mass of duffle coats infesting the rocks like cockroaches.

"They're bound to notice we're not there."

"Never mind that," said Dan. "You made a deal, remember?"

"But we've looked everywhere, Rosenbaum. It's clearly not here."

Dan desperately surveyed the Library for clues. Morrigans glared down at him from the many portraits on the walls, haughtily mocking his ignorance like knowing spectators in a parlour game. But why would they help an outsider delve into Devilston's deepest secrets? The knowledge seemed destined to remain buried behind their eyes...

Suddenly inspired, Dan darted over to the Thirteenth Duke and lifted the bottom edge of his frame enough to look beneath. He found nothing but blank wall.

"Now you're being ridiculous," said Quirk.

"Don't just stand there!" Dan snapped. "You're supposed to be helping me!"

So Quirk began to look behind the paintings too, working in the opposite direction to Dan around the curved wall of the Library until they'd checked behind all but one: the picture above the fireplace.

"Lady Caitlin Morrigan," said Dan. "I presume..."

"The very same," Quirk replied. "First Duchess of Devilston, and the scourge of every Dutchman, Spaniard and Frenchy on the High Seas."

They each took hold of a corner of the painting and pulled the bottom edge away from the wall so Dan could peer behind it.

"It's no good. I can't see far enough up. We'll have to take her down."

"But she's too big."

"A month of puddings, remember...?"

"Damn you, Rosenbaum. You're like the Devil Incarnate."

Unhooking the painting required Dan to balance precariously on a set of step ladders while Quirk struggled to hold Her Ladyship.

"She's too heavy," he groaned.

"Must be all that armour..."

Dan quickly descended to help Quirk, but he was too late. He could only watch helplessly as the painting toppled over and hit the floor on a corner.

"Quirky!"

"Don't blame me! I told you I couldn't manage her!"

Dan inspected the damage.

"Now we're for it," Quirk moaned. "I knew I shouldn't have listened to you."

"It's alright. There's a small chip in the frame but that's all. And the Duchess doesn't look too bothered."

Now the two gazed up at the great rectangle where the picture had been, whiter than the surrounding plaster. There was no secret compartment.

"After all that…" said Quirk.

It took several attempts to replace the painting, Dan holding Lady Caitlin while Quirk fumbled to hook the cord on. By the time they were finished the Librarian was a quivering wreck of worry. He made for the door.

"Hang on," Dan called after him, "what about our deal?"

"Well, I've fulfilled my part of it. We've looked all over the place and there's no sign of that Bible. I don't know what Monster Mouth's done with it - maybe he shoved it down his trousers - but I'm about to lock up, so you need to be vacating these premises pretty sharpish."

"Leave me the key, then. I'll lock up."

"Not a chance, Rosenbaum. This key was entrusted to me alone. Now, are you coming or do I need to summon a Praeposter? Come to think of it, that would be a convenient explanation for my absence. Your refusal to leave..."

"Oh..." Dan didn't usually swear but the circumstance now justified one of Tom's harsher expletives: "...bugger off then!"

"Very well. I shall."

Quirk slammed the door. His footsteps faded away as he descended the stairs, leaving Dan alone with the Morrigans. The First Duchess of Devilston was regarding him with magnificent imperiousness, tinged with the slightest hint of amusement.

"I beseech you, m'lady," Dan muttered. "Just one clue, if you please..."

Behind her the fire burned for ever, a symbol of her inner spirit. Or of the destruction she'd wreaked in her life. Or were they the very fingers of Hell, beckoning...?

Dan ducked under the mantelpiece and entered the dark chimney space, a cold wave of fear flowing through him.

Concentrating his mind on the task, he ran his hands over the brickwork - mercifully free from soot - until he felt something in the chimney breast: a rectangle of metal the size of a small oven door.

In his haste Dan scraped the top if his head against the bottom of the mantelpiece. He rushed over to the open window in time to see Quirk hurrying down the road to the match.

"Quirky!" he shouted, rubbing his crown.

"Come back! I've found it!"

Jai was playing like a demon. As scrum half he was the connection between the strength of the forwards and the speed of the backs: transferring the ball from one to the other with skill and intelligence, while dodging players twice his size as they hurled themselves towards him.

It took the perseverance of an anchorite scribe to penetrate Rockenough's formidable defence...and then there was nothing but empty sand before him. He dashed for the line - his precious charge cradled under his arm - and the crowd roared with surprised delight, Tom the loudest amongst them. A multitude of Rockenough players piled onto Jai, but it was too late. He had fallen onto the ball on the other side of the line, and for the first time in the long and bloody history of fixtures between the two schools, Devilston had scored first.

Devilston 3 Visitors 0

The home side had begun the match with the usual modest ambition of losing by a respectable margin. Now - as Jai converted his try with a long high kick from a difficult angle - they found themselves contemplating the intoxicating impossibility of victory.

Devilston 5 Visitors 0

For the visitors it was a call to arms. Defeat was utterly inconceivable and consequently Jai was targeted with extreme prejudice. Whenever he came into contact with the ball a tidal wave of blue crashed onto him, pressing him hard into the sand. Fists and boots rained down upon him, and vicious grunts.

"Bloody wog!"

"So Lady Caitlin was guarding the treasure, after all." Quirk's voice reverberated around the chimney space. "Well, now you've found it, how are you going to open it?"

They were contemplating the safe's dial in the light of Jai's torch, its battery mildly boosted by the meagre energy from Devilston's inadequate heating pipes.

"My father had a safe just like this," Dan replied.

It was behind a holiday photograph: the family on the beach at Rugen. When the Brown Shirts came they smashed the picture and took the emergency money from the safe. And then they took his father.

"Rosenbaum?"

"Ja…?"

"You were a thousand miles away."

"Sorry. What did you say…?"

"I asked you how many numbers there were in the combination of your father's safe?"

"Four pairs of digits."

It was the date of his parents' wedding: 14-02-19-18. Valentine's Day, near the end of a long and terrible war. All that hope ahead of them…

"Well, there are one hundred numbers on this dial and by my reckoning that's…" Quirk closed his eyes to concentrate, "…one hundred to the power of four possibilities…or a mere one hundred million!" He opened his eyes. "So, if we don't eat or sleep or do anything else except dial combinations then we should have it cracked by the end of our lives, presuming we make it to old age…Though it may seem like it Rosenbaum, I'm afraid rugby matches don't last that long."

"I prefer logic to guesswork," said Dan. "And if Monster Mouth is the keeper of this book then we can assume he set the combination…"

"Probably."

"Now you and I both know he doesn't like dates. He's always forgetting the years in which things happened, isn't he?"

"Numbers are the preserve of mathematicians, and let them have their jam!" Quirk boomed, in imitation of the Reverend.

"But history's the cream on top of the scone, lads..."

"So," Dan continued, "I bet it's a number even Monster Mouth wouldn't forget. When is his birthday?"

"How would I know?"

"Well you are his favourite...."

"Nonsense!" After a pause, Quirk added: "Thirty First of October."

"So you do know!"

"Only because it's Halloween. He makes the same joke every year: **I should have been called Jack O'Lantern but there's already one of those...**"

"I don't understand."

"Jack O'Lantern is the keeper of the lighthouse on Dragon Head. They say his face is so horribly disfigured no-one dares visit the place."

"How old is he?"

"Jack?" Quirk shrugged. "Haven't a clue."

"Not Jack. Monster Mouth."

"Oh, I don't know...fifty?"

"Do you think so? I'd say he was younger. Let's start at forty..."

Dan dialled **31-10-19-00**. It didn't work so he tried **31-10-18-99**, still without result. Undeterred he continued, working back in time.

Leaving the chimney space, Quirk paced nervously around the Library. He kept checking on the progress of the match through the window, and the time on the small repeater face within the clock's mechanism.

"But this is too obvious," said Dan, pausing in his work. "If **you** know his birth date then how many others do?"

"So what numbers would he use?" Quirk was addressing the lower half of Dan's body, the rest of him concealed within the chimney space. "His mother's birthday? His father's? His cat's...?"

"Does he have a cat?"

"It was a joke. What I mean is, we'll be here for ages thinking of important dates in his life. As Monster would say himself: **the show's over, boyo.**"

"Boyo...?"

"It's a Welsh expression."

"Welsh..." Now the points shifted in Dan's mind. "So what's the most important date for the Welsh?"

"Saint David's Day, I should think. The First of March."

"And the First of March was when Saint David was born?"

"Or died. I forget which."

"What year?"

"No idea. But I have a friend who'll know..."

Quirk made straight for the shelf where the many volumes of the Encyclopaedia Britannica were lined up like a guard of honour at attention, infinitely patient. He selected the correct book and opened it. Dan joined him, taking a break from the chill of the chimney space.

"Look at that," said Quirk. "It's opened in the right section. Saints…"

The entry for one particular saint was accompanied by an illustration: a semi-naked man tied to a tree. His body was covered in arrows and his face wore an expression of ecstatic agony.

"Ouch," said Quirk.

He began to turn the page but Dan stopped him.

"Wait. Who is that…?"

Quirk read the entry's heading.

"*Saint Sebastian*. Never heard of him."

"Neither have I, but you can tell this book has been opened at this page many times before. It's as if someone has had to keep referring to it. Someone with a very bad memory for numbers, perhaps…"

Now Dan scanned the entry, reading choice phrases aloud:

"*Born circa Two Hundred and Fifty Six AD … persecuted by the Romans for his Christianity… archers fired a multitude of arrows into him yet he miraculously survived…eventually beaten to death and his body thrown into a…*"

Dan faltered. The word was unfamiliar.

"A privy," said Quirk. "It's a toilet."

"That's nice...***Died circa Two Hundred and Eighty Eight AD...Catholics celebrate Saint Sebastian's Day on the Twentieth of January...***"

"This is all very interesting," Quirk interrupted, "but I thought we were looking for Saint David...?"

"Too obvious. Monster needed a more obscure number when he set the combination, but one that is still accessible in case he forgets it..."

"So you think he chose a random saint?"

"No. Everything has to have a meaning for him."

"So what does Saint Sebastian mean to him?"

"**Saint** Sebastian means very little, I should think, though Monster might identify with an intellectual martyr suffering the arrows of ignorance. But I have a feeling the name Sebastian has a deeper significance for him..."

"Why?"

But Dan didn't reply. He quickly returned to the chimney space and dialled Saint Sebastian's date of birth:

20-01-02-56

When this failed he tried his year of death:

20-01-02-88

"Damn."

"Oh well," said Quirk, closing the volume and returning it to its place in the ranks. "At least you tried. Now, can we go…?"

"How old is Smythe-Morrigan?"

"Rosenbaum, if you're going to try random numbers then we definitely **will** be here for the rest of our lives."

"It's not random. He's called Sebastian so it's very possible he was born on Saint Sebastian's Day. And I promise it's the last attempt…"

Quirk took a deep breath.

"Well, he's a Leaver so he's probably seventeen. But what's Slimy-Moron got to do with anything, apart from having the same Christian name…?"

Ignoring the question Dan dialled

20-01-19-23

to no effect.

"That's that then," said Quirk. "Let's go."

"Wait. Let me try again."

"But you've already had your last try!"

"It's the same number, only back-to-front…"

32-91-10-02

Now the little door clicked open, to Quirk's

amazement and Dan's deep satisfaction.
Historians always think backwards.

Rockenough dominated the rest of the first half, re-asserting an authority they believed to be their birth right. The enemy pack rolled forwards like a blitzkrieg, crushing all before it. Devilston put up a spirited defence - with Jai always at its heart - but the Rockenough forwards were leaner and more muscular, and stronger. Praeposters comprised the rump of Devilston's First Fifteen: a rump of considerable girth fed by a rich and privileged diet.

Devilston 5 Visitors 3

Rockenough easily converted the try, bringing the scores level.

Devilston 5 Visitors 5

For Devilston this was still an historic achievement. To be drawing with Rockenough at half-time - or at any time - was unprecedented.

The team congratulated Jai as they converged on a junior boy holding a bowl of quartered oranges.

"Well done, Rana! You were outstanding!"

Jai sank onto the sand, aching to his bones, while his team mates attacked their refreshment like wolves tearing at flesh. The oranges were huge Seville specimens, Jai noted, no doubt from one of the coffin consignments. Meanwhile the faces of the opposition contorted as they partook of the grapefruit segments provided by their hosts.

Smythe-Morrigan was drunk with the giddy prospect of captaining a draw against the mighty Rockenough. He hardly dared even entertain the possibility of a victory.

"We can do this," he said in his only attempt at a team talk. "Just get the ball to Rana."

"He's taking a hell of a beating," said the fly half. "Shouldn't we be sharing the load more?"

"I'm sure he's quite capable of looking after himself. Aren't you, old chap...?"

Head hung between his knees, Jai wearily raised a hand.

"Good man."

"You can still smell it," said Dan, his nose almost touching the ancient page. They were sitting at the Librarian's desk, Jude's Bible open before them.

"Smell what?"

Quirk was wary of getting too close to the book. Logic might have reigned supreme in his mind, but superstition was an unruly mob which required firm suppression.

It was the faintest of smells, perhaps a few molecules in a million, but Dan was sure he could detect the familiar taint.

"Smoke."

The smell transported his imagination back in time. Not to a burning chapel four centuries in the past, but to the streets of Berlin a year ago.

As Dan carefully turned the pages, the pair admired the hand-written manuscript with its sensuous illuminations. As a schoolboy might doodle during a tedious lesson, so the monk's quill seemed to have been seduced by worldly distractions, even as he had struggled to translate the biography of a god. Men and women - and even the Almighty - were invariably depicted with their clothing in the process of slipping off, revealing generous amounts of flesh.

Now Dan turned to the back of the Bible, vaulting over thousands of years of Biblical history in an instant.

"The General Epistle of Jude," said Quirk, translating the Latin. "It's the penultimate book. According to Monster Mouth, our Jude didn't get any further..."

There was excitement in his voice, and when they came to the final pages he let out a strangled little cry of shock and delight.

"So there **is** more," said Dan.

"And it's in English!" Quirk was wringing his hands. "And look! The writing is rushed and there are no illuminations! It certainly isn't the Revelation of Saint John..."

Dan attempted the title of this final chapter.

"***This being the Last***...what does that say? The lettering is difficult..."

Quirk took over.

"***This being the Last Testament of Brother Jude of the Holy Benedictine Monastery of Saint Michael on the Isle of Devilstone...***"

The two exchanged a look of wonder.

"You were right!" cried Quirk. "It's Jude's confession!"

Quirk's finger followed the words as he recited them with confidence, well-accustomed to such scripts. Then his voice diminished to a mutter.

"Aloud!" Dan urged him.

"But surely it's quicker if I read it first then give you a summary..."

"No good. You might miss something."

Dan opened the drawer in the desk, pulled out the Librarian's ledger and proceeded to tear pages out of it. Quirk was horrified.

"That's Library property I'll have you know!"

"You won't miss a few blank pages." Dan took Quirk's pencil from the drawer and licked its point. "Now start again and I'll write it down."

"But that'll take ages!"

Dan glanced up at the Library's clock.

"We've got another half an hour. Should be enough, if we get on with it..."

"Look Rosenbaum, I've got another idea. Why don't we come back next Saturday? There's no home match so we'll have more time..."

"With other pupils around?"

"I won't let them in. I'll say I'm stock-tacking or something..."

"No," said Dan. "I can't wait that long. We'll do it now."

Quirk paused, thinking fast, then said: "You realise this is much more than I originally agreed to, don't you…?"

Dan was already prepared.

"All my puddings until the End of Term."

He held out his hand. Quirk hesitated but the prospect of a stomach full of warm stodgy comfort every day until Christmas was just too tempting.

"Except Spotted Dick," he said earnestly, shaking Quirk's hand. "But I'll still have the custard, mind..."

And so they set to work, Quirk dictating and Dan transcribing, while outside a whistle blew and another cheer went up.

Apart from two Leavers in the Library the

whole school was behind the home team, their cheers like a favourable breeze propelling a pirate galleon towards its glittering prize. But the enemy shore was well-fortified: the visitors defended their honour ferociously and the match ran aground.

Something different was needed to break the stalemate. So when the ball found its way to Jai from a scrappy line-out, instead of passing it down the line he kicked it high and ahead then darted at full speed through the enemy ranks. He judged it perfectly, cleanly catching the ball as it tumbled back to earth then sprinting for the try line. With the enemy thundering at his heels there was only one more man to beat.

The full back aimed low for his legs so Jai took to the air, bounding over the defender like a young buck. He placed the ball between the posts, the Reverend-referee blew his whistle and the school roared.

Devilston 8 Visitors 5

The whole team converged on Jai, including their skipper:

"Nice work Rana"

"Thanks."

Jai's reply was guarded. He was waiting for the sting.

It was apparent to Smythe-Morrigan that

their star scrum half was receiving the lion's share of the glory. He was also well aware of Jai's leadership qualities: the calm manner in which he communicated with the forwards in set pieces, and the cool efficiency with which he organised the backs. Being a second row forward, Smythe-Morrigan was caught up in close-quarter combat for much of the time, thus denying him the larger perspective which Jai commanded.

In truth, leadership didn't sit comfortably on Smythe-Morrigan's shoulders. While responsibility weighed dangerously upon the fault lines in the Head of School's character, Jai seemed completely natural in command. When Smythe-Morrigan issued an order he was aware of the tension present between giver and receiver, and always ready to enforce his demands with threats. But with Jai an understanding seemed to already exist between the two parties. His verbal instructions were almost superfluous.

Smythe-Morrigan derived some comfort in the knowledge that traditionally the Head of School had always skippered the First Fifteen. But traditionally Devilston always lost to Rockenough, too. Today, tradition itself seemed under attack.

And there was no doubt the crowd loved Jai. When he had the ball there was a surge in their cheers, and now their chant echoed around the island's ancient rock as he prepared for the conversion kick:

"RA-NA! RA-NA! RA-NA…!"

Smythe-Morrigan knew something had to be done to re-assert his authority. He walked over and took the ball from Jai.

"I'll take this one."

The chanting deteriorated to a confused murmur as the Head of School knelt down, as if in prayer. Hands trembling, he fashioned a small pedestal in the sand on which he placed the ball. Standing, he stepped two paces back and one to the left, like a knight on a chess board. Then he looked ahead.

The enemy had gathered before him, between the goal posts. Bristling at the insult of being behind to a people they considered congenitally inferior, they lusted for revenge.

As Smythe-Morrigan began his run-up, fifteen Rockenough players launched themselves towards him, snorting and snarling like starving bears. In the teeth of this ferocious charge the skipper's fragile nerve shattered. His foot sliced the side of the ball, sending it careering across the sand.

The crowd groaned as one.

Devilston's skipper contemplated the demolished pedestal at his feet, hoping the sand might open up and devour him, while the opposition's fury was converted into joy.

Rockenough had sniffed a change in fortune and - indeed - the ball seemed to favour their company when play resumed. When it emerged from the pack, like an egg rolling out of some strange multi-limbed monster, it was passed down their line of backs with factory precision. In this way the visitors advanced deep into enemy territory, their progress only checked by a crucial tackle by Jai.

The ensuing skirmish on Devilston's goal line was savage: a frenzy of punching, stamping, kicking and biting. The Reverend witnessed it all yet his whistle remained silent between his teeth. Secretly he was relishing the scrap, wishing he was in there himself, deep in the guts of the ruck.

At last the whistle squealed and players began to peel themselves off a pile of bodies. The last man lying on the sand - hugging the ball in a foetal position on the other side of the Devilston line - wore blue.

Devilston 8 Visitors 8

The try had been scored in the very corner of the pitch. The crowd booed but the conversion kick was long and true, and the ball would have passed between the goal posts were it not for a sudden gust of wind. The lump of leather bounced off the woodwork and the crowd cheered.

Devilston had played Her part.

Despite the miss there was no respite from the visitors' attack. Jai led an heroic defence against the onslaught, executing some spectacular tackles, but Rockenough's forwards were an irresistible force. Scooping up the ball as it rolled out of a ruck, their scrum half feigned a delivery to his fly half. Falling for the ruse Jai committed himself to intercept, only to see his opposite number drop-kick.

Even Devilston was fooled. Before She had time to raise a breath of wind, the ball was already spinning between the posts.

Devilston 8 Visitors 12

"Rosenbaum," said Quirk with unease, glancing at the clock's repeater as Dan began a new page, "we really need to go. There's only three minutes left before the final whistle..."

"But don't you want to know how it ends?"

"We know how it ends. He dies."

Dan grabbed Quirk's keys and headed for the clock's cabinet.

"What are you doing?" protested the Librarian. "Those are mine!"

Now Dan was unlocking the glass door with

the smaller key, guessing that clock-winding was one of Quirk's duties. He took hold of the huge weight on the end of the swinging pendulum and brought it to rest.

The Library fell deathly quiet, like a bathroom when the drip of a leaky tap had finally ceased. Quirk was astonished. His mouth opened and shut several times before he managed to speak.

"But...you can't stop time..."

"Well, I just have." Dan returned to the desk. "Now let's finish the job, shall we...?"

The match may have been dying but its death throes were protracted.

"I say, Captain Smythe-Morrigan...?" Rockenough's coach called over. "I make it well after half past. When's your fellow going to blow his whistle?"

"We go off the school clock and it's showing..." Shading his eyes theatrically, the Captain squinted towards the Library, "... twenty seven minutes past three."

"But it's been stuck there for ages! It's obviously stopped!"

"A mere illusion. Time's like that, you know. If She sees you want Her She'll play hard to get..."

But even with extra time Devilston needed a miracle. Following Rockenough's drop goal the red and blacks dragged themselves to what had to be the final kick off.

Jai kicked the ball deep into the Rockenough half and Devilston's forwards chased. The ball was knocked on by the visitors and a scrum given. It was the home team's last chance.

The two halves of the scrum came together like a pair of giant crabs locked in mortal combat. Jai knew that as soon as he put the ball in, the enemy's forwards would drive their exhausted counterparts backwards and the blues would win possession, yet again. Devilston's only hope was a precision delivery.

Rockenough heaved forward but Jai's service was impeccable and Devilston's hooker heeled the ball back for Jai to pick up as it rolled out of the scrum.

Jai held the ball as if about to make a drop-kick and his opposite number stretched his arms upwards to block. but then - in an exact reversal of the enemy scrum half's earlier trick - Jai passed the ball to his fly half.

Jai shadowed the ball as it flew along Devilston's line of backs, a progress arrested abruptly by a crashing tackle on their winger. Released, the ball could have bounced in any direction but somehow found its way into the arms of its favoured guardian.

His heels flicking up sand like wisps of smoke as he sprinted, Jai could hear the tall full back closing in on him from behind, his longer legs eating up the distance between them. As Jai approached the try-line the predator dived, stretching to clip his prey's ankles. Jai fell between the posts but retained his hold on the ball. The whistle blew and the crowd was a riot of celebration.

Devilston 11 Visitors 12

Rockenough protested, pointing at the clock still stubbornly fixed at twenty seven minutes past.

Jai was swamped by his team.

"Hang on chaps, we haven't won yet. I still need to convert it..."

"I'll do that."

Again Smythe-Morrigan took the ball from Jai, but this time he was challenged.

"Are you mad?" Tattersall was too angry and exhausted to care for the consequences of his insubordination. "You totally fluffed the last one!"

"For God's sake, S-M," said another, "give it to Rana!"

"Shut up!" shouted the Head of School, face crimson with fear and fury. "I'm skipper and I decide!"

As the Head Boy made his way towards the Rockenough goal, a tense silence descended. No-one could quite believe what they were witnessing: an epic victory about to be squandered.

"Rana," Tattersall grunted, "why the Hell didn't you say something?"

Jai shrugged.

"He's the boss."

All eyes were once more on Smythe-Morrigan as he repeated the ball-planting ritual. He could hardly believe his own audacity, trying again at something at which he'd so obviously failed. But he knew this was his only remaining hope of regaining some respect: a last desperate roll of the dice.

The crowd was hushed, knowing this would be the final kick of the match. The clock had stopped obligingly but nothing could halt the incoming tide. It wet the boots of the Rockenough players as they jeered and gesticulated on the try-line, while Smythe-Morrigan prepared to make the conversion.

Then even Rockenough fell silent, so that now all was eerily quiet but for the beat of the waves on the shore.

And a deep hum, distant but steadily growing...

A sleek slanted shape darted between the twin towers of the gatehouse. The whole Library seemed to shudder in the near-miss: ancient glass panes rattled in their lead gums, and a rush of wind from the slipstream invaded through an open window. The pieces of paper on which Dan had written Jude's final thoughts took to the air.

"Take cover!" cried Quirk, diving under his table. "It's the bloody Jerries!"

Hurrying to the window Dan saw an aircraft flying low over the bay. The black inverted cross of her shadow shot across the beach, then the sea. Then she banked, as if to show off her beautiful form: wide wings which tapered to a point at their tips, a slender tail and a mighty maelstrom at her shark-like snout. He recalled a painting of Saint George and the Dragon he'd seen in an art book: the green dragon had roundels on her wings, too. She'd been speared in the eye but she remained alive and defiant.

"It's the RAF, you idiot!" Dan laughed, gathering up his precious pages. "Let's get down to the game. It's the perfect cover…"

Extricating himself sheepishly from his hiding place, Quirk replaced Jude's Bible in the safe while Dan re-started the clock's pendulum.

Both players and spectators had now forgotten the match. All stood in awe watching the mechanical angel ascended, pointing her nose at the heavens as she rolled in a slow pirouette.

A ghostly cloud of bluish smoke drifted down onto the gathered, anointing them with the pungent smell of combusted kerosene. Then the crowd's silence was broken by a single voice:

"Spitfire!"

Now a huge cheer went up as the pupils began to descend from the rocks, pouring onto the sand: a cavalry charge of galloping youths, as if in pursuit of the aircraft now banking in a tight turn within the great blue dome.

"It's Dad!" puffed Tom as he ran. "I knew he'd make it!"

Masters and Praeposters made vain attempts to halt the flow, warning of the dangers of quicksand and disobeying orders. They might just as well have been calling upon the tide to turn about.

"Cnuts!" a pupil shouted defiantly as he dodged a Praeposter's lunge.

Alderley was sitting next to Elena on the row of Staff chairs. She was shading her eyes and smiling as she watched the aerial display. When he slipped his hand into hers she didn't look at him but her fingers entwined with his, to his delight.

The Spitfire glinted in the sun as she completed her turn, low on the horizon. The chasing boys slowed down, suddenly fearful as the machine approached them at strafing height, so low that her propeller wash lifted thin wisps of sand which curled over her wing tips.

As she shot over the crowd, many dived to the ground in fear of decapitation. But Tom remained standing, looking up at the pale belly of the beast as it flashed overhead, the roar of the Merlin engine shaking his bones. The propeller's tornado snatched the breath from his lungs as he shouted with joy, punching the air.

The aircraft climbed steeply then - rounding the island - she dived, the tone of her engine rising. Again pupils flung themselves to the sand as she swept over their heads. Then the Spitfire raised her nose towards the sun, her engine straining as she sought to break the bonds of gravity.

Tom's neck was bent back as he stood gawping up at the aircraft, now far above him.

"He's doing a loop..."

The engine groaned in pain as it pulled the aircraft around the top of the loop, then its voice rose as the Spitfire dived towards the ground. For a moment the spectators feared the pilot had lost control and they were about to witness a terrible tragedy. Then - with another great moan of effort - the plane came round to the horizontal, skimming the shore.

The Spitfire banked in a final fly-past, a dipped wing passing between two goal posts.

Tom thought he saw the pilot waving and his chest swelled with pride, tears stinging his eyes.

"Damn show off," the Captain muttered. Raising his voice he addressed those seated nearby: "That was bloody dangerous! Did anyone get his registration? The sun was in my eyes..."

The Staff shook their heads and made apologetic noises. In truth some of them had read the three letters on the fuselage but no-one wanted to be party to any disciplinary procedure. Not for the first time they were suffering the uncomfortable feeling of having their loyalties stretched between two posts.

"All that fuel he's wasting," said the Head of Science. "And with a war on as well..."

But in reality Doctor Pottinger was envying the aviator with all of his heart.

The Spitfire disappeared inland, her voice diminishing to a distant drone then fading away. The pupil body - now spread out along the beach - stood in a dazed silence, yearning for an encore.

Meanwhile Smythe-Morrigan's attention had returned to the task at hand. The Rockenough Fifteen were still lined up on the touch-line staring after the Spitfire, their backs to the ball. For all of his faults, Devilston's skipper was never slow in recognising a golden opportunity. He caught the referee's eye and the Reverend

- immediately understanding his intention - nodded and winked.

The Head of School took two paces backwards then one to the left. At the sound of the whistle Rockenough turned, but it was too late. In the absence of a charge, Smythe-Morrigan was now able to focus fully on the ball and his foot made perfect contact. The ball took off with a satisfying thud, sailing over the heads of the stunned opposition and between the goal posts.

The clock chimed half past the hour and the Reverend blew for the end of play.

Devilston 13 Visitors 12

The Spitfire had stirred the spectators deeply and yet the feeling had been an ethereal kind of pleasure, like a beautiful dream from which they'd just awoken. But now came the opportunity for the pupils to convert their joy and they swarmed onto the pitch, converging on their new heroes, greedy for contact.

Rockenough had sunk onto the sand in weary disbelief. Their coach was remonstrating with the referee.

"I think you'll find," the Reverend replied coolly, "we did nothing in contravention of the Rules, which is more than can be said of your lot. I should remind you, sir, that thuggery is no substitute for talent…"

"How dare you, sir!" fumed the Rockenough coach. "I've a good mind to put an end to this fixture! I've never been happy with having to play on a bloody beach, and there was obviously some fiddling with the clock, and then this final insult...well, this is the last straw, I tell you!"

"Surely, the last grain of sand...?"

"Mark my words, Monmouth! I shall be writing to the Schools Rugby Association about this!"

The Reverend chuckled to himself as the his opposite number stormed off with his team, foregoing the traditional round of handshakes and three cheers.

Devilston's First Fifteen had been consumed by the mob. Jai was hoisted onto shoulders, undisputed Man of the Match. He spotted Dan in the crowd, waving some pieces of paper above his head.

"Jai! I got it!"

Jai grinned.

Another reason to celebrate.

"That was remarkable," said Alderley, still sitting next to Elena as they watched the celebrations, her hand still in his. Or his in hers.

"Yes," she replied. "Such a beautiful machine, and yet so deadly..."

Alderley took a deep breath.

"Elena, why have you been avoiding me?"

"Avoiding you?"

"I've hardly seen you since that night in your place. Was it something I said, or did? I know I was a little drunk…"

"You're a nice man, Michael."

"But…?"

"No buts. You're very sweet."

"Nice and sweet, eh? I'd call that being damned with faint praise…"

Now she glanced at him and smiled. Then her hand slipped out of his and she rose from the chair.

"What's going on over there…?"

Beyond the churned pitch Elena had spotted a group of juniors pulling a boy from a patch of quicksand. As she hurried towards the huddle Alderley called to her. She stopped and turned.

"Perhaps we could go somewhere at the weekend? You know, get away from this place for a while. Saint Ives, maybe…?"

"I'm afraid I'm rather busy at present," she replied, walking backwards. "Perhaps in the Half Term holiday…"

Alderley waved an acknowledgement then made his way slowly back to school, feeling his heart trapped and sinking.

"Still in pursuit of the Spanish Spitfire, eh?" The Captain had appeared at his side, smiling humourlessly at him. "You do realise you haven't a cat in Hell's chance with that one, don't you?"

"And how would you know? Mind-reader, are you...?"

The words had fired from his mouth almost of their own volition, but their release gave Alderley some degree of relief. He didn't really care for consequences anymore. At least losing his job would deliver him from this wretched place, and his abject failure.

The Captain retained his customary composure.

"Just this once I shall forgive your impertinence..."

Alderley suddenly quickened his pace. The Captain was about to call after him when the Head of School took Alderley's place at his side.

"We did it, Father! We beat Rockenough for the first time ever!"

"We did indeed. But was that because of your leadership, or in spite of it...?" The Captain was still smarting from Alderley's show of disrespect. His words were like a cold wave dousing Smythe-Morrigan's joy. "Now I'm no expert on rugger Sebastian, but it looked very much to me like Rana was in command for much of that match..."

"I know, Father. I didn't have a very good game today."

"No, you didn't. And popular opinion suggests that Rana would make a better skipper than you..."

"But the skipper of the First Fifteen has always been the Head of School!"

"That isn't written in stone…"

Smythe-Morrigan was horrified. How would he survive the humiliation of losing the captaincy, and to a bloody foreigner? Then another thought came to him, bringing with it a glimmer of hope.

"Anyway, the skipper can't be a darky."

As he began to climb the steps cut into the rock, the Captain paused and placed his hand on the Head of School's shoulder.

"Fortunately for you Sebastian, that **is** written in stone…"

8

THE TESTAMENT AND THE TUNNEL

As the Rockenough bus retreated to the mainland the tide closed in on the Causeway like a silent cavalry, as if intent upon finishing off the enemy.

Jai returned to the dormistudy from his bath, freshly shaved. For once the water had been hot, the precious contents of the geyser a reward for his exploits in battle.

"A magnificent performance," said Dan. "I only wish I'd seen more of it."

"Oh, I wouldn't say that." Jai patted sweet-smelling after-shave on his face then began to get dressed. "I just happen to be good at sport, that's all. Tom's father's the real hero of the day..."

"So you really believe it was my dad?" Tom asked.

"Of course we do!" said Dan.

"Well, no-one else does."

"But you know the truth Tom and that's all

that matters." Now Jai was combing his hair. "Anyway, what about our own hero here?" He pointed his comb at Dan. "The Man Who Stopped Time…"

"I stopped the clock to gain a few more minutes for the transcription," said Dan. "I had no idea it would make such a difference."

"But the gods did." Jai winked. "Kali had it all worked out."

"Or Devilston…"

"So," said Tom, "what does this Jude bloke have to say for himself then…?"

From his blazer pocket Dan produced the precious sheets of paper and unfolded them on the desk in front of him. Jai and Tom assumed their favourite positions: Jai perched on the window ledge, Tom lying on his bottom bunk with his hands behind his head.

"To be honest with you," said Dan, "I haven't really absorbed it properly myself. You know what it's like when you're being dictated to…"

They knew exactly what it was like. The Reverend often entertained himself by inserting nonsense words within tracts of dictated text, then roaring with amusement as he watched his pupils obediently write them down.

Dan cleared his throat and began to read his scrawl:

"This being the Last Testament of Brother Jude of the Holy Benedictine Monastery of Saint Michael on the Isle of Devilstone in the Duchy of Cornwalle, in the year of Our Lord Fifteen Hundred and Forty."

"Are all his sentences going to be that long?" asked Tom.

"I, Jude Petherick, entered this wicked world in Pristowe, in the Year of Our Lord Fourteen Hundred and Ninety Nine. My father fished the sea whilst my mother tended to her flock of lambs, of which I was the youngest thereof. The sea and the soil did bring forth only a modest bounty and we did lack much, but not love. Our parents were our most devoted guardians.

"But then great misfortune befell our humble home. My father was taken by the sea, some say by the terrible Leviathan itself…"

"The what?"
"A sea dragon," Dan explained to Tom.

"Then demons came forth from out of Hell and took away my brothers and sisters to be slaves in the Underworld…"

"Quirky thinks he's talking about pirates from the Barbary coast of Africa," Dan added. "They regularly raided the Cornish coast..."

"My mother hid beneath her bed with her youngest child and so we were spared the fate suffered by my poor siblings. But alas, a great despond did come upon her from the loss of her husband and all of her brood save one, and she did succumb to the fever. May Almighty God have mercy upon the souls of my dear departed family...

"Now, because the spectre of misfortune hung over me, there were none in Pristowe willing to take this wretched orphan into their care, lest they might fall victim to the curse themselves. And so it was that Providence did deliver me into the hands of the Benedictine monks of Devilstone.

"I should be grateful for the succour that they did bestow upon me, and the most excellent education they did provide for me which alloweth me to commit these very words to paper. And yet these blessings were polluted by their foul influence upon my soul, the origins of which I shall now relate...

"After the fall of Rome, the land that the Romans called Britannia and the Celts called Albion was shrouded in an age of darkness. And it is said that at this time a great king called Arthur, who was of Celtic origin but whose soul was filled with the love of Christ, did rise in the kingdom of Kernowe to fight pagan invaders

known as Saxons from the land of Germania. And it is said that King Arthur made his home in the Roman fortifications upon this very island, and that to this day he and his knights lie asleep in a cavern deep within the womb of Devilstone, to rise again should the land of Albion be threatened once more."

"Camelot!" Jai exclaimed.

"Conjecture," said Dan. "As Monster Mouth says, we've no solid evidence."

"But he did say the Celts buried their dead on this island..."

"True. And Arthur's Camelot became corrupted, just like every community that has ever lived here…"

"And it came to pass that the Saxon heathens vanquished the Celts, and Kernowe came to be known as Cornwalle. Yet a small but stubborn flame of Christ's spirit remained burning here...

"Now there were two patrons of Devilstone. The first was Saint Michael, whom fishermen swore they had seen upon this island, in combat with the demon who is Beelzebub. The other was Benedict, named so because only words of goodness flowed forth from his lips as doth sweet water from a mountain spring. And from the castle that was built here in the service of war, his devoted followers the Benedictines did

fashion a monastery for the salvation of souls, as the beautiful butterfly doth rise out of the ugly chrysalis. And lo, this place became a shining beacon of goodness in a most deep and dreary night...

"But there resideth an evil within this island that is the very spirit of God's greatest foe, with whom Saint Michael did do battle. The rock is steeped in Her blood, the mist is laced with Her poison and in the hiss of the sea can be heard Her serpentine voice. And so, even as the Word of God did slowly spread like spring amongst the Saxon hoards in what became the land of Englande, that most malignant miasma which oozes from the fetid heart of Devilstone began to infect the brethren of this monastery and did penetrate the very marrow of their bones, so that they turned away from the Word of the Lord and began to take heed of their basest needs.

"With the apples once eaten for sweet nourishment the monks brewed cider upon which they became much inebriated and lustful. And they did partake of the forbidden mushrooms of the glades which addled their minds with great madness. Where previously they had ventured into the world only to bestow blessings upon the laity, now they took payment for their benedictions, and those who refused were cursed and great ills were visited upon them. And thus the monks of Devilstone, who once had been most

faithful devotees of the Benedictine Order, came to be known far and wide as the Maledictines..."

"The Mad Monks," Jai whispered.

"And when the night was afflicted by the fever of storm, the monks would set lamps upon the great promontory that is known as Dragon Head. And lo, passing ships would mistake these as the kindly lights of Pristowe offering sanctuary from the tempest, only to be lured to a most terrible end in the claws and jaws of the monster. How many wretched souls perished on those merciless rocks on account of this most devilish trickery is a matter for God's divine reckoning alone, but in the treasure washed up from those poor stricken vessels the monks of Devilstone did reap a most bountiful dividend...

"Now the folk of Pristowe and beyond were sore afraid of the residents of Devilstone and they dared not even make mention of Her name, lest they fell victim to Her dreadful curse. And many wondered how it was that the Maledictines did range abroad, debauching themselves most freely even when furious waves did besiege this island and prohibit the passage of any vessel. Some did conclude that the monks possessed that miraculous faculty manifested by Our Lord Jesus Christ Himself upon the Sea of Galilee, which they did pervert in the interests of their own wicked

ends.

"But I do now declare that there was no miracle in this watery feat, for the Maledictines walked from the Chapel of Devilstone through the very bowels of the Earth to her sister Chapel of Pristowe, thanks to the ingenuity of Rome. Many centuries before, having failed to invade by land or sea owing to the treacherous sands and the dangerous waters, a Roman army had hewn a tunnel to the island..."

Jai clapped his hands together.

"I knew there was a tunnel! And it was the Romans who built it, not the Celts!"

"Before we get too carried away," said Dan, "remember that Jude is writing this four hundred years ago. Just because it existed then doesn't mean it still does..."

"So if Devilston is the body and the tunnel is the bowels," Tom thought aloud, "that makes Pristow the - "

"Priesthole!" Jai exclaimed. "The village is named after the tunnel the monks used!"

"Hang on," said Tom. "Jude says the tunnel ends in Pristow's chapel. But there isn't one, as far as I know..."

"That doesn't mean there wasn't one," Dan replied, then continued reading.

"I do now confess that I also did take full

advantage of the great liberties afforded to this most unholy order. And my sins were all the worse because I had some remembrance of the godliness of my dear departed parents before they perished, whilst my brother monks knew only the ways of evil which they had inherited.

"And I have not yet written of the very worst of the wickedness that was perpetrated by the Maledictines, though my heart doth quake and my quill doth tremble with great agitation at the very prospect of relating it..."

Dan glanced at his transfixed friends. Secretly he relished the power he commanded over them.

"Now, in the ancient time of the Celts human sacrifices were made upon this island so as to appease its restless spirit. An end was put to this savage practice when Rome became the great bastion of Christendom, but doth not the dark shadow of sacrifice still haunt that most holy text of the New Testament? Was it not the treacherous kiss of one disciple which brought about the slaughter of the Holy Lamb of God? And if our Saviour had not been betrayed, there would have been neither Crucifixion nor Resurrection, and hence the Church of Christ would not have risen. And so the Order of the Maledictines made use of this truth in mitigation of their wicked ways, for

in the betrayal of Jesus did not great good come about from great evil?

"And thus there was another who did usurp Saint Michael and Saint Benedict as patron of this monastery: he who occupied the thirteenth chair at the Last Supper and who did betray our most beloved Jesus Christ, and whose name the brethren bestowed upon me when they first took me into their bosom..."

"He means Judas," Dan explained, seeing Tom's puzzled expression. "A variant of Jude..."

"And so, in commemoration of this betrayal, it came to pass that every thirteen years a young innocent from the locality of Pristowe was disappeared beneath the cloak of night and secreted through the tunnel. And at the midnight hour on the eve of All Saint's Day, within the Crown of Stones and witnessed by the eleven most venerable Maledictines, the Abbot would plunge his knife into the bosom of this most unfortunate youth and bring forth the heart, as might a glistening jewel be extracted from a treasure chest. Hence, owing to the number in attendance, this abominable ritual came to be known as the Ceremony of the Thirteen..."

"It's in the Chapel window." Jai remembered his idle observations. "So it isn't a cross that monk in the middle is holding…"

"And as Jesus Christ Himself had shared his own body and blood at the Last Supper, so the choicest flesh of this poor soul would be roasted then devoured by the other twelve. Not a single morsel was wasted and even the bones were boiled for broth and served up to the rest of the brethren of Devilstone."

"Cannibals!" Tom was horrified. "Now that takes the biscuit…"

"And now it doth cause me great misery to confess that, upon one occasion, I too did partake of this most dreadful sacrament. And, though my actions do now revolt me to the very core of my heart, I am most deeply ashamed to record that I did clean my plate, for the meat thereon was the most succulent I did ever taste…

"But then a great sickness possessed me, as if my very body was want to punish me for this alimentary crime. And so I excused myself from that hellish feast and my repentant stomach did vomit up that most diabolical of meals."

"Certainly sounds like a Devilston dinner," said Jai.

"And when I had voided my innards, I sought

refuge in the Chapel where I did prostrate myself before the Cross and did beg Our Heavenly Father for forgiveness for all the years I had strayed from the Causeway of Righteousness to wallow in the Quicksand of Sin.

"And lo! a shaft of morning sun did shine though the great east window and did illuminate the lectern like the very finger of God. And behold! in this celestial light the golden dragon did glow most strangely and did draw me towards its burden. And as I did look upon God's Word rendered unto English as sweet honey is reduced to base mead, a great epiphany came upon me, as if scales had fallen from my eyes. Now I saw in this open book the doorway to my own redemption and that of my brethren. I would restore the Great Bible to the language of our beloved Holy Father in Rome, in which the Word of God hath been spoken and written since ancient times.

"As the Romans had toiled to hew a tunnel out of solid rock so that this island may be permanently wedded to the world, now I would labour with my quill to carve God's Word onto virgin pages and emboss them with my ink, so that this monastery may be united again in communion with the Holy Catholic Church..."

"That's what Monster Mouth was talking about," said Dan. "Jude had found a way of absolving his sins by translating the Bible from the King's English to the Pope's Latin..."

"And so I did call upon my brethren to fashion a cell for me inside the very walls of our Chapel, lest I be disturbed in the task that God had set me upon. And in this stone womb I was sealed, with only a small window through which my daily bread and soil were passed."

Tom pulled a face.

"Mud sandwiches?"

"No," laughed Jai. "By 'soil' he means 'excrement'."

"Even worse!"

"Look," said Dan with exasperation, "they passed food in and he passed his toilet bucket out..."

"And now I must confess that if it were not for that thick skin of stone that separated me from my brethren, who were now even more rapacious in their sinning on account of being provided with a most convenient scapegoat, I might have resumed in my wicked ways, for my flesh was as weak as my spirit to serve God was strong.

"For many years I laboured thus and my brother monks showed much gratitude for my sacrifice for the sake of their sorry souls. They did regard me as the Lamb of God who taketh away all the sins of the world, who would testify on their behalf on

the Day of Judgment, should the King of Heaven be the arbitrator of their souls, after all, and not the Prince of Darkness. Thus I was brought fine food in great abundance, and I became of quite considerable circumference."

"So the monks were hedging their bets," said Jai. "Having their cake and eating it…"

"And it sounds like Jude was having plenty of cake," added Tom.

"Yes. He must have looked like Friar Tuck."

"In the light of his ultimate fate," said Dan, "that's rather an appropriate description…"

"But then it came to pass that soldiers were sent to dissolve our monastery upon the direct orders of the King of Englande himself, who most fervently desired a break with Rome. The King's men were many in number, for Henry Tudor was most determined to lance this festering boil which did postulate upon the toe of his kingdom. But like cornered wolves my brother monks put up a most ferocious resistance, as the Celts did resist the violent advance of the Imperial Legions. And they were greatly aided in this endeavour by Devilstone Herself, who consumed many soldiers in Her deadly sloughs when they tried to cross the sands, and who conjured a most terrible storm which did smash their boats to into pieces."

"So why didn't the King's men just use the Causeway when the tide was out?" asked Jai.

"Because it wasn't there," Dan replied. "According to Quirky, the First Duchess of Devilston had the road built."

"And so the King's soldiers became of the opinion that the Maledictines of Devilstone had enlisted the very forces of nature to aid them, and were hence sore afraid to confront this elemental evil in the face. So instead Henry's men did place the island of Devilstone under siege, and they did locate the entrance to the tunnel which connects the land to Devilstone like the cord from mother to unborn child and they did seal it with a knot of soldiers so that our monastery would wither on the vine.

"And thus the brethren of Devilstone did starve, for in the years of their wanton indulgence they had neglected to tend to their plots and their livestock, and to make adequate stores, in favour of the easy bounty that could be extracted from the mainland, as the tiny mosquito doth suck the blood of its host (thereby infecting it). But now the island was being garroted, and Queen Winter did reign most harshly so that the meagre land of Devilstone lay barren and waterlogged. Nor could the monks exploit the sea for her riches, for their boats lolled unloved in the harbour and all knowledge of fishing had rotted within their

heads, for want of practice.

"And thus in this most desperate time, the Maledictines did turn upon their own for sustenance, as well as to prove their devotion to Devilstone (as a man might consume his own thumb for a woman) so that She might deliver them from their plight. Hence the very same brethren with whom I had rubbed shoulders at the supper table now came with slavering lips and famished eyes and shining knives to partake of the fatted lamb. I most vehemently beseeched them not to do so, for I had not yet finished God's work which was intended to save their souls. Nor did I wish to perish under the butcher's cleaver to be served up for dinner. And, furthermore, I did remind them that thirteen years had not yet elapsed since Devilstone had last tasted human blood.

"But my brethren heeded not these most reasonable assertations as they prepared to violate my womb of stone, so I fell upon my knees and prayed most vigorously to Merciful God that my life might be spared in order to complete my service of devotion to Him. And lo! even as the first blow was struck by that chisel, I heard a shout go up and a multitude of the King's soldiers spewed forth like vengeful angels from out of the very heart of the Chapel. And through my small window upon the world I witnessed my brethren slain with great violence, like a pack of rabid

hounds.

"Thanks be to God! I cried as the Maledictines fell before the merciless sword, for I was sure that the Lord Himself had sent these soldiers to deliver me from evil. But I did soon cease in my rejoicing, for when they had finished dispatching my brethren to their next life, the King's men now proceeded with equal prejudice to poke their weapons into my hole."

"Sounds painful," said Tom.

"As I cowered in the corner of my cell, thereby avoiding the deadly thrust of their pikes, I beseeched them to desist in their offensive, crying unto them that I had been imprisoned in this place for many years (though without mention that it was of my own volition, which would surely have diluted the potency of my pleas).

"But the soldiers heeded not my most desperate exhortations. They had been directly ordered at the pleasure of King Henry the Eighth of Englande himself to raze the monstrous monastery of Devilstone to the ground, and to put to death every miserable sinner who resideth within her walls. And because I did indeed reside within one of her walls, of which there could be no denial, I was not about to be spared. Their Captain informed me with much spite that I was a Popish canker embedded in the very flesh of Christ and, if

I could not be cut out, then I should be cauterized. To this end, when our Chapel had been plundered of all valuable goods, the Captain ordered that the ancient pews be piled into a great bonfire then set alight."

"And I thought Indian history was brutal..." said Jai.

"Did this really happen?" asked Tom. "I mean, the King's soldiers killing monks and burning down monasteries and all that?"

"Of course," said Dan. "Don't you remember Monster Mouth teaching us about the Reformation?"

"I find it hard to concentrate in lessons. But I love this kind of history, straight from the horse's mouth..."

"My Day of Judgement had arrived, for a great inferno did roar on the other side of my wall like some raging monster, and my nostrils were filled with the stench of burning flesh. The flames entered the aperture of my cell like a fiery tongue lusting for my body, so I placed the King's Great Bible in its way. Praise be to God! it was a most excellent fit and afforded me some considerable protection from that terrible inferno, though I am greatly ashamed and do beg God's forgiveness. Even though that book was of Protestant origin, it was still nevertheless the Word of God.

"And thus I was saved from the full fury of the furnace, though its hellish exhalations did scorch my lungs so that they were sorely damaged. Verily my prison had become an oven and therein I sweated and basted like the goose at Christmastide, lying upon the floor where the smoke swirled less thickly.

"And lo! the Great English Bible which was my shield against the raging dragon did soon crumble into fiery ash. This I took to be a sign, for was God not destroying the text in the heathen tongue whilst preserving that written in the blessed language of Holy Rome, which I did clutch to my bosom most firmly for our mutual protection…?

"At last the flames expired and the fog of smoke dispersed and I gave thanks to the Lord God Almighty for my life, though I was much afflicted by a most violent coughing which did rattle my very bones. And now, peering through my window in the wall, I saw what great destruction had been wrought upon our beloved Chapel. All wood was consumed and the roof was now open to the heavens, as if God in His infinite wisdom had removed the lid on His house for closer inspection. And I saw that the blessed bosom that is the dome and the great eye that is the west window had both been spared, which I took to be a sign of God's mercy.

"But no such mercy had been shown to my brethren, whose bones did lie black and

smouldering like the rafters of our ravaged Chapel. Many times I called out for help but without response and my heart grew leaden with the knowledge that I was the only soul still living upon this island. Both my fellow monks and the soldiers of the King had visited great malevolence upon me, yet now this solitude filled me with equal dread. I had no tools but a wooden spoon, and what strength I still possessed was fast waning. Thus it would have taken me much time to fashion a hole large enough to permit passage of my corporeal vessel, for I had grown of considerable girth from the fine fare brought to fatten me up by my fellow monks, who now themselves lay butchered and baked."

Tom laughed out loud then stopped, his companions glaring at him.

"Oh come on, you've got to find that funny. I mean, him trying to squeeze out through that hole..."

"So now I was confronted by a conundrum which doth surely torment all who are disposed to philosophy. Should my remaining time on this earth, which in my particular state I knew to be measurable in days, be best invested in my emancipation from incarceration, so that my ravaged lungs may be soothed with the balm of fresh sea air? Or should I not devote the last

remaining breaths of my life in the completion of my work, to which I had committed my existence for so many years...?"

"But even as I pondered this dilemma I knew in my heart this was a final bid by Lucifer to lure me from the Course of Righteousness onto the Rocks of Damnation. I alone of the Maledictine Monks of Devilstone hath been spared by God so that I may complete the task He did set me upon, all those many years ago.

"Now one book remained to be translated when I was so rudely interrupted by these violent events, namely The Revelation of Saint John the Divine. Yet I could not render the English words unto Latin as they were now reduced to ashes, so instead I set about recording my own testimony in the final pages of this Bible. I do pray most fervently that Almighty God will not judge this act as blasphemy in defiling His great work with my pitiful tale, but as further atonement for the swamp of sins in which myself and my brethren did wallow, which is surely a deep and dismal stain upon this island. And I do pray that God may forgive me for using the base language of the heathen, for alas my waning body is like a dying candle which doth spit and splutter most disagreeably. Thus I lack the luxury of time to render my story unto Latin, which taketh my weary mind a much longer while. But I am consoled by the fact that God hath seemingly

spared me for this very purpose, which I do interpret as His blessing."

"That's convenient," said Jai. "He feels justified in his actions by the very fact that his god is permitting him to commit them."

"And so I write this, my last testament, in the light that God doth provide through the open roof, which doth pour most generously through my tiny window. I have survived these last days by catching rain water in my wooden bowl, as the Holy Grail did catch the very life blood of Christ. But alas, in great heaving fits of coughing, my gurgling lungs produce a most bloody concoction of phlegm, as if to make manifest the evidence of my previous evil that has been festering and fermenting within. These foul-smelling globules are verily and surely the gruesome harbingers of my own imminent demise..."

"I can vouch for that," Dan added. "The last few pages had spots of blood all over them."
"Primary evidence," said Jai.

"I am Judas, named after he who betrayed Jesus, and now I betray to posterity the dismal deeds of the Maledictines for the sake of those who come after me, to save their souls from the fiery retribution which did so ravenously devour my

brethren.

"But I am also Jude, named after our beloved brother of Jesus and Saint of Hopeless Causes, of which I surely am, for what penitence can make amends for the sins that I have committed? Yet still my heart doth hope that Our Most Merciful Father will grant me deliverance from eternal damnation and even, perchance, a place in the very humblest corner of His Most Divine and Excellent Kingdom.

"Before this day is out I shall surely be dead, and the most wicked reign of the Maledictines of Devilstone shall be finished, for I am the very last of their number. I do most fervently pray that my passing shall end the curse that for many centuries hath hung over this corner of the Earth like a fog most malignant, and that this island will at last shake off the yoke of that most terrible of names, and thenceforth be known as Godstone.

Into thy hands, Oh God, I commit my soul.

Finaliter Lux.

Judas Ultimus."

"I recognise those last words," said Jai.

"'At the end there is light'," said Dan. "Whoever carved his memorial stone simply lifted them from the text. They probably didn't even know what they meant, but being in Latin made them special..."

He folded the sheets of paper and replaced them in his blazer pocket while the other two digested what they'd heard.

"That was some confession," said Jai.

"He had a lot to get off his chest," said Dan.

"Shame he didn't get it off sooner," said Tom. "He might have been able to squeeze through that hole..."

"So the King's men must have used the tunnel," Jai thought aloud. "Jude said the soldiers came out of the very heart of the Chapel. So where would that be, Dan...?"

"Well, he describes the dome as its bosom so it would follow that the heart is directly beneath."

"Chaps, I think this calls for another expedition..."

"But aren't you exhausted after that match?"

"I was but Jude's revelations have given me a second wind."

"Really? Well here's mine..." Tom released a flatulent emission, to the disgust of his roommates. "And that's what I think of that idea."

Alderley knocked again on the door of the cottage. A fine rain was falling.

The lack of response brought some relief. He wasn't good at expressing his feelings, even fortified with fine brandy. Now at least he'd have more time to put the right words together...

"What do you want?"

He turned towards the voice. In the weak moonlight strained by cloud he saw she was wearing an overcoat but her head was uncovered. Her hair was wet and her face shone.

"You're drenched," he said. "Where have you been?"

"For a walk. Or is that not permitted here?" Anger flashed in her eyes. "Must I log my every movement on this Godforsaken little island?"

All the pretence and politeness of the afternoon was gone, as if washed away by the rain.

"I'm sorry. I didn't mean to pry..."

"You've been drinking."

"Oh, you know...Dutch courage and all that..."

She smiled, a little cruelly.

"Hasn't done Holland much good, has it?"

"No," he replied. "I suppose not..."

"Why are you here?"

"I wanted to talk to you."

"Not now. I'm expecting someone."

"The Captain?"

"What makes you think that?"

"He keeps warning me off you."

"Well, he has no right to. He doesn't own me."

"Are you having an affair with him?"

The words had spilled out almost of their

own volition. Anger tightened her face and sharpened her accent.

"And what gives you the right to ask such a question...?"

"I'm in love with you."

Now she laughed.

"Don't be ridiculous. You hardly know me."

"I know enough. I've never met anyone like you."

She stared into him, her eyes black and fathomless. Then she pushed her body against his and kissed him hard, pressing him against her door before pulling away.

"Elena..."

He moved towards her but she brushed him aside and opened the door.

"Goodnight Michael."

Before he could protest she'd stepped into the darkness, slamming the door shut behind her.

He turned away to walk along the quayside, ascending the steps onto the harbour wall and looking down into the dark water. One moment it was surging up, the next it had dropped away in swirling eddies. He imagined himself falling into it, its surface closing quickly over the easy gift. But he knew he'd never allow himself to be drowned. The cold would shock him out of his melancholy, and the fear of death would drive his limbs to save himself.

The rain had eased off. He sat on the edge

of the harbour wall to smoke a cigarette, legs dangling enticingly over the hungry water. Across the bay he could just make out Pristow in the darkness enforced by the black-out, and to his left the long dark shape of Dragon Head. In daylight he'd often wondered why the headland was named so, but now - silhouetted against the night sky - he clearly saw the spine of a great sleeping beast, rising to a head-like crest. Beyond it, the three prominent rocks were like the bent claws of the monster, half-submerged, ready to rip open the belly of any vessel that ventured too close. And there was the dark tower protruding horn-like from the creature's snout: a lighthouse without a light.

Flicking his cigarette end into the water - its tiny glow instantly extinguished - he began to make his way back along the quayside. Then he stopped, seeing something ahead. Sensing danger he moved behind the telephone box, then watched.

A figure with a walking stick was limping along the cobbled road, hunched up against the returning rain. It stopped at the door of the end cottage, very close to the telephone box. Alderley held his breath, certain that the rapid beats of his heart would give him away.

The brass end of the stick rapped against the door. It opened and a pool of light flooded out, its edge nearly reaching Alderley's hiding place.

Elena stood in the doorway, wearing a long red evening dress and scarlet lipstick. It was the first time Alderley had seen her in make-up. The Captain placed his hand on her waist as he kissed her on the cheek. As she moved aside to let him in, her eyes swept the night. For an instant she seemed to look directly at Alderley, then she closed the door.

He decided to burst in and confront them, but by the time he'd reached the doorstep his anger had receded as quickly as it had rallied. From inside the cottage he could hear music; a slow guitar intro, then male voices in perfect harmony:

I don't want to set the world on fire
I just want to start a flame in your heart
In my heart I have but one desire
And that one is you
No other will do...

He turned and walked away from her door, along the winding road that led up through the orchard to school. The branches of the apple trees moved in the wind, their dying leaves whispering ancient secrets. His mind's eye kept returning to her front room, the two of them now dancing like she'd danced with him.

He felt a sickness in the pit of his stomach.

Passing through the dark gatehouse, he

glanced over in the direction of Chapel.

The ancient windows were glowing with a faint light from within.

"So this must be it," said Jai. "The heart of the Chapel, according to Jude…"

The three were standing beneath the dome. In the torchlight they studied the floor's flag stones. Some were graves, inscribed with names and dates. None showed any signs of disturbance.

"Well," said Dan, "if there is a tunnel, either it's been filled in or its entrance has been moved."

"A change of heart," Tom muttered, still smarting from being dragged out on another dangerous and probably fruitless escapade.

Jai directed the torch's beam at the roof above them. It was the first time any of them had really noticed the dome's decoration. Now they gawped at the ancient frieze extending around its circumference. A faded mosaic depicted a battle scene: soldiers in helmets holding shields and brandishing swords, attacking a group of long-haired semi-naked figures.

"Romans versus Celts," said Dan. "Must be a memorial to those fallen in the final battle for the island."

Tom pointed at a line of letters extending

around the base of the dome.

"Is that some kind of code...?"

Jai shone his torch along the line:

U S Q U E Q U A Q U E T R I A V I A

"Usquequaque Tria Via," he read aloud. "Always Three Ways..."

"So it is," said Tom. "Well, there can't be many schools that got their motto from the Romans. But what's it got to do with killing a load of poor Kelps?"

"No idea. Dan...?"

Dan was staring at the mosaic frieze, trying to apply logic to the wayward thoughts in his mind, as the invaders had so violently imposed order upon the wild islanders long ago. Then he smiled, pointing at a detail in the picture: a Roman soldier apparently emerging from out of the ground.

"Remember what Jude said? First they tried to invade by land, then sea. Only their third attempt was successful..."

"Underground," said Jai. "And this is our third visit, so perhaps tonight we'll triumph too..."

A sudden sound froze their blood: footsteps outside. Jai switched off the torch, plunging them into almost complete darkness, but for the night-glow of the round window and a faint rectangular shape beneath it. Grabbing his friends Jai pulled them towards the altar as the door creaked open.

Electric light flooded the Chapel, so bright through the altar cloth under which the three now cowered that they felt sure they could be seen. They held their breaths as they listened to the crisp clean click of metalled heels approaching up the aisle, halting within a few yards of the altar. Tom almost prayed for discovery, to end the pain of anticipation.

"Who's there?" a voice called out, very close. "Come out and show yourselves!"

Alderley listened to the echo of his words dying away and contemplated the altar before him. He'd jettisoned religion a long time ago, yet its stubborn spell still lingered. He considered the possibility of someone hiding beneath the altar, but an invisible force seemed to be preventing him from investigating. Whether this force had its origin in the altar or himself, he wasn't sure.

Dismissing the light he'd seen as the product of spirits - alcohol-induced rather than supernatural - he walked over to the dragon lectern. With his hands resting upon the open Bible and water dripping onto the text from his soaked hair, he surveyed the empty pews in front of him. Then he spoke, mimicking the Reverend's Welsh accent, enjoying the manner in which the rich phrases rolled from his tongue and rebounded around the Chapel walls.

"Now listen, boyos. You will all burn in damnation for eternity and there's absolutely bugger all you can do, isn't it...?"

Tom clamped a hand over his mouth, stifling a laugh. When Alderley spoke again his voice had changed, now sharp and clipped:

"Now pay attention, all of you. As Headmaster of this school I want to make one thing unequivocally clear: I am the biggest bastard this side of Berlin. So remember Alderley, hands off the Spaniard."

The three beneath the altar looked at each other, wide-eyed. Then Alderley spoke a third time, in his own voice now which trembled with emotion:

"Elena Montserrat, you are driving me to Hell!"

Anger flared again within him. He was about to pick up the huge Bible and throw it to the floor, in fury at the cruel injustice of the world, but then another idea came to him: a less-destructive method of discharging his rage.

Striding over to the flight of stairs behind the choir stalls, he ascended to the tiny organ loft nestled behind the great triangle of pipes. He sat down at the three-tiered keyboard, found the switch that operated the electric air pump then pulled out every one of the many pipe stops arrayed on either side of him. For a moment his hands hovered above the keys - fingers splayed, claw-like - then he struck, his feet simultaneously stamping on the row of wooden pedals beneath.

He possessed no musical talent yet he derived some cathartic satisfaction in operating this great engine of sound. Cocooned in the random tangle of cords swirling around him he lost all track of time and space...until he sensed a presence that made him stop and turn. The echoes of his cacophony skulked into the dark corners of the Chapel, and died.

The Captain was leaning arms-folded against the doorway, wearing an expression of bemusement.

"The Phantom of the Opera, I presume...?"

"Headmaster." Alderley's confidence was bolstered by the brandy. "Good evening."

"And what precisely do you think you're doing?"

"I thought I saw some light..."

"Well, there's certainly some light now. Tell me, do you wish us to be bombed? It wouldn't surprise me, following your demolition of the Science Department..."

"Sorry. Forgot about the black-out..."

"How did you get in?"

"The door was unlocked."

"Really? Then I shall be having words with the Reverend...Now get back to Prophets and don't let me catch you trespassing again. You don't have the run of the place, you know. This isn't Butlins."

"But isn't God's house open to everyone...?"

"No."

Alderley stifled a hiccup.

"Completely understand, Headmaster. I know my place." There was more than a hint of sarcasm in his slurs. "I'm just a mere foot soldier restricted to the barracks or the battlefield. But you...you can visit any place you want, at any time you wish. And anyone..."

He rose unsteadily from the stool, aiming for the exit, but found his path blocked. The Captain had raised his walking stick horizontally across the doorway.

"Have you been spying on me?"

"Not at all. I was just out for a walk and happened to notice you entering Miss Montserrat's house..."

Now the Captain directed the end of his stick to Alderley's chest.

"I feel no obligation to explain myself to you, of all people. However, as a matter of fact, we were playing chess."

Alderley held the Captain's stare. The pressure of the stick's tip upon his chest increased.

"You know," the Captain continued, "I'm still not sure if you're either very brave or very stupid..."

"To be honest," Alderley replied, "I'm not very anything, really. Pretty middle-of-the-road, in fact. And a trifle squiffy right now…"

"Well let me remind you of something then. As I explained to you at the beginning of term, you're not expendable. And if I catch you sniffing around in places you shouldn't be again, you will be out like that." The Captain clicked his fingers. The snap echoed around the Chapel, as if the very building itself was expressing its support. "You've had two chances now. Two and a half if I count your insolence after the match today. I won't give you a third."

"I understand."

"And by the way, my meeting with Miss Montserrat tonight never happened."

"Which meeting would that be, Headmaster…?"

The Captain lowered his stick.

"Correct response. You may go."

"Thank you." Alderley made to leave then hesitated, swaying slightly. "Oh, one more thing. Just out of interest…"

"Yes?"

"Did you beat her?"

"What?"

"The game. Did you win?"

The Captain smiled coldly.

"I did."

"Really?" Alderley returned the smile. "And so

quickly..."

The Captain opened his mouth to respond but Alderley was already descending the steps.

The three beneath the altar listened to Alderley's footsteps receding, followed by the Captain's characteristic limp soon afterwards. Only when the lights had been clicked off, the door closed and the key turned in the lock did they dare to speak.

"Jai," said Dan, "you forgot to lock the door."

"I know." Jai switched his torch on and the three blinked in the new light. "My mistake. Sorry chaps."

"Then again," said Tom, "if you had locked it we wouldn't have ear-wigged all that juicy scandal..."

"True. Sticky and Helluva, eh? I wonder what Lady Carrot would think, if she knew..."

"I thought Cowardly was quite brave, standing up to Sticky like that."

"And the poor chap's clearly head-over-heels for Helluva."

"Him and the rest of the school..."

"I didn't think much of his music," said Dan. "There should be a law against abusing an organ in that way."

Jai and Tom laughed, exchanging a glance.

"What?"

"We'll explain later..." Tom began to crawl out from their hiding place. "Well, this has all been very exciting but I think I can hear my darling bed calling for me..."

"Wait!"

"What now, Jai...?"

"Look!"

Tom poked his head back under the altar cloth. In the torchlight he saw that the floor on which they'd been crouching wasn't all stone. There was a large square of dark wood set into it, with an iron ring at its edge like a door knocker.

"Bloody Hell. A trap door..."

"Of course," said Dan, annoyed at himself for missing what now seemed so obvious. "The altar is the heart of every temple..."

Jai pulled on the ring and the trap door opened, swinging over to rest on the ground. Tom closed his eyes, dreading the sight of another skeleton grinning up at him.

"Just look at that," Dan whispered with a hushed reverence.

Tom opened his eyes. To his deep relief there was no corpse. Instead, Jai's torch illuminated a narrow stone stairway winding down into darkness.

"I don't believe it," Tom muttered. "A secret passage..."

Jai began to descend the steps and the other two followed, all three compelled by the irresistible pull of curiosity. Down they spiralled, their shoulders brushing against the prehistoric basalt of Devilston's core.

"How deep does this go?" Tom wondered aloud. "To the bottom of the sea?"

"If it leads down to the tunnel," said Dan, "then deeper..."

At last they emerged from the staircase into a low passageway carved out of solid rock, stretching into blackness to left and right. The air was cold and dank and carried a faint smell of the sea, her influence reaching even here. A slow drip echoed in the dark, like the tick of a clock.

"Well," said Jai, "if this isn't a tunnel then Hitler is a Hindu."

"Remarkable," said Dan, hardly believing his eyes. "It really exists..."

"So which way do we go?" asked Tom. "Right or left?"

In the spiral descent all three had lost their bearings.

"Well, Cornwall's in one direction," said Jai, "and in the other...who knows? Ireland? America...?"

"I've got a coin..." Tom dug into his pockets, producing a handful of detritus from which he fished a shiny penny. "Heads left, tails right."

The coin caught the light as it span in the air. Tom grabbed at it, and missed. Dan picked it up, in the torchlight studying the side facing upwards: a woman wearing a Roman helmet and holding a shield and a trident, a lighthouse in the background. It could have been Devilston depicted in female form.

"Tails it is," said Jai.

They walked hunched over due to the low ceiling, and with the tunnel's upward gradient Tom struggled to keep up. He was relieved when they came to its end: a small door of ancient wood, studded with thick-headed nails and secured with three large iron bolts. Jai began to slide them open.

"Hang on," said Tom, out of breath. "What if there's something dangerous behind that door…?"

"Like the Hound of the Baskervilles?" Jai grinned.

"Or the Dragon of the Morrigans?" Dan suggested, thinking of gargoyles."We can have a look first…"

Dan opened a small viewing panel in the door. The torch beam sliced through the darkness beyond, sweeping across a large circular space with a domed ceiling constructed of uneven stones.

"Can't see any monsters," said Jai.

He slid the final bolt and pushed on the door. It opened with a painful creak and the three found themselves at the top of a flight of stone steps leading down to the floor of the chamber.

The probing torchlight found many recesses built into the curved wall, containing objects which looked at first sight like collections of ornaments: vases, carvings and jewellery, perhaps. A familiar smell hung in the air, reminiscent of Jude's tomb. As Jai led the way down the steps, Tom realised the true nature of this collection of artifacts: not man-made, but made of men.

"Bones…"

Each of the dozens of recesses contained a skeleton yellowed with great age, in parts crumbling to dust. All lay in extreme stillness, their jaws hanging open in silent screams, their black eye sockets gazing vacantly into space, as if in contemplation of eternity. The three should have turned and fled at the sight, but their encounter with Jude seemed to have provided a degree of immunity to panic.

"A burial chamber," said Dan, in awe. "But who are they…?"

"Well they're not Morrigans because they're all in the Crypt," said Jai.

"No. These are much older. Roman, possibly. Or even Celts…"

"Remember what Jude said, about King Arthur's knights…?"

Dan was struck silent by the magnitude of that possibility.

"So where's their armour?" Tom was trying to

avoid the skulls' dark stares. "Their swords and shields and what-not…?"

"Probably stolen," said Dan. "You know what Devilston's like…"

"Or hanging in the Dining Hall," said Jai, only half-joking.

"Do you really think these could be the Knights of the Round Table?"

Tom was beginning to doubt his own inherent skepticism.

"Perhaps," said Dan, "though I can't see much sign of them coming to life to save the nation…"

"So which one's King Arthur…?"

Now Jai's torch beam lingered on a skeleton.

"Him."

Tom's heart skipped a beat.

"How do you know?"

"Because he just winked at me."

"Not funny, Jai."

"I think we'd better leave them in peace," said Dan, "whoever they are…"

For once Tom took the lead, keen to vacate the place.

"Well that's enough excitement for one night," he said as Jai slid the bolts home. "For one lifetime, actually…"

"But don't you want to see what's at the other end?"

Jai shone the torch along the tunnel.

"We might as well," said Dan, "while we're

down here. In for a penny, as the British say."

"That reminds me…" Tom was distracted from his anxiety. "Could I have my coin back please? It's my lucky penny, you see…"

"Of course." Dan produced the coin from his pocket and gave it to Tom. "Sorry. Forgot about it in all the excitement…"

The three made their way along the tunnel, Jai in front with Tom at the rear. The threat of skeletons in pursuit kept Tom's pace up, and the fact that it was a downhill journey, at least until they reached the staircase entrance. Beyond, the slope levelled out.

"All that rock on top of us," Tom panted as they walked.

"Not just rock," said Jai. "The tide's in so just think of the extra weight of water…"

"Thanks for that."

"Don't listen to him," said Dan, re-assuring himself as well as Tom. "This tunnel has been here for two thousand years."

The tunnel's construction appeared solid enough, the walls looking as fresh and smooth as if they'd been carved yesterday.

"What's this?"

Jai stopped abruptly, the other two bumping into him and cursing. They'd come to an opening in the left-hand wall of the tunnel. It was ragged-edged and asymmetrical, as if some huge and blundering creature with no respect for human craftsmanship had forced its way through. Jai shone his torch into the hole: another tunnel led into darkness, its ceiling supported by timber beams, some cracked and looking close to collapse. The floor of this passageway - littered with debris - was higher than that of the Roman tunnel.

"Looks like some kind of mine," said Jai.

"Bit messy," said Tom.

"The work of modern explosives rather than Roman slaves, I should think…"

"Why is the floor at a different level?"

"They might have broken into this tunnel by accident," said Dan. "It's probably part of the tin mine on the headland."

"A door into a corridor of more," Jai pondered.

"Well, I think we should leave that for another day."

"How about never," said Tom. "It looks highly dangerous…Now what are you doing…?"

Jai was climbing into the hole.

"Just having a quick shufti…"

The mine tunnel was even lower than the Roman one, Jai having to stoop to avoid the beams. As he walked he wondered how far he should continue, the pull of adventure versus the drag of his duty to his friends.

He came to an abrupt stop, the decision made for him. The floor had disappeared and he found himself teetering on the edge of a large hole.

It extended across the width of the tunnel and deep into its walls on either side, as if some great blade had slashed clean through the rock.

He shone his torch into the void but its depths lay beyond the stretch of the beam. So he picked up a stone and lobbed it over the edge, then waited.

Not even the faintest report of its impact returned.

"Jai!" Tom's voice was distant. "Come back!"

"Hang on!"

Jai's attention had caught on something glistening in the tunnel's ceiling, just beyond the edge of the hole. Placing his torch on the floor, he drew his kukri from its sheath. Then - leaning over the edge with great care - he managed to reach the shining object with the tip of his knife, jabbing at it until it was dislodged. But in catching the falling fragment he nearly lost his balance and only some frantic windmilling prevented him from toppling into the abyss.

"Where have you been?" Tom demanded when Jai returned. "Do you know how long we've been standing here in the pitch black?"

"Of course he does," said Dan wearily. "He's been away for the same length of time."

Dan was just relieved to see light again. In the darkness he'd been fighting a constant battle against his fear, Tom's grumbling his only distraction. He hadn't won, but then neither had he lost himself to blind panic.

Jai licked a spot of blood from his finger, having nicked himself with the kukri in keeping with its lore. Then he held up his small but glittering prize.

"Gold…" Tom muttered in deep reverence, eyes wide.

Dan took the small rock from Jai for closer scrutiny.

"Fool's gold."

Jai's smile vanished.

"Are you sure?"

"Iron pyrite. You can tell by the crystals."

"Worthless then."

"Not quite." Dan pocketed the rock. "I know a good use for it…"

"What?"

Tom was only half-interested now, his dreams deflated.

"Sh!" Jai hissed suddenly.

"I only asked."

"I can hear something. Listen…"

The three stood still, their ears straining the air. The faintest sound came to them, hardly more than a thought.

"Singing," said Jai. "And it's coming from the end of this tunnel…"

Now he began to walk in the direction of the sound, as if enchanted.

"As per usual," Tom mumbled as he and Dan followed. "Onwards into danger…"

As they progressed the singing grew louder. There were many voices: some tuneful and harmonious, others raucous and discordant, but all singing as one. Echoing down the tunnel, the song seemed eerie and unearthly.

"Sounds like pirates," said Tom.

"Or smugglers," said Dan.

"Is there a difference…?"

They came to an entrance leading to another spiral stairway. At its top they found a space barely big enough for three, with curved wooden walls and a round hatch in front of them. Jai put his ear to the little door and listened.

"I don't think they're on the other side," he whispered. "Sounds like they're further away…"

Tom was still out of breath from the climb.

"That doesn't mean…there isn't somebody else…on the other side…"

Jai switched off the torch.

"What are you doing?" Tom protested in the darkness.

Dan remained quiet, grappling with his fear again.

"Well," said Jai, "if there **is** someone on the other side we don't want to make it easy for them, do we…?"

He took hold of the handle in the centre of the

hatch and pushed. It didn't move so he pulled, still without success.

"Try turning it," said Dan.

"But it's fixed to the door..."

"I know. But just try anyway."

With a groan the whole hatch now turned and opened like the lid of a jar, allowing light to flood into the space. Jai was impressed.

"How did you know that?"

"Always three ways, remember...?"

Dan was smiling, relieved he could see again.

After carefully laying the hatch on the floor in front of him, Jai surveyed the territory beyond. Warm light was leaking down a flight of stone steps from a slightly-open door at the top, illuminating a cellar containing large wooden barrels piled on their sides. At first he thought of gunpowder and Guy Fawkes, but a familiar bitter-sweet tang hung in the air which reminded him of his father. Now he saw that the strange round space from which he was peering was a large beer barrel, lying on its side on the bottom row of a pile: the perfect disguise for a secret entrance.

The singing was loud now, coming from the doorway at the top of the stairs. It was difficult to make out the words of the verses - possibly because many of the singers were themselves unsure of them - but there was no doubting the chorus:

And shall Trelawny live?
And shall Trelawny die?
Here's twen'y thousand Cornish men
Will know the reason why!

Jai passed his torch to Dan then moved swiftly across the cellar floor, pausing at the foot of the stairs. He glanced back at the open barrel and glimpsed the illuminated faces of his two friends watching him, then he ascended the steps.

Peering through the slight crack in the door, he saw the low-beamed saloon of a public house filled with drinkers: men and women with glowing faces and shining eyes brighter than any gold, some swinging glasses and mugs in the air, their contents sloshing about. The gathered were singing with all their hearts and Jai could feel the warmth of their common humanity. He found himself longing to be among them, this glorious and unruly congregation.

In a slow and roaring crescendo the song came to an end, followed by a great cheer and the smashing of several glasses. Most of the crowd was soft-headed and misty-eyed on a brew of alcohol, nostalgia and Saturday night revelry, but one pair of eyes retained a sober vigilance. They belonged to a huge bearded man - undoubtedly the landlord - standing behind the bar, his folded arms like two great headlands before the massive mainland of his chest. Next to him stood a girl in a floral summer dress with a curly cascade of golden hair. Crouching down to get something from beneath the bar she disappeared from view, only to immediately re-appear within feet of Jai's hiding place, carrying a handful of empty glasses. Jai was confused by this girl's casual disregard of the laws of physics, and bewitched by her beauty.

What manner of magic is this...?

Something caused the landlord to look over to the cellar door. It was ajar and - in the gap - he thought he saw an eye blink in a dark face. For a moment the eye looked back at him, before vanishing. The landlord hesitated, wondering if he'd imagined it. Then he steered his massive frame in the direction of the cellar.

"Where's old Cador off to?" someone called out.

"Prob'ly someone helpin' themselves to free beer," said another.

"Or his girls!" The comment was met with a roar of amusement. "Reckon I'd brave his wrath for a kiss off of one o' them beauties!"

Darting down the cellar steps, Jai dived back into the barrel and fumbled to replace the hatch behind him. His command to his two friends was swift and unambiguous:

"Run!"

"So what did you see?"

Dan was slumped in his chair, safely back in their dormistudy.

"The King's Head..." Jai had resumed his perch on the window ledge, still restless with excitement. "The pub must stand on the site of Pristow's chapel."

"No doubt destroyed by the King's men at the same time they routed Devilston..."

"You should have seen it. The place was full of punters, having a splendid old time."

"So why all the rush?" asked Tom, lying exhausted on his bunk.

"I thought the landlord had seen me but now I'm not so sure... My God, the size of the man. He was like a veritable mountain..."

"Perhaps he **was** following us but got stuck in that barrel..."

"Well Jai," said Dan, "you might be right about the tunnel being a smuggling route, after all."

"I bet the landlord is the other end of the operation," Jai thought aloud, "distributing all the booty..."

"We should go to the police," said Tom.

"There was a policeman in the pub, even though it was past closing time. The local constabulary are probably in on it as well, enjoying the rewards for turning a blind eye..."

"So what do we do then?"

"Well Tom, we can sit and sweat it out, wondering if they know that we know about the tunnel. Or we can make the most of our discovery. Then if they do catch up with us, at least we haven't wasted the opportunity..."

"What opportunity?"

"What opportunity?" Jai was flabbergasted. "Tell him, Dan."

"Well..." Dan began, then faltered. "What opportunity, Jai?"

"I don't believe I'm hearing this. Gentlemen, we've just discovered a secret passage to the wonderful world of women..."

Now Jai recalled the lovely double-vision in the pub.

"Girls..." said Tom dreamily, as if hearing talk of mythical creatures. With his hands behind his head, he closed his eyes and smiled.

9

MINUS ONE

I t was Sunday evening. Tom was wrestling with the maths prep he'd put off until the fag end of the weekend until - with a deep sigh - he disengaged from the problem, allowing the numbers and symbols to entangle themselves again.

"I'll help you in a minute, Tom…"

Dan was working on some unidentified device. Various scavenged materials littered his desk.

"Come on then," said Jai. "Aren't you going to tell us what are you up to?"

Sitting on the window ledge he was savouring the last of the Cuban cigars liberated from the Crypt, careful to blow the smoke out of the open window.

"It's a surprise," Dan replied. "You'll just have to wait and see…"

"I think it's a time machine," said Tom, "so we can save poor old Jude the Last from his ultimate fate…"

Now Dan sat back to admire his work.

"There."

He'd fixed the cylindrical cigar container to the base of a wooden pencil box. Copper wire 'borrowed' during one of Alderley's chaotic lessons had been tightly wrapped round the cylinder. A length of thicker wire rested on this coil, its other end fixed to the base with a small screw. From this screw protruded an arc of fine wire, its other end touching the heart of the machine (secured by a lump of chewing gum): a small nugget of gleaming ore.

Closely studying the mysterious construction, Tom pointed at the iron pyrite.

"Is that the fool's gold from the mine?"

"It is," said Dan. "You see? There's a use for everything…"

Now standing on his chair, he used a knife smuggled from the Dining Hall to unscrew the wooden cover of the tannoy speaker above the door.

"Is that a good idea?" Tom worried. "If Sticky finds out he'll have your bowels for braces…Oh great. Now I'm an accessory to the crime…"

Dan had handed the cover to Tom. He then connected two wires running from his contraption to terminals within the tannoy's innards. When he'd stuck these wires to the edge of the door frame with more chewing gum and replaced the tannoy's cover, only the keenest-eyed would have noticed that the speaker had been tampered with.

He took another long piece of wire which was fixed to the device and wound it several times around the leg of his desk. A small lead fishing weight he'd found on the rocks was tied to the other end and this he handed to Jai, instructing him to lower it out of the window.

"Well, this is it..."

Dan operated the rudimentary switch on his instrument - a paper clip and two drawing pins - and they heard the faintest hiss from the loudspeaker above the door. As he slowly moved the end of the thicker wire along the cylinder, the loudspeaker emitted strange unearthly notes which twisted and warped in pitch; then - very distant yet unmistakable - the music of a dance band emerged from the jungle of noise.

"It's a wireless!" Jai exclaimed. "Dan, you're a genius!"

"Not really." But Dan couldn't help feeling pleased with himself. "My father made one of these when we had to sell our radio. It's called a cat's whisker crystal set. There's the cat's whisker..." He pointed at the fine length of wire that touched the iron pyrite, then at the lump of rock itself: "...and there's the crystal."

"Where did you get the whisker?" asked Tom.

Dan smiled.

"From the cat that Curiosity killed…"

"But what produces the power?" asked Jai. "I can't see any battery…"

"The radio station provides the energy," Dan explained. "The radio wave passes along the aerial hanging out of the window and into this crystal, where the signal is separated from the carrier wave. Then the loudspeaker converts the signal into sound waves."

"So moving that bit of wire along the cylinder is how you tune in to different stations?"

"Exactly. By altering the number of coils I'm changing the frequency of radio wave that can be picked up."

Dan demonstrated and the music faded into a hiss, as if submerged once more beneath an invisible sea. It was replaced by an urgent voice:

"…**calling. Germany calling. Germany calling…**"

Tom recognised it immediately.

"Lord Haw-Haw!"

"Lord Who…?"

Jai was unfamiliar with wireless broadcasts, his father rarely listening to them. Through his close contact with the London elite, the Maharaja of Jaisalpur derived most of the news from its source.

"He's this British traitor in Berlin," Tom explained, enjoying imparting knowledge for a change.

In a nasal drone the voice was reporting on a pact between Germany, Italy and Japan:

"...three great peoples uniting in the most formidable military force this world has ever seen. And so, in the shadow of this historic alliance, what hope remains for a certain little island and its withering colonies...?"

"Change the station," said Jai as the voice gloated over the tonnage of British ships sunk since the last transmission. "This man is annoying me..."

But Dan was reluctant to re-tune. It was coming from Germany and - as repulsive as its sentiments were - it felt like a connection to his family.

"...which brings me to a story from which the British newspapers have been making something of a meal, but one that rather sticks in the throat: namely, the recent sinking of the *SS Star of the Ganges*..."

Dan removed his hand from the device, his attention now riveted on the flat voice emanating from the box above the door.

"Mister Churchill has seen fit to condemn this tragic incident in which a vessel carrying civilian passengers - many of them children - was torpedoed at night, resulting in the loss of her entire complement. However, your esteemed Prime Minister conveniently failed to mention that not only was this ship sailing

unlit and unmarked, it was also the flagship of a convoy escorted by warships of the Royal Navy. Now Mister Churchill knows very well that these factors made it a legitimate military target according to the Rules of War: a war, incidentally, that the British government chose to declare upon Germany.

"And to ordinary Britons, whom I believe to be a sensible and reasonable people who deserve better than their corrupt and mendacious leaders, I put this simple question: how many submarine captains are equipped with x-ray devices which allow them to identify the cargo of a potential target...?

"So Mister Churchill, who are the true villains of this piece? None other than His Britannic Majesty's Royal Navy, for recklessly herding children across the Atlantic like so many lambs to the slaughter..."

"Those poor people..."

Tom was trying to imagine being trapped in a sinking ship in the middle of the night, in the middle of the Atlantic.

"Can you find some music again?" asked Jai. "I think we need to lighten the mood..."

Dan was staring into space.

"Dan?"

"*Bitte*...? Oh yes. Of course..."

He adjusted the tuner until he found the dance band again, then rose from his chair.

"Are you going to play along?" asked Tom, seeing his friend taking the violin case from his small wardrobe.

"No." Dan smiled as he extracted the old violin and its bow from the case. "I'm just going outside to practise..."

"At this time of night?"

"I'll be alright. I just need some time alone."

"What's up?" asked Jai, seeing a deep sadness in his friend's eyes.

Dan paused before replying. He'd wanted to avoid contaminating the evening any further.

"He didn't mention there were Germans onboard, but I suppose British people would have less sympathy if they knew that..."

"How do you know there were Germans onboard, Dan?"

"Because my friends were on that ship. And I was due to sail on her myself..."

Dan slipped out of the room and quietly closed the door behind him, leaving his friends to digest his words in dismay.

As if drawn by some supernatural force Dan found himself heading for the raised circle of dark shapes at the corner of the cricket pitch. He entered the Crown of Stones and sat on the low rectangle of rock in its centre. Noticing a small slit in the middle of it, he wondered if this might be the very stone from which King Arthur had extracted Excalibur...

Now he looked out across the sea. As cloud moved across the waning moon, his thoughts grew darker. The tide was coming in and the pitch where Devilston's epic victory over Rockenough had been played out was now a black and restless mass. The rock pool Charlotte had told him about - and in which he had yet to swim - was a boiling cauldron. Upon the same rocks where the school had gathered to watch the match, waves were violently sacrificing themselves.

There was some order in the way these rollers advanced relentlessly to their doom, but he knew they were driven by the chaotic force of a mighty storm far out to sea. And in their final death throes, anarchy reigned again.

Somewhere in that same sea are my friends, buried in a steel tomb.

He looked down at the violin on his lap, remembering Herr Bruschell's warm smile as he'd pressed it into Dan's arms.

"Remember us when you play her."

He lifted the violin to his chin. The tune came randomly to him, the tips of his fingers crafting a kind of melody from the raw material produced by the sawing of the bow. Though the music soothed his heart and calmed his mind, he was aware of the grief shifting deep within him like some restless animal.

A noise behind made him stop: the thud of heavy footfalls on the mown grass and a deep reverberating snort. Dan stood up - turning - to see a great form entering the circle, slowly advancing on him from out of the night: a huge white creature almost luminous in the moonlight, with a long head and big black eyes.

For a moment, and in spite of his commitment to the power of reason, Dan believed he was confronting a great dragon. Then a voice came to him, from a figure mounted on the beast.

"What beautiful music…"

Dan watched the rider dismount: an elderly woman who now led the horse by its reins towards him. She wore riding breeches, boots and an overcoat. Her face looked as old as rock but her eyes shone fresh in the moonlight and when her silvery hair blew across her face she'd stroke it aside, like a young woman in a summer breeze.

"What were you playing?"

"Oh, not much," Dan replied shyly. "I was just making it up."

"Really? It sounded quite…" she searched for the word, "…ethereal. I could hear it from the beach, as if I'd tuned into something." She smiled. "What's your name?"

"Rosenbaum."

Despite the kindness in her voice, Dan had responded automatically with his surname, trained by the system.

"Ah yes. Charlotte told me all about you, and your talent..."

"Are you the...Dowager Duchess of Devilston?"

"Rather a mouthful, isn't it? My friends call me Jennifer. What do your friends call you...?"

"Dan."

"Hallo Dan."

They shook hands.

"I read about your husband's life in the Chronicle."

"He was a good man. Sadly, too good for this place...."

She stroked the horse's neck lovingly. Taking her lead, Dan ran his hand along the soft warm flank, wary of the animal's latent power.

"Is this Merlin?"

"It is. Getting on a bit now but there's still plenty of life left in the old boy. We've been down on the sands. He loves to gallop through the shallows, just like Julian used to ride him..." She glanced in the direction of the beach, as if expecting to see her husband down there. "So Dan, what brings you out here at this ungodly hour...?"

"I just needed to be alone for a while. I've received some bad news, you see."

"Your family?"

"My friends. They were on a ship that was sunk…"

Listening to himself saying the words was like hearing the news for the first time and now he felt the grief rising to the surface. Seeing the pain in his eyes and hearing his voice break, Jennifer stepped forward.

"You poor thing…"

As she embraced him Dan remembered his mother hugging him for the last time at the station, as if she knew she'd never see him again. In the interests of maintaining a manly composure, he hadn't cried then. In fact, he couldn't remember the last time he'd discharged the emotion which seemed to press on his chest like an invisible hand; sometimes lightly, often chokingly heavy, but always there.

Now at last he allowed himself to weep, in deep satisfying waves which seemed to ease the ache inside him and resolve the conflict between his head and his heart; for his head could not comprehend that his friends were dead, while in his heart he knew it was true.

"Be careful Daniel," the Duchess whispered, so softly that Dan almost believed he was hearing her thoughts. "This place isn't safe…"

A sharp voice broke their embrace and startled Merlin, causing him to shift around uneasily.

"So what's this?" said the Captain as he joined them. "A secret rendezvous in a sacred circle, eh? I smell the whiff of intrigue, or is that just the horse...?"

"Daniel's received some bad news."

The Duchess's voice had hardened.

"Ah yes. That awful sinking, I presume...Still, lucky for you, eh Rosenbaum? You must be feeling pretty relieved you came here instead..."

"Not really, sir. All my friends were onboard."

"Well done, Ralph." Now there was a bite in the Duchess's voice. "Always ready with the right word for every occasion."

"But tell me something," the Captain continued, ignoring his mother-in-law, "how did you hear about it...?"

Dan didn't reply. Sensing he was hiding something, the Duchess came to his aid.

"I told him, though it should have been you..."

Now the Captain found himself on the defensive.

"But why cause unnecessary upset? After all, Rosenbaum's friends were heading for Canada. He'd probably never have seen them again anyway."

"They promised to write," said Dan. "I'd have at least heard from them again..."

"Well, that's all conjecture now, isn't it? But you must be brave. War is a terrible thing indeed, but we have to face adversity like men."

"And certainly not women," the Duchess added, dryly.

"Now off you go back to your house, Rosenbaum. Considering the circumstances, I shall overlook the fact that you've been trespassing."

The Duchess laughed bitterly.

"How magnanimous…"

Dan was keen to remove himself from a hostile arena.

"Good night."

"Good night Daniel," said the Duchess as he left the stone circle. "And remember what I said…"

The Captain waited until Dan was out of earshot. In spite of his anger his voice remained calm and cold:

"You know, I find it particularly unhelpful to have my authority undermined in the presence of a pupil."

The Duchess smiled.

"Anything I can do to make your job more difficult, Ralph. And by the way, I take exception to your implication of impropriety in what was a simple gesture of condolence."

"Apologies for my misinterpretation." The Captain's words dripped with insincerity. "After all, you have an unblemished reputation to protect."

"But don't we all, Ralph…?"

Ruffled, the Captain changed tack.

"Your efforts to weaken my position are quite futile, you know. I now enjoy the full support of the Staff, while you have...what exactly...?"

"The Law." Placing a foot in Merlin's stirrup, the Duchess hoisted herself back into the saddle. "And as long as a Morrigan resides on this island, Devilston will belong to us. And I mean a Morrigan by blood, not marriage..."

Now the Captain pointed his stick at her, his anger stoked by the Duchess's air of arrogance and her elevated position over him.

"You people just don't get it, do you? The normal rules which have protected your privilege for centuries are falling apart around you, and yet still you speak as if you own the Universe. But ask yourself this, Your Ladyship: when you're gone, what will be left of the Morrigans of Devilston, except for **my** wife? And **my** son...?"

"**Your** son?" The Duchess paused, revelling in the spectacle of her son-in-law in such a state of agitation. "Are you quite sure about that, Ralph...?"

Like a volatile gas, the Captain's fury ignited.

"You...bitch!"

He raised his walking stick then brought it down hard on the horse's flank. Merlin reacted in pain and alarm, rearing up on his hind legs and toppling the Duchess from the saddle. Her head struck the corner of the centre stone as she fell, her cry instantly extinguished.

He was hiding in the secret compartment. Someone outside was incessantly tapping, as if trying to torment him. Others were huddled around him, very close. He could feel their cold touch on his skin. Not the cold of fear though, but death. And not people but skeletons.

Dan woke with a jolt, the nightmare instantly dispelled. Relieved, he lay in the darkness, waiting for his thumping heart to calm. But the tapping continued: rapid but irregular, and metallic. It was coming from the vertical heating pipe near his head. He shifted so that he could put his ear to it, his movement waking Tom in the bunk beneath.

"What's going on...?"

"There's a noise coming from the pipes," Dan whispered.

"Probably some air trapped in the system," Jai muttered from the top bunk opposite.

"No. I think it's man-made. Someone above is tapping with a pen or a foot or something, like people do when they're nervous. The pipe is amplifying it."

"Probably Cowardly," said Tom, "worried sick about having to blag his way through another lesson."

"Or beside himself with unrequited love for Helluva," Jai chuckled.

"Actually, I don't think it's either…"

Dan switched on the light. Tom protested noisily.

"Some of us are trying to get some shut-eye, you know?"

"Sorry but I've just thought of something…"

Dan climbed down and pulled his suitcase from under the bunk bed. Carefully lifting out his home-made wireless set, he placed the device on his desk and connected it to the loudspeaker and aerial.

As he operated the wire tuner the radio dipped in and out of talk and music, like a train travelling through stations, before halting at a stream of blips and bleeps.

"Sounds like a robot with verbal diarrhea," said Tom.

Now Jai sat up, suddenly wide awake.

"It's synchronized with the tapping."

"So Cowardly's tapping along to the wireless. Very interesting. Now, could you put the lights off please…?"

"But he's not tapping along with it, Tom. He's producing it. His desk must be touching the pipe."

"What?"

"Cowardly is transmitting a message," Dan explained. "I only wish I knew Morse Code."

"Wouldn't make much difference," said Jai. "The message would be encrypted anyway. So, it appears our science teacher is batting for the other side…"

Tom pondered for a moment.

"Really? He's pretty crazy about Helluva…"

Jai laughed.

"Not in that way."

Dan began to rummage beneath his mattress, Jai's cricket reference reminding him of something he'd forgotten in all the excitement of Jude's revelations and the discovery of the tunnel. He extracted the thin black book from its hiding place, quickly flicking through the pages of the Chronicle until he found the photographs.

"What do you think of these…?"

Jai studied the pictures.

"Well, how about that? It's Alderley when he was a pupil here."

"I can't put my finger on it but there's something not quite right about him…"

Now Jai looked closer.

"He's right-handed."

Dan clicked his fingers.

"Of course…"

Tom yawned.

"So what's that got to do with the price of eggs?"

"Nothing." Dan was puzzled by Tom's turn of

phrase. "But our Cowardly writes with his left hand."

"Well, maybe he can use both."

"And he's not much of a sportsman to boot," said Jai. "I haven't seen him so much as pick up a ball..."

"Hang on," said Tom. "Are you two suggesting Cowardly isn't actually Alderley...?"

"We are," said Dan. "Just like *The Man in the Iron Mask*."

"Who?"

"He was a doppelganger who replaced the King of France."

"A what?"

"A look-alike," Jai explained.

"It all makes sense," Dan continued. "That's why he's so bad at his job."

Tom remained confused.

"The King of France?"

"Alderley," said Jai, impatiently. "Or rather, Cowardly."

Dan thought aloud:

"They needed someone who could pose as an Old Devilstonian. That way he'd easily get a teaching job here. Of course he'd have to speak perfect English too, but a knowledge of science would have been a minor issue because he wouldn't need to be here for long. As for his left-handedness, they took the risk that no-one would notice..."

"Are we still talking about the French?" asked Tom.

Jai sighed.

"He's talking about the Germans. Our Cowardly is clearly a spy."

Tom immediately regurgitated the thought.

"I'm sorry but that's just ridiculous. I mean, why would there be a German spy here, in the back of beyond...?"

"Because the British are expecting an invasion of the south coast," said Dan. "An attack on North Cornwall would be a complete surprise..."

Jai completed the picture:

"So the Germans have sent out spies to survey the best landing places. And what better beach head than this island...?"

"A stepping stone," Dan added. "The Devil's Stone..."

The three were quiet for a while as they listened to the busy bleeping monotone from the loudspeaker, each imagining his own version of a dark army streaming along the Causeway into Britain, like an injection of some toxic concoction. Then - abruptly - the message ceased.

"Bloody Cowardly," said Tom. "I always thought he was a wrong 'un. Fancy our teacher being a Nazi..."

"Not for the first time," Dan muttered.

"We have to tell someone."

"Who?"

"Well, someone we can trust, I suppose..."

Jai laughed.

"In this place?"

"I think I have the solution," said Dan. "Jai, why don't you send another coded message to Jomsom and tell him to inform your father? He has lots of contacts in the government, hasn't he? He'll know who to talk to."

"Excellent idea. But I'll bypass Papa. He'll probably think the message a product of an over-active imagination. I'll instruct Jomsom to contact the authorities himself..."

The weathered union flag on Devilston's highest point flapped at half-mast all week. Now - on Friday afternoon - it hung limply, as if exhausted by its exertions. The ramparts were shrouded by a veil of low cloud and a cold sweat of fine but drenching drizzle darkened the castle's ancient stone. Each passing minute was marked by a distant chime ringing out across the bay, from the fog bell of the Dragon Head lighthouse.

The extended family of Morrigans converged on the ancestral pile for the Duchess's funeral. Their cars and taxis were like a line of black ants, come to pay homage to their dead queen.

The Captain delivered the eulogy and, for

once, the Reverend was relieved to defer to his authority. The news of the Duchess's death had been a lightening bolt to his heart. It had required the best part of a bottle of port for him to even countenance conducting the ceremony, and the rest of it to navigate his way through the fog of the service.

The Captain concluded his tribute with a confession:

"I'm sure Her Ladyship would have agreed with me that she and I did not, on occasion, see eye to eye..."

He looked over at the coffin. Its gravity had drawn the attention of all the gathered, as her presence had always demanded in life. Then he stole a glance at his wife on the front row, appreciating how black complimented her pale complexion and red hair so favourably, and how in sorrow her beauty seemed strangely enhanced.

"However," he continued, "what never faltered was my absolute respect for her inimitable spirit, boundless energy and life-long devotion to this place. She was truly the manifestation of Devilston in human form, and this tragic accident has impoverished all of us."

Charlotte stared back at her husband, with eyes drained of emotion.

Even you, Ralph...?

Having to concentrate hard with each step, the Reverend led the small procession down to the Crypt as the final verse of the late Duke and Duchess's favourite hymn swirled about them:

O Trinity of love and power,
Our brethren shield in danger's hour;
From rock and tempest, fire and foe,
Protect them whereso'er they go:
Thus evermore shall rise as one
Glad hymns of praise from Devilston.

As he helped carry the coffin, Sebastian Smythe-Morrigan was fighting a desperate rearguard action against a rising tide of grief, knowing his father's opinion of emotion. But the thought that his warm and wise grandmother - who'd loved him unconditionally, for all his faults and failures - was now lying cold and lifeless in the darkness within was the heaviest of loads.

With as much dignity as was possible in placing a long box into a hole in a wall the Duchess's coffin was slid into its final resting place, alongside the Duke's gaping tomb which still waited to receive him.

"We now commit the body of Lady Jennifer Morrigan into the safe-keeping of Devilston," said the Reverend in a fragile croak, "the place in which her soul came into this world and from which she has now departed. Earth to earth, ashes to ashes, dust to dust, in the sure and certain hope of the resurrection to eternal life..."

When the inscribed tombstone had been lifted into place by Garsten and Trevail, the select few who'd witnessed the entombment made their way up the steps, but the Reverend remained behind.

When he was sure he was alone, he placed his hands on the tombstone and rested his face against it. Then, at last able to express the full extent of his grief, he wept from the bottom of his heart.

The downpour seemed incessant. By Sunday evening it felt like it had been raining for a thousand years. But the dirty curtains of precipitation provided good cover for clandestine operations...

As usual Jai led the way, over to Chapel then under the sea to the cellar of the King's Head. This time the door at the top of the stairs was shut and the noise beyond much less than on their first visit. The filthy weather and the prospect of work the following day had kept all but the most faithful in their homes.

Jai risked switching on the torch. Numerous black lozenges scuttled across the cellar floor in all directions, heading for cover.

Tom shuddered.

"Cockroaches."

"Feeding on all the spilled beer," said Dan.

"Not as big as the ones back home," Jai grinned. "The size of your hand..."

"Well, they're big enough for me," said Tom. "Listen...you can hear the buggers scratching around behind those barrels..."

"Actually," said Dan, "that's probably a rat."

"Feasting on all those cockroaches that have suddenly come his way," Jai added.

The image turned Tom's stomach.

"Can we get out of here, please...?"

Jai pointed the torch at the ceiling in the far corner of the cellar. There was a trap door in it, with a wooden ramp leading down to the floor.

"That's where they deliver the barrels. It must open onto the street..."

A sharp click cut through the air and Jai switched off his torch. The cellar door opened, allowing light and sound to flood down the steps from above. The three scrambled for cover beneath the ramp, like rats themselves.

They heard heavy footsteps descending the stairs, wheezing breaths and a tune whistled softly between teeth. With a deep grunt a barrel was lifted very near to them then carried up the stairs. Only when the cellar door was closed did they dare breathe again.

Jai switched the torch back on.

"Let's get out of here before he comes back for another."

Ascending the ramp, he slid open the bolt and lifted the trap door enough to peer into the night.

"Looks like the coast is clear..."

"It's not the coast I'm worried about," said Tom.

Closing the trap door, Jai turned to his two friends.

"I've just thought of something. The landlord might notice the trap door's unlocked and bolt it again, locking us out. Someone needs to stay behind..."

"I'll stay," said Dan.

"Are you sure?"

"Yes. It will give me the opportunity to address this irrational fear of mine, once and for all."

But he was also remembering the words of the Duchess:

"Be careful. This place isn't safe."

But where did she mean? Devilston? Britain? Or the whole world...?

Banishing dark thoughts, he helped his friends arrange wooden crates underneath the ramp, piling some old sacks on top for a mattress.

"Not much of a bed but at least you'll be off the

floor," said Tom. "Away from all those nasties..."

Dan smiled wryly.

"Can they not climb...?"

"Here." Jai offered him the torch. "This'll keep 'em away."

"No thanks. If I'm to conquer this phobia then there must be no easy escape. Besides, you might need it..."

"You're very brave," said Tom. "If it was me I'd want a bloody flame-thrower at least."

"Bolt the door after us," Jai instructed Dan as he ascended the ramp. "We'll give three knocks when we get back."

"And we'll find a girl for you," Tom added.

"Thanks." Dan smiled as he saw his friends off, holding the trap door open while they crawled out. "Just don't be too long."

After he'd lowered the door and slid its bolt home, Dan found himself in almost absolute darkness, save for the tiny sliver of light beneath the cellar door at the top of the steps. He heard the movement of the rats and remembered the soldiers on the other side of the thin wall, thudding clumsily around the apartment in their search for treasure.

Then he lay down on the makeshift bed, pulled some sacking over himself and closed his eyes. He tried to imagine he was somewhere far way in time and space: on a warm bright beach in the summer, with all of his family together again.

He was returned to the moment by something lightly brushing his hand: an insect's exploratory feeler perhaps, or a rat's whisker.

Jai and Tom emerged in a narrow side street. The rain was still falling and water splashed from a broken gutter nearby. Because of the black-out there was no street light and every window was heavily curtained, but a faint glow in the distance drew them to an open doorway. Taking shelter from the rain they found themselves in a foyer. Behind the window of a ticket kiosk sat an elderly woman, knitting.

"It's already started," she said, without looking up from her work.

"What has?" asked Jai.

"What do you think? The picture."

She nodded at something behind Jai and Tom. They turned to see a beautiful woman in the arms of a disfigured man. The poster bore the title: *The Hunchback of Notre Dame.*

"How much is it?"

"One shillin'." Now the woman glared at them over the top of her spectacles. "Each."

"Can we not get in for less if it's already started…?"

She continued knitting without reply. The

two retreated to the doorway, out of sight.

"How much have you got on you?" Jai whispered. His last poker game had cleaned him out of what gains he'd made on his cigar sales. Until the next raid on the Crypt to replenish stock, he was skint.

"Only my lucky penny and I'm definitely not using that." Tom squeezed the coin tightly in his pocket. "Anyway, why do you want to see a picture? I thought we were looking for girls."

"Think about it, Tom. It's a love story..."

Tom looked at the poster doubtfully.

"Is it?"

"Never mind." Jai's voice was louder now. "We'll just have to come back when we've saved up enough..."

Puzzled, Tom followed his friend out into the street. Then Jai immediately doubled back into the foyer, crawling on hands and knees beneath the window of the kiosk, beckoning Tom to follow. They stole silently along a corridor towards a door at its end. Beyond could be heard amplified voices and dramatic music.

Jai opened the door and the two slipped into the dark auditorium. In the flickering light they saw that the cinema was almost empty. A middle-aged man sat at the front while at the back two young lovers were taking more interest in each other than the main feature. In a middle row sat two girls, glancing over at the new entrants with curiosity. They looked familiar to Jai, then he remembered.

"Of course…" he whispered to himself.

"Of course what?"

But Tom was addressing thin air. Already his friend had placed himself in the row directly in front of the girls.

"Good evening," he said, turning round in his seat. "My name is Jai Rana and this is my good friend Thomas Barrow. How do you do?"

Taking the seat next to Jai, Tom marvelled at his friend's boldness. The girls shook hands with them, both wearing the same expression of amused surprise. It wasn't the only feature they shared: though their dresses were different, their long blond hair was similarly arranged and their faces - illuminated by the screen - were identical.

"My name's Tamsyn," said the girl behind Jai.

"And I'm Merryn," said the one behind Tom.

"You have…interesting names…."

Fettered by shyness, Tom stumbled over the words.

"They're Cornish," said Tamsyn. "Pa's very patriotic."

"So," said Jai, "how's the picture?"

"Well, if we were allowed to watch it we'd be able to tell you."

"Oh, I'm so sorry if we were disturbing you…"

"Don't listen to her," said Merryn, giving her

twin a nudge. "We've already seen it twice. There's not much else to do in this place on a wet Sunday evenin'..."

"I've not seen you two round here before," said Tamsyn. "Where are you from?"

"Rajputana," said Jai.

"It's in India," Tom replied to the girls' puzzled looks, relieved to have a means of re-entering the conversation. "I'm from Lancashire."

"India?" Tamsyn's interest was growing. "How exotic."

"My dear," Jai gushed, "Rajputana is the most exotic place in the world. It is a great desert, where the earth meets the sun and there is insufficient water to quench their burning desire for each other..."

"I like the sound of that."

"So what has Lancashire got?" Merryn asked.

Tom scratched his head.

"Blackpool Tower...?"

The two girls were amused. Tom wasn't sure if they were laughing with him or at him.

"We shall be delighted to show you the beautiful sights of our respective places of origin," said Jai, "which will provide a most fitting backdrop to your presence."

"Hang on," said Tamsyn, eyeing him warily. "That's a bit forward, isn't it? We've only just met and you're promisin' us the world..."

Jai smiled.

"Actually, I've seen you both before. You work in the King's Head, don't you?"

Tamsyn looked surprised.

"How do you know that? We've never seen you in there…"

"…and I'm pretty sure we wouldn't have missed you," Merryn added.

"Suffice to say," Jai continued, "I was under the illusion the two of you might be a single entity, blessed with the supernatural ability to transport herself instantaneously from one place to another…"

"Well, you've certainly got the gift of the gab," Tamsyn chuckled.

"I'm not sure about the garb though…" Merryn's eyes narrowed with suspicion. "You're from across, aren't you…?"

"My dear," Jai's head bowed in acknowledgement, "you are not mistaken in your deduction."

"I didn't think they let you lot out durin' term time."

"Oh," Tom piped up, "there's a secret - ow!"

A shoe had connected sharply with his shin.

"A secret we would gladly share with you," said Jai as Tom rubbed his leg. "But first we'd need to be further acquainted. After all, you might be working for the other side…"

He winked.

"We're not Jerries, you cheeky thing," said

Tamsyn.

"I meant our school. You see," Jai leaned forward and spoke in a whisper, "we are absent without leave."

"Well," said Merryn, "we've no dealings with that place so your secret is safe with us."

"My dear, everyone in this locality has some connection to our school. It is like the Kraken, its many tentacles extending into every nook and cranny…"

The man at the front turned round.

"How about pipin' down, you lot? Some of us are tryin' to watch this picture…"

In reality he was the only one still engaged in the film. The couple on the back row remained oblivious to the outside world.

"What'll happen if you two get caught?" Tamsyn whispered.

"I assure you, my dear," Jai replied, "the pleasure of time spent in your delightful company would more than compensate for the pain of a good caning."

The two girls laughed. Tom could only watch in admiration as Jai worked his charm. The man on the front row turned round again.

"Look, I'm goin' to give you one last chance…"

"My sincerest apologies, sir."

When the man turned back to the film Jai pulled a face at him. The girls covered their mouths to stifle their laughter, but in vain.

When he looked round a third time he caught Jai as Quasimodo.

"Right! That does it!"

"Jai, we'd better go," said Tom as the man marched out.

"You two goin' to turn into pumpkins?" Merryn chuckled.

"Not exactly," said Jai, "but we're likely to be reduced to a pulp similar to the flesh of said vegetable should school find out about our little excursion. But why don't we arrange to meet again…?"

"Well, there's a dance on Halloween Night in the Village Hall. We could get you some tickets…"

"Perfect." Jai flashed another smile. "We'll see you there."

"It's fancy dress," said Tamsyn.

"Really? Then we'll just have to dust off our fancy dresses…"

Both girls burst into laughter again. They were silenced by a bright light and a stern voice.

"Right, you two! Out!"

The woman from the ticket kiosk had arrived, brandishing a large torch. The man from the front hovered behind her.

"Well ladies," said Jai, "it would appear we've over-stayed our welcome. So, until we meet again, we bid you adieu…"

Jai took a girls' hand in turn and kissed it. Tom

felt obliged to do the same and his ears burned as he did so, but the scent would linger long in his memory.

"Well, that one's certainly not backwards in comin' forwards," said Tamsyn when the two escapees had gone.

Merryn smirked.

"You like him, don't you?"

"Well, he is good lookin' you've got to admit. And charmin', too…So, what did you think of Tom…?"

"Oh, I see. Already paired us up, have you? Actually he's quite nice, isn't he? But very shy…"

"You've got to watch the shy ones. They're the worst."

"I loved his ears. I was dyin' to have a play with them…"

Again the two girls dissolved into cackles. With a theatrical exhalation of air the man at the front got up and made for the exit again.

Jai and Tom hurried back to the King's Head through the rain. They crouched down next to the trapdoor and Jai knocked.

"Just wait until Dan hears about those two peaches. He'll be green."

"Bugger," said Tom.

"What?"

"We forgot to tell them to bring a friend."

"Never mind. I'm sure they'll be plenty more at the dance."

"And there's Merryn, I suppose..." Tom reflected.

"What do you mean?"

"Well, she wasn't interested in me, was she...?"

"Nonsense, man. She was interested, believe me."

"How do you know?"

"Just take my word for it." Jai knocked again on the door. "Come on Dan, where are you?" He tried pulling on the handle, without success. "It's still bolted."

He knocked a third time, as loudly as he dared, but still there was no response.

"He's probably gone back along the tunnel," said Tom.

"Without the torch?" Jai shook his head. "I doubt it."

"Do you think he's been caught?"

"I don't know. Come on..."

At the harbour they saw the incoming tide hadn't yet covered that part of the Causeway they could make out in the dark.

"Is this a good idea?" Tom asked as they began to walk down the stone ramp. "The sea comes in really quickly here..."

"Well, we can try at least," said Jai. "If we can't cross then we'll just have to come back and think of another plan."

So they left the comforting arms of Pristow's harbour walls and struck out for the dark shape of Devilston, crouching ahead of them like a slumbering sea monster.

Halfway along the Causeway they stopped. The beam of Jai's torch played across the surface of a large pool covering the road. The water looked too deep to wade through so Jai shone the torch around its edge. To the left it was connected to a stream of sea which was feeding it, but to the right sand could be seen, still exposed.

"We'll go round," said Jai.

Stepping off the Causeway they began to circumnavigate the pool, their shoes sinking in the wet sand.

"It looks firmer further on..."

Now Tom hurried ahead of Jai, keen to get back to the safety of the road.

"Be careful!" Jai called out, then heard a cry. By the time he'd found his friend, Tom was waist deep in quicksand.

"Help me, Jai..."

Tom's voice trembled with fear. His eyes in the torchlight were wide and pleading as his fingers dug into the quivering sand which surrounded him, seeking some kind of anchorage. He could feel himself being slowly dragged down, as if some malevolent creature beneath was pulling on his legs.

Jai took off his duffle coat and - kneeling as close as he dared - threw it towards his friend. Tom grabbed one arm of the coat and Jai pulled on the other.

"It's no good!" Tom gasped. "It's not working!"

He had now sunk to his chest and his breathing was becoming impeded, as if his lungs were in a cold vice which was gradually tightening. Jai spread the duffle coat out in front of him and inched forward on his knees, until he was able to take hold of Tom's wrists. Tom gripped his friend likewise, then Jai pulled.

At first there was no movement and Jai was seized with dread: that he was about to witness his friend disappear before his eyes, and now this fear was converted into a great anger at the prospect. Bellowing with rage, he heaved with every sinew of his strength.

With the great black mass of the island looming beyond, it seemed to Jai as if he was locked in a tug-of-war with Devilston Herself, and for a terrible moment he thought the battle was lost. But - at last - Tom began to shift; painfully slowly at first but gradually rising from the quicksand until he was able to breathe properly again, kicking with his legs to free himself from the pit's last efforts to consume him.

Lying on Jai's duffle coat, caked in wet sand,

Tom wept with relief.

"You saved....my life..."

Jai had collapsed nearby.

"If I hadn't led you off the straight and narrow..." he wheezed,"...I wouldn't have had to."

"But you saved my life...all the same..."

When they entered their room their hearts sank. There was no sign of Dan. Then a huge figure loomed in the doorway. Tom retreated behind the end of his bunk bed, out of sight.

"Do you think I'm deaf?" Tattersall sneered.

Jai thought it best not to mention all the times they'd successfully negotiated the corridor while the Praeposters had snored.

"Where the Hell have you been, anyway?"

"We were looking for Dan," Jai replied. "He went for a walk a while ago but he hasn't returned yet. We were worried about him. He's not himself at the moment. His friends were on a ship that was torpedoed."

"So you've been out of bounds...?"

"No."

"Is this true, Wheely?"

"No sir," said Tom, still out of sight. "I mean, yes sir."

"Why are you hiding there? Come out so I can see you..."

Tom moved into view. His teeth were chattering.

"No need to be frightened, Wheely. I'm not going to eat you."

"I'm not frightened, sir. Just cold and wet."

The Head of House was annoyed by the response. He expected more fear on the part of an inferior.

"So explain this to me: if you weren't out of bounds then why is there a trail of wet sand up the corridor here? And why are you covered in the stuff...?"

"Well," said Jai, seeing Tom's mouth gulping like a fish as he grappled for an answer, "the truth is, while we were walking round the island looking for Dan my friend here fell into some quicksand."

"So you **were** of bounds?"

Anger flared in Jai's eyes.

"What does it matter? Dan is missing, that's the main issue...and besides, I think you'll find the area immediately surrounding the island is still officially part of the school, at least when the tide's out..."

Tattersall's forehead creased and he pointed a thick finger at Jai.

"You should have come straight to me rather than taking it upon yourselves to organise a search party. Now it's Muggins here who'll get it in the neck for waking the Rev up...So get this corridor cleaned up and I'll see you both on the Cutters next Sunday."

"What neck?" Jai muttered as Tattersall clumped away. Tom looked utterly dejected.

"First Dan goes missing then I almost die, and now we're on the bloody Cutters again…"

After lights out the two lay staring into the darkness, unable to sleep.

"Jai, where do you think he is?"

"I don't know."

"I wish I'd let him keep my lucky penny."

"Then you might not have made it out of that quicksand…"

"Do you think he's alright?"

"I'm sure he is. He probably couldn't bear it in the cellar any longer so he came out looking for us. He'll be somewhere in Pristow right now, waiting for the tide to go out. Then it'll be all three of us on the Cutters again."

"But what if he tried crossing the Causeway like we did, Jai? What if he came to that same pool of water and tried skirting round it, just like we did…?"

"He wouldn't have done that."

"Why not? We did."

"Because he's cleverer than we are, that's why."

"But just say he did get stuck in the quicksand.

He'd have no-one to help him out…"

"Just don't think about it," Jai snapped. He was tired and finding it difficult himself to suppress dark thoughts. "Dan's alright, I tell you. We'll wake up tomorrow morning and he'll be here. You'll see…"

Tom closed his eyes and tried to sleep, but the weight of the blanket on his chest reminded him of the sand pressing against him. In his mind's eye he saw Dan being sucked down into the darkness, his throat filling with wet sand, smothering his cries.

10

REVOLUTION AND REVELATION

The early morning exercise regime was even more of an ordeal than usual for Tom, with the extra weight of worry on his shoulders and one less guardian angel. As he and Jai dressed after their cold baths, the anxious silence was broken by a voice barking from the speaker above the door:

"Do you hear there? Headmaster speaking. Barrow and Rana will report to my study at zero nine hundred hours. That is all."

The Captain's message and Dan's empty place invited the inevitable inquisition at the breakfast table.

"Has he run away?"

Jai kept his head down but Tom rose to the bait.

"How do I know?"

"Always looked a bit sad, that one."

"Orphan, isn't it?"

"And Jewish."

"What's that got to do with anything?" Tom retorted.

"Well, maybe he's gone off to find the Promised Land."

"Or he's upstairs, emptying our pockets…"

Now Tom exploded.

"Why don't you all just bloody well shut up? He might be dead and all you lot can do is make nasty jokes…"

He struggled to extricate himself from between bench and table then hurried out of the Hall, to the accompaniment of whistles and jeers. Jai watched with disgust as a multitude of forks homed in on Tom's untouched breakfast. In seconds the plate was empty.

"Try to think positively," Jai urged as they circumnavigated the cricket pitch, the Headmaster's large Victorian house looming ahead. "Chances are Dan's safe and well. In fact I bet he's in Sticky's study right now, waiting for us."

"I'd really like to think you're right," Tom replied gloomily, "but I've got a very bad feeling about this…"

Spotting something in the distance, his unease deepened. The tide was out and a line of tiny figures extended across the sands.

"Looks like a search party," said Jai.

Tom's heart sank.

"That means he's still missing…"

"Just leave the talking to me. And remember, absolutely no mention of the tunnel."

"But shouldn't we be telling the truth?"

"No we shouldn't. As long as they don't know we know, we've got one up on them…"

The doorbell was answered by a funereal Garsten. They were led without a word to the study, passing a young and pretty maid. In spite of the gravity of the moment, Jai couldn't resist giving her a wink. She smiled back, blushing.

The Captain was sitting behind a large desk in his study. On a chair nearby sat a crag-faced policeman. Jai recognized him immediately from his foray to the King's Head.

Dan was absent.

The two stood side-by-side in front of the desk. Jai was calm, a veteran of numerous interrogations. Tom was trembling.

"Gentlemen," the Captain began, "this is Sergeant Polzeath of the local constabulary…" The policeman nodded gravely. "Now, I'm sure I don't have to explain the seriousness of the present situation. We have a missing pupil on our hands and we need to know as much as possible about his last known movements. You two are Rosenbaum's room mates and I understand you're also his best friends…?"

"Yes sir," the two replied in unison.

"Then all the more reason for you to be absolutely truthful with us from the start. The fate of your friend might very well depend upon the information you provide for us. Do you understand?"

"Yes sir."

"Good. Sergeant?"

"Thank you, Headmaster." Polzeath's dark eyes scrutinized them from beneath thick eyebrows. "So lads, when was the last time you saw Rosenbaum?"

"Last night, sir," said Jai. "In our room. It must have been about eight o'clock when Tom and I left..."

Polzeath began to write in his notebook.

"Where did you go?"

"To Pristow, sir."

Tom glanced at his friend.

"And what did you do in Pristow?"

"We went to the pictures, sir."

"Indeed you did," said the Captain. "I received a telephone call first thing this morning from the manageress of the Palace Cinema, informing me that two of my pupils had sneaked into the evening show..."

"So what time did you return to school?" asked Polzeath.

"It must have been about ten o'clock," said Jai.

"By that time the tide would have been comin' in."

"Yes sir. It was starting to cover the road."

"And Rosenbaum wasn't with you durin' this little expedition?"

"No sir. As I said, he stayed behind."

"So why didn't he go with you? You three are best friends, after all..."

"We invited him but he declined."

"Did you taunt him?"

"Taunt him, sir...?"

Polzeath looked up from his notebook.

"You know. Make fun of him for not wantin' to come with you."

"Why would we do that, sir? He's our friend."

"But even friends can be mean to each other sometimes..."

"We'd never do that to Dan," said Tom, angered at the thought.

The policeman studied both of them for a moment before continuing:

"Well, you know what I think happened, lads? And you're not goin' to like the sound of this one bit... I think your friend changed his mind after you left and followed you across the Causeway. And while he was wanderin' the streets of Pristow lookin' for you both, you were returnin' to school, havin' been ejected from the Palace...

"But when Rosenbaum came back to the Causeway - having given up on his search - he saw the sea comin' in real quick. Now his wisest course of action would have been to report to the police station. He would have been in a lot of trouble that's for sure, and he would have spent a night in a cell, but at least he would have been safe. But instead he chose to risk it. He decided to try another route across to the island..."

"Another route, sir?" Jai asked innocently.

"That's right. When the road's covered there are still areas of sand exposed...Now a local wouldn't ever dare venture off the Causeway at night. Every Pristovian worth his salt knows those sands are treacherous. But to Rosenbaum's untrained eye it would have looked safe enough to cross. Only, once she's set upon comin' in, the sea don't wait for no man round here, and your friend would have soon found himself besieged by water. So maybe he panicked and started to run, which is the worst thing to do when it's dark and with all those sand traps around...Just imagine that, lads. Stuck fast with all that cold black water closin' in on you..."

"How do you know that's what happened?" Tom blurted out.

"I don't." Polzeath closed his notebook and slipped it into his breast pocket. "But do you have a better explanation for Rosenbaum's disappearance...?"

Tom looked at Jai but his friend remained staring ahead, saying nothing.

There was a knock at the door and a second

policeman entered, young and fresh-faced with wet sand on his shoes and trouser bottoms. He was carrying a black bundle.

"Sir, we've just found this on the rocks..."

"Did you have to bring it in here?" said Polzeath, annoyed. "It's drippin' all over the Captain's carpet."

"Sorry sir, but I thought you might want to see it..."

"And take your helmet off inside, man."

Polzeath took the bundle from his junior and unravelled it as the Constable removed his helmet. Now Jai and Tom looked at each other with dread. It was a duffle coat like Dan's... but similar to all the other duffle coats in school, which offered the slightest hint of hope. Perhaps someone had left it on the rocks after the Rockenough match...

"Any idea who's this could be, Headmaster?" Polzeath asked.

"Well," the Captain replied with some exasperation, "I should think the name tag inside might give you a clue..."

"I've already checked the tag," said the Constable, pleased with himself. "It isn't Rosenbaum's."

Tom breathed a sigh of relief but Jai remained tense, recalling something.

"May I have a look, sir...?"

Getting the nod from the Captain, Polzeath

handed the coat to Jai. It was cold and heavy, as if steeped in death. Jai fumbled with it, in search of the tag.

He stared at the name for some time before he spoke.

"S.P. Yorke…"

Now Tom remembered, and groaned.

"Yorke?" The Captain looked puzzled. "But he was killed in an air raid. He never made it here."

"Dan used his clothes," said Jai quietly. "He didn't have any uniform of his own."

"So Rosenbaum would prob'ly have been wearin' this at the time of his disappearance?" Polzeath deduced.

The Captain sighed.

"Yes, Sergeant."

My God, they're like blind children.

"Then I'll need to keep this as evidence for the Coroner."

"Of course."

Polzeath took the duffle coat from Jai.

"I'm afraid findin' this coat just about wraps up the case, lads. Rosenbaum would have taken it off to allow him to swim better."

"Or to give him somethin' to lean on while he tried pullin' himself out of the quicksand," the Constable added, with a degree of relish. Jai and Tom required little mental effort to imagine the scene.

Polzeath picked up his helmet and rose to his

feet.

"Well Headmaster, I don't have any more questions for these two, for now anyway. We'll continue with the search until the tide comes in, though I expect the body would have been carried out to sea. The currents are pretty strong in this bay. But it'll prob'ly wash up somewhere along the coast, in time…"

"That's if he drowned," said the Constable. "If he was sucked down then the worms will have got him…"

"Yes, well thank you anyway, gentlemen." The Captain rose to see the policemen out. "I'm sure you'll keep me informed of any developments…"

"Of course, Headmaster." Polzeath turned to Jai and Tom. "And I hope this tragedy will be a lesson to you both, should you ever be fancyin' another reckless adventure…"

The Captain closed the door. Tom was sobbing softly while Jai stared out of the window beyond the desk. The Crown of Stones on its raised mound now resembled a ring of graves.

"No doubt you're crying because of the punishment you're anticipating," said the Captain as he returned to his seat.

"No sir," Tom sniffed. "I'm crying because we've lost our friend."

"And what about you, Rana? No tears…?"

Jai's gaze shifted from the stones to the

Captain.

"Must a storm always bring rain, sir?"

"Ah yes. Some of that Eastern philosophy... Well, both of you should at least be thankful that Rosenbaum was an orphan..."

Tom blew his nose into a dirty handkerchief.

"But he wasn't, sir."

The Captain's mouth slid sideways.

"Well, strictly speaking he wasn't..."

"Why should we be thankful, sir?" Jai asked.

"Isn't it obvious? You won't need to face his parents as the ones who led him into this disaster."

"We didn't lead him anywhere. Dan had a mind of his own. He made his own decisions."

The Captain's voice hardened.

"I'm not sure I like your tone, young man. You need to remember exactly whom you're addressing..."

"Sorry sir," Jai lied.

"And you need to know that this very serious breach of school rules cannot go unpunished."

"Isn't losing our best friend punishment enough?"

"I'm afraid not. Imagine how it would affect discipline in this school if there were no consequences for such blatant disobedience?"

The Captain opened his desk drawer. Tom and Jai glimpsed a cane, and a revolver.

Tom was instructed to remove his blazer then

stand with his hands on the arms of the sofa by the fireplace. The cane swished through the air as if taking a quick breath before each strike, every time finding its target with a neat thwack.

With each of the six strikes Tom cried out, yet in the burning pain he found some relief, some focus for his grief; but when it came to his friend's turn, Jai made no noise. Even though the pain of each strike was intense, stinging his backside then sweeping through his body like a swarm of needles; and even though his fingertips dug deep into the arm of the sofa, he suppressed all reaction. Interpreting Jai's silence as a failure on his part, the Captain increased the force of his strikes.

"You didn't make a sound," he observed at the end, breathing heavily and smoothing back his white hair while Jai put his blazer on. "That's never happened before."

"A storm isn't always accompanied by thunder, sir..."

"Indeed. But here's a bit of my own philosophy for you: I always give a warning. Should either of you ever be foolish enough to venture off this island again without permission, you will find yourself permanently expelled from this school. Is that clear?"

"Yes sir," said Jai and Tom together.

"Barrow, you may go."

As Tom hobbled out, the Captain returned to

his seat. His stare remained fixed on Jai as he spoke, and Jai held it.

"I sense a great deal of defiance in you, Rana. I expect that's a result of your upbringing. No son of a Maharaja is going to be a wall flower, after all. You're obviously a natural leader and something of a rebel to boot, but there's something you must understand: your father has given me strict instructions to whip you into shape, and if it's whipping that's literally required, then so be it. His words, not mine. So next time you're considering stepping out of line, just bear that in mind. I am in command of this island and I will not tolerate insubordination."

"I understand, sir."

"Very good. You may carry on."

Yes, Jai thought to himself as he left the study, *that's exactly what I shall do...*

The day dragged, as if even time itself was determined to wring as much pain from events as it could. Jai and Tom longed for the sanctuary of their room, where they could rest their raw backsides on a soft bed and escape the lurid speculation about Dan's fate.

Surprisingly, Smythe-Morrigan didn't participate in this morbid conjecture, making no reference to Dan's disappearance in the course of the day's lessons. Then - during evening prep - the Head of School darkened their door, with Tattersall and his deputy in tow.

"Sorry to hear about your friend, chaps. He seemed like a good egg."

Unable to sustain the pain of simulated sincerity any longer, Smythe-Morrigan's face resumed its lop-sided sneer.

"Still, bit more space for you both, I suppose...?"

"We'd sooner have Dan back," said Jai.

Seeing the pink warning glow in Tom's face, Smythe-Morrigan pressed on. The loss of his beloved grandmother still ached deep within him, a pain that required exorcism.

"First Yorke and now Rosenbaum..." He glanced at the number on the door. "Seems thirteen is unlucky, after all. Or is this all part of Wheely's masterplan, to create a little Lebensraum for himself? You'd better watch your back Rana or you might be next..."

"You...bastard!"

The room fell silent, all stunned by the verbal bomb Tom had just detonated. Then shock creased into anger on Smythe-Morrigan's face.

"What did you say?"

"You heard!"

Though shaking with fear now, Tom's eyes were wide with exhilaration. The Head of

School took hold of the lapels of Tom's blazer.

"Just who the Hell do you think you're talking to?"

Tom's view was filled by Smythe-Morrigan's face and suddenly he felt charged with rage by the invasion. He pushed the Head of School away, into the other Praeposters, surprising himself with his own latent strength.

Smythe-Morrigan's reaction was immediate. Collecting himself he swung a wild punch which caught Tom on the jaw, sending him sprawling backwards onto Dan's desk.

What happened next occurred with Blitzkrieg speed: three hard blows landed in swift succession on the Head of School's face, dropping him to the floor where he lay on his back, gasping.

The two Praeposters looked down at their superior, now clutching his nose from which blood had begun to flow; then they looked at his assailant, standing over their fallen master. Jai's fists remained raised, the tiger-fire of pure ferocity burning in his eyes.

"Don't just stand there!" Smythe-Morrigan cried nasally from the floor. "Hit him!"

But neither Tattersall nor his deputy had any intention of confronting the beast.

"Get out," Jai growled and the two obeyed.

"Come back!" Smythe-Morrigan shouted after them. "Bloody cowards!"

By now others had gathered in the corridor outside, like sharks drawn to blood. Still holding his nose, Smythe-Morrigan scrambled to his feet and stumbled through the small crowd, leaving a trail of blood spots along the corridor.

The news of Jai's strike against the system diffused swiftly through school. Already exalted by his sporting exploits, his reputation now soared to messianic heights. Thus his attendance at breakfast the following morning was greeted by a spontaneous cheer, evolving into a chant in which every pupil - except only the Duty Praeposters - became engaged. Accompanied by a rhythmic banging of fists which rattled the cutlery on the tables and even the weapons on the walls, the mantra echoed around the Dining Hall like the voice of Valhalla hailing the arrival of its latest hero.

"RA-NA! RA-NA! RA-NA...!"

Desperate to suppress the demonstration, the Duty Master and Praeposters marched around the tables dispensing threats; but the gathered only laughed and grinned and increased the volume, flush with a febrile mix of fear and excitement, feeding off each other's defiance in a spiral of rebellion which threatened to become a tornado.

Then a gun shot rang out, instantly quashing

the din.

A multitude of eyes now turned to the source of the blast, like those of a single creature. A small quantity of plaster and splintered wood fell from the ceiling, and the pungent smell of cordite tainted the air.

The Captain stood at the centre of the Hall, cold blue eyes surveying the field of heads. One hand leaned on his walking stick while the other brandished his revolver, a thin wisp of smoke curling from the end of its barrel.

For some time he said nothing, manipulating even the silence to his own ends and allowing the tension to stretch to breaking point. When at last he spoke, his voice was calm and measured, only emphasising the malice implicit in his words:

"So...who started this?"

The pupils remained still and quiet, each concentrating on avoiding the Captain's roving stare.

"You know, right now I have a good mind to pick someone out at random and shoot him on the spot. Pour encourager les autres...Explain to these ignoramuses what that means, Mister Quirk..."

"Sir..." Quirk was terrified at being singled out and his voice faltered, "to encourage the others...?"

In his haste to get to the Hall, the Captain

had loaded only one bullet into his Webley. Now, placing his walking stick under his arm, he broke the revolver's spine. Every ear heard the sound of the single spent shell dropping onto the stone floor. Then, producing a handful of bullets from his pocket, he proceeded to slide one into each of the weapon's six chambers. All eyes watched this slow and deliberate ceremony with dread.

"In any institution," the Captain continued as his hands worked, "be it a school, a squadron or - for that matter - a nation, the maintenance of discipline is paramount. Any lapse must be dealt with swiftly and decisively, lest the functioning of said institution be compromised. This is especially so in time of war, because there is nothing quite as dangerous as a crowd that has lost control...

"Now, I know exactly what you're all thinking at this moment. You're wondering if I'm really contemplating - for the sake of good order - the summary execution of a random pupil...Well let me tell you, such is my anger right now, I could quite easily empty the entire contents of this revolver into one of you."

A metallic snap cut through the air as he closed the weapon.

"You have not only betrayed yourselves this morning, you have betrayed those who have invested substantial sums in the belief that you will leave here both educated and civilised. And - most seriously of all - you have betrayed your school. This ancient and historic place is your home, to be respected and revered. Not reviled like a pack of baying savages…

"Gentlemen - and I use the term with the utmost irony - your bestial behaviour has insulted Devilson to Her very core, and so Devilston must have Her retribution. Mrs McCarthy…?"

The large cook appeared at the kitchen door, wiping her hands on her apron and eyeing the Captain's revolver.

"Headmaster…?"

"All hot meals are cancelled until further notice. Strictly bread and water until I'm satisfied the lesson has been learned."

"But breakfast has already been prepared, sir…"

"Then feed it to the pigs. They deserve it more than this collection of filth. If the pupils in this school want to behave like convicts, then let them be treated accordingly…"

"So…" Sitting behind his desk, the Captain eyed the pair before him, "perhaps one of you could explain why two students in their final year of school - and one of them Head Boy, no less - were fighting like the common proletariat last night..."

"He started it." Smythe-Morrigan's voice betrayed a swelling of his nose, and his right eye was besieged by a purple bruise. "Rana came at me without any warning."

"He hit Tom," Jai responded. "I was simply defending my friend."

"Barrow pushed me, Father. And he called me a bastard."

"Did he, indeed?" The Captain appeared unimpressed. "Actually, who precipitated this nonsense is of no concern to me. The important question is, how will it end? And I have to tell you Sebastian, it isn't looking good for you."

"I'm not sure what you mean, Father..."

"I mean, in losing the fight you've clearly lost the respect of the school."

"Fight? But it wasn't a fight. Not a fair one, anyway."

"You're right," said Jai. "Three against two certainly isn't fair."

"Enough!" After a pause to emphasise his annoyance, the Captain continued: "Sebastian, having given this matter some considerable thought I've reached the conclusion that your only real hope of salvaging any authority lies in a contest with Rana here. A boxing match. One against one."

Smythe-Morrigan was astonished.

"What?"

"Rana, would you be willing to participate?"

"I only fight in defence, sir."

"So if your opponent was to throw the first punch...?"

"Then I will defend myself."

"Sebastian?"

"But...if I lose I won't be Head of School anymore!"

"It was pretty evident from that little insurrection at breakfast that you've effectively forfeited that particular responsibility already. You will be fighting to regain your title. And should you lose then I shall have no choice but to re-appoint."

"Rana..." Smythe-Morrigan choked back the emotion. "But a darky can't be Head of School. You said so yourself. It's written in stone."

The Captain remained un-moved.

"Very occasionally events force one to smash the stone and re-write the rules. I refer you to the story of Moses..."

"Why are you doing this to me?"

Smythe-Morrigan's voice had risen in pitch.

"You've created this situation yourself, Sebastian. I'm merely offering you a way out..."

"But you're Headmaster! You decide who's Head of School, not some...chanting mob!"

"I'm afraid there are some things that are beyond even my control. You see, a king's rule is unquestionable, but he must be served by an effective executive who is respected by the masses. This school needs a Churchill, not a Chamberlain... The fact is, I can't carry you anymore, Sebastian. From now on you'll have to fight your own battles."

"But you've never carried me. To carry someone you've got to be close to them, and you've never been close to me..."

Smythe-Morrigan began to sob.

"Dear Sebastian," the Captain sighed. "Always so melodramatic..."

"I'm a failure in your eyes, aren't I? No matter what I do, it's never enough. I only agreed to be bloody Head of School to please you...and now this!"

With that he rushed from the room, slamming the door behind him. The Captain smirked.

"Running to Mummy, no doubt..."

He opened a silver box on his desk and pushed it towards Jai.

"Cigarette?"

"No, thank you."

In truth, Jai would have loved a smoke. He knew it would be the finest quality tobacco, from the Crypt. But he resisted the temptation, aware of the power-play that was taking place. He watched as the Captain lit a cigarette, took a deep drag then blew the smoke slowly out of his nostrils, like a dragon.

"Sebastian is weak," he said, at last. "The result of too much indulgence by his mother, I fear...But tell me, Rana. Is it true you don't know who your mother is...?"

"I was lucky enough to have many mothers, sir."

"And they spoiled you?"

"They loved me, and I them. I don't think love can spoil anything. Not real love..."

"I suppose not...You know, I never knew who my real mother was either."

Jai was genuinely surprised. The offering of the cigarette was unexpected enough but this was completely new territory, and not entirely comfortable.

"I grew up in a home for unwanted children." The Captain clenched a fist reflexively. "Terrible place. I was beaten so much I ran away in the end. Life on the streets was infinitely preferable to that miserable existence. Does it surprise you Rana, to think that once upon a time I was nothing but a filthy urchin...?"

"Clearly you have done very well for yourself, sir."

"Yes, I have. From the slums of the East End to Headmaster of an exclusive public school, through sheer bloody-minded determination. Of course I've cracked some skulls to get here - metaphorically speaking - but you can't make an omelette, and all that...Sebastian, on the other hand, has enjoyed an altogether easier life. I suppose he doesn't possess the same hunger as me. But I also sense a hunger in you, Rana…"

"That'll be a reflection of the quality of the meals here, sir."

The Captain smiled.

"Banquets compared with what I endured in that orphanage, I can assure you. But I think you know what I mean. You've enjoyed a life of great privilege yet still you're driven to challenge the boundaries, and this puzzles me. But it's all in the breeding, I suppose…"

"Actually sir, in my case I'm not sure it is."

"I don't follow you…"

The Captain had confided in Jai. It only seemed fair to reciprocate.

"My father couldn't sire any children of his own. He believed a curse had been put on him by the Maharaja of Malwar, ruler of the neighbouring state and sworn enemy. Then, in a dream, he saw the place where he would find a son and heir. When he woke he went directly to the village of his vision, and found me. My real father and mother were very poor. Of course they were sad that I was being taken away from them, but happy that I was to have a new life and they'd be left with one less mouth to feed. I believe they were also handsomely remunerated for their trouble…"

The Captain looked astonished.

"So you're not really a prince, after all? You're just peasant stock…?"

"I think of myself as both, sir. We are all royalty to those who love us, and peasants in the eyes of our enemies…"

Jai held the Captain's stare.

"You certainly spout a lot of philosophy, don't you?"

"I am from India, sir. It comes with the territory."

"Are you really going to fight Slimy-Moron?"

Tom lay on his bunk trying to keep himself from thinking of Dan, and the burn that still lingered in his backside from the bite of the Captain's cane.

"If I have to," Jai replied.

"And do you think you'll beat him?"

"If I have to."

"Well, you're full of conversation tonight."

"Sorry. I just want to find out what's going on in the world…"

Jai was sitting at his desk in his pajamas, Dan's wireless crystal set before him. Moving the tuning wire, he listened to the haunting contortions of the airwaves. They seemed to him like the distant calls of creatures floating through the ether, like beasts of the sea. He crossed islands of music and talk, then paused in his quest.

So," yawned Tom, "have the Jerries invaded yet?"

"Sh!"

"What?"

"Can't you hear it?"

Tom listened hard. Somewhere within the low hiss coming from the loudspeaker above the door, he could just make out the high-pitched dots and dashes.

"Well, I can't hear any tapping from Cowardly's room this time."

"He must be sending it from somewhere else," said Jai.

"Why would he do that?"

"Maybe it wasn't received last time. Maybe he needs to be higher up in order to reach Germany..."

"Now where are you off to?"

Jai was putting his dressing gown on.

"For a shufti. Coming?"

"Have you already forgotten what Sticky said?"

"Don't worry. We're only going upstairs..."

They crept past the Praeposters' rooms and up the spiral staircase at the end of the corridor, passing Alderley's door then the Reverend's.

At the top of the steps they came to the little arched door that led to the roof. It was usually locked, but not tonight. Jai carefully opened it enough to see beyond.

In the moonlight they glimpsed a silhouette standing at the battlements, wearing headphones connected to an open briefcase on the wall in front of the figure. Another wire ran from the briefcase to a halo-like loop which the figure was holding up. At Jai's angle of observation, the black finger of the lighthouse on Dragon Head was encircled by the device.

"Caught red-handed..." whispered Tom, peering over Jai's shoulder.

Now the figue looked towards them, as if having heard Tom.

Jai closed the door and pushed his friend towards the stairs, but as they descended Tom collided with a large ascending body. Both were sufficiently upholstered to soften the impact.

"What the Hell are you doing, lad?" blared a slurring Welsh voice. The Reverend was carrying a bottle in each hand, the sweet smell of alcohol hanging about him like the Holy Spirit. Beneath his overcoat he was wearing pajamas, and keys hung from the chain around his neck.

"Sir, we've just been up to get some fresh air..."

Jai spoke in a loud voice, hoping to deter the

figure from descending.

"On the roof? But that's strictly bout of hounds..."

As well as addling his faculty of speech, drink had muddied the Reverend's sense of right and wrong. He was struggling to muster up a quantity of disapproval appropriate to their crime.

"We know, sir," said Jai. "But we were missing Dan..."

"Oh...I see..." Now the Reverend abandoned all pretence of anger. "Yes....Well, I've been meaning to talk to you both about all that business. Now is as good a time as any, I suppose..."

He shepherded Jai and Tom into his rooms and closed the door.

Shifting some piles of exercise books from the leather-upholstered couch in his sitting room, he indicated for them to sit. He then opened one of the bottles and poured a generous measure into three glasses. He handed a glass each to a grateful Jai and a more reticent Tom.

"Oh come on, lad. This'll put hairs on your chest. It's finest cognac."

Then the Reverend raised his glass.

"Here's to...what was the lad's name again? I'm terrible with names... names and dates....God knows why I'm an historian...the stories, I suppose..."

"Rosenbaum sir," Jai prompted him.

"Ah yes. To Roundbosom! Fine fellow, if I remember rightly..."

The Reverend gulped down a mouthful. Jai took a long sip while Tom sniffed his glass doubtfully.

After stoking up the fire, the Reverend shuffled over to a corner of the room, to an old gramophone which resembled a huge and exotic flower sprouting from a wooden box. He selected a record from a pile nearby, upsetting the rest and sending them cascading to the floor. Ignoring the carnage he concentrated on the challenging task he'd set himself, his shaking hand making the positioning of the needle difficult and creating some scratchy false starts. Eventually they heard the slow, dark and ominous introduction to a piece of music Jai had heard before but couldn't name.

Dan would have known it.

"Siegfried's Funeral March." The Reverend gratefully collapsed into his armchair by the fire, taking another gulp of brandy. "From Wagner's Guttermadderdung... I mean, Gotter...dammer...ung. Bloody German..."

"What does it mean, sir?" asked Jai.

"Whatever you want, boy. Such is the nature of great art..."

"The title, I mean. What's the translation?"

"What? Oh...Dawn of the Dogs or

something..."

"Really?"

"Twilight of the Gods!" the Reverend exclaimed as the name came to him, thumping the arm of his chair and causing a small cloud of dust to rise from it. "Rather appropriate, really..."

Now Tom took a small careful sip from his glass and swallowed. He'd had beer before but not spirits. It tasted bitter and dry, catching the back of his throat and burning viciously as it went down. He coughed reflexively, to the amusement of the Reverend and Jai. At first it wasn't a pleasant experience at all, but then a comforting warmth began to flow through his body. It wasn't long before he'd taken another, bigger sip.

"Yes...loss is a terrible thing," the Reverend was saying, gazing into the fire now. "But better to have loved and lost, I suppose..."

"Have you loved and lost, sir?"

Tentatively Jai sought to take advantage of the Reverend's vulnerable state, which seemed to be allowing rare access to the inner keep of his soul.

"Not sure, to be honest. Loss suggests it was in my possession to begin with..."

"I don't understand, sir."

"Well, the one I love belongs to someone else, doesn't she? Someone who treats her like one of his baubles. Like his precious car or that boat, or this whole bloody island for that matter. Just another spoil of war…"

"Are you talking about the Headmaster, sir?"

Jai glanced at Tom sitting next to him but his friend seemed more interested in the brandy.

"Who else?" the Reverend rumbled as the music swelled. He took another gulp which seemed to settle him. "But I shouldn't be telling you this. I've said enough already."

"Sometimes it can help to talk, sir."

"Yes…" The Reverend looked at Jai for a while, his dozy bloodshot eyes slowly blinking, his mind soothed by the alcohol, time itself on hold. He'd never talked to anybody about the weight he'd carried for so long, and now here he was opening up to a mere pupil. "But what does it matter anymore?" he thought aloud. "I'm not long of this Earth, anyway…"

"What do you mean, sir?"

"Something wrong inside. Lots of pain. Probably my liver…"

"Have you seen a doctor?"

"Meddling do-gooders, prodding and pontificating…And what do they care, really…? No, this is the only medicine I need…" The Reverend grinned, holding up the bottle. Then he poured some more brandy into his glass and, leaning over, topped up his guests'. "Don't want to know, to be honest. Let Mother Nature take Her course...Into Her capable hands I commit myself..." He raised his glass in another toast and drank some more; then he regarded his guests, his eyes brimming with sadness, moved by the dark swirl of the music and his memories. "Make the most of your youth, lads. Won't be long before your bodies grow old and corrupt and begin to betray you..." On that note the Reverend broke wind. His guests struggled to hide their amusement. "Excuse me."

No-one said anything for a while, all three watching the flames devouring the wood, listening to the music reaching its redemption. Then the Reverend spoke again:

"So tell me, boys...what do you really think of me? Apart from being an old soak, that is..."

Lost for words, Jai and Tom looked at each other for inspiration.

"Well sir," said Jai, "you're an excellent teacher."

"Oh, come on now! You can do better than that! A bit of honesty on my part deserves some re-prick...pre-piss...bloody brandy, swells the tongue...can't speak properly..."

"Reciprocation, sir?"

"That's the one. You think old Monster Mouth's a bastard, don't you?"

"Well, you can be quite strict sometimes..."

To Tom, the two voices appeared to be growing more distant. His head felt close to floating away. He began to wonder if he was dreaming.

"It's all an act, you know," the Reverend continued. "In fact, I'm riddled with tunnels of doubt. Mined with insecurity, I am. In constant danger of falling in on myself." He hiccupped violently. "I'm not really a bastard, you see. But I am a Bastard. In the Biblical sense..."

"Sir?"

"Ineligible...I mean, illiterate...no, that's not right..."

"Illegitimate, sir?" Jai ventured.

"That's it. Born out of wedlock, I was. I shouldn't have happened at all, but I did. Here, as a matter of fact. On this very island."

"But I thought you were from Wales, sir..."

"That's where I was brought up, true enough. Welsh and proud of it!" He raised his glass again, then drank some more. "I was spirited away from this place as soon as I was born but Devilston is where I entered this world, and where I shall depart it. She called me back, see. Didn't know it at the time, of course, all links having being severed but for the ethereal which no mortal can break. You might say I was reeled in by..." he paused before the hurdle, "...an invisible umbilical...

"I was a young man, embarking on my very first parish, all ready to do God's work. But slowly Devilston weaved Her web about me, sank Her fangs into me, filled me with Her poison, as She does with all those foolish enough to tarry here. Don't linger for too long lads, or She'll have your souls, too. Your souls… our souls…arseholes…"

He chuckled sadly to himself.

"What happened, sir?"

"I just told you what happened, didn't I? Pay attention, lad!" Monster Mouth had returned, fleetingly, then the Reverend's features softened again. "What happened was, I fell in love…"

"With Lady Charlotte?"

"How was I to know who she was?"

Jai was confused.

"You didn't know who Lady Charlotte was?"

"Well, of course I knew who she was! What I mean is, I didn't know who she really was…"

"I'm sorry, sir. You've lost me."

"Probably just as well." The Reverend had settled back now, his eyes closed. "Let sleeping dogs lie, I say…"

Soon his great mouth had dropped open and deep snores began to rumble forth from the cave. It was as if he'd been exhausted by the effort of his revelations. His empty tumbler slipped from his hand and thudded onto the balding rug.

The music had now come to an end and the gramophone's ornate trumpet emitted a sequence of scratches, constantly repeating until Jai put the cycle out of its misery.

"Well, he's out for the count," he said, then realised he was speaking to himself. Tom was also fast asleep, his hands cradling an empty glass on his lap. Jai cursed under his breath. "Why can't these British take their drink…?"

He shook Tom but his friend hardly stirred. So, with great effort, Jai took hold of both of Tom's arms and pulled him from the chair, then helped him out of the Reverend's rooms and down the steps.

The movement disturbed Tom's insides. He was suddenly overcome by a wave of nausea.

"Need the bog…feel sick…"

They just made it to the lavatory before Tom's abdomen contracted noisily. His stomach ejected a great arc of half-digested bread, brandy and bile. For Tom, the spasms were excruciating but - at the same time - strangely welcome. It felt like righteous punishment.

"Oh God…" he groaned mournfully, his voice echoing around the old veined porcelain as he knelt at the great vessel. "I'm never going to drink again…"

"I'll remember those words," Jai chuckled.

Finally - when his innards felt completely emptied - Tom pulled the chain, wiping his mouth on the back of his hand.

"It's all our fault," he groaned, now sitting on the toilet, his head in his hands.

Jai was leaning against the door frame, arms folded.

"What is?"

"Dan dying. If we hadn't found that bloody tunnel..."

"We didn't force him to come with us."

"But we left him in the cellar."

"He volunteered, remember...?"

Tom looked up at Jai, with tired sad eyes.

"You don't really care, do you?"

"What do you mean?"

"It's all a game to you, isn't it? Just one adventure after another. And if someone happens to die, well that's just the way it goes..."

Now Tom saw anger invade his friend's face, the same frightening possession he'd witnessed when Jai had confronted Smythe-Morrigan: clenched jaw, flared nostrils, bulging eyes as he loomed over Tom, fist cocked and ready to strike. Then something flickered in his eyes and he stormed away, slamming the cubicle door behind him.

"I'm sorry, Jai!" Tom called after his friend. "I didn't mean that!"

But his words only echoed uselessly around the ceramic.

Only a select few were permitted to watch the boxing match in the Crown of Stones:

Praeposters, Leavers and Dormitory Captains. It would be the latter who would promulgate the result to the rest of the school, but it was the Praeposters who - as always - enjoyed the prime positions. Each of the twelve prefects stood in a gap between the stones, while the rest of the crowd beyond - Tom and Quirk among them - craned over shoulders.

There were neither rounds nor scoring. The match would continue until the fall of the weakest, or night.

"No kicking, biting, head-butting or hitting below the belt," grunted Tattersall, officiating as referee. "The best man will win. Give him Hell, S-M!"

He slapped the Head of School on the shoulder then stepped back into his recess, as the spectators cheered on their respective champion. Wearing vests - Jai in red, Smythe-Morrigan in white - with black shorts, plimsolls and leather boxing gloves, the two viewed each other across the flat middle stone. Smythe-Morrigan saw a serene detachment in Jai's expression, while in the eyes of his taller and heavier opponent Jai recognised raw fear.

The crowd fell quiet. Using his teeth Jai was now unfastening the string of his gloves, like a terrier gnawing at a bone. As he pulled them off and threw them away, his eyes remained fixed on Smythe-Morrigan's. Interpreting the gesture as a sign of surrender the Head of School grinned at his Praeposters in triumph, and relief.

But Jai was standing his ground - clenched fists now raised in front of his face - and the Head of School's grin vanished. The stakes had been raised and - feeling a deep sickening in his stomach - he found himself discarding his own gloves.

As Devilston's clock began to strike the hour a hungry roar of expectation went up. The Praeposters were cheering for their leader, and the preservation of the old order. Most of the rest supported Jai, and the hope of an end to their miserable lot.

But there were some who simply relished the prospect of witnessing pain, injury and the spilling of blood, and they weren't to be disappointed. After a phony war in which the two contenders circled the middle stone to the accompaniment of the crowd's slow clap, the battle began.

Smythe-Morrigan leaped over the central plinth and launched himself at Jai, unleashing a furious onslaught of punches. The clapping ceased and the Praeposters bellowed as one, their faces leering at Jai from between the standing stones.

The Head of School's tactic was simple: an all-out offensive to deny his opponent any opportunity to strike back. He knew that - while he might possess the greater strength - Jai had more speed and stamina, and a killer accuracy.

But it was a frantic panic of an attack, lacking in long-term strategy and expensive in energy. As many wild swings missed as connected, while Jai raised his forearms to his head and absorbed the power of those that landed. Cringing behind his fingers, Tom winced with every blow.

Inevitably Smythe-Morrigan began to tire, unable to sustain the broadside. Now Jai dropped his hands, lifted his head and skipped around his stumbling opponent. He'd taken a punch to the nose and blood streamed over his mouth yet he seemed almost gleeful, beckoning Smythe-Morrigan to do his best as the Head of School lumbered breathlessly around the ring in pursuit.

The crowd was in uproar, either urging Smythe-Morrigan to finish the job or willing Jai to deliver the vengeance they so desperately lusted after. Smythe-Morrigan was the very personification of all that this latter group despised, and Jai their great dark hope for a new dawn of righteousness in their lives.

"So there you have it, Edward." The Captain handed his binoculars to the Reverend standing next to him at the window. "The violent waltz of nature. Nietszche's Will to Power made manifest before our very eyes…"

Through the field glasses the Reverend studied the drama taking place in the stone circle at the far end of the cricket pitch. He'd been invited to watch the match from the Captain's study.

"Red dragon fights white," he said cryptically, lowering the binoculars and taking another mouthful of brandy.

"Sorry?"

"Well," continued the Reverend, "it is said that King Vortigern tried to build a castle to protect himself from the people he'd betrayed. But no matter how strong he designed it, the castle kept falling down. His druids told him the only cure for the curse was to sprinkle on the castle's foundations the blood of a fatherless child, sacrificed. But just as the sword was about to fall, the child begged the king to look beneath the foundations…and there Vortigern discovered the real reason for the castle's instability: an underground cavern in which two dragons were fighting to the death. One red, the other white…"

The Captain looked puzzled.

"You see, Headmaster," the Reverend explained, "it was Vortigern who first invited the Saxons to come to Britain. The red dragon could be said to represent the people he betrayed: the Celts."

Now the Captain understood.

"And the white represents the Saxons. And presumably it won...?"

"If you wish..."

"What's that supposed to mean?"

"It's a myth Headmaster, and a metaphor. The fight between the two dragons could just as easily represent the struggle between the mystical and the rational, or the old and the new, or the Yin and the Yang...or - for that matter - the war that rages within all of us, between good and evil..."

The Captain smiled.

"All of us...?"

The door flew open and Charlotte stormed in, her face flushed with anger. The Reverend was thankful for the desk between them. She looked a formidable sight in red and black.

"It's polite to knock," said the Captain.

"What the Hell is going on out there?" his wife demanded.

"Well, it would appear Sebastian is currently negotiating that perilous transition from boy to man..."

"The rite of passage," the Reverend echoed, draining his glass then peering through the binoculars again.

"But why aren't you stopping it?"

"My dear," said the Captain with false incredulity, "why ever would I want to do that...?"

"Because he's going to get hurt!"

"He's certainly taking a pasting," muttered the Reverend.

"That's our son out there, bare-knuckle fighting like a gypsy!" There was a catch in Charlotte's voice. "And all you two can do is watch and make droll comments!"

Now the Reverend looked round and met her stare, for a moment sharing some of her pain, before retreating again to the sanctuary of the binoculars.

"I think you're getting things rather out of proportion," said the Captain. "It's only a bit of sport, after all..."

"A bit of sport?" His wife's eyes were wide and wild. "They're beating the Hell out of each other! Well, if you won't stop it then I shall!"

With that she marched out of the room, slamming the door behind her.

The Reverend had been accurate in his assessment of the match: Jai had launched a spectacular counter-attack, landing blow after blow on Smythe-Morrigan who cowered behind his arms. While the Praeposters were silenced by the sickening possibility of defeat, the rest of the crowd was almost hysterical with blood-lust and the heady prospect of a new leader.

In a final desperate surge, the Head of School lashed out blindly, hooking the back of Jai's neck and pulling him in. As they leaned on each other, their heads close, Jai whispered breathlessly in his opponents' ear:

"How much...do you want this...?"

"I have to win..." gasped Smythe-Morrigan.

"Then lay off Tom....No more fagging...No more bullying..."

"Alright..."

"And all Leavers treated the same as Praeposters...No punishments...Hot baths... The same meals..."

In spite of his exhaustion, Jai's demands horrified his opponent.

"Impossible!"

"No it isn't...You can make it happen, Sebastian... You're Head of School, remember...?"

The crowd was hushed. Ears strained, trying to tune in.

Smythe-Morrigan nodded wearily but Jai pressed him.

"Promise."

"I give you my word."

"And if you break it..." Now Jai's lips brushed the Head of School's earlobe as he snarled. "I'll fight you again...and I'll beat you."

He broke away and the crowd greeted the resumption of hostilities with a savage joy. But now the contest was very different: Jai made a few token lunges at Smyth-Morrigan, but there was little power in these punches and he hovered in front of his opponent, his fists low, his head unprotected, looking suddenly spent.

Seeing the opportunity open before him - as in the final fatal kick against Rockenough - the Head of School focused his remaining strength into a swinging right hook.

After the impact Jai tottered for a moment, legs buckling, eyes rolling, head lolling. Then, like a puppet with its strings abruptly cut, he fell.

As Jai lay sprawled and motionless across the middle stone, Tattersall stepped forward and began the count. Now all had fallen silent, stunned by this unexpected turn of events. On ten, a raucous cheer went up from the Praeposters, while the rest of the crowd groaned and booed, hardly believing this cruel twist: a certain victory snatched from their hungry grasp.

A dazed Head of School was raised onto the shoulders of his praetorian guard and paraded round the ring. Their elation was driven by an intense relief. The old order had been saved. Their own precarious positions had been preserved.

Tom pushed through the crowd to kneel by his fallen friend.

"Jai? Are you alright…?"

Fresh streams of red trickled from Jai's nose and a split lip, following the routes already forged by darker, dried blood. He was breathing but his swollen eyes remained closed while his mouth hung open, ominously.

"Is he dying?" asked Quirk as he surveyed the wreckage, all hope of a new era of enlightenment dashed. The rest of Jai's supporters were already making their way forlornly back to school, to disseminate the sad news.

"Don't just stand there gawping!" Tom shouted up at Quirk. "Get Matron!"

On his way to the Sanatorium Quirk passed Lady Charlotte heading for the battlefield.

She found her son sitting on the grass, back against a standing stone, his white vest stained with blood, his fingers gently exploring his bruised and bloodied face. The clot of prefects around him parted for her.

"Oh Sebastian…"

Her son looked up and smiled, feeling the dried blood cracking.

"I did it, Mother. I won."

"But look at the state of you…"

As she knelt down to administer maternal balm to the son she hardly recognised, he looked beyond her, towards the house. In the study window he could just make out two figures.

He raised a fist and - to his deep delight - he saw one of the figures respond.

The Captain lowered his hand.

"So white wins again…"

"I'd say more of a capitulation than a victory," the Reverend replied, seeing off another glass of brandy.

"Well Edward, to paraphrase Machiavelli: it isn't how one triumphs that's important."

"I suppose not."

"And thus equilibrium is restored in the Universe. Cheers." The Captain raised his glass and the Reverend responded, though his was empty. "You know, I've just had a thought… Those two dragons of yours could quite easily be you and I: the red dragon of Wales versus the white of England. The two of us locked in mortal combat, struggling for command of this school…"

"But you already command Devilston, Headmaster."

"In the secular sense, yes. But in matters spiritual you still exert a considerable influence."

"I hardly think leading Chapel services

constitutes real power…"

"Oh but you underestimate yourself, Edward. I may be the Head of Devilston and the pupils Her heart. But you…" The Captain pointed a finger his way. The Reverend towered over him, yet he always felt diminished in the Headmaster's presence. "You represent the very soul of this place…"

"Well, I'm very flattered that you hold me in such high esteem."

"Only the thing is, I don't just want Her head and Her heart." The Reverend felt the Captain's blue stare burning into him like Bunsen flames. "I want Her spirit…"

"The Holy Trinity, eh?" The Reverend smiled nervously. "One People, One School, One Leader…"

"Something like that."

"Well, you're very welcome to it." The Reverend picked up the bottle of brandy and replenished the Headmaster's glass, then his own. "I hereby present you with the Spirit of Devilston. Cheers…"

"I appreciate the gesture," said the Captain, "but I think you've misinterpreted me. What I'm talking about is neither holy nor alcoholic. It's something much more ancient, and potent. And it isn't yours to give…"

Now the Reverend understood, as if the cognac in its bulbous glass had provided the magic eye.

"So that's what the Extraordinary Meeting is all about…?"

The Captain replied with a smile.

The brandy did little to comfort the cold dread in the Reverend's heart. He quickly drained his glass.

"Well, no rest for the wicked, as they say…"

The Captain nodded, saying nothing until the Reverend was almost out of the door.

"Edward?"

"Headmaster…"

"This Vortigern chap…what happened to him, in the end?"

The Reverend had paused on the threshold.

"He was killed, Headmaster. By those he betrayed."

The Sanatorium was a small Victorian building standing alone outside the castle walls, as if itself quarantined from the rest of school. It was always cold; intentionally - it was said - so as to discourage malingering. Now a draught blew across the polished parquet floor like the wind across the Siberian Steppes, chilling Tom's ankles as he kept vigil by the side of his friend's iron bed.

Jai's eyes remained closed. But for the shallow rise and fall of his chest, he lay completely still.

His face was swollen from the battle and several plasters indicated wounds, but at least the blood had been cleaned off.

"I'm so sorry Jai," said Tom, wringing his hands and rocking slightly in his chair. "I didn't mean to say what I did. It wasn't your fault we lost Dan. And you do care...Please don't die. If you do then I'll be on my own again..."

Tom was diverted from his misery by the rattle of crockery on a trolley trundling past, trailing an interesting smell. It was pushed by a plump middle-aged woman with a warm smile. Tom found himself watching her generous bottom rhythmically sway as she headed for several patients at the far end of the ward.

"Eyes off," said a voice nearby. "You're already spoken for, remember?"

"Sorry, I was just..." Then Tom realised who owned the voice. "You're awake!"

"I've been awake all along, you numbskull."

"You mean, you weren't knocked out...?"

"Me? Of course not."

"So...you heard everything?"

"I did, and I accept your apology."

"Well, now you owe me one."

"Why?"

"I thought you were dying."

"Far from it," Jai grinned. "I just needed a quick exit from all that fuss."

"How are you feeling?"

"Well..." Jai winced as he raised himself into a sitting position, "apart from a head like a split melon..."

"But what happened? You were easily beating Slimy-Moron then it all went tits-up..."

"I struck a deal. He promised to lay off you if I let him win."

Tom was astonished.

"You lost the fight for me...?"

"There were some other concessions, too. But I didn't really want to win anyway..."

"Why not? You'd be a brilliant Head of School."

"And how long would that last, before Devilston would have Her wicked way with me and I'd become corrupted myself, drunk on power and privilege with no respect for those beneath me...?"

"But you wouldn't be like that. You're different."

"Am I? You know, when my father was young he dreamed of making Jaisalpur a better place, and improving the lot of the poor. Now look at him, pissing his wealth away while his kingdom crumbles like a sand castle. By the time he kicks the bucket there won't be anything left of either, which is just as well as far as I'm concerned..."

"What do you mean?"

"I don't want to be the next Maharaja of Jaisalpur.. Give me friendship and adventure, and you can keep all the rest. Oh and women too, of course..." Jai was watching Matron bending over to collect some cutlery from the trolley's bottom tray. "Which reminds me. We've got a date..."

"What?"

"It's Halloween Night soon. Remember the twins? The invitation...?"

"Jai, we'll be expelled if we get caught absconding again."

"Then we'll make sure we don't get caught."

"Like last time, eh? Anyway, we can't use the tunnel now. Dan had the key for the Crypt."

"But you've still got your key...?"

Tom patted his pocket. "Of course. And yours...?"

"Think so. Perhaps you could check..."

With a sigh Tom rummaged around in the pile of clothes on the bedside table, delving into Jai's pockets then staring in confusion at what he produced.

"Two keys...So who does the other one belong to...?"

"Seek and ye shall find." Jai smiled smugly, his arms folded. "It was in Dan's duffle coat. I secretly acquired it when we were in Sticky's study, while I was looking for the name tag."

Tom shook his head.

"Always one step ahead of the game..."

They were distracted by a rolling rattle which

stopped at the foot of Jai's bed, and a gentle Irish lilt.

"So Jack Dempsey's back in the land of the livin' is he? And how are you then...?"

"My dear Matron," Jai replied, "my head feels like the poor abused clanger within Devilston's bell."

"So you'll not be wantin' some of my stew then..." She lifted the lid from the pan on the trolley, releasing its magical aroma. "The Head may have closed the kitchens but I won't be havin' poorly boys on bread and water."

"Well, if you've made it yourself then it would be exceedingly rude not to try some..."

Matron eyed Jai with amusement, raising an eyebrow.

"Thought you might."

She began ladling the thick and lumpy concoction into a bowl. Jai noticed Tom's eyes were fixed upon the steaming stew, his mouth moving as if masticating imaginary morsels.

"Matron..." said Jai tentatively as she handed him his supper, "you couldn't by any chance spare some of your fine fare for my good friend here, could you? You see, he's in a state of psychological shock on account of the vicissitudes of the day and I feel he'd greatly benefit from the palliative effect of some quality cuisine..."

Jai winked at Tom. Matron sighed and rolled

her eyes; then, to Tom's joy, she began to fill another bowl with stew.

"Here you go," she said in a low voice as she handed the bowl to Tom, mindful of the eyes and ears at the other end of the ward. "But not a word to anyone, do you hear? It's risky enough cookin' stew for my patients, let alone dolin' it out to every Dick and Harry..."

Tom nodded as he began to wolf down the hot and delicious chunks, hardly allowing them to cool in his mouth before dispatching them to his yearning stomach.

"Thank you Matron," said Jai. "We'll be out of your hair just as soon as we've finished this splendid grub."

Matron fixed him with a stern eye.

"You'll not be goin' anywhere, young man. You're under observation for the night."

For once, Jai seemed willing to defer to authority.

"Whatever you say Matron…"

11

THE MOUSE TRAP

Hunched over against the elements, Alderley negotiated the track along the spine of Dragon Head as if traversing the ramparts of some huge and ancient castle under siege. The up-turned collar of his overcoat formed his own battlements against the sting of the rain's arrows, but it was scant defence against the gale. Fearing he might be scooped up and hurled into the raging maelstrom below, during the most violent gusts he stopped to crouch down, as if bowing to a greater power.

A ruin loomed before him: the roofless shell of a stone building with a tall chimney at one corner. In the twilight gloom the structure resembled a huge fist extending an accusatory finger towards heaven. Another time he would have lingered to explore, but the white tower was very close now, drawing him in...

He knocked on the door of the lighthouse

then braced himself. He'd heard many descriptions of the keeper. Youth could be cruel, judging the old and the ravaged against its own unattainable standards.

But there was no answer; only the wind howling in the gallery far above him.

Then something sharp scratched his scalp, and suddenly the air about his head was a fury of feathery agitation and loud shrieks. He raised his hands to repel the attack, glimpsing a black winged creature with red legs, crimson beak and beady black eyes full of violent intent. This defence failing, he tried the door; to his relief, it opened.

Shutting out his assailant he leant against the door for a few moments, allowing his breath and wits to return.

He was in a circular room illuminated only by what light remained outside, filtered through tiny windows in the curved wall. The space felt cold and damp. At its centre a thick pipe ran vertically from floor to ceiling, like an iron spine. The air was charged with the smell of paraffin oil. As his eyes adjusted to the dark he became aware of a large storage tank. He walked to the foot of a flight of wooden stairs. Seeing an opening at the top, he called up.

"Hallo! Anyone in…?"

No answer came so he ascended through the open hatch into a smaller, more homely place.

A large cast iron cooking range was throwing off heat for the benefit of the empty armchair in front of it. There was a small table with two chairs, a dresser and a deep sink.

Again his eye was drawn to the thick pipe running up through the centre of the room, and another flight of stairs. Climbing to the next level, he found himself in a space smaller than the one below, with only enough room for a single bed, a small wardrobe and a chair; and, in the centre, the pipe.

Something brushed against his ankle. A black cat was rubbing up against his leg, back arched, mewing softly. There was a short stump where its tail should have been. He crouched down to stroke it. Then, having gained its confidence, he picked it up and carried it with him up the next flight of stairs, harbouring a desperate notion that holding his cat might diffuse any aggression on the part of its keeper.

The next floor housed the lighthouse's machinery. Enough twilight radiated down from the open hatch above for Alderley to make out a complicated mechanism of valves, shafts and cogs, like the intimate workings of a giant clock; all steeped in the pungent smell of lubricating oil.

Now the symbolism of ascending through these levels occurred to him: the fuel room at ground level - containing the residue of fossilised species, millions of years old - represented to him the very origins of life; the living room above it provided heat and sustenance, the basic necessities of physical existence; then there was the bedroom, where the creatures of the deep subconscious roamed during slumber; and here - where he now stood - was the machine room, containing an engine of logical rationality. This motor should have been toiling away in its predictable routine, yet it stood silent and motionless, as if paralysed in thought.

A final set of steps took him to the top floor. In Alderley's analogy, the glass lantern house was the highest level of consciousness; the one all the others existed to serve: the lofty realm of enlightenment. The whole structure gently creaked and moaned, as if encouraging the wind's attentions.

In the centre of this circular space stood a huge lamp the height of a man and the breadth of his out-stretched arms. It possessed three faces, each consisting of a circular lens of over-lapping glass slats radiating from a central point, like ripples in a pond. In its myriad of polished surfaces, the world was shattered into a thousand shards. Alderley could see a multitude of aspects of his own face, magnified and grotesquely distorted; and - behind him - the fragmented form of another human.

Turning quickly he saw - through the glass of the lantern house - a figure leaning on the rail of the gallery outside, its back to him, apparently unaware of his presence. It was wearing an army great coat and - above the up-turned collar - Alderley could see the top of a bald head. Beyond this figure - out to sea - stood three dark sentinels of rock, indifferent to the angry water's violent assaults. Thick cloud choked the sky but for a narrow sliver on the horizon where a red sun bled into the sea.

In impatient protest the cat sprang from Alderley's arms with a strangled cry. The figure's head rotated slightly at the sound then resumed its seaward gaze.

Alderley took a deep breath. With one hand inside his coat pocket, tightening on the grip of his revolver, he opened the door. Stepping outside, he glimpsed the ground far below - through the wrought iron lattice of the gallery's platform - and his mind reeled.

The rain had stopped but the wind remained unruly, pushing at the door with such force that the handle slipped from his hand. The door slammed shut and the figure turned towards him, growling.

"Who's there...?"

Alderley was gripped by a sudden terror. The face that now contemplated him - illuminated an unearthly pink by the dying sun - was like the countenance of a corpse. The pale clouded eyes lacked lids or brows and stared unblinking in his direction. There were small holes where the nose and ears should have been, and the mouth was devoid of lips so that the yellowy teeth seemed set in a permanent snarl. Scarred skin was stretched over sharp edges of bone so tightly it looked on the verge of tearing.

Alderley fumbled to extract the revolver from his pocket as the ravaged face loomed up to him, reeking of tobacco and alcohol.

"Is that you, my darlin'...?"

The eyes squinted as much as the scars that besieged them allowed and a cold hand moved across Alderley's face, reading it. Then its fingers found his throat and he felt a great force pushing him against the guard rail, his gun falling from his hand. He was aware of an immense strength bending him backwards over the rail, threatening to send him plummeting to the ground. The clamp on his neck tightened, squeezing the arteries in his neck, until the skeletal face began to fade.

"Please..." Alderley croaked, consciousness slipping away. "I'm a schoolmaster...from Devilston..."

The hand released its hold and Alderley slumped to the wrought iron floor, coughing and caressing his throat as his sight returned. The death mask was glaring down at him.

"What the Hell are you doin' trespassin' in my home?"

His accent was as thick as cream, his deep voice clotted from under-use and soured by life. Evidently he hadn't seen the revolver. If he had then Alderley was sure he would have followed it over the rail.

"I was just out for a walk..." he wheezed. "I knocked but there was no answer..."

"So how do I know you ain't some burglar, eh? Or a murderer...? I could throw you over right now. Police wouldn't be askin' questions. Not round these parts."

The keeper's breathing was laboured and now he coughed: a horrible bubbling gurgle, his lungs dredging up a mouthful of bloody phlegm which he spat over the side of the rail. Then he wiped his mouth with the back of his hand.

"So, what do they call you then...?"

"Michael Alderley."

Alderley extended his hand, then remembered. However, to his surprise, the keeper's hand made contact with his own. He felt the strength again, now pulling him to his feet.

"Jack. Folk in Pristow call me Jack O'Lantern, and across, I should think..." He nodded in the direction of Devilston, now a black and ragged pyramid in the middle of the bay as twilight descended into night. "So, what are you after...?"

"I just wanted to talk to you about this place. I've always been fascinated by lighthouses but I've never been inside one…"

"Is that so? And the thought of meetin' old Jack in the flesh didn't put you off…?"

What was left of Jack's mouth widened to reveal more teeth, the remnants of a grin. Alderley was trying not to stare, forcing himself to look beyond the face; but a grim compulsion kept dragging his gaze back.

"I suppose it was a case of curiosity overcoming fear."

"Was it, now? Well, I'd wager you've not seen a fizzog as frightenin' as mine, eh…?"

Again Alderley struggled for a diplomatic answer. He had seen faces just as disfigured but they were Devilston's gargoyles, their features almost obliterated by the elements.

"Well, you certainly look like you've been in the wars…"

What Alderley had interpreted as a smile now vanished.

"Only the one."

Jack opened the door to the lantern house and entered. Alderley followed, closing the door behind him and shutting out the wind. The sound of the sea was reduced to a deep rumble. The last evidence of sunset was dwindling in the eye of the huge lamp.

"So you do all the maintenance yourself,

Jack?"

"I'm the keeper, ain't I? Or don't you think I'm up to it…?" He laid a scarred hand on the lens. "Twen'y years I've been lookin' after this old girl. Reckon I know every single inch of her…." Now, slowly and silently, the lens began to move. Jack removed his hand and the rotation continued, as if his gentle loving touch alone had brought it to life. "Proper work of art, ain't she? Floats on a bath of pure mercury…"

"Presumably the engine below provides the power," Alderley thought aloud. "And the oil's pumped up through the pipe into it. I mean, her…"

"Well, that's where you're wrong, Mister Schoolmaster. There's a motor underneath, sure enough, but it's clockwork. The pipe contains a weight on the end of a chain. As it's wound up, so the weight rises, just like a cuckoo clock…The oil in that tank below is for the lamp; and it ain't pumped up, either. Old Muggins here heaves it up by hand. Reckon they planned it that way so as to keep the keeper busy, the bastards…"

As he watched the lamp turning, Alderley pondered its design. He liked its asymmetry: a mechanism driven by the cold pure forces of physics, but its light fed by a sweating cursing creature toiling against the laws of the Universe. Reason and passion working together like the mind and the heart, but in harmony.

The sunset flashed across the kaleidoscope of the revolving lenses like spatters of blood; and yet - as beguiling as it was - Alderley knew this show was nothing compared with the blinding glory of the lamp when lit.

"So how do you know the light's working if you can't see it, Jack...?"

"I ain't completely blind, that's how. I only see shadows mind, but when daylight starts to fade I know it's time to put her in. Sometimes I'll stand right in front of her, as I am now, starin' into her light. Almost like seein' prop'ly again, and then I get to thinkin', maybe if I do it for long enough I'll get my sight back..." Alderley imagined Jack's face bathed in white light, washing away all the ugliness. "Can't do that now, though. Not in the black-out...Nearly a year since this old girl's shown her full glory, and there's been a few small boats caught on them Claws in the meanwhile." He nodded in the direction of the three rocks out to sea. "Only a matter of time before a big 'un comes a cropper on those beauties..."

"Doesn't make much sense really, keeping this light off," said Alderley. "I mean, no bombing raid is going to come from Ireland, is it?"

"Maybe not, but an invasion force might find this light handy enough..."

"You think the Germans could invade here?"

"I ain't for botherin'. I just let the world get on

467

with its dirty business while I get on with mine. As far as Jack's concerned, the sooner this old girl's back in action again, the better."

"So you've no interest in the outcome of the war?"

"I just told you, didn't I?" Jack snapped. "Don't you think I've had my fill of war, lookin' at the state of me? And why are you so interested in what I think, anyways?"

"I'm sorry," Alderley replied quickly. "I didn't mean to pry. I suppose I'm just as interested in the thoughts of a lighthouse keeper as the workings of his lighthouse, that's all." He searched for a means of dousing the anger he'd just ignited. "So what about fog, Jack? How do you know when to operate the bell...?"

"My other senses are tuned up, that's how. I can taste mist on my tongue. And I can hear the fog."

"You can hear it...?"

"That's right. No wind, and the sound of the sea ain't the same. Or the calls of the gulls and the choughs. Or my own voice, for that matter. I talk a lot to my light, see. I ain't crazy, though. In fact, prob'ly keeps me from goin' doolally, my conversations with the old girl..."

"Chuffs?"

Jack grunted.

"Call yourself a schoolmaster...? Sea raven. Black with red beak and legs. And very clever.

Some say they're the re-incarnation of King Arthur himself. Expect a lifetime of bad luck if you kill one..."

"I was attacked by a bird matching that description when I knocked on your door."

The permanent rictus gurn of Jack's mouth broadened.

"Charlie. Found him down on the beach a while agone, a-hoppin' and a-screechin'. Injured wing, peppered with shotgun lead. Your Cap'n's prone to shootin' gulls, and just about anythin' else that's airborne, the bastard...Well, I nursed old Charlie boy and he mended well enough, though he'll never fly prop'ly again. I still feed him and he's taken up residence in the old mine...But don't take it personally, him goin' for you like that. Reckon he's only protectin' his friend from unwanted visitors..."

Now Alderley saw his opportunity.

"Do you get any visitors here, Jack?"

"Nope."

"But just now you thought I was someone else..."

Jack turned away without reply and began to descend the steps. Alderley followed, down through the bedroom and a deepening darkness to the living space. He was fully expecting to be led down another floor and shown the door, and he cursed himself for his clumsiness. But instead Jack took off his coat then shuffled around the kitchen area, his hands like large spiders in the gloom, finding things. Alderley heard something being pumped then a match was struck, illuminating the room with a fragile and flickering light. Jack lit a hurricane lamp then held it towards Alderley.

"Here. Hang this on that hook above the table there. Not much use to me but you'll probably appreciate some light…"

"Thank you."

Alderley took the softly-roaring lamp and hung its handle on what looked like a meat hook, while Jack opened the door of the range and threw more coal onto the glowing embers within. Slamming the iron door shut, he then set down a bottle and two tin mugs on the kitchen table.

"You chackin'…?"

"Well," said Alderley, joining his host at the table, "as a rule I don't usually drink during the day, but since it's almost dark…"

"Always dark for me." Jack poured a generous gush into each mug. Alderley could just make out the bottle's label: finest cognac. As if reading Alderley's thoughts, Jack added: "Gift from a friend….Cheers."

"Good health," Alderley replied as they touched mugs.

"Good health?" Jack grinned then gulped down a mouthful. "Prob'ly a bit late for me, eh...?"

Two hundred miles eastwards, up the leg of the great peninsula, Doctor Paul Fischer was standing at the edge of the dance floor of Bristol University's Great Hall, sipping at a pint of beer. He had chosen the warm bitter concoction as the least worst option, having a low tolerance of stronger liquor.

The Great Hall, on the other hand, was most welcoming to spirits. Its vaulted ceiling of dark oak, lofty arched windows and wrought iron candelabras made it the perfect venue for the annual Halloween Ball. Some had questioned whether such an event should be taking place in the shadow of an imminent invasion, but the argument that Halloween had always been a defiant celebration of life over death had won the night; and the uncertainty of the future - if there was to be a future - seemed to add an extra frisson of spice to proceedings.

Fischer likened the gathering to a collection of atoms displaying a range of behaviours. There were the most attractive particles at the centre of each clique, with the little crowd of hangers-on they'd acquired in their orbits. Then there were the energetic, hurling themselves and their partners around the dance floor to the rhythm of the band, while on the boundary lurked the inert: the elderly, the un-musical and the shy.

Fischer was on the cusp between two energy states but not yet old. He was also a music lover, though he struggled to convert his appreciation into a quality of physical expression that was socially acceptable. But what firmly placed him in the third category of his atomic analogy, thereby condemning him to the outer peripheries of all social circles, was his congenital shyness.

He'd hoped that the fact he was wearing an eye-mask - in common with every other guest - might have made a difference on this particular night. In the manner of a comic book superhero it had at least given him something to hide behind, though he doubted any of those characters wore spectacles on the outside of their masks.

In truth, all his disguise had done was transfer the focus of his self-consciousness from the otherness of his facial features to his diminuitive physique, emphasised by a borrowed dinner suit slightly too big for him.

Fischer glanced up at his escort standing next to him, towering above him, the pint glass rendered a half in a huge fist. With his massive torso looking about to burst out of his dinner suit, the Scotsman very much resembled the superhero at leisure. From behind his mask he was scanning the dance floor, assessing the physical merits of each woman.

"Archie, why don't you dance?"

Fischer had to raise his voice above the band. Archie smiled down at his charge.

"I'm on duty, remember?" His deep voice rumbled beneath the music. "But feel free to have a wee dabble yourself, Doc. Within sight, of course…"

"Oh, I wouldn't know where to start. Put me in a laboratory and I'm in my element, if you'll pardon the pun. But here I feel like…"

"A fish out of water?"

"Yes," Fischer laughed. "Exactly."

"Well, in that case you need to dive into the pool…"

"Are you suggesting I should just walk into that heaving mass of humanity? Utterly unconscionable."

"Alright. If you don't want to take the plunge then spot your fish and cast your line."

"But it's all so random. So arbitrary."

"Rubbish. It's all determined."

"By God?"

"By Woman. All the single females in here have already chosen the males they're interested in. And some of the married ones, too. You just need to tune in to their broadcasts…"

"You make it sound like a science."

"It's an art and a science, Doc: the art of the conversation, the science of the signals. Like hers, for instance. That's the second time she's looked your way..."

Archie nodded towards a woman with flowing red hair sitting at a table on her own. She wore a black evening dress, long black gloves and a black eye-mask decorated with glistening sequins. A cigarette smouldered in the slender holder between her fingers. Fischer immediately disregarded her as a viable prospect.

"Simply too glamorous for the likes of me."

"Think like that and you've failed before the race has even begun. You need to remember who you are: a scientist so important he has his own personal protection." Archie tapped his temple with his finger. "It's all in the mind, Doc. A boffin like you should know that. By the way, she's just glanced over again…"

"She is obviously looking at you, my friend."

"I don't think so. Go over and ask if you can join her."

"I can't. You go."

"But I'm working, remember?"

"Ah yes. England expects every man to do his duty…'"

"Only, I'm Scottish."

"Well, in that case you are off the hook, as you British say. Anyway, I thought I was supposed to be your tutor, not the other way round..."

"Alright. If you're not going to do anything about it, then I will. She's just too ripe to be left dangling. But don't wander off, Doc. I'm doing this for you, remember...?"

Fischer watched with admiration as Archie strolled over to the table and introduced himself. He bowed slightly as he shook the woman's hand then took a seat next to her, while Fischer felt the familiar flow of self-pity within him. Once again he was the outsider, spurned by the mainstream.

When he'd first come to England he hadn't expected women to fall at his feet, but - being a foreigner and hence exotic - he'd hoped for at least some curiosity on the part of the native fauna. In its apparent absence (which - in the light of Archie's thesis - may have been a fault of his own faculties of detection, he conceded) he'd buried himself in his work, converting social failure into scientific achievement. And as Hitler had mutated - in the eyes of the British, at least - from the saviour of his country to the menace of Europe, Fischer's nationality became a dirty word and his sense of isolation was only compounded. The irony was not lost on him.

He took another mouthful of beer and the shock of its bitterness brought him to his senses. What was he thinking? He should only be grateful that Britain had given him sanctuary. The restriction of his personal freedom and the drought of female intimacy were mere inconveniences compared to what his fellow Jews were suffering at the hands of the Nazis.

"Doc!" Archie was gesticulating. "Over here!"

Fischer walked over, feeling like a dog being called to do tricks.

"May I introduce Lady Charlotte Smythe-Morrigan?" Archie grinned proudly, as if he'd conjured her out of thin air. "Lady Charlotte, this is my tutor, Doctor Paul Fischer..."

"I am..." Fischer stuttered, "...very pleased to meet you..."

As they shook hands he was thankful she was wearing gloves as his palms were moist with sweat. Her face was a ghostly pale, her lips scarlet, her eyes dark behind the mask. It was a potent combination, all really too much for him. He felt quite faint.

"Are you alright, Doctor?" she asked. "You don't look well."

"I am fine...It's just this English beer...I don't think I'll ever get used to it..."

"Why don't you sit down...?"

"Thank you."

Archie gave him a wink as he pulled up a chair for him.

Everything is just a big game to these Britishers.

"Lady Charlotte is from Cornwall."

"Really?" Fischer had no idea where Cornwall was but he was very aware of his hands. He couldn't decide whether to rest them on his lap or on the table. "So, Your Ladyship...what are you doing in Bristol...?"

In his nervousness the question sounded like a demand.

"Please, call me Charlotte."

"Then you must call me Paul..."

She smiled. With her eyes mostly hidden behind her mask he found himself frequently glancing at her mouth.

"Well, to answer your question Paul, I was a drama student here. I try to visit as much as I can, to catch up with old friends. I also took in some theatre earlier. Two birds and all that..."

"Is that the name of the play?"

Fischer had recalled the common term for British women, and he found himself speculating on the play's subject matter.

"It's an old saying, Doc," Archie chuckled. "To kill two birds with one stone means doing two things at the same time..."

"Oh. I see...So, which play was it?"

"Salome," she replied. "A matinee performance at the Old Vic."

"Forgive me but I am not familiar with the theatre. What is the play about?"

"Sounds like an Italian sausage," said Archie.

"It's the story of a woman who dances for a

king," she explained, "in return for the head of a prophet."

"Goodness," said Fischer. "That sounds rather serious…"

"These days I find myself drawn to weightier topics. I think it's the war. The fear of death rather concentrates the mind…"

"Quite."

"So…are you a doctor of science, medicine or philosophy?"

"Oh, most definitely science. I couldn't even countenance medicine. I hate the very sight of blood. As for philosophy, you could say I dabble…"

"So it's all bubbling test tubes and lightning conductors, is it?"

"Nothing so exciting, I'm afraid. My work concerns very small things."

"How small?"

"Oh, smaller than the human mind can imagine."

"How very interesting." She rose from her seat. Fischer's heart sank as he and Archie also stood. "Gentlemen, would you excuse me for a moment…?"

"Very small things," said Archie with exasperation as they sat down again. "Come on Doc, you can do better than that…"

"But I thought I was supposed to play down my work, not draw attention to myself."

"Don't worry. This one's quite safe."

"You're absolutely right," said Fischer, forlornly. "Safe from the likes of me, that's for sure. I doubt very much she will return."

"Oh, don't be so certain about that. She hasn't finished her drink yet. I think she's definitely nibbling at the bait..."

Archie stood up again.

"Where are you going now?"

"I hate being the gooseberry. But don't worry, Doc. I won't wander far. Just relax and be yourself..."

His huge hand patted Fischer on the shoulder.

"Archie..."

But his minder was already heading for a tall blonde woman by the bar who'd been casting unambiguous glances his way. Then, to Fischer's horror and delight, his new acquaintance returned to her seat.

"Where's your friend?"

"He said he didn't want to be a goose berry, though I'm not sure what birds and fruit have got to do with anything..."

She laughed and he felt his heart lift. Perhaps Archie was right. Maybe he had the tiniest scintilla of a chance with this woman: a quantum of potential energy...

They sat in silence for some time, listening to the music and watching the dancers. Fischer was desperately searching for the right words.

In the pressure of her presence, his mind seemed to have evacuated.

Nature abhors a vacuum...

He was simply incapable of generating small talk, that essential dynamo that drove polite society. Unless of course the conversation was about the smallest particles in the Universe, though now he wasn't sure he could recall even a single fact from the vast galaxy of his scientific knowledge. She seemed to have exerted a mysterious force upon him, rendering him not only mute but ignorant.

Her fingers were toying with the stem of the cocktail glass which reminded him of an item of laboratory apparatus and, to his relief, an obvious solution came to him.

"Could I get you another drink...?"

"That's very kind of you. Another dry martini would be lovely..."

He tried to catch the eye of a waiter but they were all busy, or perhaps ignoring him, so he excused himself and made his way to the bar.

It seemed like an age before he was served. He kept looking over to her, checking that no-one had slipped into his place. She was watching the dancers and now he was certain she'd lost interest in him. The reaction had cooled, the experiment had failed.

He brought her drink over and another pint of beer for himself, even though he hadn't finished the last. He spilled some of it as he sat down. In retrospect, he thought, a half pint would have been better, but then she might have questioned his masculinity.

"So what work do you do, Paul?"

"Well, I can't go into too much detail but it concerns the structure of the atom."

"Fascinating..."

"Are you being sarcastic?"

"Not at all. Tell me, is it true there are more atoms in each of us than there are stars in the Universe?"

"It is." Fischer's confidence was rallying again. "And in the nucleus of every one of those atoms is stored a colossal amount of energy."

"So what does one have to do to get this energy out?"

"The atom must be split. Or its nucleus, to be exact..."

She lifted the cocktail stick out of the glass. A green olive was skewered on it as if harpooned, the red pimiento at its centre like blood.

"Do you like olives, Paul?"

"I have never tried one."

"Really? But you don't know what you're missing..."

Now she guided the olive into his mouth. He had no choice but to slide it off the cocktail stick with his teeth, remembering his friend's words.

Now who is taking the bait, Archie?

He felt it split in his mouth. Its taste was bitter, but better than his beer. She watched with interest as he chewed.

"They say one either loves them or hates them. So, what do you think…?"

"I'm not sure…"

"That must be the scientist speaking. Always keeping an open mind…"

"Always."

Now she leaned closer, her voice lower.

"So what makes one particular atom become attracted to another, Paul?"

Fischer swallowed the olive, coughing a little.

"Sorry….Well, it's partly chance and partly the receptivity of each atom."

"But what if none of it was chance? What if every atom in my body was meant to be exactly where it is, right now? And every person in this room was meant to be with whomever they're with…?"

"You mean, everything determined by God?"

"Not God necessarily. But everything in its rightful place. Things changing all the time, of course, but always in a pattern. Like a kaleidoscope…"

"Then I think that would be a tedious universe. I believe we hold our destinies in our hands."

"Now you're sounding a tad like Adolf…"

She said it with such charm that he wasn't at

all offended.

"More Friedrich, I'd say…"

"Nietzsche? But wasn't he just as deranged?"

"He was a visionary. I suppose when you have stood on a high mountaintop, returning to the valley can be difficult. So you are interested in philosophy…?"

"Very. I think I'm an existentialist. I like the idea of being whoever you want to be." She gazed across the floor, where Archie was now dancing with the blonde. "We're all actors really, trying out different roles. All the world's a stage…"

"Actually," said Fischer, "I've always seen it as more of an experiment."

"Really?" Behind her mask her eyes narrowed as she studied him. "Well, if that's the case then let's test an hypothesis."

"What hypothesis?"

"I'm wondering if scientists can dance…"

"Oh," he laughed. "I'm afraid this particular scientist has no talent whatsoever in that area. I think the expression is, two left feet."

"Then I'll teach you…"

She stood and took his hand, leading him into the warm and pulsating heart of the dance floor. Fischer could hardly believe what was happening. He just hoped Archie could see him.

The window flashed with lightening like a tiny cinema screen, followed by a grumble of distant thunder. Their sparse conversation had dwindled into nothing. Jack seemed content to just sit and drink.

Presently the black cat materialised from the darkness beyond the circle of lamplight and jumped onto the keeper's lap, purring as he stroked it.

"That's a lovely cat," said Alderley, grateful for the cue. "What's its name?"

"Sid."

"Was he born without a tail?"

"Nope. Some bastard in the village cut it off."

"Why would they do that?"

"Well, they say a black cat's lucky, don't they? So, if you cut off its tail you've got yourself some luck without havin' to look after the whole cat. But a black cat without a tail ain't considered so lucky. Quite the opposite in fact, which is why old Sid ended up here, well out of range of Pristow. Seekin' sanctuary, you might say..."

"You're a kind man, Jack."

"Not sure about that. But I like animals, sure enough. You know where you are with 'em. Humans on the other hand..."

"But you have friends?"

"And what makes you think that?"

"Up there you mistook me for someone else. A woman, I presume...?"

The lamp swung slightly in a draft, causing the shadows to move across Jack's ravaged features.

"Well Mister Sherlock, you presume correctly. I do have a friend and she is indeed a female, and a beautiful one at that....And now I reckon I know what you're thinkin'....What would a beautiful woman want with a man lookin' the way I do?"

"Not at all..."

"My arse," Jack grunted. "I'd be thinkin' exactly the same if I was sittin' where you are....But now you're thinkin', how would I know she's beautiful, me being devoid of sight?"

"I have to admit, the thought had occurred to me..."

"Well, I'll tell you how...Because hers is the kind of beauty even the blind can see, as I'm seein' that light..."

He looked up at the lamp, his milky eyes glowing.

"She sounds very special. Would I know her...?"

Jack's hand found Alderley's wrist and gripped it tightly. Now there was threat in his voice.

"She's none of your business, you understand?"

"Yes. Of course. I'm sorry..."

The keeper withdrew his hand and took

another gulp of brandy. The wind moaned outside and the lamp roared quietly. Alderley sought to change the subject.

"That building nearby...It's an old tin mine...?"

Jack nodded slowly.

"The mouth of the monster...and swallowed some of Pristow's finest men, she did. Fact is I was prob'ly the first male of my kin who didn't start his workin' life in Dragon Head, hackin' away at the marrow of Mother Earth...and all on account of my bein' in the right place at the right time. A good fifty years agone it was, yet still as fresh as yesterday..."

Now Jack was staring at the flickering window, as if seeing his memories projected before him.

"There I was, standin' on the beach watchin' the sea demolishin' a sand castle, wonderin' what I was goin' to make of my own dreams, when this heavenly vision came ridin' out of the twilight: the fairest of maidens, gallopin' through the shallows on a handsome white horse, sittin' high and proud in her saddle, golden hair flowin' behind her. And as they passed she looked my way, and at that very moment her mount tripped over the mound of that sandcastle. Well, the poor animal went arse-over-tit and this angel in human form fairly flew off his back..."

His chuckle deteriorated into a cough.

"She was bleddy lucky the water broke her fall. Well, I led her to dry sand to gather her wits while I retrieved the horse. He'd bolted down the beach, see. Beautiful Arab, but highly-strung and easily-spooked. So I walked up to him real slow, whisperin' softly to gain his trust 'til he let me take his reins and led him back to his mistress...Now she'd been watchin' all this, and when I handed him over she said I'd a natural way with animals, and she asked me there and then if I'd like to look after her horses. And when I looked into those rock-pool eyes of hers, it finally dawned on me who she was..."

"The Duchess?"

"Who else? She weren't no Duchess then mind, only Lady Jennifer...Now hark at me. 'Only Lady Jennifer' he says, as if she was some poor commoner like me and not the wife of the heir to the Duchy of Devilston..."

He took another gulp of brandy.

"So it was that Jack here came to be lookin' after the Morrigans' horses. The last stable boy had run off with the milk maid see, hence the vacancy. Poor Trevail was beside himself, the girl havin' been his fiancée..."

"Trevail the gardener?"

"The same. Still across, is he?"

"Certainly is," Alderley laughed. "No wonder he's so miserable."

Jack fell silent for a moment, as if considering something. When he spoke again, his voice was grave.

"Not sure why I should be tellin' you all this - some stranger trespassin' on Trinity House property - but I reckon maybe this is a confession of sorts, you bein' fairly anonymous to me and that. I was a good Catholic boy once see, before my soul was burned out. And quite a looker in my youth. Hard to believe, considerin' what Jack looks like now, eh…? So Lady Jennifer took a shine to me, and me to her. Wasn't difficult on my part mind, she bein' the loveliest woman I'd ever set eyes upon…"

"But she was married, you say?"

"She was but let me ask you a question, Mister Alderley. Ever fallen so head-over-heels for a woman that the rest of the world just don't matter anymore? Like her horse did that day, unseatin' all common sense and reason…?"

"Yes. I think I have."

"Then you'll know exactly how I felt. Heart ragin' with love for her, loins boilin' with lust, and a head full o' smoke and steam all blurrin' my judgement. We'd ride out together to our secret place in the woods above Pristow where we could just be man and woman together, like…"

"Her husband was away?"

"North West Frontier." Jack took another

mouthful. "Now don't think I didn't feel guilt for what I was doin', Mister Alderley. And don't think she didn't neither. We both burned with it - and we'll prob'ly burn for it - but we were young and our desire burned fiercer..."

"You sound like a bit of a poet, Jack."

"S'pose that's what bein' in love does to you..."

"So what happened?"

"What do you think? An affair between a Major's lady and a miner's lad ain't goin' to end in a rose-covered cottage now, is it...? Well, she fell pregnant and there was no doubtin' who the father wasn't, her husband bein' away in Afghanistan...Now, she could have gotten shot of the baby and everythin' would have carried on as normal, as tends to happen with the upper classes, not wantin' to make a mountain out of a molehill... Only, Lady Jennifer wasn't for gettin' rid of the child so this particular molehill swelled up, until there was no keepin' the secret...

"They say the Duke and Duchess - bein' of the Anglican persuasion - were all for their son makin' a clean break and divorcin' the woman, and to Hell with the scandal. And you'd have thought her husband would have been in agreement when he came back to find his wife full of a child that wasn't his. But Julian Morrigan was made of a different mettle, Mister Alderley. He blamed himself for the catastrophe, on account of bein' away for so long, and so he forgave his wife. That's the kind of man he was, see? A good Christian soldier, with a great big heart brimmin' over with forgiveness...

"Now personally I'd have much preferred it the usual way, with the cuckolded husband turfin' out his unfaithful other 'alf. Then maybe there'd have been some hope for Lady Jennifer and me, though she'd have struggled livin' on a miner's wage with no horses or servants or fine linen and such like. But she knew which side her bread was buttered on....So she became the dutiful wife, presentin' her husband with two fine children of his own. As for me...well, I ended up down Dragon Head, after all. Felt like I was going to Hell for my sins, considerin' the mine belonged to the Morrigans. Or maybe Purgatory's a better likenin', bearin' in mind what was to come...I was still a God-fearin' soul in those days see, before the war brought me round to thinkin' that the Almighty had forsakin' this miserable world long ago...Ever been down a workin' mine, Mister Alderley...?"

"No."

"Heat and dust so's you can barely breathe. Noise of the pumps so's you can hardly hear yourself prayin' to any god who'd have you. Bent double all day, which is really a permanent night...And deep in that private mine inside your own head, there's this terror lurkin' of all that rock comin' crashin' down upon you. Or a flood, which for me was a worse fate 'cause it meant a longer death. The mine goes far out under the sea you know, way beyond those Claws out there. And sometimes, on days like this when the wind's makin' her mischief and the ocean's flexin' her mussels, you could hear the boulders movin' around on the sea bed above, like giant chess pieces bein' shifted about...

"S'pose I was lucky enough not to be workin' at the seam, 'cause all day pickin' away at the same open wound would have sent me mad, for sure. But because of my time in the stables across I was put to lookin' after the pit ponies instead. Beautiful animals those, Mister Alderley. Not to look at mind, all stubby and stocky and no match for the thoroughbreds across. But such a kind and calm nature, and bleddy clever. Once I was leadin' this old girl called Beth pullin' a truck when suddenly she stopped dead and wouldn't budge no further, no matter how much I cussed her and pulled on her rein and pushed on her fat arse, though I'd never use the stick on any animal...

"Well, just then there was this great rumblin' and the earth shook and clouds of dust filled the air. And when it cleared and the lamps were lit again, I saw that the tunnel ahead had collapsed. Beth had sensed it comin', Mister Alderley, which is why she'd stopped, see...? Lovely beasts, those. Born in the mine and spent their whole workin' life down there, never seein' the light o' day until retirement. Always fancied it must have been like arrivin' in Heaven for 'em, walkin' out of that darkness for the first time...But it was only a short stay in paradise, before they were off to the knacker's yard for glue. Broke my heart when I watched old Beth bein' led away..."

Jack drank some more, wiping his mouth with the back of his hand.

"I had to get out of that place, Mister Alderley. All the lads I'd grown up with were down there with me, but they didn't seem bothered. It was a job after all, and the good times on top - the women and the drinkin' and the larkin' - seemed to make up for the bad times down below, for them anyways. But not for me. S'pose you might say I had a little more imagination in me. I saw a better life for myself than scratchin' around in the bowels of that bitch of a bal...

"And sometimes, when I'd crawl out of that arsehole of a pit at the end of a shift, covered in filth and blinkin' in the sun like some poor godforsaken mole, I'd see the boys from your place chasin' a ball across the beach, with their lives all neatly marked out in the sand and the whole world before 'em like a wide blue horizon.

Those lads might just as well have been on another planet, for what was my future but a dead end of rock in the darkness...?

"They say a man can suffer most things so long as he knows nothin' better, like those pit ponies born and bred down the mine. Problem was though, I'd already tasted a piece of Heaven and the yearnin' for more kept chippin' away at my insides. I just couldn't get Lady Jennifer out of my head, and it didn't help that the island was always there, just beyond my reach. But there were no waves goin' to break down those castle walls. No time long enough to wash away those memories...

"And then the Great War came along and I joined up. Not so much to serve my country though, but just to get out of that bleddy mine. Fancied myself in the cavalry, shipped off to the far corners of the Empire to return a hero, trottin' through Truro on my big horse in my scarlet tunic, with all my medals sparklin' in the sun, and ribbons streamin' from the end of my spear like a knight of old. And all the girls a-sighin' and a-swoonin' as the band played *The British Grenadiers*, with my chest filled to burstin'...And do you know what my greatest dream was, Mister Alderley...? Ridin' into that castle over yonder like Sir Lancelot himself, to win back the hand of my only true love, havin' proved myself in mortal combat..."

Jack's voice broke. He finished off the contents of his mug then replenished it, allowing him the opportunity to regain his composure. Then he felt for Alderley's cup and shakily poured some more in, ignoring his guest's half-hearted protests.

"So I wrote a letter to Lord Julian Morrigan himself. Some years had passed by now and he'd inherited the Duchy and taken up Headmastership of the school. I was reckonin' maybe his wounds would have healed, though mine were still pretty tender. Still are...

"Anyways, I apologised for what had happened between his wife and me all those years back and I accepted full responsibility, like a man. No mean feat for me Mister Alderley, seein' as though I wasn't the only guilty party, and her bein' older than me and hence more worldly-wise...Then I asked him if he might see it in his heart to arrange for me to join his old cavalry regiment, him havin' been a staff officer and no doubt able to pull a few reins..."

"Did he reply?"

"What do you think...? But everyone's got their limits, eh? Like that one particular bastard of a seam that just won't yield for no man, no matter how hard you slug away at it...But what stuck in my craw was all the talk of his Christianity. Wasn't often Jack here darkened a church door or bothered a Bible, but that don't mean I'd forgotten what Jesus said about forgiveness. And surely I'd served my penitence, toilin' for the Morrigans for all those years down that Hell-hole...

"Anyways, I expect my letter ended up on the fire, while I ended up in a foreign country, after all. But it was only Belgium and the weather was no better than Blighty. What I saw of it, that is. You see Mister Alderley, on account of that experience underground they made me a sapper, plantin' mines under the Hun to blow the poor bastards up. Out of the fryin' pan and into the fire, you might say..."

Jack paused for a moment, as if himself mining his mind for the darkest memories.

"Messines, West Flanders. Rightly named 'cause we made a fair old mess of it. Spent a year diggin' tunnels underneath the enemy lines, while the Boche were diggin' their own tunnels, tryin' to find us. Sometimes there'd be a breakthrough and then we'd be at each other's throats in the dark, fightin' with pick axes and shovels and whatever else you could lay your hands on, just like the bleddy Dark Ages...

"Well, eventually everythin' was ready for the Big Push. Twen'y-one mines in all, stuffed like a goose on Christmas Day with half-a-thousand tons of high explosives, to be discharged dead-on three o'clock in the mornin'..."

Now Jack produced a tin and a pipe from

his pocket. He banged the pipe on the table to empty it then proceeded to re-load it with fresh tobacco from the tin, pushing the flakes into the pipe's cup with a thumb.

"The blast was to signal the start of the British attack, like a gun startin' a race, see? The battle that followed was a real blood bath, Mister Alderley. I think you might have heard of it, bein' an educated man. July 1917..."

"Passchendaele."

"That's the one....So anyways, three o'clock was fast approachin'. We checked the charges one more time then we were scurryin' home through the tunnels like rats, as fast as we could go bent double, when I realised we'd left Chalky..."

"Chalky?"

"Mouse we carried with us in a little cage, in case we came across any natural gas. Or the man-made variety..."

"Like a canary."

"That's right. Only Chalky was white, and he couldn't fly..." Jack chuckled darkly. "Now me bein' an animal lover, I couldn't leave the poor little fellah to be blown to animal heaven, so I turned back. Prob'ly should've let my oppos know, but they'd only have given me a ribbin' for bein' soft...and anyways, I reckoned I'd be back with 'em soon enough. But what I hadn't reckoned on was my carbide lamp givin' up the ghost...

"So there I was, stumblin' through the blackness, and not even able to shout out to the boys for fear of alertin' Fritz. I was lost Mister Alderley, and in more than one sense of the word, 'cause three o'clock came and those mines had to be blown...

"My mates told me afterwards they'd begged to delay the attack, just for five minutes at least so they could look for me. But the officers weren't havin' any of it. My own fault for gettin' detached in the first place, they said. Strictly speakin', it was desertion. They could have had me court-martialled and shot, though they never bothered in the end. Reckon they considered what happened to me punishment enough..."

Alderley was horrified.

"You mean, they detonated the charges knowing you were still down there...?"

Jack struck a match and lit his pipe, sucking at it until the tobacco glowed and smoke curled from his mouth.

"Funny, ain't it? It wasn't the bleddy Boche who did for me in the end but good old Blighty. Sacrifice it was Mister Alderley, pure and simple. The mines had to be blown at three o'clock dead, 'cause that was the time the enemy watch was relieved. That way more of 'em would be killed, see. The ones being relieved and those relievin' 'em, too. And what was one more dead sapper, after all, on top of all those other wasted men? Or beneath them, I should say...They said it was the biggest explosion mankind had ever seen, though I daresay there'll be a lot bigger in this war. Man kind. Now that's a good 'un...

"I was told so much earth was lifted into the air by that blast that the followin' day was like night. They reckon Lloyd George himself would have heard the bang, all tucked up and snug in his mistress's bed in Surrey... Ten thousand Germans perished that mornin', Mister Alderley, and all they found afterwards was a single foot in a boot. How about that...? All those souls gone in the blink of an eye, and a poor little white mouse who'd done no harm to no-one..."

"Do you remember anything of the explosion?"

"Not much. Prob'ly just as well. Only this blindin' flash like a dragon's breath which I s'pose was all the gas catchin' fire... Next thing I knew, I was lyin' in a field hospital, wrapped from head to toe in bandages like King Tut himself, hearin' the padre readin' my rites. They'd given me up for dead, see. Didn't think anyone so badly burned would make it through the night, let alone the next twen'y years. But we Cornish are a tough breed, Mister Alderley. When all else is washed away in the Final

Reckonin', we'll still be clingin' on to the Rock of Ages with our fingernails...And so I hung on, even though the pain of my scorched flesh was like the claws of Hell draggin' me down. Imagine some bastard's peeled away every inch of your skin with a potato knife, then dunked you in a pan of boilin' salt water..."

Alderley winced.

"So anyways, I recovered. Well, in a manner of speakin'... By the time I was well enough to be shipped back home, the war was over. My mates were cheered as they marched through Bodmin - those who'd survived, that is - but not me. I wasn't invited on the victory parade on account of my lookin' like Death Himself, in the flesh. Mine was the true face of war and no-one wanted to see that, not even my family. I don't think Ma and Pa could believe it was really still me in this mask. Took one look at their son and ran away weepin', bless 'em. Never heard from 'em again...

"So I was kept out of sight in a sanatorium like a dirty secret, until I was almost goin' out of my mind. I'm a practical man you see, Mister Alderley. I need to be doin' things to keep me distracted from all those memories flashin' inside my head like cannon fire. So in the end they made me the keeper of the Dragon Head light and everyone was happy: my family 'cause I was out of the way, and me 'cause I'd sort of come home and at least I'd have somethin' to do....Well, 'happy' is probably not the right word for it but I ain't too good at expressin' myself..."

"You've expressed yourself extremely well," said Alderley quietly.

"So, poor old Jack never did get to join the cavalry and see the Empire, but that's the way life goes. For some of us, anyways..."

"You're a very brave man, Jack."

"That's what they all say, but I reckon bravery's got nothin' to do with it. It wasn't bravery that kept me alive all those long dark nights in that field hospital, listenin' to the cries and the moans of the dyin' all around me, feelin' my skin burnin' like it was still on fire. It was plain selfishness, Mister Alderley. I wanted to live, that's all. I was greedy for just one more gulp of sweet cool air, and then maybe another... Pure survival instinct, that's what it was. Jack wasn't goin' to give in to the Grim Reaper without a fight. And so Jack fought..."

"And won."

Jack's ravaged mouth curled up at one side.

"Considerin' the state of me, I'd say more like a draw..."

"And do you think it was all worthwhile?"

"Well, I'm still alive, ain't I?"

"The war, I mean..."

Jack shrugged.

"They said it was the war to end all wars,

didn't they? But here we are twen'y years on, starin' down the barrel of another. And this one's goin' to be even worse, mark my words. The killin' machines they have now will make the last one look like medieval times. If you were the cynical type, you might think it was all a con so that a few bastards can get rich from sellin' weapons. Problem is, there ain't no shortage of boys volunteerin' to use 'em so's they can prove themselves men...If you ask me, Mister Alderley, if they want to put an end to war for ever then they shouldn't be makin' it so bleddy profitable and glorious. In my reckonin' it's just another dirty job. Like minin', only it ain't minerals you're after but other men's scalps..."

"Do you think we'll win this one, Jack?"

"I don't know and I don't really care. It don't make much difference to Jack who's in charge of the world, 'cause the world don't want Jack to be part of it. As long as I've got my light they can all burn in Hell..."

"So you'd still be looking after this place if the Nazis invaded?"

"I work for nobody but myself. Take care of Number One, that's what I say, because no-one else is goin' to...Speakin' of which," Jack patted his stomach, "it's way past Jack's dinner time. I can tell 'cause he's gettin' a tad grumpy..."

Alderley looked at his watch.

"Gosh, it is getting late. The tide will probably be in. Might have to spend the night on the mainland…"

He was angling. He knew it was rather desperate but he needed to talk more. He'd been so engrossed in the story he'd neglected the reason for his visit.

"Well," said Jack, rising to un-hook the lamp and ignoring the bait, "no doubt there'll be a room for you in the King's. But I wouldn't be hangin' around for too long down there. They ain't too partial to outsiders round these parts, Mister Alderley. Especially not folk from across…" Jack put out his hand. Alderley shook it, again feeling the strength. "I'd see you out, only I can't see…" He snorted with brief amusement, then the levity was gone. "Watch yourself on that path now. Nights like this there's been folk blown clean off. And give my regards to the Duchess from me…"

Alderley cleared his throat. He'd been hoping to avoid having to break the news.

"Jack, there's something I should tell you…"

"Oh God," the keeper laughed then coughed. "You ain't my long-lost son, are you…?"

"The Duchess had a riding accident."

"An accident…?"

"I'm afraid she's dead."

Jack slowly lowered himself into his seat. He said nothing for some time, his ghostly eyes staring ahead. There was no sign of tears and Alderley wondered if even his tear ducts had been damaged in the onslaught that had destroyed his face.

Or have his emotions been cauterized?

"I had a feelin' in my bones," Jack said, at last. "Fell off her horse, did she? And this time there was no Jack there to help her...

"You know, sometimes I catch myself wishin' I'd never met her on the beach that day. That nothin' had ever happened between us. Then I may have made it into the cavalry after all, and not ended up in this state....But then I think of that short time I had with her: the brightest days of my life Mister Alderley, shinin' like a seam of gold inside my head, even in the darkest nights....And so I always come to reckonin' that the Hell I faced under Dragon Head, Flanders and all that was fair trade for that little piece of Heaven, when she was mine and I was hers..."

"Was she the one who visited you, Jack? The one who gave you the brandy...?"

Jack's pale eyes looked straight at Alderley, as if seeing him clearly for the first time.

"Reckon you should be goin' now, Mister Alderley. You wouldn't want to be over-stayin' your welcome, would you...?"

After Jack had closed the door on him, Alderley lingered in the doorway for a while. Sheltered from the wind, he lit a cigarette and contemplated all that he'd heard. He tried to imagine himself living through what Jack had endured, and failed.

Finishing the cigarette, he began to search the ground surrounding the lighthouse. The storm had broken and a full moon lit the night with a milky radiance, but his quest was hindered by a black feathery shape continually swooping down on him, as if intent upon thwarting his efforts.

At last he found the revolver, gleaming in the moonlight, its barrel stuck into the soft turf. But something still pestered his thoughts, like the bird that flapped around him.

Gripped by a feverish impulse which overcame his fear of the keeper, he knocked loudly on the door. Presently he heard heavy footsteps descending the stairs, and a familiar cough. In spite of the gun lying heavy in his pocket, his courage was quickly evaporating. By the time the door had opened he was ready to flee.

"Get away, boy!" For a second Alderley thought the keeper was shouting at him. "It's alright Charlie, it's only that schoolmaster come to mither me again…" The chough squawked as if in reply, then flew away into the night. "I'm presumin' it's you Mister Alderley, since I don't often get two visitors in the same month, let alone within minutes of each other…"

"I'm sorry to bother you again Jack, but you never said what happened to the child…"

"And what's it to you?"

"Well, yours was such an extraordinary story but it didn't feel quite finished, somehow…"

"So you thought you'd disturb me from my supper for one more precious nugget…?"

Jack's skeletal face was illuminated momentarily by a lightening flash on the horizon.

"Well, His Lordship would have been someone special indeed to have brought up a bastard child, wouldn't he…? Never saw the boy myself, which is prob'ly just as well. Better for him to have a new start in life, and all that. Adopted by a family in Wales, they say…"

She was leading as the band played a warm slow number. In her heels she was taller than him, and she was probably taller than him out of them. Finding her perfume and proximity intoxicating, Fischer occasionally stepped on her toe.

"What is this song?" he wondered aloud. "The melody is beautiful."

"Stardust," she replied. "One of my favourites."

"How appropriate."

"Why?"

"Stardust could be another name for atoms…"

He was feeling wonderfully relaxed, the intricate cogs of his mind now effortlessly free-wheeling.

"So what kind of an atom would love be?" she asked.

"Now that's a very good question. Where would it fit in the periodic table? Noble gas or volatile metal…?"

"There's another question you haven't asked me yet…"

Now the cogs grated on the unexpected gear change.

"What question?"

"Well, I'm wearing gloves so you can't see if I have a wedding ring…"

Not for the first time, she seemed one step ahead.

"So," he said, hesitantly, "are you married…?"

"Yes…"

He found himself relieved by the news. She'd clearly been indicating an interest, but this exciting prospect had also generated some considerable agitation within him. The immediate future presented a multitude of possible outcomes, and he didn't cope well with choice. However - in the light of her revelation - the dull but familiar face of certainty had returned to his universe. Now he could relax and resign himself to comfortable disappointment, knowing that factors beyond his control had determined the result. There was nothing he could do about it. He was off the hook.

"...but not happily."

His inner turmoil immediately returned to the boil.

"I'm seeing someone else." Her eyes watched him from within her mask. "Does that shock you, Paul?"

His inability to reply answered her question.

"He's here tonight. Over there. With the woman in the tiara..."

He followed her line of sight, seeing a plump grey-haired man stuffed into a dinner suit. He was dancing with a woman of similar girth in a straining ball gown who looked like a female version of her partner.

"You're having an affair with the Vice-Chancellor of the University?"

"I know. Rather wicked, isn't it? But then," she added, after a thought, "he is the Chancellor of Vice..."

Fischer hoped the Vice-Chancellor wouldn't recognise him in his mask though he knew this was unlikely, considering he'd instantly identified the Vice-Chancellor; and the spectacles perched outside Fischer's mask would have dispelled any traces of doubt.

"It gives him a thrill," she continued. "All the

subterfuge. I'm sure there are other women of his here tonight..."

"Do you love him?"

"No. But I like his company."

"If you were mine I wouldn't give another woman a glance."

"Funnily enough, that's exactly what he said to me once..."

"But I mean it."

She looked at him and smiled. Then she drew closer and whispered in his ear.

"Paul, I want to take you home."

He panicked.

"Now?"

"No, next Christmas..."

"Next Christmas?"

She laughed at his obvious disappointment.

"Of course I mean now."

"I'll have to tell Archie..."

He'd spotted his escort on the dance floor, now entwined with the blonde woman.

"Is Archie your chaperone?"

"Of course not." His denial was more forceful than he intended. "He's just one of my research students. He thinks I need looking after."

"And do you?"

"No. I can look after myself."

"Very well then..."

She took his hand tightly and led him quickly to the exit. He glanced back. Archie was kissing the woman. He hadn't noticed them leaving.

As they left the Great Hall - its dark gothic tower glowering down upon them - the slow eerie wail of sirens filled the night air. For a moment Fischer believed Archie had seen him leave and had raised the alarm, then he checked himself. Sometimes his ego knew no bounds. He was more than a little drunk but he remembered the drill.

"It's an air raid. We'll have to get to a shelter."

"No. We'll take the car and drive out of the city."

"What car?"

A black Rolls Royce pulled up alongside the pavement next to them. A uniformed chauffeur got out and opened the door for her.

Guests had begun to spill out of the huge arched doorway of the Great Hall. The anti-aircraft guns had opened up - a distant thumping - and searchlight beams swept the black sky.

Now she was sitting in the car, waiting for him. The slit down the side of her dress displayed a considerable section of her thigh. Her fingernails were blood red. The chauffeur rested a hand on his shoulder.

"What are you waiting for, sir...?"

Fischer looked at the chauffeur who winked at him. Then he found himself getting into the car beside her, the heavy door clunking shut on him like the lid of a casket.

As the car began to move, there was a knock on the window. He looked round to see Archie's big face. The car accelerated but his escort was still there, standing on the running board, holding onto the edge of the roof. In his mask he looked like a highwayman. For a second Fischer was struck by the comic absurdity of it all.

The car started to weave at speed along the road, its driver trying to throw Archie off. Fischer glanced at the woman beside him. She was rummaging in her handbag, perhaps for her lipstick, he thought. He wound down the window, allowing Archie to get a better hold.

"What the Hell are you doing, Doc?" cried Archie, then he shouted at the driver: "Stop the car! I'm a police officer!"

There was an explosion to Fischer's left, instantly deafening him in that ear. At first he thought a bomb had dropped close by, then he saw the smoking gun in her hand. Archie was still on the running board, his hand fumbling inside his jacket. The gun fired again and the Scotsman dropped out of sight. The smell of cordite filled the car. Now she pointed the gun at Fischer.

"You shot him…"

He choked on the words. She replied in German.

"And I'll shoot you too if you don't do exactly

what I say." In her mask it was now she who looked like the outlaw. **"Wind the window up.** Schnell!"

He obeyed, his hand trembling. Bombs were starting to land now, some of them quite close: bright flashes and deafening crashes like the heart of a lethal thunderstorm. They overtook a fire engine, its bell clanging frantically.

"You shot my friend."

He hadn't spoken - or even thought - in his mother tongue for an age. The words felt clumsy on his lips.

"Your Special Branch minder, you mean." She'd reverted to English. "He had a gun and I didn't want to give him the opportunity of using it. It was either him or me. War is a messy business up close, isn't it...?"

"He was married. He had children."

"And he was getting on very well with my colleague back there."

"So she was an agent too...?"

"You're a very big catch, Paul. We had to be sure of getting the pick-up right."

He was slowly regaining some degree of control. He was feeling sick at the loss of his friend, but he also felt a cold and selfish emptiness within. She had no interest in him after all, other than as a commodity. The whole artifice of the evening had collapsed to reveal a terrible truth. His star had turned into dust.

"But I should have known from the beginning. You never asked me the question..."

"What question?"

"'Where are you from?' Everyone asks me that when they first hear my accent. But you already knew..."

"I know everything about you, Paul."

"While everything you told me was lies..."

"Not all of it. What do you call it when a particle can be two things at the same time?"

"Quantum Theory," he replied gloomily. "And the Vice-Chancellor...?"

She smiled.

"A little improvisation on my part. I hadn't the faintest idea who he was until you said his name."

The car turned into a dark side street and stopped. The sound of bombing was behind them now. She slid open the glass partition and passed the gun to the driver.

"Keep him covered."

Fischer felt surprisingly calm. He'd resigned himself to his fate and now he was preparing himself for his punishment, for investing too much trust in human beings.

"So it was curiosity that killed Schrodinger's cat," he muttered in German.

"Bitte?"

She'd taken a small bottle out of her hand bag. Removing the top she tipped it up, holding a handkerchief over its neck, while the chauffeur pointed the gun at him, smiling vaguely.

"Not really," said Fischer, in English. "Just rather annoyed at myself, that's all. So what are you going to do with me...?"

Now she closed in on him, clamping the handkerchief over his mouth and nose. He tried to remove her hands but felt his consciousness waning. A smell had filled his head and it wasn't bitter at all, but really rather sweet.

"I already told you, Paul." Her face was fading, and her voice. "I'm taking you home..."

J.J. Greenwood

12

MISCHIEF NIGHT

The deep hum of a busy pub dwindled, all eyes on the stranger as he entered the King's Head.

"Good evening," Alderley said to the huge bearded man behind the bar, whom he presumed to be the landlord. "I wonder if you have a room for the night...?"

The reply rumbled like the sea in a cavern.

"Might have..."

"Well... if you did, how much would it be...?"

The landlord contemplated the stranger with deep-set eyes.

"Who are you?"

Alderley offered his hand. It was ignored.

"Michael Alderley. I'm a schoolmaster at Devilston."

Now there was silence. All present made the sign of the cross, the landlord included.

"We don't use that word over here."

"What? Schoolmaster...?"

Alderley wondered what horror they'd experienced in their school days.

"The name of the island," growled the landlord.

"Oh, I'm sorry. I didn't realise....Well anyway, I've been beaten by the tide so...would you have a room, by any chance...?"

"For you? Nineteen shillings, sixpence and a ha'penny."

The landlord cast an amused glance at an old man sitting on a high stool by the bar, smoking a pipe.

"Nearly a pound..." Alderley patted his coat pockets reflexively. "I'm afraid I don't have that much on me. I wasn't expecting to stay out tonight, you see..."

"So you'll be payin' me first thing tomorrow. Or else I'll be havin' words with your Captain, whom I happen to be well acquainted with..."

"Of course." The sting of being fleeced was soothed by the relief of securing a bed. "Any chance of a bite to eat...?"

"Kitchen's closed."

Alderley glanced at his wristwatch. It wasn't particularly late.

"Bar's still open though," the landlord added.

"Right. Well, I'll have half a cider, please."

"Don't do things by halves round here..."

The landlord filled a pewter tankard with cider then set it down in front of Alderley.

"Two shillings."

A huge hand hovered over the bar.

"Could you put it on my bill?"

"Another loan, eh? I ain't the bleddy Bank of England, you know."

The old man chuckled.

"If I was you I'd be payin'..."

Alderley dug out some coins, his hand by-passing the revolver in the deep pocket of his overcoat. The other drinkers resumed their conversations.

"So, what do you teach across?" the landlord asked.

The cider was strong and sour. Alderley winced.

"Science."

"Prefer history, me. Like to know about the past, and where I've come from..."

"Well," said Alderley, encouraged by the apparent thaw in the landlord's manner, "one could argue that science is just as important, being all about the present. And the future..."

"Who said anything about arguin'?"

The landlord's glare remained cold.

"Anyway," said the old man, pipe-smoke pouring from his mouth, "history can be about the present and the future, too. In fact, there's a great big block of it standin' right there in front of you..."

He grinned at Alderley's confusion.

"Our landlord's a Pendragon, see. Direct descendant of King Arthur himself, he is..."

The old man pointed the wet end of his pipe at the landlord like a wand, a cloud of smoke drifting across the bar.

"But I thought King Arthur is only a legend..." Alderley ventured.

"Oh, he existed alright. And there's your proof..."

To Alderley the landlord seemed the physical antithesis of the mythical king. Henry the Eighth would have been a better likening.

"And one day Cador here won't just be our landlord, he'll be the lord of our land...."

Now Alderley wondered if he was being toyed with, as a naïve outsider.

"But we've already got a lord of the land. He's called the King."

"Not the King of England," said the old man. "That's the land across the Tamar, whose business is none of ours. I mean the King of - "

He was interrupted by a clattering intrusion. Soldiers in full combat dress carrying rifles had entered the pub.

"What's goin' on?"

Pendragon placed his big hands on the bar, like a chieftain at his castle wall.

"We're searching your premises," said the young officer in charge, then continued to direct his men. Some went upstairs, others searched the ground floor while a third group descended the cellar steps. The patrons looked on in silence, their eyes dark with contempt for the intruders.

"So where's your warrant then?"

The landlord was clearly struggling to control himself. Alderley noticed his nostrils dilating as he breathed, like those of a bull under restraint.

"Not necessary," the officer replied. "We're at war, in case you hadn't noticed…"

"And what are you lookin' for?"

"You don't need to know that, but your full cooperation is appreciated."

"Seems I don't have any choice in the matter, do I?"

"Correct." Now the officer was surveying the shelves behind the landlord, crowded with bottles. "Quite an array of spirits you have here, Mister Pendragon. And no shortage of foreign brands, I see…"

"They're not rationed."

"No, but I haven't seen such a variety since before the war. Surprising, considering our nation is effectively under siege…"

"We don't get through much in the way of foreign liquor," said Pendragon. "Folk round here prefer my cider."

"Of course they do," said the officer, unconvinced.

Presently his soldiers returned from their

search and began to exit.

"Apologies for the inconvenience, Mister Pendragon. Oh, and by the way…" the officer pointed with his stick at the brass clock behind the bar, "you haven't put your clock back for winter."

Now Alderley noticed the time on the clock. It was still an hour ahead.

So that's why the kitchen's closed.

Pendragon feigned slight surprise, anger still seething beneath.

"You're right. So I haven't…"

When the soldiers had gone the drinkers cheered. Whatever the invaders were looking for they hadn't found and this qualified as a victory. Then the hum resumed, the landlord moving to the other end of the bar to serve some new-arrivals. The clock remained untouched.

"All the clocks in Pristow are an hour ahead," the old man explained to Alderley. "And one day soon it'll be the same right across Kernow. This is a separate country see, and now the time is nearly upon us to seize our freedom…"

He clenched his fist. Alderley was astonished.

"You mean, an uprising…?"

"Not exactly. Let's just say, deals will be done…"

"Deals? Who with…?"

The old man's reply was a wry smile as he puffed on his pipe. Alderley was aware that the cider - in combination with Jack's brandy - was having an effect on him, stoking his confidence. But it was also bringing illumination to parts of his mind usually in shadow, like dappled summer sunshine falling on ripening apples.

"Well," he pondered aloud, "they do have an interest in that kind of thing, what with Wagner and all that...I suppose it's possible they could put a puppet king on the throne of Cornwall..."

A sudden loud thud brought silence again. The landlord had slammed his huge hand down on the bar and his eyes was boring into Alderley again.

"Puppet king?" he boomed and Alderley's blood froze. "Poppycock!" Now the landlord pointed at him. "Mark my words, schoolmaster. As soon as the power's in my hands I'll drive all you bleddy foreigners out of this land, once and for all. My ancestor led an army that crushed the Saxons, and we'll do it again!"

Pendragon reached under the bar and produced an object which caused Alderley to fear for his life. With its glistening golden hilt and gleaming steel blade, the huge sword seemed to cast a spell over the room.

"Behold Excalibur..." muttered the old man, his eyes wide with enchantment.

Holding the sword horizontally in front of him - one hand gripping the hilt, the other encircling the blade - the landlord bellowed three words over the heads of the gathered. His men roared their approval, stamping feet and pounding on table tops. Alderley had to raise his voice above the din.

"What did he say?"

"'Onan hag all'," the old man replied. "One and all..."

It was an impressive display. Alderley could easily imagine Pendragon in full armour on a huge war horse, at the head of an army of Cornishmen. But what match would Celtic ferocity be against the Nazi war machine?

It would be History versus Science...

Not long after the soldiers had vacated the cellar of the King's Head, two 'monks' crawled out of a large barrel lying on its side at the bottom of a pile. They stood in the dripping darkness, listening to the chanting in the pub above.

"What's going on up there?" whispered the plump one.

"No idea," replied the other, dark-skinned with eyes that gleamed in the meagre light, "but I'm not hanging round to find out..."

He crawled up the barrel ramp, unbolted the trap door and opened it enough to peer into the night. Satisfied the street was clear, he climbed out and his accomplice followed.

The pair raised their hoods. It had been Tom's idea to borrow two of the habits from the Crypt. Not only were the garments a perfect Halloween costume, they also conveniently concealed their identities.

"The Village Hall must be up this road," said Jai.

"What makes you think that?"

"Because important buildings are usually at the top of hills...."

As they hurried up the steep cobbled street they heard a shout behind them.

"Oi! You two!"

They accelerated their pace.

"Hang on there!"

Jai cursed under his breath.

"No point running. It'll just make them suspicious."

So the pair stopped and waited for the two figures to catch up. One had a deathly-pale face, with slicked-back hair and two fangs protruding from a bloodied mouth. The face and hands of the other were covered almost entirely in what looked to be dog hair, badly glued on.

"Evenin'," said Dracula, with some difficulty. "You two off to the do...?"

Jai grunted. He and Tom were hunched over, their faces hidden within their hoods.

"So who's in there, anyway?" asked the

Wolfman. "Let's have a look at you…"

He reached for Jai's hood but a hand grasped his hairy wrist.

"Oh, you don't want to be doin' that…"

Tom stifled a snigger at Jai's theatrical Cornish accent. Fortunately, alcohol had blunted their inquisitors' critical faculties.

"Beware, m'lads…" Jai continued, "for anyone settin' eyes upon the face of a Mad Monk will suffer the Curse of Devilston…"

The two Pristovians laughed heartily, knowing it was all just make-believe. But both made a swift sign of the cross, all the same.

"Come on, Davy," said Dracula. "It's gettin' late and there won't be any scrumpy left."

"True enough, Will," the Wolfman replied. "Or girls, for that matter…"

They moved on, but cast nervous glances at the hooded figures following behind.

As the two ghouls entered the Village Hall, the monks held back.

"We'll let them go in first," said Jai. "We don't want any more awkward questions…"

Approaching the entrance, they could hear music from within. But there was one more obstacle to negotiate: at a trestle table in the entrance hall sat a triumvirate of stern-faced elderly women.

"Here we go," Jai muttered to Tom. "The three-headed gatekeeper…"

"Tickets," said the first of the ladies, coldly.

"We're friends of Merryn and Tamsyn," Jai replied with confidence. "They've got our tickets."

"The twins have already gone in," said the second. "They were waitin' out here for the best part of an hour for you two. Gave up in the end and left your tickets with us to sell on."

"Well, that won't be necessary now because we're here." Jai held out a palm. "So, if you would kindly hand them over, madam…?"

"Too late," said the third. "We've just sold 'em to Will and Davy there, and they were the last I'm afraid…"

She appeared to be more gleeful than afraid.

"But that's not fair!" said Tom. "Those were our tickets!"

"Serves you right for leavin' two lovelies in the lurch," said the first, smiling smugly. "It's the quick and the dead round here."

"Yes," Jai murmured, "and we know which of those you are…"

"What was that?

"Couldn't you just let us in anyway?" Tom persevered. "It's quite late now…"

"But that wouldn't be fair on the others who've paid," said the second. "Besides, there are fire regulations, you know."

"Who are you, anyway?" The third was trying to catch a glimpse of the faces within the hoods.

"You don't sound from round here…"

"Well," said Jai, "I'm the Thane of Cawdor and this is my best friend Banquo. But you three should know that already…" Before they could answer, Jai was walking out. "Come, my friend. We'll find a better party than this…"

"A better party?" said Tom as they descended the steps outside. "This is the only party in town. Unless you were thinking of the King's Head…"

"King's Head, my arse," Jai retorted. "Do you really think we're going to let three miserable old hags defeat us…?"

Tom followed Jai round the side of the building.

"So where are we going now?"

"If they've got fire regulations then they must have a fire escape. And lo and behold…"

They had come to a closed door with no handle. From within they could hear the muffled sounds of merriment.

"You can only open it from inside," said Tom dejectedly. "Well, that's that then…"

"Not yet…"

Jai knocked loudly on the door. When no response came, he thumped at it until a warm wave of sweaty heat engulfed the two, and the noise of a party in full swing. In the open doorway, clutching a pint glass and swaying precariously, stood the Hunchback of Notre

Dame.

"Sorry to disturb you, old chap," said Jai, "but while we popped out for a breath of fresh air some unkindly soul closed the door on us..."

Ignoring them, Quasimodo staggered past and proceeded to urinate against a drainpipe, burping and breaking wind simultaneously.

Halloween was the one night of the year when Pristovians could escape the stifling confines of village life and be anyone - or anything - they wished. Now the Village Hall was crammed with a multitude of grim refugees from the Underworld. Every light had been covered in coloured cellophane - painting the scene in a wash of blood red - and cigarette smoke hung thick in the air, as if from the very fires of Hell.

On the stage a skeleton band comprising accordion, banjo, fiddle, horn-pipe and drums played as if possessed: veins bulging, eyes popping, skull-faces shining with sweat. Before them, the Dead and the Undead reeled and jigged together, while in dark corners some cavorted in closer proximity...

Tom had seen nothing like it in his life. For Jai it was reminiscent of the festival of Kali, when the world was turned on its head and normal rules thrown to the wind. In keeping with this spirit of anarchy, he helped himself to a couple of mugs of cider left by revellers too tangled in the web of dance to notice. Passing a mug to Tom, they toasted their success then each took a swig.

The first mouthful was a shock. Tom grimaced.

"What kind of apples do they make this with?"

Jai looked into his mug.

"Probably Devilston's rejects..."

But the two returned to their mugs for more as they stood on the edge of the dance floor, surveying the scene.

"Any sign of them?" asked Jai.

"It's hard to see anything in this light," said Tom. "And this bloody hood doesn't help."

"What we need is a closer look..."

Jai downed the rest of his cider then dissolved into the bubbling cauldron of the dance floor. Tom followed, trying hard to avoid contact with the dancers. But his efforts seemed only to increase his clumsiness, bumping into bodies and connecting with knees, hips and elbows, while the cider began to cloud his mind with its insidious magic...

The sight at the centre of the seething mass brought him to his senses.

One sister wore a long red dress, clinging to her like the skin of a snake, her body undulating in time with the beat of the drum. Her pale face was partly obscured by a long black wig, revealing glimpses of mascara-ed eyes and scarlet lips.

The other wore a ghostly white dress. A tiara of flowers crowned her golden hair, and her skin appeared to glow with a spectral pallor.

Together the twins seemed like the very embodiment of worldliness and innocence. As they danced they weaved a bewitching spell upon Jai and Tom. But each was accompanied, a truth rendered even more painful by the identity of their dancing partners: Dracula and the Wolf Man.

Tom's heart sank.

"We're too late."

"Not yet," said Jai. "The game isn't lost until the final whistle, remember?"

"But we're two tries down."

"Two tries down but neither converted. We just need to wait for our window of opportunity to open..."

As he watched the girls dance, Tom felt a sweet sickness churning within: the coming together of what he wished for and what he knew would happen, like two currents - one warm, the other cold - meeting in a violent whirlpool of frustrated desire...

A whistle shrieked and the house lights came on. The music stumbled to a halt and all looked to the door, blinking in the harsh white glare as if woken from an exotic dream. Armed soldiers were entering the Hall. Their officer addressed the crowd.

"Your attention, please! We're conducting a search of these premises! This is a security matter of the utmost importance so your full cooperation is required!"

As he spoke his soldiers fanned out, moving amongst the crowd, some climbing onto the stage to search the wings and dressing rooms beyond.

"Wonder what they're looking for," said Tom.

Jai shrugged.

"German paratroopers disguised as nuns…?"

"Well, they've got their work cut out. Everyone's in disguise here."

"Yoo-hoo!" Hitler called out. "Over here, boys!"

The soldiers ignored the faux Fuhrer but the rest of the gathered cheered and whistled. Then some began to boo and slow-clap, taking advantage of the anonymity of their costumes to express their displeasure at the interruption.

Or was it more than that? Jai wondered. Were they displaying some deep resentment of authority: a distant and disinterested government in a city far away…?

The soldiers returned to their officer, the lights were switched off and the band launched into another number. Jai noticed that Dracula and the Wolf Man were still distracted by the departing troops, their young and malleable minds seduced by the allure of uniform, guns and a clear purpose. While they gawped he seized the opportunity.

"Come on, Tom. Now's our chance…"

Darting into the crowd he took the hand of the girl in white. Tom did likewise with her red-dressed sister, though clueless of Jai's intentions.

"What's goin' on?" the girls protested. "Who are you?"

"Don't be afraid," said Jai from beneath his hood. "We just need to talk with you."

The twins were perplexed yet intrigued. Jai led the other three outside, through the fire escape.

"We shouldn't be usin' this door," said the girl in white. "It's only for emergencies."

"This is an emergency," said Jai. "We're rescuing you from the clutches of two dangerous predators."

Now he pulled the hood from his head and Tom followed suit. The girls exclaimed.

"You two!"

"We thought you'd forgotten!"

"Forgotten?" said Jai with theatrical astonishment. "How could we possibly forget such a bitter-sweet rendezvous as this? With Macbeth's scheming wife, and the ghost of fair

Ophelia...?"

"You're the first person to get that right," said Lady Macbeth. "Davy thought we were the bride and bridesmaid of Frankenstein..."

"Philistine."

"Phyllis Stein?" asked Tom. "Is that Franken Stein's wife...? "

The girls laughed. Jai slapped his friend on the back.

"Good old Tom. Always ready with a gag up his sleeve..."

Tom wasn't aware he'd made a joke.

"Actually Tamsyn..." Jai began.

"It's Merryn."

"Actually Merryn, it's a remarkable coincidence that you should have come as Lady Macbeth. Who did we pretend to be at the door, Tom?"

"Er...Nathan Corduroy, was it? And his best friend's banker...?"

The girls exchanged a puzzled look then burst into laughter again.

"You two are funny," said Merryn.

"You should be a double act," said Tamsyn.

"Actually we're a triple act," said Jai, "only our third man couldn't make it...Anyway, should we dance?"

"Let's."

Seizing the initiative in the manner of her alter-ego, Merryn took Tom's hand and led him back through the fire escape, returning to the maelstrom. Tom glanced behind him, a look of elated disbelief on his face. Jai pointed to his hood and - remembering - Tom raised his. Then the couple were consumed by the party.

"So what about us?" asked Tamsyn. "Don't you want to dance...?"

"To be honest," Jai replied, "I just wanted to get rid of those two. Didn't want to share this beautiful full moon with anyone but dear Ophelia..."

"You're very greedy..."

Now she was looking at his mouth and Jai took the cue. It was by no means the first time Jai had kissed a girl, but - after an enforced hiatus of half a term - it felt like it.

The band was playing a slow number which even Tom could negotiate. He was holding Merryn close while they shuffled. Her cheek felt so soft against his, and the smell of her hair filled his head.

"You're so lovely," he whispered in her ear. It was an obvious line but he couldn't think of anything better.

"Thank you," she replied. "You're not so bad yourself..."

"Could I...kiss you...?"

There was a pause. Tom feared he'd gone too

far and - not for the first time - he blamed Jai. But then her face moved close to his and their mouths met, and it felt like his life had just begun.

He was standing with Elena on the battlements of Devilston. Black clouds cloaked the sky and the lighthouse flashed on Dragon Head. In the rocky formations of the headland, he thought he could make out Jack's ravaged face.

Like menacing beetles, panzers were crawling along the Causeway towards the mainland. Dark masses of ant-like troops followed on behind, while from a grey sky Stukas screamed over the defenders on the beach: Celtic warriors with spears and shields, in complete disarray as the bombs rained down upon them. In their midst he could see Cador Pendragon in full armour, his sword raised but struggling to control his terrified horse.

One bomber peeled off from the rest and dived on the castle, its whine terrifying. Not an aircraft at all but an eagle: black with a red beak, its crimson claws releasing a deadly load.

The bomb slammed into the castle wall and exploded.

Alderley woke.

A car reversing outside had been the bomber's whine, a door closing the thud of the bomb. He wanted very much to remain buried in the warm and musty bedclothes, but duty dragged him to the window.

A large black car occupied most of the dark alleyway below, its engine idling. Alderley saw two male figures - one of them tall, the other large - lifting something from its open boot, while a female figure watched over them. At first he mistook their load for a dead weight - a carpet, perhaps - but then he glimpsed arms hanging limply, and a head slumped to one side.

The two men carried the body into the gaping mouth of a trap door, the woman following. Presently the tall man re-emerged from the hole in the ground, closed the trap door then got into the car and drove away.

Alderley dressed quickly. Retrieving his revolver from under the mattress he carefully opened the door - its hinges whingeing as if rudely woken - then slipped out of the room.

In the dark he felt his way slowly along the wall, thinking of Jack moving around his lighthouse. Reaching the stairs he carefully descended, testing each step before committing his full weight, dreading the treacherous croak of a loose-tongued board.

After the din of the night before - the

raucous drone and the drunken roars - he found the silence of the pub deafening, its darkness oppressive. But a small amount of light was getting in, through the gap at the bottom of a door near to the bar. He walked quietly over and placed his ear against the door, believing the figures he'd seen were beyond.

He was suddenly aware of heavy breathing and a large presence behind him. He felt the yolk of a massive arm around his neck, while a huge hand clamped his wrist like a steel manacle.

"Drop the gun," rumbled a deep and familiar voice in his ear, "else I'll break your bleddy neck..."

The revolver clattered onto the stone floor. Alderley's right arm was forced painfully up his back as he was pushed against the door.

"Sleepwalkin', eh?"

"I heard something..." Alderley gasped. "I thought you were being burgled..."

"And do all you schoolmasters across carry guns? The boy's that bad, eh?""

It felt like the socket of his arm was about to pop out.

"Please..."

"I knew you was trouble the moment you set foot in my pub. Who you workin' for, then?"

"That's enough."

A female voice, from the other side of the room. In the corner of his eye Alderley glimpsed a shadowy figure walking towards them, heels clicking. The woman entered the weak pool of light. She wore a black evening dress and an eye-mask, and she held a pistol. Her long hair was a flaming red.

"Lady Charlotte. Thank God…"

"I thought you might make an appearance, Michael. Or rather, Arthur…"

Now she took hold of her hair at the fringe. To his astonishment it came away, taking the mask with it. A crop of curly black hair was revealed which she ruffled back to life., and familiar eyes.

"Elena…"

"Nothing is ever what it seems, is it?" She picked up his revolver and put it in her handbag. "Let go of him."

Pendragon paused for a moment before releasing his grip, uncomfortable at having to defer to another, and a woman at that. It wasn't the expected behaviour of a future king. But she was holding a gun and he wasn't sure she wouldn't use it. He never really knew where he was with this one.

"Now open the door."

The landlord unlocked the door and pushed it open, revealing a flight of stone steps leading down. Elena smiled, gesturing with the gun for Alderley to descend.

"After you, Arthur…."

"But you'll give the game away," Pendragon protested.

"It doesn't matter. He's out of the game now."

Descending into the cellar, Alderley saw a slight dark-haired man lying on his side on a makeshift bed of sacks. He was wearing a dinner suit too big for him, and an eye mask.

"Don't worry," said Elena, "he isn't dead." Then, louder, as she prodded him with her foot: "Just sleeping off the effects of a long journey, aren't we Herr Doktor...?"

The man began to stir. Blearily he sat up, removing the face mask to reveal dark tired eyes blinking in the glare of the bare light bulb.

"Where am I?" He squinted up at his visitors, then winced. "Scheisse, mein kopf...."

"You're quite safe, Herr Doktor."

From her handbag Elena produced a pair of spectacles. The man put them on and looked around.

"Doctor Paul Fischer, allow me to introduce Arthur Alderley of His Majesty's Secret Intelligence Service. MI5 isn't it, Arthur...?"

"What?" Pendragon looked at Alderley with astonishment. "Why didn't you tell me? I'd have had him done over..."

"Exactly why I didn't tell you."

"I'm touched by your concern for me," said Alderley.

She smiled.

"Don't be. It was all about protecting the mission, not you."

"So when did you find out?"

"I had a feeling from the first time we met. Call it a gut instinct, confirmed by the sodium pentathol in your wine..."

"Truth drug. That explains the epic hangover. And here was me thinking it was a love potion..."

Elena laughed.

"A love potion?"

"You know, like Tristan and Isolde. They drink the magic concoction then fall helplessly in love with each other."

"Poor Arthur. Always the romantic. But not really cut out for espionage, are you?"

"And are you cut out for National Socialism...?"

Her expression hardened.

"What makes you think I'm a Nazi?"

"Well, you **are** pointing a Luger at me..."

"I work for myself. But the Abwehr compensates me well, true enough..."

"So where are you from?" Fischer was slowly rubbing his face as his wits returned. "Britain? Germany...?"

"Catalonia," said Alderley and Elena together, then shared a smile.

"Well senorita, I salute your acting skills," Fischer touched his forehead, "if not your moral choices."

"Danke Herr Doktor, though you made it very easy for me. I was expecting a little more skepticism from a scientist of your calibre."

"I'm very much at home with atoms, my dear. With humans I have rather more difficulty…"

"Evidently." She turned to Pendragon. "Tie their hands."

Sighing heavily, the landlord began to rummage around his cellar for spare rope.

"So," said Alderley, "are we waiting for the tide to go out? Or do you enjoy the use of the Captain's boat as well as his car…?"

Elena smiled again.

"Neither. We'll be taking the short cut, darling…"

"Where's Pa?" Merryn wondered.

Tamsyn checked her watch.

"Well, wherever he is he'd better hurry up. It's nearly midnight…"

The four of them stood on the periphery of the dance floor. Tom noticed a bearded bull of a man entering the Hall, carrying a barrel on his shoulder which he delivered to the temporary bar. With a sheathed sword hanging from his belt he looked like a smuggler of old.

Tom nudged his friend.

"Wouldn't like to get on the wrong side of

him..."

"I already have," Jai muttered in reply. "That's the landlord of the King's Head..."

"Pa! Over here!"

The girls were shouting above the din, and waving. To Tom's horror the landlord waved back.

"Pa...?"

Jai couldn't resist a spot of mischief.

"Your father looks a tough 'un. Bet he doesn't take any nonsense from anyone..."

"Oh, he's a big softy really," said Tamsyn. "Ever since Ma died we've been lookin' after him. He wouldn't admit it, mind..."

"What's with the sword?" Tom asked, still anxious.

"He thinks it's Excalibur," Merryn explained. "Passed on to him down the generations."

"Ma wasn't havin' it any of it though," said Tamsyn. "She knew a bit about antiques and didn't reckon it was much more than a hundred years old."

"And he carries it everywhere he goes?" asked Jai.

"Only on special occasions. Like tonight..."

Spotting his daughters, Pendragon made his way towards them, the dancers parting respectfully like the Red Sea. His great arms encircled the girls' shoulders.

"So where have you been?" Merryn asked as

they kissed their father.

"Oh, just tyin' up some loose ends..."

"Well, you're only just in time," said Tamsyn. "You've got to pick the names, remember?"

Pendragon pulled a face.

"I really ain't in the mood tonight..."

"But it's your job," said Merryn. "You do it every year, and this one's no different."

"Ain't it?" he muttered under his breath, then turned to the hooded figures. "So, who are these two reprobates who ain't got the manners to show their faces?"

"Pa," Tamsyn sighed, "they're supposed to be Mad Monks from across. They don't show their faces. That's the whole point."

"Anyway," Tamsyn pushed at the huge mass of her father, "get up there and do your job. It's nearly time."

Wearily Pendragon clumped up the steps and onto the stage as the band brought the number to a hasty end. The crowd cheered and clapped then fell silent for their landlord, and leader. Pendragon's voice easily filled the hall:

"Ladies and gentlemen, it's nearly midnight on Halloween, and as usual it's incumbent on me to draw the names of those lucky ones who'll be meetin' our special visitor in the flesh..."

More bawdy cheers. The Wicked Witch of the West - with green-painted face and hooked false nose - had joined Pendragon on the stage, and now she invited him to withdraw the winning tickets from her upturned hat. Jai was sure he'd seen her somewhere before, and it wasn't in Oz.

As Pendragon read out each name a roar went up, loudest when the names of Merryn and - right at the end - Tamsyn were announced. Good-natured shouts of 'Fix!' peppered the cheers, while a smiling Pendragon insisted there'd been no tampering.

A space was cleared on the dance floor and the chosen eleven formed a circle. Consulting his pocket watch, Pendragon led the assembled in counting down from ten. Another great cheer went up as the hour arrived, then a silence spread through the gathered, until it was so quiet that the faint chimes of Devilston's clock could be heard.

The band's drummer began a soft roll which steadily grew in volume, now joined by the other musicians who sustained a long quivering note. Then a trapdoor in the stage slowly opened and a figure emerged as if invoked by the music, like a snake from its basket. It was dressed in red from head to foot, with stumpy horns and a long forked-tail. Its one-piece hooded suit fitted tightly, emphasising its distended belly.

Now the crowd screamed and recoiled with ecstatic terror as the Devil came down amongst them, brandishing a trident and darting this way and that whilst jabbing the air with his weapon in time with the frantic music. For Tom, the most terrifying aspect of the creature was his nose-less face, with lifeless eyes and a lipless mouth. He stepped back in alarm when the creature loomed up to him during its manic rounds.

"Bloody horrible, that."

"It's only a mask," said Jai.

"I know. But still…"

They watched as the Devil now entered the circle, weaving between the chosen eleven. He lingered around the females especially, particularly Merryn and Tamsyn who smiled awkwardly.

Pendragon drew his sword from its scabbard and descended from the stage, to another cheer. At a dignified speed - and with a look of bemusement on his face - he pursued the Prince of Darkness. His red quarry skipped and dodged about, until at last confronting Pendragon in the centre of the circle. A short bout of gladiatorial combat culminated - to the delight of the audience - in the wooden trident snapping under the superior force of the sword. And when its sharp tip pierced the monster's belly, the crowd gasped.

Now the 'wounded' creature stumbled around the circle. In turn the chosen eleven delved into the gash in the Devil's false stomach with a genuine look of disgust and pulled out a large bar of chocolate, each extraction accompanied by a cheer. When all the prizes had been distributed, Beelzebub fell to the floor, rolling and thrashing about in his death throes as the music reached a frenzied crescendo.

Then all was still and quiet.

After an appropriate pause Satan rose from the dead and took a bow, breathing heavily from his exertions. The crowd cheered and applauded, except one. As Jai had witnessed these strange proceedings, a cold wave of realisation had washed over him.

"It's tonight..."

Tom could hardly hear his friend over the noise.

"What is?"

"The Ceremony of the Thirteen." Jai's hooded head was close to Tom's now as he hissed: "Pristow is acting out what happens on Devilston."

"What do you mean?"

"Bloody Hell, have I got to spell it out? The sacrifice is happening tonight, in the Crown of Stones!"

Tom laughed, incredulous.

"How much cider have you had? Sacrifices don't happen anymore, Jai. Maybe in the time of our friend Jude, but not nowadays."

"So what happened to the last Headmaster, then? Lord Julian Morrigan…?"

"I told you. He was caught in the quicksand."

"But they never found his body. How convenient. And when was that?"

"I don't know. Sometime in the Twenties, I suppose…"

"It's on his memorial stone in Chapel, remember? Nineteen Twenty Seven."

"And?"

"How long ago was that, Tom?"

"Jai, I thought we we're supposed to be having fun tonight, not doing maths…"

"It was thirteen years ago, exactly. Just like Jude said: every thirteen years, at midnight on the eve of All Saint's Day. That's Halloween night, Tom. That's tonight!"

Tom was wavering.

"Well, it's passed midnight now. If there was a sacrifice, we've missed it."

"No we haven't. It's only eleven o'clock by my watch. For some reason they're an hour ahead here. We've still got time…"

The twins returned.

"And you thought you had some strange customs across," grinned Tamsyn.

"Anyone for a bite…?"

Merryn showed off her prize. Tom recognised the label: the same make of Swiss chocolate he'd taken from the coffin.

"No time for booty," said Jai. "I'm afraid Tom and I must bid you adieu."

Tom shook his head.

"I don't believe I'm hearing this…"

"But don't you want another dance?" asked Tamsyn, confused.

"My dear," said Jai, taking her hand, "I would surely dance with you until the end of time. But alas, a matter has arisen which demands our immediate attention…"

Not wanting to risk lowering his hood, Jai had to make do with kissing her hand.

"I'm really sorry about this," said Tom, as he kissed Merryn's hand. "It isn't my idea…"

"Will we see you again?" Tamsyn asked.

"Of course!" Jai cried, leading Tom towards the exit. But his path was blocked by two ghouls with clenched fists.

"You too ain't going anywhere." Dracula showed his fangs. "We've got a lesson to teach you for stealin' our girls."

"That's right," growled the Wolfman. "We had first dibs."

"We're not your girls," said Merryn sternly.

"We had one dance with you," her sister added, "and that was more than enough, quite frankly."

"So there you have it," said Jai, from within the shadows of his hood. "Now kindly step aside, gents. We wouldn't want this turning ugly." Contemplating their countenances, he added: "Or any uglier…"

A crowd had gathered around the scene, smelling blood. Emboldened by the weight of numbers, someone pulled down the strangers' hoods and the onlookers gasped. The house lights came on, Jai and Tom cringeing in the glare.

"They're from across!" shrilled the Wicked Witch of the West. Now Jai recognised the face beneath the make-up: the manageress of the Palace Cinema.

Hitler jabbed a finger at Jai.

"He's from farther away than that!"

Something deep and dark in the collective consciousness of the village had been stirred: an ancestral memory of faceless visitors from Devilston who'd brought fear and death to Pristow, a long time ago yet only half-a-dozen life spans away…

"Look!" Jai shouted, pointing towards the door. "It's the Devil! The real one!"

All eyes were momentarily diverted, Tom's included.

Jai dived through a gap in the crowd, pulling Tom with him. They ran onto the stage, barging through the band and disappearing into the wings. Startling the undressing Lucifer in the room beyond, they made for the back door.

"I must say…" gasped Tom, his habit hitched

up to allow him to run unimpeded, "your timing is bloody diabolical!"

"You're right!" Jai replied from ahead. "We should have worked it out ages ago!"

Dan would have.

As they reached the King's Head and turned the corner into the side alley, they could hear their pursuers: a sizeable number, aroused by the hunt and thirsty for blood. Their territory had been violated by two outsiders: one of them English, another even more foreign; both of them from that most feared and hated of places.

Jai pulled on the handle of the trapdoor. It didn't budge.

"Damn. Bolted again."

"And the tide's in!" cried Tom, panic-stricken. "What do we do?"

"Run!"

Tom followed Jai back round the corner, straight into the path of two fishermen stumbling out of the pub.

"Grab 'em!" the approaching mob shouted. "They're from across!"

Had they been quicker in the strike, the men might have had two prize catches on their hands; but cider had slowed their wits and the fugitives dodged them, disappearing down a side alley.

Jai and Tom fled through the village like two fish in a reef, desperate to throw off the sharks in pursuit but quickly getting lost. The labyrinth of passages reminded Jai of Jaisalpur's ancient backstreets, some alleyways barely wide enough for one person.

But the fishermen knew their village like their fishing grounds, and the quickest route to get there. The escapees soon found themselves trapped in a ginnel, a drunken fisherman closing in on them from each end.

"Looks like we're in for a lynching," said Jai, with uncharacteristic defeatism; and - uncharacteristically, too - Tom made a spontaneous decision.

Head down and emitting a bellowing war cry, he charged towards the smaller of the two men. The top of Tom's head struck the fisherman's belly, knocking him on his back. The impact forced a slosh of scrumpy from his stomach to his gullet, like sea water up a blow hole.

As Tom lay on the choking Pristovian, he glimpsed what looked like the tail of a black cat on a cord round the fisherman's neck.

Hurdling both of them, Jai pulled Tom to his feet and the two made good their escape. Reaching the edge of Pristow, they scrambled over a wall and dashed across open fields until Tom could run no more. He collapsed behind a hedge, within a small wood offering welcome cover from the dangerous moonlight.

"Well done, old boy!" said Jai.

Tom was coughing and wheezing, his vapourised breath billowing out of his mouth like exorcised spirits. He could hardly speak.

"We're not....out of the woods...yet...."

They could hear the shouts diminishing. Denied the consummation of their anger, it sounded like the villagers were satisfied with seeing off the outsiders and keen to return to the party.

"We'll have to lie low...until the tide goes out...then sneak across."

Jai shook his head.

"We can't wait. We've got to stop the ceremony."

"You must be off your rocker, chum...I mean, fancy abandoning the two most beautiful girls in Cornwall for the sake of some false hunch... and I'm not talking about Quasimodo back there..."

"We'll see them again."

"Really? First thing tomorrow we'll be hauled in front of the Head Bastard himself, you'll see. We might as well just cut our losses now and get out of Cornwall. I'd sooner face the Blitz than the wrath of Sticky. Does it have a spare room, that place of yours in the Big Smoke...?"

"More spare rooms than you possess fingers and toes," said Jai, "but we're not going to London. We're going back to school."

An owl hooted nearby, testing Tom's already

stretched nerves. The call was answered by a distant shriek.

"So you really think a sacrifice is going to take place on top pitch in broad...moonlight? This isn't the Dark Ages, Jai. That kind of thing doesn't happen anymore."

"But what if I'm right?" Jai's eyes were wide now, like two bright moons with dark hearts. "What if there is a killing tonight and we don't do anything about it?"

"So let's go to the police."

"They'll be in on it too. You know what these locals are like. Thick as thieves..."

"What about those soldiers then?"

"I doubt they'd believe us. Besides, they had other business on their hands by the look of it. They've probably moved on to the next village by now."

Tom folded his arms.

"Well, count me out of any more capers. From now on I want a nice warm bed and an easy life."

"Easy evil, hard good..."

"What?"

"It's an old Indian proverb."

"Well I'm the Devil and I don't give a damn."

Jai laughed.

"You're just sour because we left the girls."

"You're bloody right I am. For the first time in my life something was actually going right for me, and then you had to spoil everything with all this superstitious claptrap. This isn't India, in case you hadn't noticed. You're in England now..."

"Cornwall actually, and they've more in common than you'd think..."

Tom looked away, bristling with frustration, eyes brimming.

"Anyway," Jai continued, "we couldn't have stayed any longer at the party and survived."

His friend wiped his eyes and rubbed his nose on his sleeve, then stared forlornly ahead.

"So what do we do?"

"Well, we could wait here until the tide goes out and sneak across, as you suggested. But it'll be way past midnight by then..."

"And we'd probably die of pneumonia in the meantime."

Now that he'd cooled down from the chase, Tom was aware of how cold the night had become since the rain clouds had cleared.

"Or we could steal a boat from Pristow..."

Tom shook his head.

"Back into that lion's den? No fear."

"Well, there is a third alternative..."

"There is?"

"Always Three Ways, remember? Land, sea and...?"

"We can't use the tunnel, Jai. The door's bolted."

"But that's not the only route..."

"What do you mean?"

"Remember the passage that had broken into the tunnel? It must be connected to that old mine building, up near the lighthouse…"

"But that's Jack O'Lantern's territory…"

Tom shivered, remembering dormitory tales of a ghastly creature who ate trespassers.

"Just another myth, " said Jai, "like the Mad Monks. No doubt promulgated in order to keep curious schoolboys away from treacherous mine workings. If there is a lighthouse keeper still there, I bet he's a perfectly ordinary chap, with a wife and a dog."

"So Jack and the Mad Monks are myths but this ceremony of yours is real…"

"That's different."

"Is it?"

Jai didn't reply.

"And your plan is to climb down a disused mine shaft and then somehow find our way along miles of dangerous passages…?"

"We could at least have a look. It's better than sitting here twiddling our thumbs…"

"If we'd stayed at the party we'd be doing more than twiddling our thumbs," Tom retorted.

"If we'd stayed at the party we wouldn't have any thumbs to twiddle…"

Jai was already moving on, tired of debate. With a groan and no other alternative, Tom hauled himself to his feet and tried to keep up.

As they ascended the path along the headland through the low heather a mist began to creep in from the sea. It arrived in thin wisps like the advance party of a ghostly army, gradually reinforced until the land was besieged by a thick fog. The full moon that had earlier been a bright lantern was now just a faint disc: a single eye paled by cataract. Jai had resisted using his torch to save its battery but now the moonlight was so weak he feared they might stumble off the cliff edge to their left.

The lighthouse had responded to this slow invasion by sounding its clockwork bell every minute: a deep and melancholy knell which grew louder as they approached until they could feel the air vibrating around them, the resonance of the last toll still lingering even as the next rang out.

"What's the point of having a black-out when you've got that bloody thing clanging away?" Tom complained.

"I doubt bombers would be able to hear it."

"Really? I bet Adolf can hear that in Berlin."

A dark shape loomed out of the fog ahead: a shell of a building with a tall chimney, guarded by a sign hand-painted in large and uneven lettering.

TRESPASSERS WILL BE PERSECUTED

"I don't like the sound of that," said Tom.

"A mistake I'm sure," Jai replied, unsure.

Tom followed his friend into the roofless mine building, deeply uneasy about ignoring the warning though its tall walls offered some respite from the din of the bell.

A sudden raucous croak from above startled them. The torch beam found a small dark shape perched high up in a corner. A black beady eye shone in the light, scrutinising the intruders.

"It's just a crow," said Jai, with some relief.

The bird squawked again, correcting him.

Sweeping the ground with the beam, Jai soon found what he was looking for: a square of rusty iron. He pulled on its handle. To his surprise, the hatch lifted.

"That's a stroke of luck. It isn't locked…"

Tom moved carefully to the edge as Jai shone the torch into the deep shaft. Iron rungs set into stone led down into the blackness.

"Jai…are you seriously thinking of going down there…?"

"Well we haven't come all this way for the view."

"In that case, good luck to you."

"So you'll be staying here, will you?" Jai smiled, his face cruel in the torch light. "With old Jack O' Lantern to keep you company…?"

"Hang on. I thought you said he was a

perfectly normal bloke…?"

"Probably…"

"Now that's not fair and you know it! You've completely changed your tune! Anyway, I won't be hanging around for long."

"So you're going to take your chances back in the village…?"

Tom didn't reply.

"We'll just have a recce, that's all. As soon as it starts looking dangerous we'll turn back."

"Why don't I believe you, Jai…? I'll tell you why: because you're always shifting the bloody goal posts!"

"Keep your voice down. We don't want to wake old Jack."

"I doubt he'll be sleeping much with that bell so close…" Tom peered anxiously into the void then shook his head. "I can't do it Jai. I suffer from vertigo, you know that…"

"You won't see a thing in the dark. Just pretend you're climbing down from the top bunk."

"But I'm on the bottom bunk."

"Well you made it up to our window, remember? Compared to that, this is a piece of cake."

The thought of cake distracted Tom for a moment.

"So," Jai continued, "when I get to the bottom I'll shine the torch up so you can see the rungs…"

In order to facilitate their descent the two removed their costumes, Tom struggling to get out of his habit. With the torch hanging by its strap from his neck, Jai then descended into the hole. Tom watched his friend slowly recede into the dark until all he could see was a tiny light, like the faintest of stars.

"I'm down!"

Jai's faraway voice echoed eerily round the walls of the shaft.

"You can do it, Tom! Just take your time!" Then he added, as an afterthought: "Not too long, mind! It's not far off midnight!"

"Not far off midnight..." Tom mumbled to himself, trying to keep his mind from the appalling prospect of what he was about to do. "What's going to happen at midnight? We're going to change into bloody pumpkins or something...?"

The thought reminded him of Jack O'Lantern. He took one more glance around the gloom then lowered himself into the hole, legs quivering as his foot felt for each rung, hands tightly gripping the rusty iron.

He kept his eyes shut throughout the descent, the torch beam pointed up at him completely wasted. He could hear Jai's words of encouragement getting gradually closer, and the restrained impatience in his voice.

At last he felt the ground beneath his feet, and

the slap of Jai's hand on his back.

"Well done, Tom. I knew you'd do it."

Tom opened his eyes. They were at the end of a narrow passage, its low ceiling supported by beams.

"Come on." Jai had already set off. "We haven't long…"

They trudged along the winding passageway for some time, skirting piles of fallen rocks, ducking under sagging beams and passing numerous openings to their left and right.

"How do we know one of those isn't the right way?" asked Tom.

"Because the passage that's connected to the Roman tunnel is a main route like this," Jai responded confidently, "not a side one."

As he spoke they came to a dead end of solid rock.

"A main route, is it?"

"Not to worry," Jai replied jauntily. "All we have to do is go back to where we started from…"

They began to re-trace their steps, but as time passed Jai felt increasingly uneasy. They seemed to have walked much further than the journey in.

"My kingdom for a ball of string," he muttered.

"What?"

"*Theseus and the Minotaur…*Theseus takes a

ball of string into the maze so he doesn't get lost."

"So the Mine O'Tor is the maze…?"

"No. The Minotaur is the monster at the centre of it. Half-man, half-bull…"

"Full of bull, more like."

But Tom checked behind all the same. He didn't turn back in time to avoid walking into his friend.

"Sorry."

Jai had stopped at another dead end. Tom sighed heavily.

"Admit it, Jai. We're lost, aren't we…?"

It wasn't often he had to confess to failure, but Jai was spared the discomfort by a sound: a faint tapping, distant but getting nearer…

The light vanished, replaced by a complete darkness neither of them had experienced before. It wasn't just lack of light, as in a room without windows which could be dispelled by the simple opening of a door. This was darkness of a much purer quality: of a passage carved out of solid rock, deep beneath the sea.

"Jai…why have you switched the torch off?"

"Quiet!"

Now they heard shuffling footsteps, and a heavy breathing punctuated by frequent hacking coughs; all accompanied by the incessant tapping…

It came to a sudden halt. The wheezing was

now very close, as if the mine itself had begun to respire: ancient lungs of rock inhaling their first breath...

The two felt the light touch of a stick exploring their bodies, like the antenna of some huge subterranean insect. They could smell a bitter-sweet concoction of sweat, tobacco and alcohol. Then a voice spoke, deep and muffled:

"So...what have we here, then....?"

Jai switched on his torch and Tom cried out in shock. A dark figure stood before them in a heavy army greatcoat, its head covered by a canvas hood with two round eye-holes. What lay behind these glass portals was hidden in shadow, but a cackle from within indicated that the wearer was amused by the reaction he'd elicited. The laughter deteriorated into a bout of coughing.

"Are you...the lighthouse keeper?" asked Jai.

Before replying the figure turned away for a moment, lifting his mask just enough to allow the unimpeded ejection of what had been dredged up from his lungs.

"I am indeed...I'm also guardian of this mine, and you two are trespassin'. You'll be from across, I s'pose..."

"That's right."

"Thought as much. What is it with you folk tonight, wanderin' abroad where you shouldn't be...?"

Tom began to babble.

"We're really sorry, sir. We were just trying to get back to school. We've already been done for absconding once. If we're caught again we'll be expelled. But the tide's in you see, so we couldn't use the Causeway…"

"Actually, I don't see."

"Oh…Sorry…"

"Sorry? You responsible for me losin' my sight, boy…? What you really mean is, you're sorry for poor old Jack….Well, don't be. Jack can look after himself, right enough. My other senses have taken up the slack, see. Helps to have an alarm system, mind. Charlie woke me up, a-peckin' and a-squawkin' at my window…"

"The crow," said Jai, remembering.

"Chough," Jack corrected him. "So I goes out to investigate, and sees a certain trapdoor open…"

"My fault," said Tom to Jai. "Should have closed it behind me."

"Found some abandoned garments, too…"

"Fancy dress costumes," Jai explained. "We were at the Halloween Party."

"Were you indeed? So you'll have met my twin then…"

"Your twin?"

"I'm told folk have takin' to pretendin' I'm the Devil himself this time o' year, for a lark….So what do you think of me, lads? Old Jack O' Lantern ain't that bad in the flesh, is he now…?"

"No sir," said Tom nervously, "not that bad at all."

"Well, that's only because Jack's wearin' his old gas mask, so as not to scare the horses, so to speak...Anyways, what makes you think this mine'll get you across...?"

"We know about the Roman tunnel," said Jai. "And we've seen where it connects to the mine system."

"My but you have been busy...Well, I'll tell you boys somethin' now, for free. You should be real grateful to my Charlie. Him raisin' the alarm back there saved your lives...Mind you, if a certain other creature hadn't forgotten to lock the trapdoor...but that's another story...Get lost down 'ere lads and you'll never see the light of day again. And you **are** lost, ain't you...?"

The two didn't answer.

"Plays tricks on you this mine, don't it? Almost like a livin' thing herself, a-movin' and a-shiftin' around in the dark like some great dragon-snake. Couldn't say how many lost souls are still wanderin' round down 'ere. Some nights I reckon I can hear 'em..." He paused for effect. "But she'll never get the better of Old Jack. He knows this passages like the scars on the back of his hand. Might not be able to see 'em, but I can feel 'em, sure enough..."

He struck a wall with his stick.

"Jack, will you show us the way to the

tunnel?" asked Tom.

"Mister Petherick to you. Don't they teach you manners in that place…?"

The two exchanged a look.

"Did you say Petherick?" Jai asked.

"You deaf as well as rude?"

"Sorry. It's your hood. It distorts your voice…"

"So you want me to take it off?"

"No!" cried Tom. "I mean," he added, embarrassed by the outburst, "that won't be necessary…"

"Are you any relation to Jude Petherick?" Jai persisted.

"Never heard of her…Now, are you two just after polite chat or are you wantin' safe passage home…?"

"Home please," said Tom. "Or back to school, at least."

He felt a weariness creeping over him. It had been a very long night and he ached for his bed.

"So what's it worth…?"

"I'm afraid we haven't any money," said Jai.

"What? Rich brats like you…?"

"I've got a penny," said Tom, adding hopefully: "It's a lucky one…"

"Save it," Jack replied, sniggering. "I'm only havin' you on. I'll show you the way, so long as you'll be promisin' never to venture down here again. Next time he catches you, Jack won't be so forgivin'…"

"We promise," said Jai.

"Thanks Jack," said Tom.

He felt the stick strike him quite hard on his head.

"Ow! What was that for?"

"I just told you. It's Mister Petherick to you. Now follow me, and stay close. Easy to wander off the wrong way down a mine like this, and I'm speakin' from experience…"

Jai walked behind Jack, holding the torch, with Tom the nervous back-marker. Jack's stick continually rapped against the ground and the walls like a magic wand conjuring the right direction out of nothingness until they came to a hole in the floor. It spanned the width of the tunnel and extended deep into the walls on either side, as if two halves of the world had been pulled slightly apart.

"We're here," said Jai, relieved.

"As I said," growled Jack, "sometime's feelin' is better than seein'…"

"Where are we?"

Tom was just grateful for the opportunity to rest.

"The hole I came to from the other side," Jai explained. "That first time in the tunnel…"

"The final obstacle," said Jack. "Abaddon's abode."

"Abaddon…I've heard that name before…"

"Book of Revelation."

"That's it. Remember Monster Mouth's Bible readings, Tom? Abaddon is the Angel of the Bottomless Pit…"

"Oh." Tom had no idea what his friend was talking about. "Really."

Now Jai shone his torch into the hole, its beam petering out in the blackness.

"Don't be starin' too long into the abyss, lads," Jack's voice reverberated ominously around the void, "else she'll be starin' into you…"

Tom shivered.

"How deep is it?"

"Nobody knows. Natural fault, see. One day the rock shifted and, lo and behold, there was this new hole in the ground. For all I know, might go all the way down to Hell itself…"

"Perhaps it's something to do with Devilston being volcanic," Jai wondered aloud.

Dan would have known the answer.

"No idea. But I do know it spelt the end of this mine. Things were desperate by then, what with the price of tin collapsin'…And then this bleddy great crack opened up, like a miracle. Maybe there was somethin' else down there, they thought. Gold p'raps. Or even diamonds…"

"A last ditch effort," said Tom.

"Some ditch," said Jai. "Did they find anything?"

"Oh, they found somethin' alright. Set up a makeshift winch, but they was so hasty to get a man down there they didn't check their equipment prop'ly. Seems somethin' broke and the whole contraption fell down the hole, and that poor soul with it. Put a jinx on the entire mine. The final blow..."

"So what was it they found?"

"I already told you." Close to the torchlight, Jack's eyes could now be seen within the mask, wide and staring like a fish. "The Angel of Death..."

Jai and Tom stood in silent contemplation for a moment, imagining the horror of a final plummet through the cold darkness, waiting for the impact. Then Jai glanced at his watch, aware of midnight fast approaching.

"How do we get across, Mister Petherick?"

"Well, how do you think...?"

Jai assessed the gap. It was probably within his capability, but the consequences of getting it wrong chilled his spine; and he knew Tom would never make it. Then, shining the torch beyond the hole, he saw something lying on the floor, up against the wall of the passage.

"There's a plank on the other side. I don't remember seeing that the last time I was here..."

"Prob'ly because it was on this side of the hole," said Jack. "A certain someone's used it since then..."

"Presumably you?"

"Don't be presumin' anythin', boy. Not round here. I've no business in the land of the livin', but that's not to say there ain't others who have good reason to cross..."

"Who?"

"Now that would be tellin', wouldn't it...?"

Jai handed Tom the torch.

"Point this at the other side, and keep it still."

As Tom watched his friend pace into the darkness of the passageway, a sickness grew in his stomach.

"You don't have to do this, Jai. We can just go back..."

"Just keep the torch steady!" boomed Jai's disembodied voice from out of the dark.

There was a pause. Tom heard a deep inhalation of breath, then accelerating footfalls.

His friend shot into the light like an express train from a tunnel, arms and legs piston-ing furiously. His right foot planted itself on the very edge and he launched himself into space like Jesse Owens, head tipped back and limbs flailing as if struggling to propel him through thin air.

Tom held his breath.

Jai's toe caught the opposite edge, then slipped. For one terrible moment Tom thought he was about to see his friend swallowed by the hole. But Jai's body toppled forward with the momentum of the jump and he sprawled onto the floor in a heap on the other side.

Tom clapped ecstatically.

"Well done!"

Jack wasn't impressed.

"Well done? I've jumped trenches wider than that in my time. You young 'uns don't have a bleddy clue...."

Jai picked himself up then proceeded to slide the plank across the gap. When it was in place, Tom noticed there wasn't much overlap at the edges. Nor was it the thickest of planks.

"Tell you what, Jai. Why don't you carry on and I'll go back with Jack? I mean, Mister Petherick."

"I ain't goin' back with no-one," Jack grunted. "I ain't some bleddy tour guide, you know."

"Come on Tom," said Jai. "You can do it. I'll hold the plank steady."

Tom contemplated the gap with a deepening dread.

"Why doesn't someone build a proper bridge over this, anyway?"

"And have every man and his dog sniffin' around my mine?" Jack sneered. "No thanks. This is my moat...Now give me that torch and get your whingin' backside over there so's I can be goin' home. Some of us have got important business to attend to tonight..."

Handing Jack the torch, Tom tried to prepare himself for what promised to be the most frightening thing he'd ever do in his life.

Jack's big hands explored the torch.

"Where did you get this?"

"A friend of mine gave it to me," Jai replied from across the chasm between them.

"Boche was he?"

"No. He got it from a dead soldier...How did you know it's German?"

"I've got history, that's how..."

"Were you in the Great War?"

"Well I didn't get this face in a croquet accident, did I...?"

While they'd been talking Tom had begun to cross, his mind using their voices for support like invisible ropes. His whole body was trembling as he concentrated on putting one foot in front of the other, his arms stretched out like a tight rope walker, his eyes trying to focus on the narrow section of wood in front of him but unable to ignore the well of darkness beneath.

"That's it, Tom," said Jai. "Nice and slowly does it..."

But now his friend had reached the middle and the plank was sagging alarmingly.

"Jai..." Tom's voice was shaking. "I think it's going to break..."

"No it isn't."

In truth, Jai wasn't so sure. Then all became black.

Tom cried out in panic.

"What's happening?"

"Jack!" Jai shouted. "What the Hell are you doing?"

They heard raucous laughter mutate into a cough, then another ejection of phlegm.

"Showin' you somethin', that's what. And it's Mister Petherick. How many times do I have to tell you...?"

Jai was struggling to contain his fury.

"Mister Petherick, how can you show us something when we can't see a bloody thing?"

"But that's exactly what I'm showin' you, boy. What nothin' looks like, 'cause that's what it's like for me, all the time...This mine's a great leveller see, like the war, or the sea. No airs and graces down here, lads. No rich and poor, or black and white. No-one better than anyone else, like up there. Down here, we're all in it together. Us against the darkness..."

Instinctively Tom had lowered his centre of gravity, first kneeling on the plank on his hands and knees then lying down, his arms and legs wrapped around it, his face pressed against the rough wood, his body trembling.

"Mister Petherick," he muttered softly, "please...switch the torch back on..."

"Why are you doing this?" Jai demanded. "Tom's done nothing to you!"

"No, but that bleddy place across has, and

you're a part of it…" All the amusement had vanished from Jack's voice now. "Breakin' our backs down here to keep the Morrigans in fine wines and fancy livin', we were. Then I signed up to do my bit, and I asked His Lordship if he'd recommend me for the cavalry. Lord Julian Morrigan himself, hero of Omdurman and recipient of the Victoria Cross, no less…And what was His Lordship's reply? Square root of Sweet Fanny Adams. Just like what you're seein' now…"

"He might just have forgotten!"

Tom's voice had risen considerably in pitch.

"And that's supposed to make me feel better, is it? Bein' forgotten? Like I was by a certain resident of that island, who once swore she'd be mine for ever? Like I was beneath those Boche lines, when they blew those charges and robbed me of my good looks and any chance of a decent life? Like I was by my own kith and kin, when I came back from the war lookin' like Death fresh out of the oven…? And who ordered those charges to be blown, by the way? Officers that's who, from schools like yours. All well-tutored in the fine arts of the rulin' class. All playin' the bleddy game, with the likes of me as their gamblin' chips. 'Might have just forgotten' eh? Well maybe they might have, but here's somethin' you two ain't goin' to forget for a while…"

The light came on again. Jack had removed his hood and was holding the torch beneath his chin. Jai saw again the Devil from the Halloween party, now in long trench-coat and heavy boots but the grinning skull-face was the same: a monstrous visage devoid of lips, nose, ears and hair.

"Don't look round Tom!" Jai shouted.

"Why not?"

"Just keep looking ahead!"

Tom began to pull himself along the plank, as Jack proceeded to kick its end.

"Stop it!" cried Jai, crouching down and reaching out for Tom's hand, seeing the terror on his friend's face. "How's another death going to make things better?"

"But She always makes things better." Jack's kicking was knocking the end of the plank towards the edge in small increments. "The Angel of Death looks out for everyone…"

The plank dropped.

Tom cried out as Jai took his full weight, grasping both his wrists and pulling with all his strength, once again dragging his friend to safety.

The plank hit the side of the hole as it fell, sending out an echoing crash which - eventually - diminished into nothing. Jack tossed the torch after it, plunging the passageway into darkness again.

"See?" he chuckled in the dark. "You made it after all, and one day I reckon you'll be thankin' me. Life's all the sweeter when you've tasted a little death, lads. Only, don't be takin' too big a bite out of it, like Jack did…"

Then he shuffled on, tapping his stick in front of him and singing under his breath:

"It's a long way to Tipperary
It's a long way to go,
It's a long way to Tipperary
To the sweetest girl I know…"

Jai opened the trap door beneath the altar. The pale moonlight that fell upon them was like dawn after the longest night.

The faint toll of the Dragon Head bell marked the death of each minute as they hurried from the Chapel to the edge of Top Pitch. Crouching behind a buttress of the castle wall, Jai surveyed the scene while Tom regained his breath.

The full moon shone down on a white blanket of fog which smothered both sea and land, except for Devilston's mount and the headlands on either side of the bay. Top Pitch was veiled in the upper layer of this tide of mist, but Jai could just distinguish the dark shapes of the Crown of Stones at the far end of the field.

"Can you see anyone?" Tom whispered.

"Not sure…"

"What time is it?"

Jai checked his watch.

"Ten to twelve. Come on. We need to get closer…"

They edged round the pitch, keeping to the castle wall until they were close enough to the Crown of Stones to see what lay within it. Then - casually - Jai walked over to the monument, as if on a Sunday morning stroll. But for the flat stone in its centre where he'd fallen in the boxing match and the mist hanging in the air like the tattered remnants of ghosts, the circle was empty. Tom joined him and the two sat on the middle stone.

"Maybe the stones come alive at midnight," he said, seeing his friend's dejection. "They look almost human…"

"Very funny."

"Cheer up, Jai. No-one's going to die tonight, after all…and I thought I was a goner back there, I tell you. If it wasn't for you I'd be lying at the bottom of that pit…"

"If it wasn't for me you wouldn't have been in the mine in the first place."

"True. And we wouldn't have met those girls."

"Or lost Dan…."

"Now you're starting to sound like me." Tom nudged his friend with an elbow. "Cheer up, mate. It might never happen."

"Well it's not happening here, that's for sure…"

"Why are you so disappointed, anyway?"

"I just had a feeling, that's all…"

They sat in silence for a while, Jai deep in thought, Tom feeling the cold beginning to seep into his bones. The fog had thinned and now he could see the white tower on Dragon Head glowing in the moonlight. The toll of its bell was like the call of a church, speaking to its congregation of one. He imagined the keeper hauling himself out of his mine and making his way home.

"Poor Jack…"

"Poor Jack?" Jai grunted. "He nearly killed you."

"I know, but just think what kind of a life he must have…" Tom was beginning to shiver. "Jai…?"

"Still here."

"What was his face like?"

But Jai was distracted now, sniffing the air.

"What's that smell?"

"Not me."

Tom's insides were unsettled but he wouldn't have dared violate the sanctity of the Crown of Stones.

"It's smoke." Jai turned round. "It's coming out of this hole…"

Now Tom saw a wisp of grey rising like a

spectral form from the slit in the centre of their seat, where it was said that Excalibur itself had once resided.

"Maybe the volcano's about to erupt. Wouldn't be surprised, after today..."

"Of course!" Jai sprang to his feet. "The Crown is on top of the King!"

"What?"

"That burial chamber we found, where King Arthur is supposed to lie? It must be underneath this circle!"

"I'm sorry but you've lost me there."

"Don't you get it?" Jai gripped Tom by the shoulders, eyes full of a new energy. "It's happening beneath us! Underground! Come on!"

"Bloody Hell. Not again..."

Tom rose wearily to his feet and once more heaved himself after his friend.

All the Chapel's candles had been removed so they had to venture down the spiral stairway without light. By the time they reached the bottom, they were again submerged in absolute darkness.

Disorientated from their winding descent and with only their touch to navigate by, it was only when they came to the ragged mine entrance that Jai realised their mistake.

"It's almost as if She doesn't want us to get

there," he said as they re-traced their steps.

"Who?"

"Devilston…"

Now sensing the floor of the tunnel sloping upwards, Jai held out his hand as he walked, until he felt the door in front of him. The bolts had been slid open and - placing his ear to the ancient oak - he could hear a sound from within: the deep muffled drone of a male voice. His hands found the small panel and he carefully slid it open, releasing a dim but welcome light which shone on their two faces as they peered in.

In the chamber beyond, all the candle stands from Chapel had been arranged in a large circle. In front of each flickering flame stood a figure dressed in a monk's habit, each head concealed beneath a raised hood. The candlelight's glow illuminated the bones and skulls in the surrounding recesses, and cast long shadows from the monks which converged in the middle of the ring.

Eleven candles for eleven monks. A twelfth - in white robes, contrasting sharply with the others - was standing in the centre of the circle, over a dark-haired figure in school uniform kneeling on the ground. The white monk was chanting monotonously in what sounded to Jai like Latin. The prostrate figure was facing the door - his features glowing pale in the

candlelight - and Tom gasped in recognition.
   "Dan!"

13

AN EXTRAORDINARY MEETING

T he white monk - walking with a limp - moved over to the tallest in the circle and accepted a chalice. Holding the receptacle aloft, the leader recited another burst of Latin which the circle repeated. Handing back the cup, he was then presented with a great sword by the broadest of the gathered.

After each monk had kissed the sword at the base of its hilt - declaring allegiance to the inverted cross - the white monk returned to the centre of the circle and consulted his wristwatch.

Jai checked his own watch, set from Devilston's clock. It was the final minute before midnight. The second hand was relentlessly advancing upon the twelve, like a tiny sword itself.

The monks stood in quiet obedience as the faintest sound of chimes seeped into Devilston's core. Jai and Tom exchanged a glance, both dreading what had to be done. Jai's hand found the handle of his kukri, sliding the knife from its scabbard.

Gripping the sword with both hands, the white monk gently rested the edge of its blade on the nape of Dan's neck. Then, on the eleventh strike of the clock, the sword was raised...

The door flew open and two intruders descended the steps, screaming. Jai's call was a battle cry as he brandished his kukri, Tom's a shriek of pure fear. They halted in the centre of the circle of monks, breathing heavily.

The white monk lowered the sword and Dan lifted his head. He was trembling and his face was deathly pale but his mouth flickered with a faint smile as he recognised his friends.

For a moment all was still, then the spell was broken.

"Well, don't just stand there gawping!" the leader shouted. "Seize them!"

Now the circle converged on the invaders. The two felt the grip of many hands, forcing Jai to drop the kukri. The white monk lowered his hood.

"Good evening....Headmaster..." said Jai breathlessly. "Apologies for disturbing...your little reception..."

"Just can't stay out of trouble, can we? Like a pair of moths to the flame..."

"You...evil...bastard!"

The Captain smiled crookedly.

"Not really, Barrow. I'm merely carrying out the wishes of a higher authority."

"You mean, a lower one," said Jai.

"I mean, Devilston." The Captain's smile vanished. "And if it's the blood of three She wants tonight, then so be it…"

He nodded and the pair felt hands on their shoulders, pushing them down. Tom acquiesced, feeling the cold hard ground on his knees, but Jai resisted.

"Always the awkward one, aren't you?" The Captain carefully directed the tip of his sword to a place beneath Jai's chin, just above his Adam's apple. "Defiant to the end…"

Jai felt the point pressing into his neck.

"Stop!"

It was a female voice. She lowered her hood to reveal a head of red hair, and from her robes she produced a revolver. Her hand shook as she raised the weapon but her dark eyes were fixed on the Captain. Now Charlotte wielded a power over her husband which wasn't to do with beauty or title, and it felt good.

"That's my Webley!" he protested. "How dare you?"

"Always so possessive, Ralph…"

"You're ruining everything, as usual."

She smiled.

"Then you shouldn't have invited me. If you

really thought I'd stand by while you committed a murder then you are truly deranged. As I am, for all those wasted years of my life."

"Wasted years? But darling, you love me..."

He moved closer to her, his shadow falling across her face. His voice had adopted a strange tone: soft, affectionate, and insincere.

"No," she replied. "I hate you."

He shrugged.

"Hate? Love? Merely two edges of the same sword, my dear. Some things are more important, in the grand scheme of things..."

"Power?"

"Yes." He was close to her now, his eyes shining in the candlelight, his voice low but sharp, testing her resistance like the tip of an invincible sword. "Devilston's power. Can't you feel Her presence, Charlotte?" He looked around the chamber, aware of the unease in the many eyes watching him. "That's what we must preserve..."

"I'll pull this trigger if you come any closer!"

He laughed.

"Really?" Now his chest was inches from the gun. "But my dear... I'm your husband."

His grin vanished. Grabbing the barrel he wrenched the pistol from her grip then struck her face with his other hand.

Retribution was almost instantaneous. He felt a metal object connect with the side of his head with great force. The sword clattered to the floor as he dropped but he retained his grip on the gun.

Now the tallest monk stood over him, dominant at last with huge fists raised, one still clutching the chalice. Dazed and with blood running from a ringing ear, the Captain smiled up at his assailant.

"Sir Lancelot, I presume…"

"Should have done that a long time ago," a Welsh voice rumbled. "Are you alright Charlotte…?"

She nodded, her hand at her jaw.

"But look at us, old boy…" said the Captain. "Just like those two dragons of yours, slugging it out beneath the castle. Red and white, weren't they…?" He smiled as he raised the revolver. "And I'm afraid white wins again…"

The gun's shout echoed around the chamber as the tallest monk crumpled to the floor. He lay clutching his stomach, blood pouring into the chalice still clasped in his hand. The hood had fallen back to reveal the Reverend's red face, creased with pain.

Aided by two monks, the Captain rose to his feet. He waved his revolver at the rest of the gathered.

"Now all of you get back to your positions! We're going to finish this ceremony if it kills me…"

"No we're not."

Another female voice, and the sound of a machine gun being cocked. The Captain turned to see a Schmeisser pointed at him. The monk pushed back her hood.

"Sorry Ralph," said Elena, "but mine appears to be bigger than yours..."

"Oh, for Satan's sake..." he groaned. "I knew I should have banned women from this event. Always sticking their noses in..."

"Drop the gun."

"But what about our agreement?"

"You mean, you the Gauleiter of Cornwall and me your acquiescent little frau?" Elena smiled. "You of all people should know the dangers of doing deals with the Devil, Ralph..."

"Wait a minute!" boomed a broad Cornish voice. "You promised me I'd be King of Cornwall! And you said you'd be my Queen!"

The largest monk had now thrown back his hood. Pendragon's face was flushed with anger, like a child denied Christmas.

"Sorry to break it you both," said Elena, "but I have it on very good authority that Goering has his greedy eyes set on Cornwall, with Devilston as his seat. Though I'm not so sure it will be big enough for his fat backside..."

"So what do I get for helping you?" the Captain demanded.

"And me?" added Pendragon.

"Well gentlemen, I believe a brace of Iron Crosses awaits you in Berlin…"

The Captain wasn't impressed.

"Iron Crosses?"

Pendragon looked dismayed.

"Iron…?"

"Poor Cador," Elena laughed. "Didn't your mother warn you about women who promise you the Earth?"

Pendragon's massive shoulders had visibly drooped as the news sunk in.

"I'm afraid you're just not my type," she continued. "And as for you, Ralph…I wouldn't marry you if you were the last man on the planet. You repulse me."

The Captain sneered.

"You've a very strange way of showing it…"

"What happened between us was purely for the sake of my mission…I'm sorry you have to hear this, Charlotte…"

The Captain's wife was tending to the wounded Reverend.

"Don't be. You weren't the only one."

"He told me everything." Elena's eyes remained fixed on the Captain's. "He thought it would impress me….Your father didn't disappear in the quick sands. Ralph killed him, in a ceremony just like this, thirteen years ago. And he killed your mother, too. He hit her horse with his stick. That's why she fell."

Charlotte looked up at her husband.

"Is this true?"

The Captain laughed, still holding Elena's stare.

"Darling, of course not. This woman has just proved she's a congenital liar. She'll do anything for the sake of her precious mission. She even pretended to be you."

"But why would she lie now? She has nothing more to gain."

He took a deep breath, as if about to explain a complicated concept to a small child.

"Look…your father was leading this school into ruin. All that nonsense about nurturing the soul…No wonder the place was in financial crisis. No responsible parent is going to invest good money in sending their offspring to a school for pansies, after all. As for your mother….well, she just couldn't keep herself from interfering, could she? Another meddling bitch…"

"You killed my parents."

Charlotte's voice was flat, devoid of emotion.

"I did what I had to do," her husband replied, equally coldly. "Devilston's legacy must continue…"

"Through more deaths?" Elena asked and now the Captain turned to her. Beyond him she saw Charlotte rising to her feet and heard the faint ring of metal scraping against stone.

"Well, it's not as if there's a shortage of boys on this island." He smiled. "And Devilston must have Her blood…"

"Then let it be yours!"

Charlotte lunged forward, grunting bestially with the physical effort demanded by the task.

The Captain's body jolted, as if electrocuted. A long silver blade had emerged from his chest, a dark stream flowing from the tear it had made in his white robe and splashing on to the floor. He looked down at the ghastly protrusion with an expression of surprised curiosity. Then the realisation came to him, and the pain.

The revolver dropped from his hand and he reeled around, sending a candle stand crashing to the ground, its light dying. Before his mind drained away, he saw his wife standing before him, her eyes darker than he'd ever seen them before.

"You shouldn't have turned your back on me, Ralph…"

With a long sigh the Captain dropped to his knees, then fell onto his side. A pool of blood grew from his lifeless body, like a hole opening in the ground.

"Now get out!" Elena shouted. "All of you!"

But the monks remained motionless, a flock frozen in shock and in need of some encouragement.

The industrial clatter of the machine gun was

deafening, its side-snout spewing out a stream of spent shells which tinkled as they hit the ground. Elena had aimed at the open doorway to avoid bullets ricocheting off the chamber walls, but she was also reluctant to disturb the bones of the dead.

Now the monks were galvanised into action, rushing up the steps and forming a frantic bottle neck in the doorway. Dan, Jai and Tom moved towards the exit in their wake but they were stopped by Elena.

"You'll stay here. They won't raise the alarm," she nodded in the direction of the fleeing monks, "but you three are a different matter..."

Pendragon also remained, his loyalty to Elena overcoming his instinct to escape. Despite her betrayal, she still exerted an irresistible force upon him.

Charlotte stayed too, struggling to stem the flow of blood from the Reverend's wound with a handkerchief.

"He needs a doctor!" she called out in despair.

"No my dear..." The Reverend squeezed her hand, the ghost of a smile passing across his pale lips. "Too late for that..."

Elena removed her habit, revealing black battledress and boots. Kneeling next to the Reverend, she carefully lifted his head and placed her rolled-up robe beneath it.

"Goodbye Edward. I think you are a good man,

in spite of everything."

"No Elena...I'm a bad man because of everything...I was weak...I allowed a wicked world to get the better of me..."

She kissed him on the forehead. Then she moved over to a pair of shadowy figures beyond the circle of candlelight, sitting on the floor with their backs against the wall. Jai and Tom hadn't noticed them until now.

"Come, Paul." Elena drew a knife from her belt. "Time for us to leave the party again."

"Elena," Alderley pleaded, next to Fischer, "you can't do this. Think of the consequences for the world..."

She cut through the rope that bound Fischer's wrists and ankles, sheathed her dagger then regarded Alderley with depthless eyes.

"I'm sorry Arthur. I suppose I just can't see beyond the consequences for myself..."

She touched his cheek with her palm and smiled with a hint of sadness. Then she helped Fischer to his feet and escorted him up the stairs. The door clunked shut behind them, and three bolts slid home.

"Well," said Dan, "you two took your time. Talk about leaving things to the very last minute..."

"Sorry old chap," Jai grinned, slapping Dan on the back. "But better late than never, eh...?"

Tom shook his friend's hand vigorously.

"We shouldn't have left you in the cellar. Then all this wouldn't have happened."

"They would still have got me," Dan replied, "one way or the other."

"I knew you were still alive." There were tears in Tom's eyes. "I just knew it."

"What?" Jai exclaimed, bemused.

They were interrupted by a voice from beyond the circle of candles.

"Hate to be a party pooper chaps but if one of you would kindly do the honours…?"

Jai picked up his kukri and hurried over to Alderley. The blade made short work of the bindings but before returning the knife to its scabbard he dipped its tip in the Captain's blood, under the blank gaze of lifeless blue eyes.

"So who was that other bloke, sir?"

"He's a scientist, Rana." Alderley stood, rubbing his wrists back to life. "Right now, probably the most important in the world…"

"Why?" asked Tom. "What has he done?"

"It's not what he's done but what he knows. Doctor Fischer has treasure in his head which the Nazis desperately want to dig up…"

"The Fisher King!" Charged by the power of legend, the Reverend had experienced a surge of energy. "Keeper of the greatest treasure of all: the Holy Grail…"

His grip tightened around the chalice he still held, as if it alone was keeping him alive.

"An interesting analogy Edward, but isn't the Grail supposed to bring eternal life, not death...?"

"But that's the point, Alders! Death is itself an act of creation. Sacrifice is essential for the maintenance of life. Rana will tell you all about that, won't you lad? That idol of yours is a goddess of both creation and destruction, isn't she...?"

"With respect sir," said Jai, "I'm not sure now is the appropriate time for theological debate."

"I'm dying," the Reverend moaned. "What better time...?"

Jai turned to Alderley.

"Sir, if Doctor Fischer is so important, shouldn't we be trying to get him back?"

Alderley raised his hands helplessly.

"How? We're locked in!"

"There used to be a another entrance to this chamber," the Reverend gasped, each sentence now demanding a substantial investment of energy, "for the Celts to visit their dead...The Roman tunnel broke into here by accident... That's why that door isn't at ground level, you see...? When the legionaries finally emerged the poor Celts must have thought their ancestors were coming back to life..."

He chuckled, then winced.

"Most interesting Edward, but hardly relevant."

"History is always relevant, Alders...How did the Romans exit this place? Through the original entrance, of course..."

"So where is this entrance?"

The Reverend lifted a hand. Alderley picked up a candle stand and walked over to where he was pointing. In the candlelight he could just make out the shape of a doorway, now filled in with stone.

"Well, if we start now we should be out by Christmas..."

"What about that?"

Dan pointed at a small square hole at the foot of the wall near to where Fischer and Alderley had been sitting, covered by an iron grate.

"Usquequaque Tria Via," said the Reverend. "Always Three Ways, remember Alders...? When Devilston was a castle this chamber was its dungeon...A tunnel was cut down to a natural blowhole connected to the sea... That way they could slosh out the detritus from all those tortures and executions... Notice that the opening is just big enough for a body..."

Alderley had now crouched down next to the hole and was pulling on the grate. The three Leavers joined him to help but the bars were stuck fast.

"Let's try pushing instead of pulling," said Jai. "It might open inwards..."

But still the grille stood firm.

"Remember lads," laughed the Reverend, hearing their frustration. "Usquequaque Tria Via..."

"For God's sake, Edward!" Alderley shouted in frustration. "Why does everything have to be a bloody riddle?"

"Because it's more fun that way!"

"Right..." Alderley strode over to where the wounded man lay. "Are you going to help us get out of this place or just lie there giggling like some demented jester...?"

The Reverend coughed liquidly, his lungs filling with blood.

"Please don't talk to him like that." Charlotte was gently stroking his head, trying to soothe his agony. "Can't you see he's dying...?"

"Forgive me," said Alderley, struggling to remain calm, "but a great many more people are going to die if we don't get Fischer back... Edward, you've got to help us..."

"Or else what?" The Reverend grinned up at his colleague, beads of sweat glistening on his brow. Or it might have been a grimace of pain. "You'll kill me...?"

Now Alderley knelt beside him, his voice softer:

"Do you believe in Hell, Edward...?"

The Reverend's eyes widened.

"Oh yes," he whispered. "Oh yes, I do..."

He took hold of Alderley's wrist and gripped

it hard. His face was grey and contorted with pain.

"Then please, tell us how to open the grate. If the Nazis get their hands on Fischer, all Hell will be unleashed."

"I've always hated fascism, Alders..." The Reverend's voice was failing now. "I have no sympathy for the Nazis...You know that, don't you...?"

"So why were you involved in the Ceremony?"

"For Devilston...The Captain was right about that, at least...Devilston must have Her blood... and now She has..." He looked at Charlotte with eyes full of love, a faint smile on his lips. "She's safe now...for a while, anyway..."

"Edward, the grate. Please..."

"Edward the Great..." the Reverend muttered deliriously, his grip tightening on Alderley's wrist with the last of his strength, struggling against the strongest of currents. "Edward the Eighth...bloody traitor...Traitor's Gate...I can see it now, Alders....I can see Hell's gate...only, it isn't a gate at all...it's like Devilston's...a port - "

Now his face was full of fear, as if he'd glimpsed something beyond Alderley's shoulder. Then his grip relaxed, his eyes froze and his lungs released their last breath, in a final sigh of relief.

Charlotte's head bowed, her red hair covering the Reverend's face like a veil. Alderley rose wearily to his feet and walked over to the three Leavers. His expression conveyed the news.

"What did he say?" asked Jai

"Not much of sense. Just something about the gate of Hell being a port, like Devilston…"

"But Devilston isn't a port. It's just a small harbour…"

"Not a port!" Dan exclaimed. "A portcullis!"

Now they each grabbed a bar of the grate and pulled upwards, having to cluster together to do so and thus compromising the force they could apply. But still the grate wouldn't shift, welded by centuries of rust.

"Let me have a go…"

Pendragon had been sitting on the steps by the door, ruminating on his foolishness in becoming entwined in such mischief. His wife would never have stood for it. But now an opportunity had arisen for him to make some amends.

The four made way for his huge bulk, watching him crouch down like a weightlifter, gripping the grate then committing himself to the task. Veins bulged in his thick neck, his contorted face turned pink and - venting all the anger and frustration boiling within him - he let out a great roar.

With a long and painful screech, as if in sympathy with Pendragon's agony, the grate ascended.

"There," he muttered, breathing heavily. "That's as much as I can do. I'll never fit through that hole."

"You've done enough," said Alderley. "Thanks."

"No..." Pendragon's eyes brimmed with regret. "I've done too much...I only hope it's not too late to set things right. I hate the English sure enough, but Nazis....Well, better the Devil you know, I suppose..."

They peered into the hole. In the light of the candle they could see a narrow tunnel descending at a steep angle into darkness. They smelt the rich tang of the sea and heard her lapping far below, like some huge and ravenous creature smacking her lips.

"The tide's in," said Alderley. "This could be tricky..."

The others watched with great deliberation as he removed his jacket and lay it neatly on the floor like a condemned prisoner. Then, sitting on the ground, he shuffled himself feet first into the tunnel, until gravity took over.

He tried to slow his descent by pressing his legs and arms against the rough rock, but his speed increased at an alarming rate.

The three heard a loud splash below, then a shout.

"Jesus!"

"Are you alright, sir?" Jai called down.

"Fine!" Alderley replied, treading water, struggling to breathe with the shock of the cold.

Fine. What a ridiculous word to use in the circumstances.

In the darkness he sensed from the echo of his voice that he was in a small space. He could see the tunnel entrance far above him, a distant moon with three tiny faces within it. Climbing back up was impossible. There was only one way out, if it even existed.

"I can't see any exit!" he shouted up. "It must be underwater! I'll have to dive for it!"

"What should we do, sir?" Jai asked.

"Just wait there!"

The three Leavers heard Alderley take a deep breath, and another. Then, after a third, all was quiet in the chamber below.

"And to think we called him Cowardly," said Tom.

"And we thought he was a German spy," said Dan.

The three were sitting by the hole. Jai felt something sharp in his side.

"Damn. Should have given him my knife..."

"Not sure it would be much use against a machine gun," Dan said.

Encouraged by his success with the grate, Pendragon climbed the steps and tried pulling on the door handle; but the bolts were strong and held fast. Then he sat on a step with his head in his hands, humbly requesting forgiveness from God, and his wife.

Charlotte remained kneeling by the Reverend. She'd raised his hood to cover his face and crossed his arms on his chest so that he resembled the statue of a knight lying on a medieval tomb. She wasn't asking for God's mercy, either for herself or the dead man before her. She knew it was probably too late for that. Instead she prayed for her son, who would have been a better person in different circumstances.

But perhaps now there is hope for him...

"So what happened, Dan?" asked Jai. "We came back to the pub that night but the cellar door was bolted."

"Then they found your duffle coat on the beach," said Tom. "Everyone thought you'd been caught in the sands."

"Mister Pendragon found me," said Dan.

"He'd fallen asleep under the barrel ramp." Pendragon had over-heard the conversation. "Snorin' like a baby, he was. When I woke him he told me he'd come over on the Causeway and taken cover in my cellar from the rain....Wish I'd never found him now. Then all this would never have happened..."

"Ralph was planning to abduct Daniel anyway," said Charlotte. "You just made it easier for him. He wanted a Jew for the sacrifice. That's why he sent me to the Isle of Man, where he knew there were refugees. That way he'd be able to demonstrate to Miss Montserrat his devotion to the Nazi cause, and provide a sacrificial offering to satisfy Devilston…It was all nonsense really, though. You saw for yourself how impressed Elena was, and Ralph had no real belief in the Ceremony. He had no belief in anything, really. Except himself, of course. He just wanted to consolidate his power…"

"Over who?" asked Jai.

"The Staff. They were all here tonight, kissing the sacrificial sword and thereby implicating themselves in the crime…"

"What went wrong with him?" Tom wondered. "He was a hero in the last war, wasn't he?"

Charlotte shook her head.

"He wasn't even in the last war. That bad leg wasn't a wound. He contracted polio when he was a child, and it almost killed him…He was no war hero but he was a survivor, I'll give him that. I was the only one who knew the truth, but by then I was already under his spell, along with my father. Mother always suspected him though…"

"But I don't see what this has got to do with that doctor chap," said Jai. "All that stuff about treasure buried inside his head…"

"Who knows?" Tom shrugged.

"I do," said Dan. "Just before the Ceremony I was locked up in here with Doctor Fischer and Mister Alderley and they told me everything." It felt to Dan that his near-death experience had earned him the right to divulge the truth. "Doctor Fischer has been working at Bristol University, studying the quantities of uranium required to trigger a chain reaction…"

"Right…"

"Don't you remember that science lesson, Tom? When we were talking about Einstein and all the power contained in a single atom?"

"Vaguely."

"Well, the British have been trying to find a way of harnessing that power in a bomb, which would be a million times more destructive than an ordinary one. The Nazis are working on such a weapon too, but they're hampered by the fact that many of the best German scientists were Jews who fled Germany when Hitler came to power. Like Albert Einstein, and Doctor Fischer…"

"How ironic," said Jai.

"But that's not the only reason it's taking them so long. You see, until now the Nazis have mistakenly believed they needed enormous amounts of uranium to make a single bomb: the weight of a large battleship, in fact. That much uranium would take many years to mine.

And besides, how would you get a bomb that size anywhere near the enemy, without him knowing about it…?"

"Dig a tunnel under the channel…?"

Tom's suggestion was ignored.

"But then the Germans found out about Doctor Fischer's work. The doctor has calculated that you only need an amount the size of a turnip to make a bomb big enough to destroy a city. The Nazis already have more than enough uranium for that, and it could easily be carried in a single aeroplane. All they need now is the doctor's knowledge, which is why they've employed Miss Montserrat to take him back to Germany…"

"But surely they can't force him to tell them," said Tom, "if he doesn't want to…?"

Dan and Jai exchanged a glance.

"They'll torture him," said Jai.

"More likely they'll round up his relatives and torture them in front of him," said Dan. "After all, they wouldn't want to risk killing the goose that lays the golden egg…"

"But if the Nazis build this bomb they'll easily win the war," said Tom, horrified. "They'd only need to drop one on London and we'd be finished."

The other two nodded gravely.

"So what are we waiting for then?" Now Tom was on his feet, the quickest his friends had ever seen him move. "We need to help Mister Alderley get the doctor back!"

"He told us to wait here," said Jai.

"And what's he going to do if we disobey him? Put us on the Cutters? Sometimes you've got to ignore orders, Jai. You should know that, of all people..."

Tom helped Dan to his feet but Jai remained sitting. All the fight seemed to have drained from him.

"What's the matter, Jai?" asked Dan. "This isn't like you."

"Please don't tell us you're a Nazi spy," said Tom. "I don't think I could take any more shocks tonight..."

Jai fidgeted awkwardly, scratching his head and stroking his chin, struggling to put the words together.

"Well chaps, it's like this," he said at last. "You see, I can't swim."

There was a pause while the news sunk in.

"I don't believe it!" Tom blurted out. "You mean, you're actually scared of something?"

"Now I never said I was scared..."

"Well if not then you're putting on a bloody good act. How come you can't swim, anyway? I thought you could do everything...?"

"Look," said Jai with mounting irritation, "I was brought up in the middle of a bloody desert, alright? There wasn't much opportunity for swimming..."

"I thought you looked a bit worried when you climbed into that cutter," said Dan. "Well, in that case you'll just have to wait here. I must say, that'll be a first..."

The mere suggestion of sitting out on something so important was offensive to Jai's very being, but the sound of the sea slopping around at the bottom of the tunnel filled his heart with dread.

"I've got an idea," said Pendragon.

Tormented by the past and keen for redemption, he'd begun to collect up all the rope he could find from the monks' robes, starting with the one tied around his own expansive waist. Charlotte contributed hers, as did - involuntarily - the two dead men. Along with Elena's discarded length, Pendragon managed to accumulate a considerable amount.

"Should be long enough to pull someone through to the other side." Now he began tying the ropes together into one. "But one of you'll have to swim through first..."

Tom looked again down the drain hole. His initial surge of enthusiasm had waned somewhat.

"I'll go." Dan had begun to remove his blazer. "I've been in this place long enough."

"Are you sure?" asked Tom.

"No, but when have we ever been sure about

anything...?"

Dan took the rope from Pendragon and tied one end round his waist. Then he positioned himself on the cusp of the drain hole. Jai patted him on the back.

"Best of British."

"British what...?"

"Luck!" Tom pumped his hand. "Bloody good luck to you!"

The other end of the rope was wrapped around Pendragon's waist and - as Dan descended - the landlord maintained the tension in it. In this way Dan's entry into the water at the bottom of the tunnel was more dignified than Alderley's had been, yet still he gasped in shock as he slid into the pool of black.

Treading water in the tiny space, he felt the cold seeping into his bones. Breathless, he called up:

"You can let go now, Mister Pendragon!"

The rope slithered down the slope. Teeth chattering, Dan took its end and fastened it around an outcrop of rock.

"Tom, follow the rope along and it should lead you to me!" He paused to catch his breath. "When it's your turn Jai, tie the end round your waist then pull it tight and give three tugs! That'll be the signal for us to pull you through! And remember to take a deep breath..."

"Right." Jai looked doubtful. "But what if the

rope's not long enough…?"

"Well, I'll soon find out if it isn't… See you on the other side!"

Dan filled his lungs, then dived.

The water was as cold and black as death. It made no difference whether he opened or closed his eyes. He pulled and kicked through the darkness, panic his principle propulsion, half-expecting to bump into his science teacher's lifeless body.

His back rubbed against a rough surface. Even with the weight of his clothes he was fighting against his own natural buoyancy, pushing him upwards against solid rock.

Against Devilston.

"Well," said Tom, "I suppose it's my turn now…"

He shook hands with Jai then entered the hole, feet first.

With no rope to slow his descent, he accelerated down the chute, hitting the water in an impact that seemed to freeze his brain. He coughed and spluttered for air, clutching the outcrop of rock while he regained his wits.

It was as if he had dropped into a giant toilet. He only wished someone might pull the chain and make the next part easier for him. But now there was nothing for it but to take the deepest breath he could manage and dive under the rock, pulling himself along the rope into the darkness, the cold like a vice tightening around his skull.

"So," said Pendragon, "just you left then…"

"Yes. Just me…"

Uneasy, Jai took up position on the edge of the hole.

"You know, I used to think you were a lot of spoiled brats, lordin' it up over here in your own little world. But you're a brave bunch, you three. I'll give you that…"

"I'm not sure bravery has much to do with this, Mister Pendragon," Jai replied. "To be honest, for me it's more about saving face…"

"And the world," said Charlotte, still kneeling by the Reverend's body.

As ridiculous as her words sounded, there was truth in them. The three of them were Alderley's reinforcements: the cavalry riding to the rescue. Only, Jai's horse seemed to be lame.

"I really don't think I can do this," he muttered.

"Yes you can!" roared Pendragon and shoved him off his perch.

Jai found himself sliding at increasing speed down the shaft. He cried out as he plummeted, a cry that was instantly extinguished by an explosion of cold. Thrashing around in a blind panic, his hands found the rocky outcrop. He clung to it for dear life, terrified by the prospect of what he was about to do.

Now he remembered what a holy man had said to him once: a naked saddhu with white beard and trident, and eyes that burned with life:

"Greed, desire and fear are three heads of the same beast, sahib. What you hunger for will devour you, what you desire will burn you, and what you fear will kill you..."

But I must fear nothing, for I am a Rajput prince...Yet my father found me in a village so my bravery is not in my blood or my bones. It is but a ghost in my head...

And he recalled the story one of his many mothers in the zenana had told him, of a pregnant woman who lived in a village in the forest far from Jaisalpur's desert. While she was bathing in a lake, a tiger came down to the water's edge to drink. She hid among the reeds, waiting for the huge animal to go. But the shock brought on her labour and - half-submerged - she gave birth to the child.

Was she my real mother, telling me the story of my own birth? And is this why I fear water so, because my mother was so full of fear as I passed out of her...?

"I'm no Rajput prince!" Jai cried aloud in despair. "I'm not the true son of the Maharaja of

Jaisalpur!"

"And I'm descended from King Arthur of the Britons," bellowed a voice from above, "and a fat lot of good that's done me! Forget about where you came from, boy! Just think about where you're goin'..."

"Yes," Jai muttered to himself. "Just think about where I am going..."

Holding onto the rock with one hand, he untied the rope with the other and fastened its end to his belt. Then, shivering, he took a deep breath he knew might be his last and dived beneath the rock.

His thoughts were swamped, as if the water itself was flooding into his mind, dousing all reason. Suspended in the darkness he flailed around as if in some strange dance of death, feeling the rope wrapping itself around his neck like a sea snake.

The rope! I forgot to pull on the rope!

Jai caught hold of the umbilical cord and yanked three times. Then - as the cold water pressed at his lips like a deadly lover and consciousness faded - he felt himself being drawn towards a dim light, as if ascending to Heaven...

"There he is!" a voice called out as Jai's head broke the surface. "Quick! Haul him in!"

He felt rough rock beneath him, and fingers fumbling with the rope round his neck. He coughed up bitter salt water then gulped down sweet fresh air.

"Now you know how I felt after climbing that wall," grinned Tom.

Jai looked about him. A thick mist still hung in the air and the moon was a ghostly face beyond it, but there was no mistaking where he was.

"The rock pool..."

"Come on!" said Tom. "We've got to get down to the harbour!"

"Not the harbour," Jai gasped. "It's too obvious...She'll be using the smuggler's cove..."

Intent upon raising the alarm Alderley ran along the path to school, water squelching in his shoes, his sodden clothes heavy.

He was thwarted by an ancient barrier of wrought iron. The portcullis had been lowered, Devilston's mouth shut tight. Quickly giving up on trying to lift the massive lattice, his mind fumbled for an alternative plan, his body trembling with cold and urgency.

The bell of the Dragon Head lighthouse tolled again, marking the passing of another minute. He knew there wasn't time to run down to the telephone box by the harbour. He had to try to stop her himself.

Negotiating the path skirting Devilston's

walls, he noticed the sea was as calm as he'd ever seen it. It was almost as if Devilston Herself had conspired to create the perfect conditions for tonight's shipment of priceless goods.

The tiny beach at the most northerly point of the island was the perfect disembarkation point, facing open water and concealed from prying eyes on the mainland. To save time he left the path and made straight for the little cove, picking his way carefully over the sharp edges of rock. As he approached he saw the shadowy form of a boat floating in the shallows, a bow line securing her to the island: the sleek lines of *Llamrei*, enhanced by the blue moonlight.

Seeing two figures standing on the sand his concentration was distracted. His foot slipped, sending him sprawling painfully onto the rock.

"Who's there?" Elena called out to the dark shape above. "Identify yourself or I will fire!"

"Only me." He picked himself up, furious at his clumsiness. "Arthur."

"Well, hello again." There was amusement in Elena's voice now, but she kept her weapon pointed at him as he climbed down from the rocks onto the little beach. "Didn't they teach you stalking skills in the Secret Service...?"

"My training was a little rushed." Alderley rubbed his grazed leg. "I'm sorry, Doctor. I'm afraid I've made a bit of a hash of your rescue."

"At least you tried," said Fischer. "So how did you manage to escape?"

"There's a sluice drain that connects to the rock pool."

"Clever boy," said Elena. "The Devil really is in the detail, isn't she...?"

"Elena, I've put the call out. This place will be crawling with soldiers very soon...Leave Doctor Fischer and I'll tell them you used the tunnel to escape. That should give you enough time to get away in the boat..."

"Nice try, darling. But I know you haven't been back to school because Garsten closed the portcullis after us. And I don't believe you could have escaped, run down to the telephone then made it all the way out here in the time since we left..."

His bluff called, Alderley played his final card.

"You do know who Doctor Fischer is, don't you...?"

"Indeed. We are very well acquainted. Aren't we, Paul…?"

"Elena, if the Nazis build an atomic bomb they'll destroy London."

"And if the British build one they'll do the same to Berlin..."

"We'd only use it to end the war. But Hitler would hold the whole world to ransom. Who do you want to win? Civilisation or the barbarians…?"

"Any side using such a weapon would be committing an act of barbarism."

"And any person helping to make it would be an accessory to the crime," said Fischer. "That includes all of us, in one way or another..."

Elena turned to her hostage.

"So perhaps I should kill you right here, Paul? Then neither side will get their hands on your dirty little secret..."

"Perhaps you should." Fischer smiled sadly. "It would certainly be a solution..."

"But then I wouldn't get my money."

"Aren't some things more important, Elena?" Alderley implored.

"No."

A light flashed from the direction of Dragon Head and a beam began to sweep the bay, like a great arm trying to dispel the fog. Elena checked her wristwatch.

"Bravo, Jack. Right on time..."

Now Alderley spotted a crouched shape approaching over the rocks behind her. He needed to sustain the conversation, to keep her distracted.

"Of course. The lighthouse...You don't want your taxi coming a cropper on the Claws, after all...So what are they sending for you? That smuggler's boat, perhaps? Or an E-boat...? Yes, that would make sense. E-for-Elena. Very fast, those beauties..."

"You'll find out, soon enough."

"And Jack's also working for you?"

Alderley imagined the keeper staring into the light and seeing again, all of his ugliness washed away.

"He's the most dependable of the lot."

"Another of your conquests…?"

"I do what has to be done." Her voice was cold now. "Judge me as much as you like. I don't care."

"I don't believe that. And I don't believe you'll go through with this…"

The figure on the rock was close now. Alderley glimpsed a dark face, and a blade glinting in the lighthouse's flash.

Commando…?

Now she saw the figure's reflection in his eyes. As she turned he threw himself upon her before she could fire, both falling on the sand. He was physically stronger but her ferocity was relentless.

"Use the boat!" Alderley shouted to the newcomers jumping down from the rocks; not commandos at all but three soaked Leavers. "Get Fischer to the mainland!"

Jai guided Fischer to the boat and helped him in. When Dan and Tom had climbed aboard he untied the rope, pushed *Llamrei* into deeper water then clambered aboard himself.

"Start her up!" he ordered Tom, who'd found

himself in the driving seat.

"There's no key, Jai! Helluva must have it!"

"Damn…"

Jai scanned the boat, searching for inspiration. Dan and Fischer were sitting on the long passenger seat. Now he recalled the Captain's rescue of the Head of School.

"Gentlemen, if you don't mind…?"

Dan and Fischer stood and Jai lifted the seat.

"Bingo…"

He took out the two short oars and handed one to Dan. Sitting at each side of the boat, the two began to row while Tom steered the wheel. As *Llamrei* slowly turned her nose away from the island, her occupants saw the two dark figures still grappling on the beach.

"For God's sake, Elena!" Alderley grunted as they fought, smelling her sweat which only stoked up his passion. "Give it up! He's gone!"

"Never!"

She was like a wild animal but he'd managed to grip her wrists, aiming to sit astride her and pin her to the sand. His plan was foiled by a knee rising swiftly and connecting with his groin.

Rolling off her, he curled up in nauseating agony. Grabbing the gun, she scrambled to her feet.

"Go on then!" Alderley cried out, tears

streaming from his eyes from the sickness in his belly and the thwarted love in his heart. "Finish it!"

She unfolded the metal stock and lifted the machine gun to her shoulder, squinting along the barrel; not at Alderley but towards *Llamrei* as the boat slipped into the mist. Her finger rested on the trigger.

"No Elena! Not them!"

She lowered the weapon, but it had nothing to do with his pleas. She'd spotted something in the water, beyond the boat.

The deep ache in Alderley's abdomen began to subside. He sat on the sand, elbows resting on his knees, taking deep breaths.

"So...what you told me was all lies...?"

"Not really." She was still looking seaward. "It was mostly the truth. I just turned the chess board round, that's all. White became black. It wasn't Franco's men who butchered my family but Anarchists. My lust for revenge was jut as strong, though..."

"And did you get it?"

"Of course. I joined the Falangists and hunted down every last one of the bastards. The Abwehr spotted my natural talent for killing and sent me to Germany to be trained in the dark arts. I was happy to leave my mother country. I'd had a bellyful of her...

"I was something of a novelty in Berlin. I

even met the Fuhrer himself. Wasn't impressed, to be honest. Smaller than I expected and a bit of a bore, the way he ranted on....Then I was posted here on my first mission: to survey Devilston as a possible invasion point at first, then to organise the Fischer operation. Turned out there was quite a lot of sympathy for the Nazi cause in these parts, which made my task rather easier..."

"So you've no qualms about working for them?"

"Why should I? They pay well and provide interesting work."

"You make it sound like a game."

"Isn't it?"

"Not when so many are dying, Elena. And with so many more at risk..."

Now she turned to look at him.

"And what do you know about death, Arthur?"

"My brother was killed at Dunkirk."

"And I witnessed my entire family being slaughtered. A part of me died with them, you know? The part that cares about the fate of others. My soul, I suppose..."

"But you stopped the execution."

"I was getting bored."

"So if you really don't care, why didn't you shoot at the boat just now?"

"Because a dead Fischer is of no use to the

Germans."

"But the Germans won't get him now."

"Really?" Elena smiled, looking out to sea again. "Are you quite sure about that...?"

Dan and Jai rowed like galley slaves, trying to carve as much distance as they could between *Llamrei* and Devilston. But for the plough of the boat's bow and the chop of her oars the water was a glassy calm, the thin mist drifting across its oily black skin like smoke over gun metal. Occasionally the full moon would reveal her beauty through a hole in the fog, only to quickly conceal herself again, as if suddenly coy. Her intermittent radiance was mimicked by the regular flash of the Dragon Head light - diffused by the mist - while its bell tolled patiently on.

During one of the moon's reveals, Jai glimpsed something off the starboard - seaward - side: a thin shape like a blade slicing through the surface of the sea, slowly closing in on them.

"Not to worry," said Tom, deeply worried. "It's probably the fin of a basking shark. They're completely harmless, you know..."

Now the sea immediately surrounding them began to transform into a pale constellation of rising bubbles, growing in size until *Llamrei* was besieged by white water as if dropped into a boiling cauldron.

"More likely a whale than a shark," Dan observed.

"Just keep rowing!" Jai shouted.

They dug deep into the churning mass, their oars like spades in snow. The dark blade had risen from the water, and now they saw it was attached to a great column ascending from the sea like the turret of some long-submerged castle.

With a sickening groan the bottom of the boat ground against something hard. Its four occupants felt themselves being lifted as if by a great hand. Tom glimpsed an image on the rising tower - a fist gripping a sword, emerging from water - before *Llamrei* flipped over, tipping the four into the sea.

Dan grabbed Fischer's collar. Seeing a grey wall in front of him, he reached out with his other hand and felt cold hard metal. Water was gushing from a row of rectangular holes in the wall. Gripping the edge of one, he hauled Fischer to his side as the cascade subsided.

Jai was floundering, unable to reach the steel wall, his head repeatedly dipping beneath the water then emerging again, the sea smothering his desperate cries. Then he felt an arm around him, and a familiar voice in his ear.

"I've got you, Jai!" gasped Tom, swimming with him to the body of the monster.

Clinging to its streaming skin next to Dan and

Fischer, they looked up at the huge fin above them, and the large black figures painted on it:

U-724

Glancing over his shoulder, Tom caught *Llamrei*'s final seconds, her beautiful rear disappearing as she headed nose-first for the sea bed.

"We'll have to swim for it!"

"But I can't swim!" spluttered Fischer.

"That makes two of us…"

Jai managed a swift smile at Tom, in gratitude.

"We'll never make it that far," said Dan. "Doctor Fischer, you're our teacher and you don't speak German. Do you understand?"

Fischer nodded, shivering. His spectacles had been swept off his face, rendering the real world even more of a confusing blur.

A hatch clunked open in the deck ahead of the submarine's conning tower and men with rifles clambered out. Then an officer appeared in the tower above and barked down orders in German as the four were plucked from the sea.

"Elena, you can't let this happen…"

Between the veils of drifting fog, they'd watched the submarine surface and pick up the four. Now - with the deck cleared - the steel sea creature began to sink into her preferred habitat, the hiss of released air from her ballast tanks like a sigh of relief.

"I'm afraid it's too late, Arthur."

"But if the Nazis build an atom bomb it would mean the end of the world."

"I told you. My world ended a long time ago."

"And us…?"

"Us?"

"You could stay here. With me…"

Her laugh was spiked with disdain.

"Don't be ridiculous. I shot a policeman and kidnapped a government scientist. I'm an enemy spy. I'd be hanged."

"Not if you got Fischer back. And there's everything you know about German Intelligence. You'd be a priceless asset to MI5. And to me…"

"I'm not sure I want to be anyone's asset." She surveyed her surroundings. "Anyway, this country is so dark and cold…"

"We could go to Spain then…"

"You mean, Catalonia?" She looked at him, her black eyes gleaming in the moonlight. "I can never return, Arthur. Not after all that has happened. There's no escape for me now. Only death."

"But death is the losing side."

"Really? I was under the impression she

always won…?"

"Elena, I love you."

She smiled sadly.

"Poor Arthur. Always the romantic, right to the bitter end."

"Don't you feel anything for me?"

"If I allowed myself… Another time, another place…" She shrugged. "Who knows…?"

"Elena, please stop this. If not for our sake, then the greater good…"

"I've already told you. I can't. It's too late."

Her reply was curt, as if she'd considered the alternative then dismissed it. Their eyes followed all that remained of the submarine: a thin and distant finger moving slowly through the water towards open sea.

"No it isn't…"

The four prisoners stood shivering in the cramped command post, dripping sea water onto the steel floor. The warm air was thick with the smell of diesel oil and unwashed men. The tiny space was lit by a single red bulb, painting the scene in a dim and eerie light, like Hell.

A crewman was pointing a rifle at them. His unshaven face was grimy and glistening with sweat, his clothes oily. In another age he could have been a pirate.

Another man - bearded, in a leather jacket - was squinting through the periscope, rotating slowly as he scanned the world above. His wrists rested on the handles - his hands hanging lazily - and his grubby officer's cap was pushed back so he could get close to the eyepiece.

A third man was staring at Fischer. He was thin, clean-shaven and - despite his filthy habitat - quite smart. On the collar of his tunic a skull and crossed bones was prominent.

"Welcome aboard, Doctor Fischer," he said in German, smiling, a mocking tone in his voice. **"I am Lieutenant Hassler and I shall be ensuring your safe passage back to the Fatherland..."**

"I'm sorry," said Fischer in English. "I'm afraid I don't understand." Then he added, falteringly: "Keine...Deutsche...bitte...?"

"Really?" laughed Hassler. **"Or have you been in England so long that the cat has got your mother tongue...?"**

"Forgive me sir, but you are mistaken."

The officer turned to Dan.

"And you are...?"

"Yorke, sir. We are three pupils from Devilston School. And this is our teacher, Mister Alderley."

"You speak German..."

"Sir, I lived in Berlin before the war."

"I see. And do you also speak Yiddish...?"

"I'm not sure what you mean, sir..."

"Yiddish is the language of the Jew. And you are a Jew, aren't you?"

"No, sir."

"And yet you look Jewish, as does your 'teacher' here..." Now the officer regarded Jai. "But where is this one from...?"

"India, sir."

"India...? Well, we certainly have an exotic catch on our hands, haven't we? The only one who looks English is this fat one." He prodded Tom in his belly then turned his attention back to Dan. "So tell me, what were you doing out in a boat in the middle of the night?"

"We were fishing, sir."

"Fishing? For what? Submarines...?" Hassler chuckled, his small dark eyes looking for some reaction from the crew but getting none. "So this is what His Majesty's Royal Navy has been reduced to, is it? Schoolboys in a motor boat, armed with rods...?"

"Sir, we were fishing for mackerel," said Dan. "A full moon and a calm sea bring them close to the shore to feed..."

"Is that so...? Well, this is a coincidence because we were out fishing too, and I think we've caught a big one. The Fischer has been fished, you might say..." Hassler's face loomed close to Fischer's. "Come now, Doctor. Drop the act. I know exactly who you are."

"With respect sir," said Dan, "but he really is my teacher."

Hassler slapped Dan across his face, sending him sprawling back against a row of valve wheels. Jai and Tom moved forward to help their friend but the crewman blocked them with his rifle.

"Liar!"

Flecks of spit flew from Hassler's mouth. His anger was frightening in its spontaneity.

"He's telling the truth." The commander remained staring through the eyepiece as he spoke, two bright pinpoints of light flashing in his eyes. "She's signalling the correct call sign. She's got Fischer..."

Straightening up, he snapped home the handles of the periscope and its column descended.

"Surface!"

The crew responded immediately, operating levers and turning valves. Accompanied by the deep rumble of compressed air entering the ballast tanks like an expression of exasperation, the submarine began to rise again.

"Prepare a shore party to return this lot and pick up Fischer..."

"Captain," said Hassler, "you're not intending to release these prisoners, are you?"

"Well we're not taking them home with us," the commander replied. "We're already one man over our maximum compliment..."

Hassler glared at the commander, emboldened by righteousness.

"To free them will jeopardize this mission. They will raise the alarm. They must be dispatched!"

"This is my boat, Lieutenant, and I have no intention of presiding over the murder of three school pupils and their teacher."

Now Hassler smiled.

"Very admirable, Captain. Perhaps you are seeking atonement for sinking that passenger ship. What was its name again? *Son of Genghis* or something...?"

"I think you mean *Star of the Ganges*," said Dan, then answered Hassler's puzzled look: **"My friends were on her."**

The commander glanced at Dan.

"I didn't know there were children onboard..."

"Of course you didn't," said Hassler. **"But we are now in a state of total war. Consequently the normal rules of engagement have changed..."**

"No civilians will be executed on my boat." The commander's contempt for Hassler was undisguised. **"Is that understood, Lieutenant...?"**

"Very well. But I insist upon taking command of the shore party. The Fuhrer himself has entrusted me with the task of personally

escorting Fischer back to Berlin."

The commander returned to his periscope.

"Just get a move on. We've been sitting here for too long as it is..."

Two armed crewmen climbed in the dinghy to sit at the front, then the four captives, with Hassler at the back.

Jai and Tom were ordered to row. Eyeing their escorts' weapons and exchanging anxious glances, they wondered what had been discussed so heatedly in the submarine. Dan and Fischer knew, and dreaded their arrival.

As the little cove slowly emerged from the mist, two figures could be seen on the tiny beach: a man kneeling on the sand with his hands on his head, and a woman standing over him holding a machine gun.

Jumping into the shallows, the two crewmen pulled the dinghy to the shore and the rest of its occupants climbed out. Hassler strode up to the kneeling man.

"So this is Fischer?" The officer studied Alderley's face in the moonlight. **"Doesn't look very Jewish to me..."**

"And you don't look very Aryan," Elena replied, **"for an SS officer..."**

Hassler glared at her.

"If your friends in Intelligence had graced

us with a photograph we wouldn't have wasted valuable time on a fishing party."

"Such is the nature of our work. Trust no-one…"

Now Hassler turned to the other prisoners:

"Down! All of you!"

The four obeyed, lying face down on the cold hard sand.

"You're not going to kill them…?"

"Of course not, my dear." Hassler nodded towards the two crewmen. **"They are."**

"But they're civilians," Elena protested.

Hassler shrugged.

"Such is the nature of our work…"

The crewmen looked at each other.

"So what are you waiting for?" the officer demanded. Receiving no response he marched over to the pair, removing his pistol from its holster.

"Are you defying an order?"

"The skipper doesn't want them killed," said one of the crewmen.

"And we won't disobey our commander," said the other.

"Spineless scum! I'll have you both shot!" Hassler paced over to where Fischer lay. **"Always the same story. If you want something doing properly…"**

The officer cocked his Luger then took aim at the back of Fischer's head.

"I wouldn't, if I were you..."

Elena moved so that Hassler and the two crewmen were within the sweep of her Schmeisser.

"Drop your weapons! All of you!"

Two rifles fell onto the sand and the crewmen raised their hands.

"Pick them up and put them well out of reach," Elena instructed Alderley in English. He complied, not entirely certain she wouldn't shoot if he hesitated. **"And drop your gun too Lieutenant, or I will kill you."**

Hassler was astonished.

"What the Hell do you think you're doing, woman? You're compromising the whole mission!"

"Do it!"

Seeing unflinching intent in her eyes, the officer let his pistol fall to the sand.

"I'm afraid the mission is over, Lieutenant," Elena continued. **"Allow me to introduce Arthur Alderley of His Majesty's Secret Intelligence Service..."**

Alderley knew enough German to understand. He clicked his heels and bowed his head.

"Wilkomen in Devilston, Herr Leutnant."

Now Hassler was confused.

"But...where is Fischer...?"

"Paul," said Elena, **"would you kindly**

identify yourself?"

Fischer slowly picked himself up, making some attempt to brush the sand from his wet trousers.

"You were about to kill him, Lieutenant. Now that would have really compromised the mission."

"I knew it. I knew it was him..."

"Then you should have put more trust in your instincts. Isn't that what your beloved Fuhrer teaches...? Now lie down!"

Hassler regarded her with disgust.

"I am an officer of the SS and I will not take orders from some treacherous Spanish bitch!"

"Catalonian," Elena corrected him, moving behind the officer, and closer. **"Ah yes, one of the Fuhrer's loyal knights...But I'm afraid that means nothing, Lieutenant, because I have a gun and you don't. The strong prevailing over the weak, you might say. Another philosophy close to your dear leader's heart..."**

She planted her foot with force behind Hassler's knee and his legs buckled. Then the butt of her machine gun striking his back sent him face down onto the sand.

"You know," Elena continued as she picked up his Luger, **"many are forced into wickedness by their circumstance, like the ignorant peasants who destroyed all that I loved. But you are an educated man, Lieutenant. And you made a**

choice..."

"What choice?" Hassler sensed death fast approaching and had reverted to desperate measures. **"I was a child when I joined the Hitler Youth! This is all I have known!"**

"Oh, come now. You must realise that the murder of innocent civilians is wrong."

"But who is innocent?" Hassler pleaded, his voice higher now. He tasted salt on his tongue and grains of sand between his teeth, adrenalin sharpening his senses. **"We are all guilty, to some degree!"**

"Yes, Lieutenant. But some are more guilty than others..."

Elena offered the Luger to Fischer.

"He's all yours, Doctor."

Fischer contemplated the weapon with horror. He'd never touched a gun in his life. He looked at Elena pleadingly.

"But I'm just a scientist..."

"I see. So you merely design the weapons for others to use..."

She moved on to Alderley.

"Elena, he's a Prisoner of War..."

"Yes!" cried Hassler, in English now, in a last bid for sympathy. "The Geneva Convention!"

"Funny," said Elena, **"but you made no mention of that when you were about to murder these civilians. And besides, we're not in Switzerland now..."**

Standing over Hassler and taking aim, she added in English:

"This is Devilston."

"Nein!" Hassler shrieked. "Bitte!"

Tom's hands blocked his ears against the scream, eyes squeezed shut and face pressed into the sand. But Dan and Jai saw it all.

A single bullet silenced Hassler for ever. A pool of blood - black in the night - blossomed around his lifeless head, which Devilston soaked up thirstily.

Shocked, Alderley looked over at Elena. She shrugged.

"So whose side am I on now...?" She turned to the two crewmen, still standing with their hands on their heads, a look of fear and confusion on their faces. **"Get back to your boat. Tell your skipper the mission is aborted."**

Almost falling over themselves the two men pushed the dinghy into the water, climbed in then began to row for their lives, expecting bullets to rip through them from the strange and dangerous female on the shore. They were desperate to return to the warm and rumbling womb of their steel mother, where the risks were great but more predictable.

"They'll send reinforcements," said Alderley.

Elena shook her head.

"The tide is on the turn. The skipper will want to get away before he runs out of water. And so do I, before I run out of night….It's alright, you three. You can get up now."

The three Leavers stood, looking at Elena with new eyes.

"Thank you," said Alderley.

She smiled.

"You're welcome. But I want something in return…"

"Of course…"

He hoped he could deliver.

"I don't want Jack or Cador to be prosecuted. They were working for me, not Germany."

"And Garsten?"

"Nazi."

"I'll do my best…"

"Not enough." She fixed him with her stare. "I want your word."

"Alright." He nodded. "I promise."

Now Fischer spoke.

"I want to thank you all for risking your lives to help me."

Elena turned to him.

"Even me, Doctor? After I shot your friend in Bristol…?"

"I can't forgive you for that. But you saved my life, all the same…"

They heard a sudden loud release of air, like a whale's exhalation.

"Look!" Tom was pointing seaward. "It's diving!"

They watched as the black silhouette of the U-boat slipped beneath the surface, leaving no trace of her existence but for a set of small waves which presently lapped at the beach.

"Where will you go?" Alderley asked.

Elena shrugged.

"Not sure. Portugal, perhaps..." Then she added: "Want to come?"

He found himself considering the offer. He imagined the two of them sipping red wine under a hot and high sun. Then he remembered his brother and his family, and his country.

"Not yet," he replied. "Will you write?"

Walking up to him she placed a kiss on both cheeks, then a third on his mouth.

"Adio, Arturo. Maybe we will meet again..."

"Another place?" He stared sadly into her eyes. "Another time?"

"Perhaps." She smiled. "Who knows...?"

And then she turned and walked away, in the direction of the Causeway. Yet again the sea would be surrendering up the ancient road, only to be reclaimed later in an endless cycle.

"Helluva woman," said Jai, watching her disappear into the night.

Alderley took a deep breath.

"Yes. Wasn't she...?"

Alderley opened the bottle of champagne and

filled the glasses, handing three to his guests then raising his.

"To a mission successfully accomplished..."

"Cheers!" the others responded.

"...and to the memory of the Reverend Edward Monmouth. May his soul rest in peace..."

"Amen."

The four drank. Tom grimaced at the dryness of the champagne but their host was impressed.

"Quality bubbly. Where did you get it...?"

"From the family vault." Jai winked at his friends. "I was saving it for a special occasion."

Alderley had invited the three to his rooms for an informal de-brief. They had bathed and changed, but they still tingled from their immersion in the sea and all that had transpired.

Fischer had been spirited away, Charlotte and Pendragon had been released from the dungeon, the Dragon Head light had been doused - though its bell still stubbornly rang out through the fog - and a calm had returned to Devilston for what remained of Halloween Night.

"Sir," said Dan, "we owe you an apology."

Alderley looked puzzled.

"What for...?"

"We heard you sending Morse Code messages. We thought you were a German spy."

"Ah yes... Control informed me of your suspicions..."

"So they got our warning?" said Jai. "Good old Jomsom...Is that why you were transmitting from the battlements, sir? Because you knew we could hear you from our room...?"

Alderley shook his head.

"I wasn't transmitting that night but receiving. Direction-finding, actually...By then I was sure there was an enemy agent in Devilston who was communicating with Germany. Thought it was the Captain at first..."

"But he **was** a spy. Wasn't he...?"

"Alfie Smith was more of an opportunist. The type who'd run with the strongest pack, no matter how rabid. Preferably leading them..."

"Who's Alfie Smith when he's at home?" asked Tom.

"Alfred Smith was Captain Ralph Smythe's real name. East End gangster and career criminal, and something of a genius at assumed identities."

"You'd think such an expert would have come up with a name that didn't sound so much like his real one," said Dan.

Alderley shrugged.

"Maybe he wanted to preserve some connection with his roots. Or maybe he just liked living on the edge...Some are like that: they just can't resist leaving clues, as if they get a thrill out of flirting with fate..."

"What did he do in London?" asked Jai.

"I believe several gangland murders were attributed to him. And a few bank jobs, too. Took off for the West Country when things were getting a bit hot for him in the Big Smoke. He really landed on his feet here, charming his way into the Morrigan family, and Lady Charlotte's heart. Lying low, like a fox gone to ground...

"Then Bletchley Park began intercepting communications between Germany and this corner of the world. And when MI5 got wind of Cornish nationalists in Pristow who might be in league with the Nazis, they sent me here to investigate. I had an inkling an agent would use the highest point in the vicinity to communicate with Berlin which is why I was on the battlements that night, testing my theory..."

"Now I get it," said Jai, remembering the distant white tower caught in the wire loop. "The faint signal we picked up on Dan's crystal set was Miss Montserrat transmitting to Germany from the lighthouse. And she used the tunnel to get there..."

"Sir, will Jack be hanged for helping her?" asked Tom.

"Well, I gave her my word that Petherick and Pendragon wouldn't be prosecuted." Alderley lobbed another piece of driftwood on the fire, triggering a display of sparks. "And woe betide anyone who reneges on a promise to Miss Montserrat. Hell hath no fury and all that..."

"Why did she call you Arthur, sir?" asked Dan. "I thought your first name was Michael..."

"Arthur is my real name. Michael was my older brother. I pretended to be him to maximize my chances of getting a teaching job here. He was a scientist and an old Devilstonian. He won a scholarship here, but I failed the exam and my parents couldn't afford the fees... So you see, my only qualification for becoming a secret agent was that I resembled my brother... Ironic, really. I'd always looked up to him - always wanted to be him - and now here I was, assuming his identity. I could never really fill his shoes though..."

"Well, I think you did a fine job," said Jai. "Notwithstanding those abysmal science lessons..."

Alderley winced as he recalled his ineptitude.

"I did it for Mike. He gave his life for his country. It was the least I could do to resurrect him for a while, for the sake of the war effort..."

"And that explains the photographs," said Dan.

"Photographs?"

"In the Chronicle, sir. The Alderley in the team photos was right-handed. Presumably your brother..."

"My God," Alderley smiled, "you lot don't miss a trick, do you...?"

"Sir, what will happen to Lady Carrot?" asked Tom. "I mean, Charlotte..."

"Well, the Coroner will be instructed to conclude that the Reverend died in an unfortunate shooting accident involving the Headmaster's rather-antiquated revolver. Then, consumed by guilt, the Captain fell on his sword..."

"Backwards?"

"We don't need to go into detail, Rana. As long as everyone is singing from the same hymn sheet, as it were..."

The three nodded, Tom now recalling the sword on the submarine's conning tower.

"I still can't believe I've been inside a Jerry U-boat. Just wait until Quirky hears about it. He'll be green..."

"That never happened," said Alderley.

"You mean...we can't tell anybody?"

Tom was dismayed.

"Not for a long time, I'm afraid. But it'll be quite a story for your grandchildren: how you contributed to the preservation of Western civilisation..."

"Well," said Jai, "if we're going to have grandchildren then we'll have to meet women first....So how do you two fancy staying in my father's place in Kensington for Half Term?

We'll celebrate a successful culmination of operations with a few nights on the town…"

"But London is being bombed," said Dan, recalling the chaos of Liverpool and Bristol.

"And what about Merryn?" asked Tom. "And Tamsyn…?"

"Too dangerous by half," said Jai. "I'd sooner face the Luftwaffe than that crowd of local yokels again." Then he added, with a wink: "Plenty more fish in the sea, I say…"

A burning log shifted in the grate, as if Devilston wanted the last word.

A military staff car sped through the Cornish night, two escort motorcycles ahead of it, a truck full of troops behind.

"Are we going to Bristol?" asked Fischer in the back of the car, a soldier on each side of him with rifles resting between their legs. He was fighting the fatigue that had now crept over him, struggling to keep his eyes open. The young officer in the front passenger seat turned to him, his face in shadow.

"I'm afraid not, Doctor. Much too dangerous for you there. We're going to Plymouth instead."

"And Plymouth is safer…?"

"You won't be staying for long." The officer smiled. "You're booked on a cruise you see, as a special guest of His Majesty's Royal Navy."

"A cruise? Where to…?"

"To your new home, Doctor…"

The officer turned back, resuming his gaze along the dark road ahead.

"America."

J.J. Greenwood

AUTHOR'S NOTES

Daniel Rosenbaum was a fictional participant in an historical event. The Kindertransport programme involved the evacuation of about 10,000 predominantly Jewish children from Germany, Austria, Czechoslovakia and Poland. The children were placed in British foster homes, hostels and schools. Many were the only members of their families who survived the Holocaust.

In 1940 the British government ordered the internment of all male refugees between the ages of 16 and 70 from enemy countries (oxymoronically known as 'friendly enemy aliens'). Consequently about 1000 male youths who had come to Britain as Kindertransport children now found themselves interned in makeshift camps, many on the Isle of Man. Around 400 were transported overseas to Canada and Australia.

The *Victoria* on which Dan and Charlotte sailed

from the Isle of Man was based upon the *Mona's Isle*, one of eight ships of the Isle of Man Steam Packet Company which took part in the Dunkirk evacuation, rescuing a total of 24,699 British troops (about 1 in 14 of all those evacuated). Three of the company's ships were lost due to enemy action.

The *Star of the Ganges* is a fictional composite of two real ships: *Arandora Star* and *City of Benares.*

On 1 July 1940 *Arandora Star* sailed out of Liverpool heading for St. John's, Newfoundland. She carried nearly 1,500 German and Italian internees, bound for internment camps in Canada. Off the northwest coast of Ireland she was struck by a torpedo from the German submarine *U-47*, commanded by U-boat ace Gunther Prien. It is assumed that *U-47* mistook her grey wartime livery for that of an armed merchant cruiser. 35 minutes after the torpedo struck, *Arandora Star* sank with the loss of over 800 lives.

Late in the evening of 17 September 1940, the *City of Benares* was sighted by *U-48*, 253 miles west-southwest of Rockall. The submarine fired three torpedoes at her. The first two missed but the third struck her in the stern, causing her to sink within half an hour. Heinrich Bleichrodt - commander of *U-48* - did not know there were 90 children on the ship, being evacuated to Canada. 248 of the 406 souls on board were lost, including 77 of the 90 child evacuees. The tragedy prompted the immediate cessation of the trans-Atlantic evacuation programme.

The character of Jai Rana was based upon the young Man Singh II, who became the last ruling Maharaja of Jaipur in Rajputana.

Man Singh's father Madho Singh was a wild-spending and heavy-drinking Anglophile, with three wives and eighteen (official) concubines. Madho believed his inability to father a male child was the result of a curse by a rival Maharaja, but in a dream he saw the village where he would find the boy he should adopt. The boy became Madho's heir, and the inspiration for Jai Rana. Man's deity was Shiva, of whom Kali (Jai's deity) is a manifestation.

The character of Paul Fischer is based upon two little-known but highly-influential scientists.

Otto Frisch and Rudolf Peierls were Jewish atomic physicists who fled Nazi Germany. Working at the University of Birmingham, they devised the first technical exposition of an atomic bomb.

While acknowledging the theoretical possibility, most experts in the 1930s - Albert Einstein included - had assumed that an atomic bomb would require a huge quantity of uranium, a fact that effectively made it unviable as a practical weapon. However, what became known as the Frisch–Peierls Memorandum (dated March 1940) contained theoretical proof that previous calculations had been wrong. According to the memorandum, the critical mass of the uranium-235 isotope required for nuclear fission could be achieved with only 1 kg of fissile material. A bomb containing this quantity could be easily transported in a single aircraft.

This explosive revelation led directly to a British plan to build an atomic weapon, code-named Tube Alloys. The programme was eventually transferred across the Atlantic and absorbed by the Manhattan Project at Los Alomos in New Mexico, resulting in the bombs detonated over Hiroshima and Nagasaki.

The Dragon Head lighthouse was inspired by the Trevose Head light which lies a few miles along the coast from Padstow in Cornwall, itself the inspiration for the village of Pristow.

The character of Devilston is based upon the beautiful and mysterious St Michael's Mount, near Penzance in Cornwall: a place steeped in legend and history. In the Eleventh Century a Benedictine monastery was established there, and since then the Mount has been used as a fortress in numerous conflicts, including the Wars of the Roses, the Cornish Rebellion and the English Civil War. However - although an ideal location - there was never a boarding school on the island.

I should also include a note on the artistic licence I took with some historical facts, for the sake of narrative integrity:

The Barbary Pirates raided the coast of England in the Seventeenth Century, not the Sixteenth.

The infamous Totenkopf (Death's Head) division of the Waffen SS was formed in October 1939, a month after Dan's crossing of the Dutch border.

The German bombing of Liverpool and Bristol commenced in November 1940, not September.

By 1940 the great Bengali poet Tagore was on his death bed in India, not mingling among London's high society.

And in 1940 British Summer Time was retained. The clocks didn't go back.

Printed in Great Britain
by Amazon